D0252156

Praise for the Nov
Karen White

The Memory of Water

"Beautifully written and as lyrical as the tides, *The Memory of Water* speaks directly to the heart and will linger in yours long after you've read the final page. I loved this book!"

—Susan Crandall, author of *A Kiss in Winter*

Learning to Breathe

"White creates a heartfelt story full of vibrant characters and emotion that leaves the reader satisfied yet hungry for more from this talented author."

—*Booklist*

"Beautifully written, White's latest is full of emotional drama and well-crafted characters."

—*Romantic Times* (4½ stars)

"One of those stories where you savor every single word . . . [a] perfect 10."

—Romance Reviews Today

"Another one of Karen White's emotional books! A joy to read!"

—The Best Reviews

continued . . .

Pieces of the Heart

"Heartwarming and intense . . . a tale that resonates with the meaning of unconditional love." —*Romantic Times* (4 stars)

"A terrific, insightful character study." —*Midwest Book Review*

The Color of Light

"[White's] prose is lyrical, and she weaves in elements of mysticism and romance without being heavy-handed. This is an accomplished novel about loss and renewal, and readers will be taken with the people and stories of Pawleys Island." —*Booklist*

"The reader will hear the ocean roar and the seagulls scream as the past reluctantly gives up its ghosts in this beautiful, enticing, and engrossing novel." —*Romantic Times* (4½ stars)

"A story as rich as a coastal summer . . . dark secrets, heartache, a magnificent South Carolina setting, and a great love story." —*New York Times* bestselling author Deborah Smith

"An engaging read with a delicious taste of the mysterious." —*New York Times* bestselling author Haywood Smith

"Karen White's novel is as lush as the Lowcountry, where the characters' wounded souls come home to mend in unexpected and magical ways." —Patti Callahan Henry, award-winning author of *Between the Tides*

The

MEMORY

of

WATER

KAREN WHITE

NAL
ACCENT

NAL Accent
Published by New American Library, a division of
Penguin Group (USA) Inc., 375 Hudson Street,
New York, New York 10014, USA
Penguin Group (Canada), 90 Eglinton Avenue East, Suite 700, Toronto,
Ontario M4P 2Y3, Canada (a division of Pearson Penguin Canada Inc.)
Penguin Books Ltd., 80 Strand, London WC2R 0RL, England
Penguin Ireland, 25 St. Stephen's Green, Dublin 2,
Ireland (a division of Penguin Books Ltd.)
Penguin Group (Australia), 250 Camberwell Road, Camberwell, Victoria 3124,
Australia (a division of Pearson Australia Group Pty. Ltd.)
Penguin Books India Pvt. Ltd., 11 Community Centre, Panchsheel Park,
New Delhi – 110 017, India
Penguin Group (NZ), 67 Apollo Drive, Rosedale, North Shore 0632,
New Zealand (a division of Pearson New Zealand Ltd.)
Penguin Books (South Africa) (Pty.) Ltd., 24 Sturdee Avenue,
Rosebank, Johannesburg 2196, South Africa

Penguin Books Ltd., Registered Offices:
80 Strand, London WC2R 0RL, England

First published by NAL Accent, an imprint of New American Library,
a division of Penguin Group (USA) Inc.

First Printing, March 2008
10 9 8 7 6 5 4

ACCENT REGISTERED TRADEMARK—MARCA REGISTRADA

LIBRARY OF CONGRESS CATALOGING-IN-PUBLICATION DATA:

White, Karen (Karen S.)
   The memory of water/Karen White.
      p. cm.
   ISBN: 978-0-451-22303-6
      1. Mentally ill parents—Fiction. 2. Sisters—Fiction. 3 Family secrets—Fiction. 4. South Carolina—
Fiction. 5. Sailing—Fiction. 6. Domestic fiction. I. Title.
PS3623.H5776M46 2008
813'.6—dc22   2007032734

Set in Adobe Garamond • Designed by Elke Sigal

Printed in the United States of America

*This book is dedicated
to the original Highfalutin,
and to all those who lost so much
in Hurricane Katrina.*

ACKNOWLEDGMENTS

With many thanks to my friend and talented author Wendy Wax for your pearls of wisdom and thoughtful suggestions, which always make my books better.

Thanks also to Jill Evans and to the kind and helpful staff at Windsong Sailing Academy for your sailing pointers, and especially to Dave Crumbley aka "Captain Dave," who gave so much of his time and knowledge to share his love of sailing with me and to make sure I got it right. Any errors regarding sailing are completely mine and mine alone, and my apologies to Captain Dave.

I would also like to thank Kelly and John Deushane and their daughter, Taylor, for their charitable donation to KRCS and for the inspiration for the character of Tally Deushane.

And no acknowledgments would be complete without a nod to Tim, Meghan, and Connor for hanging in there and for always being excited when seeing my name in print.

CHAPTER I

Marnie

For thousands of years, the Atlantic Ocean has beat against the beach of my childhood, its watery fingers stealing more and more of the soft silted sand, grabbing at the estuaries and creeks of the South Carolina Lowcountry, leaving us with the detritus of old forests, battered dunes, and bleeding loss.

But the shore remains, the sand itself testament to survival—the remnants of large rocks crushed into grains of sand. Just as our family has dared to claim ownership of a parcel of shoreline and ocean for generations, our house defying the elements of nature. Strong winds buffet the sea oats and tall dune grasses, tossing sand and seabirds where it will, winding my sister's golden hair into sunlit spirals of silk until it becomes the only good memory I have of her—the only memory I allowed myself to keep. But the wind pushes on, pushes at the shoreline, at our old house, and at me. Yet somehow, we remain.

I hadn't been back to McClellanville for almost ten years—ten years while I tried to forget the sting of salt water in my eyes, the slippery feel of the tide pulling the sand out from under my feet. Of being underwater and not able to breathe as water rolled over me, cascaded around me in a watery rug, sucking the air from my lungs. And the feel of my mother's hands slowly letting me go.

I parked my rental car on the driveway of crushed rock and shells, and left the radio on, not yet ready to hear the ocean again. The white clapboard house, owned by my mother's family ever since the Revolution, had changed little. Only on closer inspection did I begin to see my sister's artistic hand. The once solid green porch swing now sported a leopard's spots, and the front walk and porch were covered with brightly hued flowers, their garish blooms radiant and mocking as if they knew they had once been outlawed by our grandfather. Blatant beauty and bright colors were once a sin to him, regardless of the fact that the Creator he worshipped had also created them.

A tire swing hung from the ancient oak tree in the front yard, its frantic movements evidence of recent occupation. Reluctantly, I turned off the radio and took my key from the ignition before exiting the car. I glanced around, hoping to catch sight of Gil, the nine-year-old nephew I had never seen, but only the empty yard and the distant sound of the ocean greeted me. I glanced up at the windows on the right side above the porch roof as a shadow seemed to pass behind the glass. I stared at them for a long time, wondering if it had been the passing of a cloud reflected in the glass and remembering my sister sneaking out of her window onto the roof, then shimmying down the drainpipe that ran from the roof to the front porch.

I'd never tattled on her. Looking back, I suppose that even then I'd known that her self-destructive behavior would simply find a more dangerous outlet. Watching her run off the first time into the darkened yard with a shadow boy, I had felt the final snap of the invisible cord that had attached us since my birth. It had first started to fray on the day our mother died and we'd been sent to live with her father. We were given separate rooms, and my sister had become a beautiful stranger who regarded me with silent eyes and weeping shoulders. My grief for my mother and my sister found no succor with our grandfather whose only recourse during times of trouble was his Bible. But it never occurred to me to question the reason for my grief; according to my mother, we Maitlands were meant to suffer. It's what happens, she once explained, when a man curses God. His children, his children's children, and their children would be cursed. From what I have seen of this family, I would have to agree that she was right.

Slowly I walked to the back of the house, a swarm of gnats following like persistent memories, down to the gravel path that led to the dunes, and finally beyond them, the Atlantic Ocean. I stopped on the old railroad tie that marked the end of the path and turned my face to the wind, stilling the first panic at the smell of salt water. I clenched my eyes, and when I opened them again, I saw Diana. She sat on an old Adirondack chair with her feet in the surf, swaddled in a quilt despite the pressing heat of the midafternoon sun. She wore her hair loose, its color not diminished by time or the miles of asphalt that had separated us for so long. Miles and years become suddenly invisible when you find yourself back where you started from, as if you've learned nothing and you are once again the person you once were.

She was watching a sailboat as it headed out into deeper water, triangular sails full and bright white. Two sailors, a man and a woman in bright yellow Windbreakers, stood in the cockpit, their faces turned into the wind. I moved through the cloying sand so that I stood behind my sister, not speaking.

"Do you remember how it feels?" She spoke without looking at me, her words deceptively soft.

I watched the sailboat bobbing on the waves as if nodding, the woman moving to adjust a sail. I could almost feel the sleek teak beneath my feet, the damp crispness of the white sails through my fingers. Hear the rushing water beneath the bow and the wind blessing my face. "No," I said. "I don't remember at all."

She faced me for the first time, the old familiar sneer darkening her once beautiful face. I had never been able to lie to her; although she was three years older, we had been as twins, inseparable as if we had shared our mother's womb, felt the rhythm of our mother's heart at the same time. Maybe we had known, in that dark corner of heaven our preacher grandfather said babies came from, that being born into our family would require an ally.

Diana reached up with paint-stained fingers and pushed her hair away from skin that appeared too sallow, too tightly aligned over jutting bones for a woman just thirty-one. I swallowed a gasp; her resemblance to our mother was unmistakable now. Long ago, when we were a normal family of mother, father, and two daughters, we had taken delight in the fact that I looked just like our father and Diana had been a reflection of our mother. But now, that reflection included all the demons of memory, and I took a step away from her as the old fears reached out and grabbed me like grasping seaweed in the darkest part of the ocean.

"Is that why you moved to Arizona? It's the goddamn desert, Marnie. I thought you, of all people, would be a little more creative than that." She fished a cigarette pack and a lighter out from under the quilt. With shaking hands she put a cigarette in her mouth and lit it, then took a deep drag. "It didn't make you forget, though, did it? You still remember how it feels."

A large wave broke near the shoreline, sending its frothing edge with bubbling fingers toward me. I jumped back and Diana laughed. "You've been living in the desert too long. Welcome back." She blew out a puff of smoke into the air between us, like the ghost of unspoken words.

"I came because of Gil."

She looked at me again, her eyes flat, her cigarette stilled in her hand. "I know." She turned from me, examining the tall mast of the fading sailboat again, as if hoping to see something new. "I wouldn't expect you to come back for me." She took another drag from her cigarette, her hand shaking so badly she could barely make it to her mouth.

"Quinn called me," I said, feeling embarrassed that I hadn't seen the need to lie. "Is he up at the house with Gil?"

Pale green eyes studied me and it was as if I were looking into my mother's face. "There's nothing you can do for us here, Marnie. Go back to your desert, to your months without rain, and leave us alone. We don't need you here, and I don't want you here. So go home."

"I am home," I said, surprising myself with the words. It had been ten years since I'd called this place by the ocean home.

She stood suddenly, the quilt falling into the sand and water. I stared in horror at her legs, merely bones with flesh clinging to them, a large white bandage bisecting the upper quadrant of her thigh. *It's been almost two months since the accident. Why is it still bandaged?* I looked up into my sister's eyes, hoping to see anything but the defiance I found there. Without a word, Diana turned and walked away from me down the beach, leaving only a trail of cigarette smoke and more hurt than could be contained in the mere vastness of the ocean.

I closed my eyes, wanting to see nothing but endless miles of sand and asphalt, the outstretched arms of the saguaro cactus and the rough-hewn crags of distant mountains of my adopted home. Instead I heard the crash of waves against the ancient shore as I turned my back on the unforgiving ocean and headed up over the dunes and back to my grandfather's house to face whatever curse God had decided to visit upon the latest generation of Maitlands.

CHAPTER 2

All is born of water; all is sustained by water.
—GOETHE

Diana

Sedona is located in Arizona's high desert under the southwestern rim of the vast Colorado plateau. Average precipitation is around ten inches per year, and the average yearly temperatures range from about forty degrees in January to a high of around eighty degrees in July. A dry, temperate zone. A great place for retirees who hate humidity, for Midwesterners who can't stand the thought of another harsh winter, and for wounded souls running from the sound of wind and ocean, not having yet realized that the ripe summer smell of pluff mud and the tang of salt in the air is part of their blood.

This is Marnie. She was raised in the Lowcountry, same as I was. But I know that there are some things you can never run away from no matter how far you go. Surrounding yourself with a lot of desert is a bit like sitting in quicksand: Sooner or later the water will find you and suck you under.

I watched my sister walk away, her feet in sensible flat-soled shoes, her dark hair pulled back neatly in a hair clip robbing the wind its pleasure of throwing it out of place. She was contained, my Marnie—the proper little schoolteacher. To the impartial observer it would appear that she was ambivalent about seeing me again. But I see things about her that other people don't. She's the other side of my soul and she's never been able to hide anything from me. Marnie may have grown older in the last ten years, but I don't think she's grown any wiser. She says she doesn't have a clear memory of the night our mother died, but she thinks she knows what really happened. And for that, I can't forgive her.

I watched her retreating back long after it disappeared up the path before deciding to follow. I knew why she'd come, and somewhere in my tired mind, I was grateful. Gil needed her. I also knew that if I could get myself to calm down and think straight, I would say that I needed her, too. But I couldn't. Hate does that to a person.

I looked back toward the ocean and at the quilt being slowly dragged from the sand into the surf, the colors blurring as it sank farther under the waves. Reds and yellows and blues wept together and my fingers itched to paint the abandoned chair and the drowning quilt. Instead, I pulled out another cigarette, needing the soothing drag of nicotine so that I wouldn't care so much that I seemed to have lost the ability to paint.

Taking another deep drag, I forced myself toward the meandering path, following it until I reached the house. I spotted Marnie as she rounded the corner, heading toward the front porch, and made to follow her but a hand on my arm stopped me.

"Give them a few minutes."

I stared into the serious dark blue eyes of my ex and Gil's father, Quinn. Out of habit, I pulled away. I had acquired an aversion to being touched and he seemed to recognize that because he stepped back and dropped his hand.

"Sorry, Diana. I don't want you up at the house right now. Gil's on the porch waiting for Marnie and I want to give them a little time to get acquainted."

He was on the offensive and I couldn't say I blamed him. Even I wasn't sure how I'd react to things anymore. Since the night of Gil's accident almost two months before, I had somehow lost myself. I had become a spectator of my own life—a life that I barely recognized and one in which I had no idea what would happen next.

Quinn stared warily at me. "Please."

I nodded, too disjointed to feel either anger or rebellion.

His eyes traveled down to the bandage on my leg. "It's time to change your bandage again. You've been picking at it."

My eyes strayed down to where he was looking. I put my hand over the bandage, over the evidence of what I had done, and I shook my head. I couldn't explain that I needed it to remind me and that I could never let it heal. "It's fine. It's scabbing up."

He looked at me again with those eyes I had once fallen in love with and took a step closer. "Just let me see."

I felt the reassuring snap of anger. "I said it's fine. I'll take care of it." I began to walk away from him. "Don't worry. I won't scare Gil with my presence. I'm going up to my studio and won't be down for dinner." I was almost running now.

"Diana—wait. Don't you want to say something to your sister? You haven't seen her in a long time."

I stopped but didn't look back. "We already spoke. Sorry it didn't turn out to be the reunion you anticipated, Quinn. There are some things even you can't fix." I continued walking to the back of the old house, not remembering to breathe until I was safely inside the crowded walls of my art studio.

⌖

Marnie

I paused on the front steps for a moment, thinking the front porch empty. I looked up at the ceiling, painted a robin's egg blue. Our grandfather had told us it was to make the bees and birds think it was sky so that they wouldn't build their nests there. But our mother always said that it was painted blue to scare away ghosts. I still wasn't sure who was right.

A small movement caught my attention, and I turned toward the old metal chairs now painted a cobalt blue with schools of brightly colored mythical fish swimming across the backs and seats. They were the old-fashioned spring chairs made to bounce as you sat on them—chairs you didn't see much anymore but that always reminded me of my childhood by the sea.

In the chair farthest from me sat a young boy, sunk back into his chair as if to blend into the ocean scene painted behind him. He sat watching me with familiar green eyes, his limbs completely still. I stared back, taking in his USC T-shirt and cutoff jean shorts, and his sun-streaked white-blond hair. It needed cutting and lay about his head in tangled waves, the long bangs acting as a barrier between his eyes and the world.

I wanted to step away, to retreat back to my car from this minia-ture replica of my sister. How could I help this boy? How could I ever learn to see past his mother to the child that lay beneath? As if sensing my thoughts, he bowed his head, like he was asking for forgiveness for something that wasn't his fault. It was an act of submission and humil-ity that I had never seen from Diana. It reached my heart and shook me from my thoughts, opening my eyes to see the troubled child Quinn had called me all the way from Arizona to come help.

Slowly I approached, afraid that any sudden movement on my part would make him bolt. I knelt in front of him, my knees cracking, and touched his arm. "Gil? I'm your aunt Marnie. I've come for a visit."

He looked up at me, those eyes meeting mine again, and simply stared back at me.

"I've come to spend time with you so we can get to know each other. You've been my nephew for nine years and we've never met. Hard to believe, isn't it?"

He continued to look at me, and I could see the comprehension in his eyes. I stared back, willing him to speak while trying to remember what his father had told me on the phone. *He won't speak. It's not that he can't—he's been doing that since he was a year old. But he won't now. Ever since the boating accident with Diana, he hasn't said a word. Neither one of them will speak of it.*

I stood, moving away to sit on the chair next to him, feeling as if he wanted the extra space between us. I was his mother's sister, after all. "I teach art to kids about your age in Arizona. Did you know that?" I didn't mention that I taught special-needs children, nor did I expect him to answer. "I thought maybe we could use the rest of the summer to paint together. We could take trips to the marsh and paint the dock and any birds or wildlife we see." *But not the ocean. I will never paint the ocean.*

I pointed to the giant live oak on the front lawn. "That tree was the first thing I ever painted. I think I was about six, and the picture resembled a mad brown cow wearing a fancy green hat." *But your mother's painting of the same tree made me weep for its beauty.* I faced him again. "Not exactly the look I was going for." I slid a sideways glance at him and saw a lip twitch. "You can have a go at it, too. Then maybe we could paint the house, or your dad, or the tire swing, or your nose, or your toes, or maybe even your belly button. . . ." I let my voice trail away as I slid another glance his way and was rewarded with a full smile. I faced him and smiled, and for a moment, his smile matched mine.

"I see you're already becoming friends."

Gil's smile faded as I turned around to find the owner of the voice. The man was tall and lean with sandy blond hair, sun-streaked like Gil's.

He continued, perched on the top step as if waiting for an invitation to move forward. "I'm sorry I wasn't here when you arrived. I was in the greenhouse and didn't see your car until just a few minutes ago. I figured you'd want to say hi to Gil first."

I stood and approached him with an outstretched hand. "You must be Quinn, then. It's nice to finally meet you."

The hand he slid into mine was strong and firm, his palm and fingers hardened with old calluses. A sailor's hand. I pulled my hand away a little too quickly. His eyes flickered slightly, and I thought I could see him looking for any similarity I had with Diana, and not just physically. After a short pause, he said, "Thank you for coming."

I looked back at Gil, who had pulled his legs up in the chair with him, hugging his knees with his arms, and I realized with a start it was the same position I'd seen his mother in when I'd first spotted her down by the beach. "I've enjoyed chatting with Gil." I grimaced, knowing how inaccurate the word "chatting" was.

Quinn took my elbow, steering me toward the door. "I've made clam chowder. I'm sure you're hungry after your long trip. Why don't we all go inside and eat and you can tell us about Arizona?"

Gil slid from the chair, lizardlike—stealthy and quiet so as to escape notice as he slipped through the front door. As if he were afraid of being caught.

As the screen door banged shut, Quinn called after Gil, "Go wash up. Then please tell Joanna to bring Grandpa to the table."

I paused outside the door. "How is Grandpa?" I hadn't seen my mother's father since I'd left, but I'd dutifully spoken to him on the phone every Saturday for five years until he'd had the stroke that had robbed him of his speech. I'd sent a dwindling number of letters in the years since, the only responses being from Joanna, his nurse, who kept me apprised of his condition, which never seemed to change. He was an old man, confined to a wheelchair and unable to speak, and I knew it was only his legendary stubbornness that made him cling to a life that no longer wanted anything to do with him. After all, he was a Maitland.

Quinn held the door open for me. "Still the same. He and Gil spend a lot of time together. I think they find some sort of comfort in each other's presence."

I looked at him in surprise, wondering how two people who couldn't speak could forge any kind of a relationship. "Grandpa never had much interest in children. Couldn't stand all the noise Diana and I made."

Again, I grimaced at my faux pas, but Quinn squeezed my elbow. "No, it's not that. There's some kind of bond between them. And I encourage it. Gil doesn't want to be anywhere near his mother, and he's begun to avoid me, probably just because of my association with her. I'd rather he be sitting with Grandpa than wandering the beach by himself. Diana had been looking into putting Grandpa in a home about a year ago, but seems to have dropped that idea. She doesn't talk to me, so I don't know why. I think he's better off here, anyway."

I nodded and preceded him through the screen door and into the house of my childhood. It hadn't changed much; it still smelled of old wood and lemon furniture polish. And always, always the cloying smell of salt water.

The chintzes and rugs were comfortably worn and faded, but were hardly noticeable for the vivid artwork on the walls. As I glanced into the dining room across the foyer, I saw row upon row of gilt-framed watercolors, depicting everything from ocean scenes to renderings of the house and the metal chairs on the front. There were several of a towheaded baby and growing boy that I recognized as Gil, and even a few of a younger Quinn perched on a sailboat, facing toward the sea.

As if sensing that I wanted a few minutes alone, Quinn excused himself, saying he'd take the luggage from my car and bring it up to my old bedroom. I could find my grandpa in his room. I nodded, then continued to study the paintings, marveling as I always had at my sister's talent. Despite my own yearnings in the same direction, it had been a long time since I thought to be jealous of it. Being second-best in our mother's affections had used up my entire well of jealousy.

I was the queen of technique and art history. I could teach art to anybody and coach talent from the youngest of students to the elderly in the classes I gave at a local nursing home. But I could never coach the liquid beauty of color and form from my own paintbrush; that talent had been given to the golden-haired Diana, who resembled our mother in so many ways.

I crossed the foyer and walked into the formal front parlor and stopped. There was no artwork in this room. Instead the walls were decorated with rectangular patches of darkened paint. I paused before the old familiar sofa, staring at the large, empty rectangle on the wall behind it, wondering about the painting that had hung there.

I heard the sound of wheels rolling on wooden floors, and I turned back to the hallway that bisected the house, connecting the front formal rooms to the kitchen and family rooms in the back. A heavyset woman wearing white nurse's shoes stood behind a wheelchair carrying an old man whose thin face was dominated by thick glasses. In his lap lay a well-worn Bible and a *TV Guide*, both bearing marks of a fluid yellow highlighter. I wanted to laugh, remembering this idiosyncrasy that he seemed to have passed on so well to me. I still cannot pick up something to read without a highlighter in my hand.

A guttural sound erupted from his throat and I moved forward. Squatting, I took his blue-veined hands in mine. They trembled slightly as I registered a slight squeeze. He made that sound in his throat again and I looked up at Joanna. "Is he all right?"

"He's having a good day. He's spent most of it at his window, waiting for you."

Grandpa jerked his hands and grunted again and I knew that he was trying to tell me something.

I held his hands tighter and stood to kiss his cheek, the unshaven and familiar bristles scratching my chin as I kissed him. "I'm home, Grandpa. I've come home."

I felt his hands relax in mine, and when I looked into his eyes again, before he turned his head away from me, I was sure that I saw tears.

CHAPTER 3

Ocean into tempest wrought,
To waft a feather, or to drown a fly.
—EDWARD YOUNG

Quinn

I've lived by the ocean all of my life. But the cold waters off New England did nothing to prepare me for the yellow-green vibrancy of the Lowcountry marsh, or the heaviness of the air that could only be escaped out on the water, clipping the waves on a sailboat.

Almost reluctantly, I fell in love with this place. I'm not sure if it was only because anywhere other than where I'd come from seemed a likely refuge, and this was the first place I'd stopped. I remember driving down Highway 10 and pulling off to the side of the marsh. The tall sawgrass undulated in the wind, like a heavy sigh from a tired earth and I knew then that I had found a place to lick my wounds and build a life.

I was easily transplanted. I had a thriving veterinary practice and a new wife all in the course of a year. I should have known better than to call myself a success before giving it more time. Raising orchids has taught me this: A plant's inability to adapt to a new climate will not always be immediately apparent. You'll try a new soil and snip off dead parts from the leaves, maybe try fertilizer. But one day you're going to walk in and find your beautiful orchid slumped over and hugging the earth whence it came.

I met Diana through one of her paintings. I'd been attempting to decorate my new house with limited funds and had walked into an antiques store in McClellanville on a hot summer afternoon. I'd seen the painting hung behind the cash register and knew that if that was the only thing I could afford in my house, I had to have it. I haggled with the storeowner for almost an hour before I could be persuaded to understand that it wasn't for sale. The artist, Diana Maitland, had lent it to the store for safekeeping. She could no longer stand to look at it, but had not wanted to sell it, either.

About a week later, after me making daily offers to buy it, Diana herself showed up on my doorstep with the painting and never went home. She still claims that I fell in love with the subject of the painting before I fell in love with her. Even now, knowing what I know, I can't really say if she was wrong.

From the stories Diana told me of her childhood, I expected Marnie to be more like her sister. When I saw Marnie on the front porch with Gil, I wasn't at all sure that the woman standing in front of me could really be related to my ex-wife. This woman was calm and cool, her hair dark and neatly held back in a smooth bun. Her voice as she spoke to Gil was soft and reassuring. But when she faced me for the first time and I saw her eyes—hazel, not green like Diana's—I knew without a doubt that she was a Maitland. There is something about their eyes that rivets you: a mix of light covering shadow so that you never really know what you're looking at. It made me think of my orchids again, of how two completely disparate hybrids look completely different, but when you put them each under a microscope, you see the characteristics that brand them as being from the same genus and species.

I sat at the head of the table, with Marnie on my right and Gil on my left, the seat next to me empty as usual. Grandpa sat at the foot of the table, with Joanna next to him, slowly feeding him. I passed the corn bread, expecting a neutral conversation about the dry climate of Arizona.

"Does Diana not eat with you?" Marnie looked steadily at me.

I paused with the breadbasket suspended in midair. Slowly, I put it next to Gil's plate, knowing he'd never take a piece as long as I held on to it. "Not usually. She hates to interrupt her painting and she's rarely hungry. Diana really only leaves the house once a week to run a few errands and visit a nursing home. She's found a friend there, apparently—an elderly woman who's also an artist."

Marnie nodded and pinched off a piece of her bread, small delicate movements that were at odds with what little I knew about her from Diana. She primly dabbed at the corners of her mouth with her napkin. She looked at Gil, as if measuring what she could say in his hearing.

"When does she spend time with Gil?" She flushed slightly. "What I meant was that I need to come up with some sort of schedule for Gil and I don't want to interfere with her time with her son."

"I don't anticipate that as a problem. Go ahead and make up a schedule, and I'll make sure Diana is aware of it."

She was still for a moment, her eyes on her plate. Finally, she nodded. "All right," she said. "I'll work on it tonight."

Gil studied his aunt as she ate small, precise spoonfuls of soup. He sat halfway in his chair, one foot on the floor, as if he were ready to bolt. I put my spoon down, my appetite gone. When had my son become this quiet, fearful boy? He'd sailed through the divorce without any problems, and I made sure I still spent as much time with him as I had before. It was only in the last year that Diana had made it difficult for me to see him, with weeks in between my visits. I thought it a good sign that Diana had taken such an interest in spending time with him. It wasn't until it was too late that I realized how very wrong I'd been.

I leaned toward him. "Gil, your aunt Marnie comes from a place where there are tarantulas and scorpions just like we have seagulls and crabs."

Gil's eyes lit up.

Marnie smiled. "Well, I don't know how accurate that is, but I will say I've seen more large, hairy spiders and stinging insects in the last ten years than I ever thought possible."

Gil smiled, and for the first time in over a month, I saw his teeth. He spotted me looking at him and quickly began to study his hands as if a smile had somehow become contraband. Marnie saw this, too, and her brows creased.

I sat back in my chair, eager to change the subject. "Do you still sail,

Marnie? I've seen all your trophies, and Diana used to talk about all your sailing adventures when you were younger."

Obviously, I'd picked the wrong subject again. Her face went still and white as she gave up all pretenses of eating. Slowly she put her spoon down by the side of her plate. "I live in the desert now." She forced a smile—a wooden smile that reminded me of a clown puppet Gil had had as a baby. "No ocean."

Stupidly, I pushed on. "I used to sail a lot—as a boy on Cape Cod." I glanced over at Gil again and saw he hadn't lifted his head. I took another spoonful of my soup, only tasting powder. I swallowed slowly. "Maybe we can go sailing together sometime."

"Maybe," she answered in the tone of voice Diana used when she meant "never."

Marnie slowly pushed out her chair and put her hand on Joanna's arm. "May I?" she asked as she picked up her grandfather's spoon. Joanna nodded and Marnie took the seat Joanna had vacated. The side of his mouth that wasn't paralyzed tilted upward in a smile as Marnie began feeding him, and I was once again struck with how very different she was from her sister.

Without looking at me, she said, "Would you please make up a tray for Diana? I'll bring it up to her when we're done here."

I sat back in my chair. "She won't eat it. I've tried, but I can't force her to eat."

She looked at me with eyes that were frighteningly like Diana's. "I'd like to try, if you don't mind."

I nodded. "I hope you succeed." And I did. Watching Diana waste away with our damaged son as a witness was one of the reasons I'd asked Marnie to come. I stood. "If you're done, Gil, it's time for your shower. Maybe afterward we can watch the Braves on the big screen in my study. They're playing the Mets tonight."

My son, the child I'd picked up at every cry as a baby, who'd allowed me to carry him in a backpack as soon as he could hold up his head on his own, and whose first word was "Daddy," shrank back from me. I let my hand drop to my side. Even I heard the weariness in my voice. "Go take your shower, Gil. I'll be up in a little bit to check on you."

Gil slid out of his chair in the quiet, catlike way he'd adopted since the night of the accident and I watched him go. "I'll go make a tray for Diana," I said as I walked toward the kitchen without looking to see Marnie's expression.

✦

Marnie

I carefully carried the tray up the back stairs to the attic where Diana had her studio. It was at the back of the house, with a distant view of both the ocean and the marsh, and a huge turret window that allowed in the outside light. It had been our mother's studio when she was a girl, and shortly after Diana and I had moved here, Diana had adopted it as her own. But whereas my mother tolerated my presence while she worked, Diana kept the door locked at all times, making it clear that I wasn't welcome. My own feeble attempts at painting had been relegated to the back shed, where the heat and humidity made canvases soggy and paint too thick to do anything with. Maybe that had been Diana's intention all along.

I balanced the tray with one hand while I knocked on the door. When there was no answer, I pressed my ear to the rough wood, listening intently. All was still. I knocked again, knowing I wouldn't get a response. I lowered the tray and placed it on the floor in front of the door, blocking the area between the stairs and the door so that she'd have to pick it up to get inside or, if she were hiding there already, before she could walk down the stairs. Maybe that was all it would take to get her to take a bite. I remembered how she'd looked to me out on the beach and knew I had to try.

Regardless of how I felt about Diana, she was my sister. Maybe blood was thicker than water, after all. Or maybe I was still trying to win affections. I'd done it all my life.

I slowly made my way down the stairs, pausing at the window on the landing. In the daylight, you could see the ocean from here, but at night it was simply a frame for absolute blackness in a moonless sky like tonight. I shuddered, knowing what was out there, and was about to turn away when I noticed a speck of orange glowing in the distance. It was a campfire on the beach and I suspected I knew who was there.

I continued my descent into the foyer, pulled toward the broadcasted sound of a baseball game in the back of the house. Pausing in the threshold, I saw Quinn on a couch with his back to me, the space next to him vacant. On the coffee table in front of him sat two large bowls of popcorn, both untouched.

Backing away, I made my way to the back door. Out of habit, I pulled open the drawer in the hall table and took out a flashlight to guide my way down the path to the ocean. I flipped it on and made my way down following the triangular arc of yellow light, my feet already knowing the way.

The beach was worse at night. At least in the daylight, I could see the ocean clearly where it pressed against the shore and keep my distance. But at night all I could see was liquid shadow, and hear the insistent murmur, like static between stations in my grandfather's old Cadillac. And I couldn't see where it swept over its boundaries, waiting to grab my feet and pull me under.

I kept to the edge of the dunes, my feet slipping in the heavy sand so that I was winded by the time I reached my sister's campfire. She sat in the sand with her arms around her knees, and I remembered times, long ago, when I'd sat next to her and we'd contemplated the universe.

"What do you want to be when you grow up?"

Diana's blond hair glistened like gold in the firelight and I almost said, "Beautiful. Like you." But even I knew how stupid that was. You were either born beautiful or you weren't. "An artist."

She looked at me, her eyes reflecting the flames from the fire and I was afraid for a moment of what she might say, knowing that if she said I couldn't, then it would never come to be. Instead, she looked into the fire and said, "Me, too. We could have our own studio and paint together. We'd be a team. And we'd always be together. Like we promised when we were little."

I nodded, afraid to feel hopeful, but satisfied anyway. I sat back, pulling my knees up to my chest, and allowed myself to dream.

I stood now facing my sister, the echoes of our past circling around us with the smoke from the fire. "You need to eat," I said.

"I'm not hungry."

I shivered despite the heat from the fire and rubbed my hands on my arms. "I brought a tray up to your studio. I know how you love clam chowder."

"I'm not hungry. And I'm not one of your little students who you can easily coerce into doing what you want."

"You need to eat. You don't look . . . well."

Her flame-eyes regarded me silently. "And you look . . . frumpy."

"Ouch," I said, watching the smoke rise over her head like a ghost. "I'm not here to pick a fight. I only mentioned it for your own well-being. You need to take care of yourself, if not for yourself, then for Gil."

She stood, kicking sand on the fire, and then leaned down to shovel big handfuls onto it, making the flames sputter and crack. "Leave my well-being to me and do what you came here for—to help Gil. Just leave me out of it."

Angry now, I faced her over the smoldering fire. "Unfortunately, I think Gil's recovery has everything to do with his relationship with you. Maybe if you pretended to give a damn about him and paid him some attention, he might not have any problems."

"Damn you!" With a sudden motion, she grabbed the flashlight out of my hand and threw it as hard as she could. It landed with a splash and cold fear lit my heart. "You don't know anything. Leave me alone, you hear? Deal with Gil and make him well, but leave me alone."

She turned and ran from me. I wanted to follow her, but I was paralyzed by fear. My feet were lit by the glowing embers of the dying fire, but the sound of the ocean behind me was like a growling animal in a dark forest, out there and waiting for me.

"Stop!" I opened my mouth to scream, but only a strangled whisper emerged from my lips. I turned my head, sure I could hear footsteps in the sand, the moonless night making me blind.

"Marnie?"

I almost fell to my knees in relief. "Quinn? I'm over here." I could see the circle of light made by his flashlight as he approached and I reached for him.

His arm was warm to the touch and I clung as a scared child would cling to a parent in the dark of the night.

"I saw the fire and figured this is where you'd gone." He made a small sound of disgust. "I don't know why she would do that. Leave you here in the dark."

I leaned into his warmth and clung to his arm as he led me back to the path. "I do," I said, as I struggled with leaden feet back to the house.

CHAPTER 4

But I have sinuous shells of pearly hue . . .
Shake one, and it awakens; then apply
Its polished lips to your attentive ear,
And it remembers its august abodes,
And murmurs as the ocean murmurs there.

—WALTER SAVAGE LANDOR

Gil

My daddy took me to Lighthouse Island once when I was five to see the two lighthouses. It was our secret, since they're closed and you're not supposed to go there, but I promised I wouldn't tell anybody. We borrowed a small motorboat and I clung to the sides of it and listened to the snapping of the tall marsh grass against the metal sides as we sped across Muddy Bay and the marsh to the island. But that's how my dad moves; he doesn't seem to know how to go slowly. It's like he thinks there's something chasing him and he can't get away fast enough.

There are two lighthouses because the first one was a mistake. I thought that was funny: having do-overs because the first lighthouse was too short. Mama tells me that I should always do it right on the first try because you don't get second chances in real life. Since Dad showed me the lighthouses, I've always wanted to tell her she's wrong. But there's something in the way she looks at me that makes me feel as if I've already made a mistake just by breathing and there's no use adding back talk to whatever else it is she thinks I've done bad.

The first lighthouse is halfway gone and is the color of a train's caboose. We walked around it for a while, looking for souvenirs but not finding any, and then turned toward the taller one. The bottom half is solid white but the top half is black and white striped. If you look at it just right, it looks like a man with a jacket on and the light itself is the man's head. It leans a little bit, as if it's tired after standing all those years. I'd like to paint it with my watercolors sometime—sometime soon. I haven't painted since the accident. I want to, but when I see the pictures that I want to paint in my head, it's like somebody's switched the channel on the TV to something I don't want to watch. It's that way with words, too. I know what I'm supposed to say, but I can't seem to make the words come out. I guess it's because Grandpa has always carried on about how liars can't go to heaven. Because if I opened my mouth now, I'd have to lie.

The staircase was missing in the smaller lighthouse, but it was still there in the black-and-white one. Dad went first, testing each step carefully, and I followed up behind him, counting the 195 steps. Without him knowing it, I stopped every once in a while to listen for the ghost of the lightkeeper's wife. I'm not supposed to know about her, but I've found that if I'm real quiet, people forget I'm there and say things that they wouldn't if they knew I was listening. That's how I knew that Aunt Marnie was coming, and that she lives in Arizona. It's how I knew that my parents didn't want to be married anymore and that Mama hates Aunt Marnie. And it's how I heard about the lightkeeper who killed his wife a hundred years ago and how she now haunts the lighthouse on Lighthouse Island.

Mama tells stories to Grandpa, not all of them made-up. I know he doesn't approve of ghost stories but I don't guess he has much say about it now. He has to just sit there while Mama tells him whatever story comes to her head. She does this when she can't paint. I don't think she's painted anything since our accident, either, because she's been spending lots of time with Grandpa.

When Dad and I got to the lantern room, we stepped out onto the little balcony and held on to the railing. I wanted to see the ghost and I kept looking inside the glass to see if she was there, at the top of the stairs. I wanted to see if she looks like Mama: see-through, but right there in front of you. And I know why she's like that. It's because of what happened the night on the boat. I think she's still there, in her head, in the ocean in the dark with the tall waves and the sails falling overboard. But that's okay because I don't think I really want to see her, anyway.

My dad took me to a doctor after the accident, and she asked me a lot of questions about what happened the night Mama and I took the *Highfalutin* out into the open ocean. I wanted to tell the doctor that everything is safe inside my head, wrapped up in a little box like it was Christmas. And I will never open it. Not ever. That's why I can't talk about what happened. Because I don't want to go to hell and that's where liars go.

Dad and I left Lighthouse Island without seeing any ghosts but I'm okay with that. I've already seen enough ghosts to last my entire life.

❧

Marnie

I sat on my old bed and stared at the familiar landscapes that my mother had painted and that had hung on my bedroom wall since I was a young girl. They were all marsh scenes: of oyster beds and nesting herons and stretches of battered maritime forests that always made me think of my mother. She'd been like one of the tall cedars clinging to the sand as the ocean washed away the earth its roots clung to, making its demise a certainty. This had been the world beyond my four walls, a world I'd never imagined leaving, no matter how flawed. Even now, I look back on my childhood as a canvas splashed with vibrancy; the paint spurted from a wild machine, and I never realized how dangerous it could be if I got too close.

My suitcases sat unopened on the floor inside the doorway, where Quinn must have left them. I tried to will myself to go to them and unpack, to hang up my functional shirts and nondescript skirts in the empty closet, but I couldn't seem to move myself forward. My resolve to leave immediately, which had started down on the beach, had lost its burn somewhere on the path back to the house. But I knew I couldn't stay. Remaining here, in this place with these people, was too hard. As my mother had always told me, I lacked courage: the courage to use purple to color the ocean in a painting and the courage of conviction had always been synonymous in my mother's mind. And I lacked both.

I stood and moved to the closet door, nudging it open with my foot. Reaching forward I pulled the string on the overhead bulb, the light illuminating the corners of the room like a recalled memory. Most of my stuff was gone, packed up and given to charity by my grandfather after I had left for college. I suppose he knew even then that I never intended to come back.

I spied the large conch shell in the dim corner of a top shelf as I reached to turn off the light. I could almost believe, as I stood near the closet doorway, that I could hear the echo of the ocean's surf emanating from the delicate folds of the shell. I stood my ground, wary of the sounds I thought I could hear and of the memories they invoked.

Quickly, I snapped off the light and stepped out of the closet, nearly tripping over Gil, who stood silently at the foot of my bed. I startled, swallowing a scream. In my agitation, I almost asked him why he didn't give me a shout to let me know he was in my room and felt instantly ashamed.

I knelt in front of him, staring into familiar eyes. "Are you all right?"

He nodded, but his lips tilted into a slight smile as if to say that his words weren't fooling either one of us. I smiled back and smoothed the hair off his forehead. He smelled of sweat and salt water and a sugar-cookie dusting of sand coated his damp skin and clothes as if he'd stood in the surf, facing its encroaching tide without fear.

"Will your dad be mad that you need another shower?"

Ignoring my question, he walked slowly around the room, his hands and eyes taking in the unpacked suitcases and empty drawers.

I sat down on the bed and patted the spot next to me and waited until he slid up on the yellow chenille bedspread. "I can't tell you how much it's meant to me to finally meet you, Gil."

He kept his head down as he stared at his hands, and I noticed again the long, slender fingers so much like his mother's. I glanced away. "I'd like to stay here longer, to get to know you better, but I don't think it's going to work out that way after all."

His fingers began pulling on the cotton tufts of the bedspread, his agitated movements mimicking my thoughts. *There's nothing you can do for us here, Marnie. Go back to your desert, to your months without rain, and leave us alone. We don't need you here, and I don't want you here. So go home.* I'd been foolish to think I had the strength to help Gil. To help Diana. To think that sixteen years after our mother's death, we could finally come to terms with each other and what happened the night she died.

A door slammed somewhere in the house, and I pictured Diana climbing the stairs, the scent of cigarettes and stale perfume trailing behind her. I watched as Gil's shoulders went rigid, his eyes wide as he shifted his gaze to the corners of the room as if looking for a place to hide. His gaze settled on the closet door and he sprang from the bed and darted into the dark closet, closing the door silently behind him.

I waited for a moment, listening for approaching footsteps that never came, remembering other nights spent in this bedroom as a young girl, waiting for Diana to come home and tell me that everything was all right again. That she wanted my forgiveness. But forgiveness is a hard thing to squeeze from a stone, and that is what my sister had become when we'd moved to this house. All of her emotions were eked onto the canvases she created, leaving no scraps for me. I'd once made the mistake of waiting for her in her room. She was angry when she'd found me asleep on top of her quilted bedspread. She'd thrown her sweater at me, and it had smelled of pluff mud and marsh grass and some other odor I couldn't identify yet. And I'd known she'd snuck off to Cape Romain and she hadn't gone alone. A button hit me in the eye and made me cry.

"Good—I hope it hurt. You should cry. You should feel so sorry for what you've done that you cry every day of your life."

I stared at her, not understanding. What had I done? I swallowed back the tears and searched for the words from one of our grandfather's sermons. I wasn't yet sure of what turn the other cheek was all about, but I did get that I was supposed to forgive those who trespassed against me. I looked at my sister, at the face and hair my mother had chosen to put in so many of her paintings, and wiped my eyes. "I forgive you, Diana."

She turned to me, her eyes dark and hateful, and I cringed. I didn't know this Diana—this girl who looked so much like the other half of my soul but had somehow become the stranger you'd cross the street to get away from.

"You forgive me? That's really rich, Marnie. That you would be forgiving me." She laughed, a sickening, hollow sound that melted my resolve of giving her my cheek to slap. I was afraid of Diana. I think it was because I'd seen that wild look before many times, but never on Diana. It was our mother's face I saw—the face she'd wear as she approached one of her episodes, like a horse galloping toward a cliff and moving too swiftly to stop before hurtling off into nothingness. It was the last memory I had of my mother's face.

I turned without speaking and attempted to leave the room but Diana pulled me back, her fingernails cutting into the bare skin of my arm. "I don't want your forgiveness, and I sure as hell don't need it." She grinned, knowing we weren't allowed to cuss in our grandfather's house. "So get the hell out of here and don't mention forgiveness to me ever again. Not ever. Do you hear me?" Her voice had risen to a shriek and I hated her then. I don't think I've ever stopped.

I yanked my arm away. "Go to hell," I said, showing her that I was just as capable of cussing as she was.

She laughed again, but her face began melting like a watercolor left out in the rain. For a moment I saw the old Diana as she stared at me from her ruined face and I lifted my hand to touch her.

Diana turned her back to me, her shoulders hunched forward. "I'm already there, Marnie. I already am."

I fled from the room and hid in my closet, wrapping my arms around my knees and praying that she wouldn't find me. It was my grandfather who pulled me out three hours later and patted my head with large, shaking hands while I sat there, trembling.

I stood before the closed closet door and tapped gently with my fingernails. "Gil? Are you all right?"

Silence.

I tapped again. "Gil? Can I come in? Just me—I'm by myself." And then, unbidden, I said the words I'd always hoped to hear on my sister's lips. "I'm lonely without you. Can't I come in?" I placed my forehead against the cool wood of the door and pressed my eyes shut. "Please."

The doorknob turned with a slight squeal, and the door was pushed open a few inches, revealing complete darkness within. The triangle of light landed on Gil's golden head, and for a moment Diana's eyes looked back at me before he ducked his head, his attention focused on the object he was cradling in his hands.

Opening the door further, I stepped in and knelt in front of him, realizing with surprise that he held the conch shell.

"Are you all right?" I asked quietly.

Without a word he held up the shell to my ear, and it was all I could do not to jerk back and knock the shell out of his hands and away from me. Instead, I remained rooted to the closet floor, listening to the tremulous echo of the ocean's waves whispered from the pearlescent lips of the shell.

I tried to move away, but Gil's hands holding the shell followed me, not allowing me to escape from the sound of my past. Finally I put my hands over Gil's and moved them away so that I could turn my head to look at him. His eyes appeared liquid in the dim light, and I realized he was crying.

I took the shell away from him and laid it aside, then drew him to me as I remembered my gruff grandfather doing all those years ago. Gil sobbed silently on my shoulder, soaking my shirt as I patted his soft head. My voice was low and seemed to be coming from somebody else. "Do you want me to stay, Gil? Do you not want me to leave?"

I brought his face around to look at me. He hiccupped once and continued staring at me but didn't answer. Instead, he reached behind him in the dark and picked up the shell again and held it out to me. I ducked my head so he couldn't see my own tears. I wasn't sure what else he was asking of me, but I knew that I couldn't leave. I saw a part of me in his neediness—the girl who'd reached for her mother and had only found salty air—and a corner of my heart softened for that young Marnie and for this lost child.

"I'll stay, Gil. For you."

His arms came around my neck, and I felt the scratchiness of the shell against my cheek. His other hand patted my back as if to comfort me, and I smiled into the darkness as I contemplated the wisdom of this young boy.

CHAPTER 5

Terrestrial orchids live on the ground, needing a constantly moist medium in which to grow. Epiphytic orchids live on the branches of other plants. They are not parasites, as they obtain no food from the trees on which they grow, but have air roots, which are accustomed to drying out in between periods of rain.

—DR. QUINN BRISTOW'S GARDENING JOURNAL

Quinn

The marsh slowly pulled a reluctant sun into the dawn, its faint light etching lines through the layers of clouds, creating thin reptile skins in the sky. That's how Gil, with his artist's heart, had once described the dawn to me. We're both early risers and Gil would usually be waiting for me as I set out for my greenhouse, and we'd watch the sun come up together. He'd join me and my orchids and ask a thousand questions while I tended to the flowers. He'd never asked if he could help me; it was almost as if he knew I needed to sink my fingers into damp mulch as much as I needed to fill my lungs with air. And he'd be right, of course. Studying orchids has taught me a lot about life, and a lot about women. Certainly more than I learned in three years of marriage. But at least with orchids you know that if you water them and treat them well, they'll reward you with blooms.

When I heard a tap on the greenhouse door, I assumed it was Gil. He hadn't joined me in the greenhouse since the accident, so I turned with pleasant surprise toward the door and tried to hide my disappointment that it wasn't him.

Marnie stuck her head through the doorway, her hair already pulled mercilessly back from her face in a tight bun at the base of her neck. I wondered absently if she ever wore it loose and what it would look like falling across her shoulders and down her back. I thought I knew, of course. I'd seen the painting before Diana had taken it from the living room wall, leaving only the scars on the paint as a reminder.

Marnie smiled. "Can I come in? Is this a good time?" Her smooth forehead puckered.

I motioned for her to come inside as I flipped on the faucet and began filling my watering can. "It's always a good time when I'm in here."

I allowed my gaze to flicker over her as she entered through the glass door and shut it softly behind her. She wore a pale knee-length skirt with a floral print and flat-soled sandals. Her sleeveless blouse was buttoned up to the neck, with only the defiant flash of a gold chain buried inside the collar. I almost smiled. She couldn't have been more different from Diana if she had tried. And I had the distinct impression that she had.

"Why is that?" she asked, smoothing a hand over the back of her head to tuck in any errant strands that would dare to push past their boundaries.

"Because Diana never comes in here." I wanted to bite back the comment before the last syllable had faded in the early-morning air between us.

Marnie turned her head, but not before I'd seen the trace of a smile on her lips. "I know what you mean." She turned back to me and flapped her hand. "No, not because we don't get along. But because I've known Diana for a long time. I know how she can suck the air out of a room just by entering it."

It was my turn to smile. "Yeah. I used to think that was a good quality in a person. Now I find that it's too exhausting for us mere mortals."

She didn't say anything but turned to examine a shadow-witch orchid, its pearlescent white petals bisected with bright green veins. She leaned forward and sniffed, closing her eyes, and I was once again reminded of the girl in the portrait. "Do you live here?" she asked.

"In the greenhouse?"

She bit her bottom lip in a move I was beginning to recognize as something she did when she didn't want to smile. "No. I meant here. On this property. Since you and Diana are divorced, I was just wondering . . ." Her voice trailed away.

I hoisted the full watering can up on the laminate counter. "I wanted to be near Gil. And your grandfather. Diana forgets sometimes that she's responsible for them." I figured I didn't need to soften my words for Marnie. As she had said herself, she'd known Diana for a long time. "We have joint custody. She was taking her meds at the time of the divorce and I didn't want to make it an issue then."

"Then?"

"Yeah. Up until about a year ago, when I noticed her behavior getting more and more erratic and I figured out what was going on. It's kind of a wake-up call when your young son calls you at two o'clock in the morning asking where his mother is."

"Was there something else going on in her life a year ago? Maybe something that might have triggered her decline?"

I remembered having the same thoughts and it made me feel a certain kinship with Marnie. Not everybody analyzes a situation trying to find a reason, perhaps to point blame on yourself for your own shortcomings that may or may not have had anything to do with it.

"It coincided with Diana trying to find a nursing home for your grandfather. I don't know why that would have triggered anything if at all; it's just that I remember what was going on then."

I relaxed my grip on the watering can, not surprised at the anger I still felt at the danger she had put our son in. And how I was no closer to understanding her demons now than I had been then. I reached for the old dish towel on the counter and began wiping off any water droplets that might have landed on the leaves of the plants. I took another glance at Marnie and saw her in what I assumed was her teacher's pose: feet together, hands clasped in front of her, and her hazel eyes impassive. She wasn't one to give anything away, I figured. Or maybe her years as a Maitland had taught her that holding back was the only way to survive.

I continued going down the line of potted orchids, watering each plant according to the little notes I kept beside each pot and feeling her gaze on me as I worked. "I tried to talk to her about it and to even

get her to go with me to see her doctor but she wouldn't. So I fixed up
the old caretaker's cottage and moved in. I didn't ask and she didn't
complain. She didn't even say anything when I built this greenhouse.
And everything was sort of working out if you could overlook her un-
explained absences and reappearances or her sudden need to visit a new
friend in a nursing home. Until the accident, anyway."

Gently, Marnie stroked an ivory petal. "You didn't really explain
on the phone what happened—only that Gil and Diana were in an accident involving your sailboat and that he'd stopped speaking. I think
that to help him, I really need to know as much about it as possible."
Her lips had thinned, turning white at the edges. "It reminds me . . ."
She stopped and dropped her hand from the flower. She looked at me
again, her face placid but her eyes stormy and bright. She continued. "It
reminds me of the night our mother died."

I nodded, recalling what little Diana had told me. How their mother
in one of her periodic manic episodes had decided to take her two
daughters sailing despite the whitecaps on the waves and the warnings
from the weather center. But as Diana had explained, there was never
any dissuading their mother once she'd made up her mind. I never had
the heart to tell Diana that she and her mother were no different as far
as that was concerned.

I brought the watering can back to the sink, trying to recall the
night of Gil's accident and explain just the facts to Marnie devoid of
the gut-twisting sense of loss I had felt when I'd walked into his room
and found it empty.

"I'd known for about a week that something was wrong. She'd taken
to spending hours and hours in her studio without eating for days on
end. And then she'd go out on the beach and build sandcastle after
sandcastle, all of them nearly identical. I tried to talk to her, to get her
to come inside and eat a meal. I even called her doctor, who said that
unless I committed her, I couldn't force her to see him. But she was
happy—happier than I'd seen her in a very long time. And because her
behavior seemed nondestructive, I decided to let her be and just keep
an eye on her. I kept trying to talk to her, to ask her about her medication, but I couldn't get through to her."

I twisted on the water faucet again to begin refilling the watering can but saw only Diana's empty eyes. My hands gripped the handle of the can, the metal edge biting into my palm. I looked up at Marnie, but her eyes remained blank, her hands folded neatly in front of her. It was then that I saw the resemblance between her and Gil: not the physical similarities like he shared with his mother, but the slightness of movement, the emotions hidden behind blank expressions as if they were trying very hard not to be noticed. Like hiding in plain sight, their wary eyes like those of a deer I'd once seen on a hunt with my father and older brother, straddling the riverbank to slake his thirst, but constantly aware of the danger of letting down his guard just once.

I turned off the water and faced her. "It was around eight o'clock in the evening. Gil and I normally sit and watch a little TV together before he goes to bed at nine. When he didn't come, I went to go check on him and found his room empty. I panicked when I discovered that Diana was also gone. I was at a loss until I got a call from the marina telling me that Diana had taken out my sailboat and that Gil was with her. They were worried because of the approaching storm and were calling the coast guard."

Marnie's lips had gone completely white now. When she didn't say anything, I continued. "As I told you on the phone, we don't know what happened. The coast guard found the capsized boat. Diana had passed out from loss of blood from the gash in her leg and Gil was somehow managing to hold on to her, keeping them both from slipping off."

Something gray and fast-moving swept behind her eyes and I saw her swallow. Her voice was strained when she spoke. "And neither one of them will talk about what happened?"

I shook my head. "Diana won't and Gil can't." A thickness arose in my throat like a fist of dried hope and I swallowed it down. "I've taken Gil to several specialists in Charleston and they all tell me the same thing: He's faced a trauma and this is how his mind is dealing with it. He'll speak when he's ready and not before."

"Is he receiving counseling?" Marnie's tone was placid, but her fingers had begun to pluck at the fabric of her skirt.

"For a couple of weeks I tried." I wiped my hands over my face, trying to forget Gil's tortured expression every time I had to take him to the doctor. "I gave up. I asked the doctor to give me a month with him to see what I could do."

"So you called me."

I stared at her nails on her clasped hands, noticing that they were short and well-kept. They were capable hands, not those of an artist at all. I wondered if that had bothered her, being in a house with artists, with a love for creating things on canvas, yet relegated to simply watch like a crow who'd found herself in a nest with nightingales. In the moment that our eyes met, I thought she knew what I was thinking. Embarrassed, I looked away.

Hoisting the watering can, I resumed my rounds of the orchids. "Yes, I called you. But I can't take credit for that. It was your grandfather's idea."

"Grandpa?"

I gave her a quick glance, relieved to finally see emotion on her face. "Yeah. He showed me a passage he'd highlighted from the Bible about sisters. His nurse gave me your address."

Her lips parted in a soft "o" as she turned her gaze to the window, toward the rising sun and the fading moon that pulled at the ocean beyond the dunes. Softly, she recited, " 'Say, I pray thee, thou art my sister: that it may be well with me for thy sake; and my soul shall live because of thee.' "

I scratched my head trying to remember what else the old man had told me. "Genesis, I think."

"Genesis, chapter twelve, verse thirteen, actually. It's about Abraham and his wife, but Grandpa thought that the words taken out of context fit Diana and me." She grinned sheepishly. "Having a preacher for a grandfather sort of stays with you, I guess."

"I guess," I said, not able to look away from her face, which had gone soft and luminous. This was the Marnie I'd only seen on canvas— the Marnie she was very careful not to let anybody see. I watched as her expression changed into the mask I was beginning to get used to.

"After last night, on the beach, I decided I wasn't going to stay. Diana and I . . . well, we don't like each other very much. I couldn't imagine being around her every day. But Gil came to my room and convinced me that he needs me here." A reluctant smile tugged at her lips. "He's a great kid. And I think . . ." She stopped and I saw her chin jut out as she searched for something different to say. "I think I can help him. I've never worked with this kind of case before, since my training and experience is with special-needs kids, but I think my methods could help. I just need you to give me free rein." She raised a hand to stop me from speaking. "I'll keep you updated, of course. But I also need you to act as a buffer between me and Diana. I'd rather not have to talk to her at all."

I recalled all the sailing trophies lining the walls in the house and the old pictures of the two sisters in their younger incarnations with their arms around each other. I'd found them in shoe boxes in the back of the hall closet and knew Diana had put them there. Looking at Marnie now, I was encouraged by the fact that Diana hadn't thrown them away. I had no idea what had happened to those two happy girls, other than their mother's death. But that alone didn't really explain their animosity toward each other. There was a story there that Diana had never shared with me despite my prompting—one that might come to the surface now that the sisters had been reunited, albeit reluctantly. But my concern was Gil, and all else had to take a backseat.

"Of course," I said. "Gil's well-being is my priority. I have a lot of faith in you." I wasn't sure why I had said that, other than that I truly believed it. There had to be strength and a sense of purpose in a woman who would turn her back on her childhood by the sea to live in the desert just to prove a point. The fact that she worked with special-needs children was just icing on the cake.

Her impassive mask remained in place. "I'll do my best."

She moved to the door but I stopped her with a hand on her arm. "What were you going to say before—about you and Gil? You stopped, but I think you meant to say something else."

She looked at me for a long moment, her eyes distant. "I was going to say how much alike Gil and I are. I didn't think you'd want to hear that."

"Why would you think that?"

"Because you married Diana and Gil's her son. I'm nothing like her."

I stopped myself before I could disagree. She wouldn't want to know the reason Diana and I had first met and how it had everything to do with how very much she and Diana resembled each other in ways not easily seen.

I didn't say anything as she pulled the door open, then stopped to face me again. "What happened to your sailboat—the one Diana and Gil were on?"

"The coast guard towed the *Highfalutin* to shore. She's in dry dock now, waiting for me to decide what to do."

She'd gone very pale and still. "You named your sailboat *Highfalutin*?"

"Actually, Diana did. She never stepped foot on it until that night, but she insisted on naming it."

Barely audible, she said, "She would, wouldn't she?"

I held the door as she stepped through the threshold into the heavy morning air, the humidity high despite the early hour. "I've seen your sailing trophies, Marnie. Maybe you'd like to come down to the marina with me some time to see her. Let me know if you think she's salvageable or not."

"No!" She shook her head, then said more evenly, "No. I don't know anything about sailboats or sailing anymore. It's been too long."

Or not long enough, I thought as I watched her stumble in her hurry to get away from me. I grabbed her arm to steady her and our eyes met. The fear I saw in them sent a cold shock running down my neck despite the heat. Her fear was real and raw, and I knew then that ten years in the desert had done nothing to dispel it. *She's as lost as the rest of us,* I thought with a sinking heart. Our knight in shining armor had turned out to be just another lonely soldier stuck in the trenches. I let go of her arm.

Glancing toward the house, she said, "I'm going to go find Gil and start our first lesson. I think it will help him to have routine and structure in his life. Can we meet you at the house at noon for lunch?"

"I'll work it out with my practice so that I'm home every day at noon. All right?"

She gave me a tremulous smile, but her eyes remained flat. "All right. I'll see you at lunch, then."

I held the door, not allowing her to close it, and she looked up at me expectantly.

"I'm thinking that maybe Gil's not the only one who can benefit from you being here."

"What do you mean?"

I was reminded yet again why I had chosen to work with animals instead of humans: I have an almost uncanny ability to say the wrong thing and animals don't seem to care. Yet I couldn't forget the look on Marnie's face when I'd said the name of my boat.

I cleared my throat. "I only meant that it seems you have some unresolved issues with Diana and that spending time with her—"

She cut me off. "I've resolved all my issues by moving away and getting on with my life. I'm here to help Gil because he's my flesh and blood and I can't see him getting the help he needs from his own mother. It is my duty to help. And when he's better, I'll go back to Arizona and get on with my life, as I've been doing for the last ten years."

She walked away quickly, her shoes kicking up gravel and sand and old crumbled shells, crushing them beneath her feet like dried-up dreams and memories she thought had long ago been relegated to dust.

*

Gil

I watched Aunt Marnie from my secret spot under the porch while I tried to decide if I wanted her to see me or not. I wanted to go to the greenhouse with my dad, but stopped when I saw her. She had that look on her face that grown-ups wear when they have to do something they don't want to. Like when my dad comes to get me for one of my doctor appointments. And for some reason my aunt Marnie looks like that all the time. But I know that's not true. In my mom's room, there's paintings of two girls that I think are my mom and her sister, and Aunt Marnie is different in them. It was like she was softer then. Like clay before it goes in the oven and hardens so that there's no memory of how it used to be before. Except for her eyes, I'd say that's how it is with Marnie.

I'd like to paint her, I think. When that thing inside of me that tells me to paint lets me know it's ready again, I'll paint her first. It's not like she's pretty like my mother. My mother is beautiful, and people always stare at her when I'm with her and it makes me proud. But Aunt Marnie is different. You don't see she's beautiful by looking straight at her; it's more like catching her from the corner of your eye that makes you know you've seen something special. And her eyes. They're not like my mom's at all. But maybe that's why I think they're so beautiful.

I crawled out of my spot so that Aunt Marnie could see me. She stopped, then waved and gave me a real smile—not the kind of smile my mom gives me when I try to tell her something. She rubbed my hair and hugged my shoulders, and I didn't want to pull away.

"Well, it's official, Gil," she said. "I'm staying. And I want us to have fun." She looked me straight in the eyes like Grandpa does and I liked that. "But it also means that we're going to have to do some school-work, too. Just you and me. I'll be the teacher and you're going to be my only student. Does that sound like fun?"

I nodded and she touched my face.

She kneeled in front of me, and I know it must have hurt her knees to kneel on the sand and broken shells but she pretended that it didn't. "You remind me a lot of someone I used to know a long time ago who was very special to me. We used to paint together and that's how we became so close. I was thinking that you and I could start out that way, too."

I blinked. I wanted to tell her that I wasn't painting anymore but I couldn't. Because then I'd have to tell her why. So I just kept quiet.

"After breakfast, let's go down to Jeremy Creek and study the water-front with the boats coming in and out. We'll just bring our sketch pads and see how we do as we get to know each other."

I nodded. I'd been afraid she'd say she wanted to paint the ocean. But I'd seen the painting that used to hang over the couch downstairs and knew she wouldn't want to go near the ocean, either. So we'll go to

Jeremy Creek and sketch boats instead. Maybe, if I'm good, she'll let me sketch her. And if I do, maybe I can draw the person I see when she thinks no one else is watching—the person in all those photographs in the album I keep under my bed that nobody else knows I have, except for Grandpa because he gave it to me.

Taking Aunt Marnie's hand, I led her inside the house to show her my shell collection. She hurried after me like somebody was chasing her, and I knew that she'd heard Mama's voice call out to my daddy and that if we stayed where we were for a few more minutes, she would see us.

Aunt Marnie stopped at the door for a moment as if trying to decide what she should do, so I tugged on her hand to help her choose and she followed. I knew she would. Aunt Marnie sees ghosts when she looks at Mama, and it's way too early in the morning for that.

CHAPTER 6

Raging waves of the sea, foaming out their own shame; wandering stars, to whom is reserved the blackness of darkness forever.
—The General Epistle of Jude 13

Diana

When I was nine and Marnie six, our mother took us to Disney World. This visit to the Nirvana of every childhood was marred by the fact that our mother woke us in the middle of the night to tell us we were going. In a frenzy she stripped the sheets from our beds and told us to throw our clothes onto the sheets and then knot the ends together. These were our suitcases, and Marnie and I thought we were on a grand adventure as we tossed our bundles over our shoulders and ran barefoot—we were still in our pajamas—out to the car.

We ran out of gas before we'd crossed the state line. We waited until dawn when Mama was able to flag down a passing trucker to hitch a ride to the nearest gas station. She left us alone in the car, and I held Marnie while she cried and cried for Mama to come back. And she did—four hours later. Four hours of Marnie crying and me trying to pretend that I wasn't scared and really believed that Mama would come back.

When Mama got back into the car smelling of gas and something else we didn't recognize, we told her we wanted to go home. But she was in the middle of one of her episodes and nothing could make her turn back once she'd got started. I didn't like the way she looked at us, her eyes like vacant skies with dark storm clouds creeping up from behind. It scared me the most because every once in a while, I could see the same dark clouds when I looked in the mirror.

We sped down the highway while Mama spun stories about our adventure, how we were princesses on the run and that we would be met at the gates of Disney World by Walt Disney himself. Mama was flushed and sparkling, as insidious in her charm as I was impervious to it. I, after all, had seen the clouds. Eventually it would start to rain.

By the time we reached Orlando, Marnie was smiling but I was girded. Mama's energy had begun to flag with the darkening sky and I reached for Marnie's hand to hold for the last hour of our trip.

We never made it inside Disney World. Mama had a breakdown somewhere between the empty parking lot and the vacated ticket windows, attracting the attention of two security guards.

I grew up that night, I think, under the celluloid eye of Mickey Mouse and two Orlando police officers, the night air around us saturated with the scent of old popcorn and spun sugar. My childhood was forever stained with the image of my little sister clinging to me in the back of a police car and then on the couch at the police station until my grandfather arrived hot and harried and smelling of sweat. I can still see two barefoot little girls in pajamas clutching dirty sheets stuffed with clothes and perched on a green vinyl couch with tufts of stuffing pressing through the seams like bleached cotton candy.

But Marnie kept her head tucked under my neck the whole time, her hand in mine, as night became morning and I grew older and older. Afterward, when we were staying at our grandfather's house and our mother had been sent away for the first of many times, Marnie told me that she hadn't been scared because I was there. She pretended that I was Superman and that I wouldn't let anything happen to her. And I didn't.

Even now, when I turn my head, I can sometimes feel her there, at my side, her warm breath like that of a suckling baby. She has always been a presence there, my sister, not a twin but the other half of my soul. My right side walks with her ghost as if without her I am not whole. We are Maitlands, after all. And what better curse could there be but for two inseparable sisters to resent the very air the other breathes?

I could feel Marnie and Gil watching me from the porch but I didn't turn to look at them. I was quite sure that they didn't want to see me any more than I wanted to see them. Instead, I made my way to the silly glass building that Quinn calls his greenhouse. It's nothing more than a kit he ordered on the Internet and he put together on a clearing between the big house and the old caretaker's cottage that he now calls his house.

If I were to paint a picture of the greenhouse, I would show Quinn on the inside of his fortress sanctuary, where he breathes life into temperamental plants and pretends that he can see everything around him just in case somebody might need him. But it's a house of glass, after all, and I would paint the fissures and holes that exist in the walls but that he refuses to see. Standing on the outside and looking in would be me and Gil. And Marnie. She's one of the people Quinn has collected because she needs fixing. He's only attracted to the broken ones. Why else would a vet not even keep a goldfish as a pet?

I didn't knock but pulled the door open, letting it slap shut loudly behind me. My bandage itched under my skirt but I dared not scratch at it and call his attention to it. I needed to be on my best behavior, so I just stood there and tried not to look as belligerent as I felt. I tried not to think about how much a prisoner Quinn had made me, and instead focused on our son. It was only because of him that I would put myself in this position. I almost smiled at the irony, considering how Gil couldn't stand to be in the same room with me anymore. Not that I blamed him.

Quinn looked up at me from the small desk on the far side of the room, and I watched as his calm doctor face settled on his features. I love the way he looks, all broad-shouldered and blue-eyed and tall enough so that when I wear heels I still need to look up at him. And yet I can't say that it was his physical looks that first attracted me to him. He had the misfortune to fall in love with one of my paintings, one that wasn't for sale, and his persistence in acquiring it and my perverseness in not letting him have it are what first drew me into his bed. The painting still belongs to me, yet it is stored with a sheet over it in my studio, where I don't have to look at it and face all of my failures.

Unaccustomed to talking, I cleared my throat before speaking. "I need the car keys. I have an appointment with Dr. Hirsch at two o'clock, and I'd like to run some errands while I'm out. I need more canvas board." I looked hopefully up at him at this last admission. It wasn't a complete lie. I did need more, but I'd needed more for almost two months. It was only after I'd uttered the words that I realized I had spoken the truth. Since Marnie's return, I'd felt drawn to my paints again. That part of me that makes me paint trembled inside like a tightly folded flower emerging into the sun, and I had begun to see light and shadows again instead of the flat colors I'd been seeing since the night on the boat with Gil. I didn't want to examine the reason why too closely, afraid that I might see Marnie's return into my life as something good. The barrier of hatred I had erected between us was not impenetrable; but should it dissolve, we would both be forced to examine the truth. And that would be my undoing.

He tapped his pen against his gardening journal. "Did you take your pills this morning?"

I managed to keep my breathing even. I managed a smile. "Yes, I did. As a matter of fact, I found Joanna and asked her for them before she had a chance to come find me."

He smiled back, but I could still see the uncertainty in his eyes. "Why don't I take you? I don't have any patients after twelve."

"No." He looked at me sharply and I softened my tone. "Thanks, but no. I'm feeling much better and I'm more than capable of driving myself to Charleston. Besides, Dr. Hirsch thinks it would be good for me to get back to visiting my friend in the nursing home. Helping others does help me, and I'm eager to see her again." My wound itched as if it were clawing at me from the inside, and I struggled to keep my fingers away from it. Quinn's eyes watched my fingers as they twitched on my skirt and I quickly clasped my hands together. Quinn was never one to miss anything.

"I still think I should drive you. It's still so soon . . ." He didn't finish his sentence, his unspoken words loud enough for both of us to hear.

I played my trump card. "But I'd be gone for most of the afternoon, and I know you don't want to leave Gil for that long. He's only known Marnie for a short while, and I don't know how comfortable he would be spending all day with her."

He stood, then hesitated only a moment before digging into his pocket for his keys. "Is your cell phone charged?"

"Yes."

"Good. I want you to call me when you get to Dr. Hirsch's and when you leave the nursing home so I'll know when to expect you."

"And if I don't?"

He didn't blink. "Then you'll be confined here or in a hospital. Either way, you won't have your freedom."

I had won a small victory, so I bit my lip to keep me from replying. Instead, I simply turned on my heel and left the greenhouse, giving the door a satisfactory slam on my way out. I didn't have to turn around to see that Quinn was already on his cell phone. First, checking with Joanna that I really had taken my pills and then calling Dr. Hirsch to verify my appointment. He would probably even call the nursing home to confirm my visit, and he would be satisfied with all the answers provided. There would be only one more question to ask, one more thing to find out. But this one last question would never be asked; I had made sure of that. Because how can you find an answer when you don't even know there's a question?

ø

Marnie

My grandfather's house is located on a strip of land sandwiched between the South Santee River and the Atlantic Ocean. The original house on the site had been built by my great-great-great-great-grandfather, Josiah Maitland, a retired sea captain who wanted to become a gentleman farmer and grow rice out of the rich, wet earth of the South Carolina Lowcountry.

He'd been fairly successful, the number of acres he owned between the river and the ocean growing at a somewhat faster rate than the number of children he and his wife brought into the world. He was prosperous and prolific and presumably content with his life until the night his wife burned the house to the ground, killing herself and nine out of their ten children. That tenth child was my great-great-great-grandmother.

Diana, after we had moved in with our grandfather, would delight in scaring me with stories of poor old Josiah, driven to curse God in his grief and forever damning future generations of Maitlands. Diana had me almost believing that on still nights when the moon nested in the open arms of the dead cypress trees, you could smell the smoke of wood burning and hear the cries of children. I never heard them. I couldn't hear anything over the sound of my own screams.

But before our mother's death, before the time our lives changed, Diana and I lived in a small house on Jeremy Creek in the coastal village of McClellanville, a short boat ride on the Intracoastal Waterway from our grandfather's house. Our parents were free spirits, artists who didn't believe in conventions like being married before having children. I suppose this was one of the many reasons why we didn't see much of our Bible-thumping grandfather during our early years.

Despite the occasional snide remarks from other children, Diana and I were oblivious to our unconventional household, immersed as we were in the joys of growing up in the Lowcountry. There were always other children to play with, barefoot like us, to climb oak trees, skip oyster shells across Jeremy Creek, or play kick the can. We were experts at crabbing and in navigating the myriad fingers and estuaries of the marsh in our small boats. And then later, when Diana and I were old enough to help hoist a mainsail, our mother taught us to sail.

I suppose it's these childhood memories that brought me back to this place and to Gil. If the child needed help, I could only imagine that this magical place could provide it. Maybe for both of us.

It was with these thoughts that I made the plan for our day's trip, and I set out with feelings of both excitement and trepidation. Gil and I were heading to my rental car to take the long route by paved road to McClellanville when we were intercepted by Quinn.

"Are you off to town?"

I nodded. I had asked for permission to take Gil, knowing that disappearing with Gil, despite my good intentions, might justifiably be cause for Quinn to worry. I tucked my sketch pad and small case of charcoal pencils more securely under my arm. "Yes. We'll be back for lunch, though."

He looked behind me to my parked car. "You're driving?"

"I'll make sure he wears his seat belt. And don't worry about me getting lost. I lived here for eighteen years, remember?" I avoided looking directly into his eyes knowing that I hadn't answered his real question.

"Why don't you take my jon boat? It'll get you there in half the time than it would take by car. Besides, Diana's told me that you could navigate the marsh blindfolded."

My gaze slid to his as I felt Gil leave my side and head for my car. After pulling the passenger-side door open, he plopped himself into the front seat with his pad of paper on his lap and shut the door.

I looked down at my feet, unable to meet his eyes as I lied. "I think Gil's more comfortable riding in the car. It's too soon. . . ."

When he didn't say anything, I dragged my eyes back to his face.

"Too soon for Gil? Or for you, Marnie?"

I glanced at my watch. "It's getting late and we're going to lose the morning light if we don't leave now."

He didn't move. "It's just the marsh, Marnie. I wouldn't dream of suggesting that either one of you should head out into the ocean on any kind of watercraft."

"It's too soon," I said again as I watched Gil staring straight ahead out the windshield.

"All right," he said and I could hear the reluctance in his voice. "But I want you to know that Gil loved the water more than anything—even more than his painting. And I will give that back to him. Even if I have to drag you kicking and screaming along for the ride."

My eyes met his, and I was surprised to see that his were dead serious.

"We'll see about that," I said under my breath as I turned and headed for the car.

"Yes, we will," he said before I could close the door. I didn't look at him as I backed the car out of the long gravel drive before heading out toward the highway.

It was a short drive down Highway 17. I flipped on the radio to erase the silence and began to sing aloud to a pop song that had been played so many times I knew every word by heart. I had no delusions about my singing talent or lack thereof, and had sometimes been accused of not being able to carry a tune in a bucket. I kept giving Gil sidelong glances to gauge his reaction and was rewarded with a dimple and a crooked smile. When I belted out the final chorus, he opened his mouth wide as if to laugh but no sound came. It unsettled me enough that I swerved on the road, my tires slipping off the asphalt onto soft grass for a quick moment. Watching Gil trying to laugh was like watching the television with the sound turned off. In his open mouth, I could almost see the sadness he had swallowed as if it were a clenched fist, letting nothing past. He closed his mouth and stared at me silently as if telling me that I didn't have the whole story, that it wasn't just sadness.

A loud honk of a horn had me swerving back into my lane, focusing on the road ahead instead of on my silent nephew. I threw a quick glance at him and saw that his face was once again passive and his gaze was trained on the yellow dotted line disappearing beneath the car. I remained silent until we spotted the first welcome sign.

McClellanville, known as the Village to locals, began in 1771 when Archibald McClellan bought land along Jeremy Creek. It's had its share of prosperity and decline, but it's come back into favor as one of those "quaint" small towns outsiders move to in an attempt to escape from the cities and suburbia and end up creating exactly what they're moving away from.

I only ever knew it as home, and all the shop owners and shrimping boat captains knew who the Maitland sisters were. We spent a lot of time on the docks, ruining our teeth chewing on saltwater taffy from Mrs. Crandall at the post office and watching the shrimpers bringing in their haul. Diana's earliest paintings are of the shrimpers with their deep-creased faces folded in on themselves like extra protection from the wind and sun. It was in watching Diana create those paintings that I first began to realize that whatever I put on canvas was simply water-diluted paint. But what Diana created was life and light and truth. I was the liar when I painted and I watched in my hurt and disillusionment as our mother began to notice it, too.

It was the first time I'd felt jealousy, and it grew into a grotesque black finger that scratched at my insides. I was sick with it and couldn't leave my bed for a week. My father, as always, was oblivious, but my mother knew. She didn't call a doctor and she didn't coddle me. She let me writhe in my pitiful state until she came and sat by my bed one night. She didn't say anything for a very long time but sat watching me with her green cat eyes—so much like Diana's yet I had never noticed until that night. Mama told me that Diana was gifted in ways that neither of us could ever understand or attain. And Diana deserved my jealousy. But I needed to stop wallowing and deal with it. *It's a blessing and a curse,* she'd said, and I turned my face to the wall, feeling the scratching inside where I couldn't make it stop. Then Mama had leaned over my bed and whispered very close to my ear. *Be careful what you wish for.* She stayed there for a long time, as if she wanted to say more, and I could feel her warm breath on my cheek, but I didn't turn my head to look at her. Eventually, she straightened and I waited in my misery as she walked out of the room.

She never spoke about it again. I got out of bed the next day and tried to pretend that things were the same between Diana and me. But they weren't. And they would never be again. The incessant scratching was still there. I learned how to keep it at bay so that sometimes I was hardly aware of it. But it became like a bruise you think has gone away until you accidentally bump against it and the pain is there again.

I closed my eyes to the memories, and concentrated on finding my way to a place I had once known like the back of my hand. I had planned to take Gil to the docks, but not today. I wasn't sure I was ready. Besides, it was too near the water for us to visit on our first outing together, and I decided to save it for another time. Instead, I headed down North Pinckney, the town's main street, toward the intersection of Oak and Pinckney where the one-thousand-year-old Deerhead Oak towered and lurched over the square plot of land where an acorn had once fallen ten centuries before.

I parked the car and waited while Gil scrambled out of the passenger side, his sketchbook clutched tightly to his chest. He looked up at me expectantly and I waited for him to speak for a moment before I remembered. I still wasn't used to his silence.

"Let's sit on one of these benches, and I'll talk about the tree for a bit, and then we can do a quick study of it in our sketch pads." He followed me to a bench and we both sat down. "And then I thought we could walk down the street and get an ice-cream cone before heading home."

He grinned and he looked so much like his mother at his age that I had to look away. I dragged my gaze back to the tree, to its swollen trunk divided into a crooked "v" and its arthritic fingers festooned with weeping Spanish moss. I began to tell one of my stories about the ancient oak, how the moss was the tears of the tree as it wept over all the things it had witnessed in one thousand years. I closed my eyes, still picturing the tree but seeing Diana at my side instead of her son. I remembered how, before Diana could paint, she'd have me tell a story first. I kept my eyes closed as I spoke, recalling a story from memory, and when I opened them again, I saw that Gil had moved to another bench, and he was busy working in his sketch pad.

I flipped mine open, too, and gave a few halfhearted stabs at it, the old familiar feelings of frustration resurfacing as I tried to re-create the play of light and shadow on the tree trunk and its branches onto paper. Something always seemed to get lost in translation, as if I were transcribing Shakespeare without being allowed to use any vowels. After about half an hour of useless scratchings on my pad, I closed it and looked over at Gil. He had stopped, too, but when I stood to go take a look, he abruptly closed the cover. I understood and I wouldn't press. His art was for him alone, but I'd make a point to discuss his sketches later. And, eventually, I hoped that he would want to open up more and tell me what he saw and how he translated that onto paper. Eventually. He stared up at me, his silence unnerving, and for the first time since Quinn's call, I wondered if Gil might be another one of my failures.

I smiled. "Are you ready for ice cream?"

He nodded and stood. Then, after sticking our sketch pads inside the car, we headed into the town's center. I was struck by how much had changed and how much hadn't. When I left, the effects of Hurricane Hugo were still visible, but now the piles of lumber and broken trees were gone, roofs repaired, buildings rebuilt. The Victorian storefronts were the same, but the names of the businesses were mostly different. I remembered Mrs. Crandall at the post office and the saltwater taffy she used to give us. I made a mental note to stop in later, but not today. I was treading lightly into my past, gently prodding at the old bruises.

There was a veneer to the town, a spit-and-polish job done for the benefit of those moving into the new suburban developments on the outskirts of McClellanville. She was like an old woman who had suddenly decided to wear makeup, and I wasn't completely convinced that it was change for the better.

We bought our ice creams from a teenager too young to know who I was, and we took our cones out to the sidewalk, where we could leisurely walk and window-shop. The humidity had crept up on the day, and I worked hard to keep the ice cream from melting and spilling down the cone before I could eat it. I kept up a one-sided conversation, still unnerved by the silence of the boy next to me. I knew he was listening, and I still paused, as if waiting for him to speak.

I was in midsentence when a storefront across the street caught my eye. It was an art store, with framed paintings displayed in the front windows and a large sale sign in red splayed across the glass. One large painting sat on an easel in front of the entrance, its deep marsh colors pulling at the eye, easily enticing browsers to stop. I stopped suddenly, feeling the old scratching again, and Gil almost ran into me. Without even looking for traffic, I headed across the street, vaguely aware of Gil following me. I stared at the painting on the easel and my throat constricted. My ice-cream cone, now forgotten, fell to the sidewalk

I didn't need to look in the corner to see the author's signature; Diana's name was all over the painting in the lush greens and yellows of the marsh at sunset, in the undulating of the cord grass, and in the punches of the storm clouds that crept into the corner of the painting. And there, in the bottom left corner, was a girl. She sat at the edge of the dock with her back to the artist. Her hands reached out to the sun and marsh in unobstructed joy, her face turned toward the wind with her brown hair streaming wildly behind her, the side of her face creased in a smile and unaware of the approaching storm.

Once, I had known that girl; she was as familiar to me as breathing. My heart broke a little as I looked at her in oils and light, knowing that she had died long ago and the only thing that remained of her was her ghost, which followed my every waking moment.

A cold, sticky hand gripped mine and I looked down at Gil, surprised to find him next to me. His eyes had that strange light in them again, reminding me of the way he had looked in the car when he had opened his mouth to laugh and no sound came. I had thought at the time it was sadness but knew now that it was much more, the word defining it dangling on my tongue but as elusive as a raindrop.

He tugged on my hand, pulling me away from the painting. Reluctantly I allowed him to lead me away, our ice cream and walk forgotten but neither of us caring. It wasn't until we were pulling into the gravel drive leading to the house that I realized what I had seen in Gil's eyes. I recognized it as the same thing I saw in my own eyes every time I saw my reflection. It was more than sadness and loss. It was grief: the grief of losing the one thing in your life that mattered the most.

I reached for his hand and squeezed it, and he squeezed back, and I knew then that whatever it took, I would be there for Gil until he was better. We were Maitlands, after all, and we had survived for centuries despite being battered against the unforgiving land. I put my arm around his thin shoulders, and we walked together up to the house, while we both pretended that we didn't see the pale face in the window of Diana's studio watching us until we moved out of sight.

CHAPTER 7

The mottled-leaved paphiopedilums have developed black spots on their leaves. Except for their leaves, these orchids are nearly identical to the solid green paphs that are potted next to them and they are doing fine. From my research, I've discovered that the black spots could be sunburn, so I'm moving them out of direct sunlight. It's remarkable that two nearly identical orchids could be so different in their requirements for survival.

—DR. QUINN BRISTOW'S GARDENING JOURNAL

Quinn

While growing up on Cape Cod with my older brother, Sean, I collected sick animals like other kids collected baseball cards. Our parents fought all the time, and Sean told me he figured that was my way of trying to fix things in a world where I felt pretty much mute and powerless. When I set the broken wing of a sparrow or rescued an abandoned kitten from a Dumpster, it was like shouting to the world, "I am here!"

But that was in the days when I kept the animals I saved. My parents were too busy with their own turmoils to take much notice that I had accumulated a small menagerie of animals in my bedroom and backyard. I divided my time between my animals and sailing, and I planned to live the rest of my life like that. But life never happens the way you plan it.

When I was ten, Sean died. My mother said that I killed him and I suppose I had. But whether you call it an accident or not, my brother was dead at fourteen, and I had to spend the rest of my life looking next to me for somebody who was never there. That's the thing about guilt,

I've learned. On the outside you look perfectly normal, going about your daily routine. But on the inside there's a little hamster on a wheel spinning furiously, urging you on to make restitution for your crime. There's no rest from it; I suspect I'll always be running and seeking until my last exhausted breath.

On the day after Sean's funeral, I began to let all my animals go. I sold some and gave others away, and the wild animals who had long since been healed, I set free. I never stopped fixing the broken ones that came into my life after that, but I never kept one again. It was as if I couldn't trust myself with the soul of another living creature.

Until I met Diana or, rather, until I saw the portrait she'd painted. But I ended up letting her go, too, and the only thing different about her departure was that I was left with Gil. The child I'd never planned on having but who became my life. I love my son more than a sail loves the wind, and it scares me, because I know what it's like to lose the one thing that matters the most. And I don't think that I could survive that again.

I missed my son—the boy that he had been before the accident—and I was willing to resort to drastic measures to bring him back. That was my entire motivation for bringing Marnie home, although since her arrival I'd begun to have doubts about my judgment. Since the night she arrived, I've been having dreams about her. Dreams where she's emerging from the water and the sunlight or the moonlight—I'm not sure which—is glinting off of her. And the light is so bright that it nearly blinds me, but I can't walk away until I can figure out why it looks like she's on fire. When I get closer to examine the light, I see that her skin is made of splinters.

After one such dream-filled night, I made my way to Grandpa Maitland's room. For a guy who doesn't talk, he's given me more peace of mind and counsel than any psychiatrist I've ever been to. Maybe it's his years as a preacher with a needy congregation that makes his presence a soothing one. Whatever it was, I always found myself in his room several times a week, hunched over a chessboard—usually losing—and talking about life.

There's something reassuring about the game of chess. It's about the

only time I feel as if I'm in control, moving chess pieces across a board
as if with the hand of God. I once even considered myself a pretty
good chess player. Until I challenged Edward Maitland to a game as
a charitable act and got my ass whipped. He's a formidable opponent,
and once you get past the shaking, yellow highlighter-stained fingers
and wheelchair, you realize that he's got a razor-sharp mind and those
Maitland eyes that don't miss a thing. I think that's why Gil spends so
much time with him. All the other people in Gil's life use words like
smoke to obscure the truth.

I moved my bishop forward within striking distance of Edward's
queen and removed my hand from my chess piece before realizing the
flaw in my reasoning. Giving himself only a few minutes to contemplate his next move—most likely done for my benefit, to pretend that I
had given him a quandary—he slid his queen forward placing both my
errant bishop and my king in jeopardy.

"Check," I said for him and he smiled.

I moved my king out of harm's way and then watched as he captured
my bishop with his queen.

I pretended to contemplate my next move as other thoughts tugged
at my attention. Finally, I looked up from the board and found him
watching me closely. I noticed for the first time that his left hand rested
on his dog-eared Bible, the open pages decorated with sporadic yellow
highlighter marks. I glanced to see what chapter he'd been reading, but
couldn't make out the tiny print at the top of the page. I sat back in my
chair and said, "I need to get Gil on a sailboat again."

I stared down at the black-and-white board, but saw only the
blue of the ocean. "I'm not a psychiatrist—not that they've done him
any good—but I have a gut instinct about this. He loved it so much
before—before the accident. And now he's petrified of going anywhere
near the water. His doctors have said that getting him back on the water
might help jog his brain, get him talking again. I just need to do it carefully and gradually. But I can't do it on my own."

I looked up to see Edward's eyes gazing steadily at me, but I couldn't
read them as easily as I usually could. "I was thinking that since Marnie
was an excellent sailor at one time that I could convince her to help me,

although I'm beginning to think that she might be as afraid of the water as Gil seems to be."

I picked up a pawn, feeling its cool stone surface against my fingers. "I don't suppose even you know what happened out on the boat with their mother the night she drowned. Diana would never talk about it. But from what I can gather from the dates on all the trophies up-stairs, Marnie—or Diana—never put foot on a sailboat again. I feel like I'm living with ghosts who won't—or can't—communicate with the living."

I put the pawn down and moved it one space forward in an un-planned move. A quirk of Edward's eyebrow made me quickly pick it up again. Instead of replacing it on the board, I gently closed my fingers around it, cradling it in my fist. "I've got to do something for Gil now. I can't just sit and wait this out." I looked up at Edward again to find his clear gaze still leveled at me. "And I think that bringing him out on the water again is the right thing to do." I sat back, still holding the pawn. "But Gil doesn't trust me anymore. Maybe it's because I'm his father and therefore connected to his mother, which is another story altogether. I need Marnie's help to do this, but I think she's going to resist the idea as much as Gil." I spotted the perfect move and replaced the pawn on the board before sliding my rook two spaces.

Edward sat forward in his wheelchair and moved his queen within striking distance of my rook.

"Are you sure you want to do that?"

He nodded and I efficiently moved my rook and took his queen, positioning my piece in proximity to his king. "Check," I said.

Instead of moving his king, he picked up my queen, a pawn, and my rook and held them out to me with shaking fingers. I opened my palms and he dropped each piece, adding to the queen I already held, the soft clinking noise the only sound in the room. Slowly he reached over to me and closed my hand over them. Confused, I stared at my closed fist, thinking I understood the two queens and the pawn. What I didn't understand was the rook.

"Are you the rook?" I asked.

Slowly, he shook his head and sat back in his seat, his eyes steadily penetrating. For a moment, while our eyes met in the quiet room, I felt a small fissure erupt in my armor, and for the first time since Sean's death, my belief in my ability to fix things and people faltered. There was something in his eyes that only hinted at the magnitude of our problems and that Gil, the small pawn I held in my hand, was just a grain of sand buried under the unforgiving coast of his ancestors.

A soft tap came from the door and I startled, unaware of how long I'd been holding the chess pieces. After a quick nod from Edward, I said, "Come in."

Marnie stood primly in the doorway and I had to look away as I felt the odd sensation of a blush rush to my face. It was seeing her there, outlined by the hallway light, that I remembered for the first time that in my dream Marnie's hair had been loose and falling around her shoulders. And she'd been naked. What was worse was that I could feel Edward's gaze on me and I had the distinct impression that he knew.

Marnie seemed agitated and I felt a stab of alarm. "Is Gil all right?"

She smiled, and her face softened. "He's fine. I've just been discovering that he's a very gifted artist, although I'm sure you already know that."

I didn't really. I'd been in sort of a denial about his talent ever since he picked up his first crayon, and he hadn't done much in the way of art since the accident. I almost considered this a blessing, seeing as how the artistic mind of a Maitland wasn't always the healthiest.

She clasped her hands together in front of her in what I had always considered a classic teacher pose, and saw that it didn't suit her at all. Neither did her hair, scraped off her face. It looked much better loose around her shoulders, like in my dream. Where she was naked. I quickly looked down at my hands, the chess pieces pressing against my closed palm.

Marnie walked over to her grandfather and kissed his cheek. "I hope I'm not interrupting."

Edward grunted and I said, "No, actually. We just finished."

"Oh, good. Who won?" she asked absently.

I glanced at her grandfather and saw that he was flipping through his Bible, each page turn a chore. "We both did. I allowed him to let me win."

She nodded, but didn't say anything and I could tell that she wasn't really listening. Moving to the window, she looked out at the gathering gray clouds, deliberately avoiding the view of the ocean. "When Gil and I were in town today, we passed an art shop. They had one of Diana's paintings on an easel in front of the store."

"I'm not surprised. You might not know this since you've been away for so long, but Diana's established herself as a fairly renowned artist. She's received commissions from all over the country."

"Yes," she said quietly. "Even in Arizona people know who she is." She worried her lower lip for a moment. "I've just never seen one of her more recent paintings and it was a bit of a shock."

Edward continued his search through his Bible while I became aware again of the weight of the chess pieces in my hand, their heaviness equal to the growing dread I felt.

She turned to face us, the darkening clouds of the sky behind her framing her pale face. "There was . . . there was a familiar person in the corner of the painting. I'm not sure that I would have even noticed the figure except for the fact that it was me."

I slid my chair back and stood. "Yes. It's become sort of like her signature. Your image always appears somewhere in her paintings. I thought you knew."

She shook her head and I noticed her turquoise earrings, shaped into shells. I almost smiled, seeing how even in her exile in the desert, her memories of home lingered—if only in her subconscious.

"No. I didn't." Her eyes held shades of panic. "Why does she do that? Why does she feel the need to include me?"

"I've asked Diana, but she'd never tell me. I thought that maybe you were her muse, somehow. That she needed you to inspire her."

The corner of her mouth dipped. "No," she said, her voice not quite convinced. "It wouldn't be that." She faced the window again and stared out at the clouds, pregnant with rain. "I don't like storms," she said quietly and I wondered if she'd forgotten that she wasn't alone.

"Neither does Gil. It was stormy on the night of his accident, too."

She jerked her head back to me, and I held her gaze as I watched something dark and tremulous pass behind her eyes.

She turned back to the window. "Even as a child I didn't like storms. Diana would let me crawl under her covers on stormy nights and stay there until it passed. She was never scared." A smile was there in her voice. "I suppose children are born one way or the other."

"Gil was never afraid. He used to always ask me to go outside to watch the ocean. If it wasn't lightning, I'd bring him to the beach. He wasn't afraid of anything—not before the accident, anyway." I sat back down and let the chess pieces in my hand clatter onto the board.

I watched as Edward slid his arm across the board, knocking all the other pieces in his lap. He continued to look at me steadily as I reached for the wooden box where we stored the pieces, and handed it to him. I took a deep breath. "I want my son back. I want him fearless again. I want him to love sailing again. It was so important to him once." Edward slid the pawn over to me and I picked it up, rubbing my thumb over the cold hardness of it. "But I need help. From someone he trusts. Someone he's not afraid of."

"No," Marnie said and she brought her hand up to the window, her fingers clenched in a fist. "That's not why you brought me here. I'm trained to use art to help children with problems. Just let me do what I know how."

"I'm not asking you to do any of that differently. And I do think that his art is also an integral part of him, and if you can help him rediscover his talents, then it can only be good. But it's not enough. I know that. And I think you know that, too."

"No," she said again, her voice wavering like the sheets of rain that had starting spilling out of the heavy clouds.

"I'm not saying that I should throw you both on a sailboat at night during a storm."

She shuddered and I wished I hadn't said that, but I pressed on. "I'd like to take you out on the marsh again in my jon boat until you're both comfortable in a boat. We'd only go in good weather, and to familiar places—and never near the ocean."

I watched as her shoulders relaxed and I was tempted to stop there.

But I felt the heaviness of the pawn in my hand and I knew that I had to go on. "And I've decided to refurbish the *Highfalutin*. It's in dry dock—away from the water—and I thought that if we all worked on it together—"

"No!" She turned away from the window and faced me, and her eyes were lit with fear and anger and something else—something that reminded me of Diana when she began to lose her grip on reality.

I stood, the enormity of what we were fighting for overriding any concern I might have for Marnie's feelings. This was about an innocent child who had lost his way and couldn't find the road back. And it seemed that I was the only one willing to fight for him.

I grabbed her shoulders, forcing her to look at me. "You're his only hope, Marnie. I've seen him with you, and he responds to you better than I've seen him responding to anybody since his accident. Don't you see? I need you." I dropped my hands, realizing too late that I shouldn't have touched her. Quietly I said, "We need you."

She backed away, rubbing my handprints off her shoulders. A flash of lightning split the sky answered by a growl of thunder. "I can't," she whispered. "I can't. You just don't know." Shivering, she backed away from me. "He'll be afraid. I'll go to him now."

I nodded, too spent and defeated to say anything else as I watched her leave the room. I didn't realize that I had been staring after her until I felt a bump on my arm. Edward had wheeled himself over and was pushing his Bible at me as if he wanted me to read something. I took the book and squinted at the small print highlighted in yellow that he indicated with a yellow-stained fingernail. It was Proverbs, chapter twenty-four, and I read it aloud. " 'If thou faint in the day of adversity, thy strength is small.' "

I started to shake my head but he grabbed my arm and squeezed it tightly. I pulled away gently and gave him back his Bible. "It's not my call, Edward. It's not up to me at all."

He began flipping through pages, wetting his thumb to make it easier to grip the paper, and finally came to rest at another passage. He pressed it open and held it up to me again, this time at the book of Genesis. Once again I read aloud, " 'Say, I pray thee, thou art my sister:

that it may be well with me for thy sake; and my soul shall live because of thee.' "

I looked at him in confusion, ready to remind him that the last passage was being taken out of context, but his chin had already sunk to his chest and his eyes were closed as his breath rose and fell in the steady rhythm of sleep. I gently pulled the Bible from his fingers and placed it on the table before leaving the room to go find Joanna. Outside, the rain began to fall hard on the house and the restless sand, shifting the color of the ocean from blue to white.

Gil

I hate storms. I didn't used to. There was something about the electricity and noise of a thunderstorm that seemed to recharge that thing inside of me that makes me paint. Sort of like putting a new battery in a flashlight makes the light stronger and brighter. I wasn't afraid because I never thought that something that beautiful could ever be so dangerous. Until that night on the boat with my mother when I learned the truth.

I figured out that if I lay on my bed on my stomach and squeezed my pillow over my head, pressing it against my ears, I couldn't hear the storm. Except that sometimes, if I pushed the pillow on my ears too tightly, I thought I could hear children crying. It always took several tries to get it just right, and then all I could hear was the swooshing of my blood and my own breathing.

I knew Aunt Marnie was in my room before she touched my back. I had heard her and my dad arguing, and I was pretty sure it was about me, even though I couldn't understand any of the words. I've learned that when you do more listening than talking, you can hear a lot more. So I kind of expected one of them to come find me when I didn't hear them arguing anymore. I hadn't felt my dad's heavy footsteps on the stairs outside my room, so I figured it was Aunt Marnie.

I flipped over on my back to see her, careful to keep the pillow around my head, and when lightning lit the room, I thought I could see a ghost by her side. I shut my eyes, and when I opened them again, it was gone, and I allowed Aunt Marnie to move the pillow away from my ears.

"Gil? Are you all right?"

I nodded, keeping my eyes on her face and away from the window.

"I don't like storms either."

In the next flash of lightning, I thought I could see her ghost and me out on the beach, staring at the storm, and we were laughing as the wind blew her hair in her mouth and the water splashed over our feet and we didn't care.

She sat down on the bed and I barely felt the bed move because she was so small.

"I had fun this morning. Did you?"

I nodded, knowing that our visit to town wasn't really what she wanted to talk about.

Her fingers plucked at my bedspread and she kept her eyes away from my face. "Your dad says that you used to love sailing."

I felt my heart tremble like a butterfly in my chest, but it wasn't because I was scared. It was because when Aunt Marnie said the word "sailing," it came dressed with sunshine and the smell of salt water in your face and all the happy memories of being on a boat beneath sails with only ocean around you. It made me remember everything I had forgotten about sailing—all that I used to love doing. And in that one word, Aunt Marnie told me that she had loved it once, too. I nodded and she touched my head, lifting the hair off of my forehead.

I watched her throat as she swallowed. "He said that it might be a good idea for you to maybe start thinking about sailing again." She put her hand flat against my head as if to stop my thoughts from jumping ahead of what she was going to say next. "Not right away, of course. But he thought maybe you—and I—could maybe start using his jon boat on the marsh and creeks." She looked out the window, where the rain was still hitting the glass like BB pellets. She smiled at me but I could see she didn't really mean it. "And he wanted you to help him fix up the *Highfalutin* while it's in dry dock."

My heart fluttered again, just like it does when the mainsail is hoisted and the boat begins to move under your feet. It was a feeling. The feeling I painted when I made my best pictures.

She began stroking my hair again. "I won't make you do it, Gil, if you're really too scared. I wouldn't do that."

Aunt Marnie's voice had gone real quiet, like she'd forgotten I was there and she was talking to herself. And then I thought that she actually was because I had already decided that it was something I wanted to do. Probably something I needed to do. I missed my painting so much that it sometimes felt like I had stepped into an elevator and forgotten to push the button. I just sort of stood there, waiting for the elevator to move on its own or for somebody else to push the button. I guess Aunt Marnie had shown me where the button was and was waiting for me to do something about it.

But there was something in her voice that wasn't right, and when she leaned forward and looked in my face, I knew why. She was thinking I could do all that stuff she talked about without her. She really had no idea that she was stuck in the elevator, too.

I grabbed her hand and squeezed and her forehead wrinkled, making her look old. "What is it, Gil? Do you want to? Would you like to give it a try?"

I let go of her hand and got out of the bed. Crouching on the floor, I stuck my hand under the bed and pulled out an old sailing trophy. It was made of blue glass and shaped like a sail, but the top of it was rounded and wet-looking, as if the sail itself was turning into a wave. I'd wanted to look at it closer so I could paint it, and had hidden it under my bed before the accident. I had to hide it because Mama didn't want me anywhere near the sailing trophies.

I handed it to Aunt Marnie, but she didn't take it at first, so I placed it in her hand. She stared at it for a long time as I sat listening to the storm move away and watched the grayness lighten as if a curtain had been pulled open across the sky. I could tell when she understood what I was trying to tell her when her shoulders drooped forward, reminding me of my dad's orchids when they haven't had enough water.

She swallowed again and I could hear it in the quiet room. "You want me to do it with you, don't you? That's what you're trying to tell me."

I nodded and her shoulders rounded even more.

After a deep breath, she said, "I guess that's what we'll have to do then, isn't it?" She put the trophy on the bed behind her, as if she didn't want to look at it. Then she smiled at me, but her eyes were dark and cloudy like the sky before a storm. She stood and put an arm around me. "Let's go find your dad and let him know, then."

We began to walk out of the room together, but I pulled away and ran back to the bed and picked up the trophy. I slid it under my bed where Mama couldn't find it, then joined my aunt to go find my dad.

As we headed for the stairs, Aunt Marnie's hand slid from my head to my ear and I felt her fingers tugging on my earlobe, just as Mama used to do when I was small and still does when she thinks I'm asleep. I guess they both must have learned to do that from the same person, and that little thing was probably all they had left that reminded them that they were sisters.

CHAPTER 8

The human heart is like a ship on a stormy sea driven about by winds blowing from all four corners of heaven.
—MARTIN LUTHER

Marnie

The one thing a person never forgets about the Lowcountry marsh is the smell. What seasonal visitors wrinkle their noses at and call rotten eggs, the longtime resident simply remembers as the aroma of home. Even in the Arizona desert in the middle of a windstorm, I could close my eyes and smell the pluff mud left behind by the outgoing tides.

Once, on a bet with Diana, I looked up the word "pluff" in the dictionary. She'd always said it meant the sound your bare feet made when you jumped over the side of your jon boat. The dictionary simply defined it as "to blow out like smoke or breath with an explosive action; to puff." I told her we were both right.

After leaving Gil with his father and passing on lunch, I made my way through the tall grasses to the long dock that stretched out into the marsh like a long finger pointing toward the ocean. All marshes here lead to creeks, the creeks to rivers, and the rivers to the great Atlantic. Even out in the marsh, the ocean always lets you know that it's near by the tangy smell of salt in the air and the seabirds that circle and cry above you. And by the sucking in and spitting out of the marsh's waters like the breaths of the ocean orchestrating the tides.

I watched Quinn's flat-bottomed aluminum jon boat lift gently in the shallow water as the ripples nudged at the bottom of the boat and at my memories. Quinn was right. I had once known these creeks and estuaries so well that I could navigate them at night blindfolded. They were the highways and byways of my childhood, not easily forgotten. And the smell, always the smell to remind you of where you came from.

Two large blue herons stood regally on an exposed mud flat watching me and the receding tide with studied nonchalance. The hot sun had already begun to bake a jagged oyster bed, laid bare by the tide, the smell mixing with that of dried salt and decaying marine life and wafting in waves around me. I closed my eyes and bent my head to my raised knees, wishing that I couldn't remember.

The sound of a footfall on the wooden dock behind me made me raise my head, and I sat watching while Quinn walked toward me. He stood in front of me, and I had to raise my hand to my forehead to block the sun from my eyes.

"Mind if I join you?" he asked.

I shrugged, still stung by his role, however unintentional, in making me face my biggest fears. I had moved to the desert, after all, yet he seemed not to notice or care that he had lured me out of my refuge like a fish from the ocean, then left me exposed on the beach with no escape from the burning sun.

He sat beside me and handed me a foil-wrapped square. I didn't take it but looked at him for an explanation.

"It's from Gil. He thought you might be hungry since you didn't have lunch. I hope you like peanut butter and jelly."

My stomach had begun to rumble and I took the proffered sandwich. "Thank you. Gil's very considerate."

He laughed quietly but didn't say anything.

"What's so funny?" I asked in between bites of sandwich.

"You don't want to know."

I stopped chewing. "No, I do. What?"

He looked at me and I noticed belatedly that he was sitting very close, close enough that I could see how very blue his eyes were. I looked down at my sandwich, suddenly intrigued by the layers of brown and red between two slices of white bread.

"I was just thinking that you're more like your sister than you think."

I polished off the last of my sandwich. "What makes you say that?"

"Well, since you asked. She's always indirect when she's pissed. Like by you telling me that Gil was considerate I knew that you were really saying that I wasn't. Which isn't always true, but in this case I'll have to agree with you. And you both twirl your hair when you're thinking."

"I wasn't twirling my hair," I said, annoyed that this virtual stranger could have figured out so much in such a relatively short period of time.

He reached over and lifted a small handful of hair that I had worked out of my bun and then twisted around my finger so that now it bore a distinct circular pattern. He didn't let the hair drop immediately, but when I looked at him to tell him to let go, I froze. He was looking at me oddly, and if I hadn't known better, I would have thought that he was seeing what I looked like naked.

I jerked my hair out of his hand and let my legs dangle over the edge of the dock, a small cloud of gnats zipping around my ankles.

Out of the corner of my eye, I saw Quinn stretch his long legs out in front of him as he leaned back on his hands. I wanted him to go away. I'd come here to think and to prepare myself. And, I had to admit, to feel sorry for myself.

Quinn broke the silence. "I wanted to thank you. For agreeing to help out with Gil. I know it won't be easy for you."

I didn't say anything, not wanting to make it any easier for him. A trickle of perspiration ran down my back between my shoulder blades, making my blouse stick to my skin. I watched the herons stand absolutely still, and I wished that Diana were here to paint it. I stopped my thought, surprised at it. I hadn't wanted Diana near me in so very long. I looked away, making a mental note to bring Gil here another day to paint.

"How did you and Diana meet?" The question popped out of me without thought, and when I looked at him, I could tell that he was as startled by it as I was.

He paused for a moment as if weighing his words. "I fell in love with one of her paintings."

He held that odd look in his eyes again and I knew there was more to this story that he wasn't going to tell me. Uncomfortable, I looked away and saw one of the herons take off from his perch, his wings splayed out against the cloudless sky in such perfect beauty that for a moment I forgot to miss the desert and its dry wind and brown creatures.

"And that was it?" I asked, testing him, surprising myself at how hungry I was for information about Diana during my years away from the water.

"No, it wasn't." He studied the remaining heron. "Did you know that the greatest threat to the blue heron is utility wires? They're at the top of the food chain out here in the marsh, yet they're completely help- less when it comes to avoiding utility wires."

I turned to look at him, trying not to notice how nice his T-shirt fit or how the sun turned the ends of his hair gold. Annoyed at myself, I said, "Are you sharing this useless information with me because you're trying to distract me from thinking about what you're going to make me do, or is it because you're a vet and you think everybody's as inter- ested in animals as you are?"

He looked hurt and I regretted my harsh words.

"A little of both, I suppose. I thought you liked blue herons. I saw the pair of paintings you did in high school. I figured you had to have really studied them for a long time to portray them so accurately."

I stared at him. I knew what paintings he was talking about, of course. I had entered them into an art competition in high school and they had placed second. Diana had placed first. I had thrown them into the garbage afterward. I later learned that my mother had pulled them from the garbage and had them framed and hung in her bedroom. I'd always thought that she'd done it as some sort of a joke. Until now.

"How did you see them?" I asked.

He looked surprised. "They're still hanging in your mother's old room. Diana moved into it after you left and, I assumed, liked them enough to keep them."

"Oh," I said, not wanting to talk about it anymore. I searched for something to change the conversation. "Since you're a veterinarian, isn't it a bit odd that you don't have even a single dog?"

He didn't say anything for a moment but raised his eyebrow. "Prob- ably," he said. "But it's not something I like to talk about."

Intrigued, I asked, "Why not?"

He turned bright blue eyes on me. "Probably for the same reason that you don't want to talk about blue herons."

"Touché," I replied, and settled back on my hands just in time to see the remaining heron stretch out his neck and take off, uttering a loud *kraak* as he spread his wings and flew out over the marsh toward the ocean.

*

Diana

I had begun to get used to Joanna's appearance every morning, as she carried a tray with food and medications. She would stay until I'd eaten every bite and swallowed both pills, as she had been directed to do by Quinn. I don't know if she ever reported back to him if I had slept in my studio again and had on the clothes I'd worn the previous day, or that I sat in front of an empty canvas with nothing to mar the white expanse of it except my hopeless ambitions.

She handed me a cup of water as I picked up my pills and put them one at a time on the back of my tongue and washed them back with a water chaser. I took my Lithium pill—for seizures—and my Prozac, and swallowed them down like a good girl, showing my empty mouth to Joanna when I was through. With a rueful grin, she turned to leave, picking up wet towels on the floor on her way out.

My doctors say I have bipolar disorder, something they suspect I may have inherited from my mother. What they don't know is that with every pill I take, the truth is pushed farther and farther away until I see it only through a congealed fog of faces and words and memories. But what I can't seem to make them understand is that in the other world, the world I knew before the pills, I saw such indescribable beauty with color and movement, and it reached out to me through my hands and my paintbrushes.

With the medication, that part of me is asleep. Living my life now is like being forced into a wheelchair when you know that you can run marathons. But it's the price I pay for not having to face the truth.

My diagnosis came after Gil was born, and I guess I owe Quinn my life. I had felt highs and lows before, but memories of my mother had somehow held them in check. But my defenses were useless in the onslaught of postpartum hormones. To give Quinn credit, he'd reacted like any good doctor when he saw me attempting to skydive out of my bedroom window with an umbrella. He had me committed to a hospital until we figured out what was wrong. I couldn't be grateful. I hated him for taking away my passion, for stealing my art. And when Gil's first word was "Daddy," I hated him even more.

Slowly, I came back to his world and even resumed painting. But the colors seemed dimmer, the nuances of movement less clear, the flow of the paintings less passionate. I still sold paintings, but I knew in my heart that they were the paintings of the drugs and not the true heart of the damaged artist.

I continued taking my medication for Gil, staying on it even through my divorce. I fought against my chains, but my son, and my avoidance of the truth, kept me bound to them. Until the night I went searching through my grandfather's papers and unwittingly became Pandora.

Yesterday, I watched Marnie and Quinn walk out of the marsh, keeping close to each other to stay on the narrow path. There was something in their posture, something that reminded me of bees dancing around flowers that alerted my senses. I felt a pang somewhere my heart used to be, which changed abruptly to a thud as a different emotion began to overtake me. My hand trembled against my chest and I could feel the clammy coolness of my fingers against my skin. It was fear I felt: fear of discovery. Separately, I could keep my secrets from them. But not if Marnie let down her reserve with Quinn. He had a way with damaged women, I knew. He could get them to tell him their most intimate secrets without them even knowing what they were doing. And then I'd have no more power over Marnie, no one at whom to direct my hatred. There could be no reconciliation; the truth would blind us both.

I stilled my hand, holding it tightly against my chest, and turned to the wall, where splashes of color reflected the light from the window. Just last night I had begun to paint again. It wasn't a portrait or a landscape, but an illustrated time line that I wanted to edge my ceiling with so that it was the first thing I saw when I walked into my studio and the last thing I saw before I turned out the light. It was as if Marnie had truly been my muse and with her return came the return of my painting. But I'd never tell her. I sickened at the thought of her returning to Arizona to her little job as an art teacher and telling everyone that she was the muse of the great artist Diana Maitland.

The skin under my bandage began to throb and itch, recalling the dream I'd had the night before, where a thousand bugs had crawled out of my wounded leg and proceeded to eat the damaged flesh. The drugs made me dream disturbing dreams, but my visits to the nursing home also had a similar effect. Both were essential to my recovery, and as my grandfather would say, God never gives more than we can handle. Maybe he was right. Or maybe I was just out to prove him wrong.

I looked down at my nightgown, splattered with paint, and wrinkled my nose. When I'd put it on the previous evening, I'd had every intention of going to sleep in my bedroom. But I'd found myself drawn to my studio, and I had escaped this life for just a few hours to paint.

There was a brief rapping on the door. "Come in," I said, thinking it was Joanna. I was surprised to see Quinn stick his head into the room as if making sure the coast was clear.

He raised an eyebrow. "Am I being allowed into the inner sanctum?"

"What do you want?" I asked, rolling my eyes. "If you're just here to make sure I took my pills, you could have asked Joanna. She just left."

"I did," he said, entering the room and closing the door behind him. It had been a very long time since Quinn had been in my studio, and when I saw the way he filled the space and disturbed the air, I knew that I'd been right to keep him away. He still had the power to suck the air out of my lungs by just walking into the same room. I would admit to no one that I was still half in love with my ex-husband, because that would make me an even more pathetic person than I already was. Besides, marrying a man who was in love with somebody else was already one failure too many according to my calculations. Being second-best seemed to be a running theme for me, and the less I admitted to it, the better I felt.

I remained sitting on the futon in the corner of the room, the unraveled sheets and blankets testament to the fact that I had slept there. I watched his eyes take it all in, including the fresh paint on the walls and me, and the large sheet-draped canvases on the other side of the room. I felt a strap from my nightgown slip off my shoulder, and I let it fall, exposing the top of my breast. His gaze flickered over that, too, before settling on my face.

"How are you feeling today?"

I shrugged, knowing the action pressed my breasts a little closer to the neckline of my nightgown. "Fine. Not full-blown crazy, but just a little crazy."

He raised his eyebrow. "You're not crazy, Diana. You have a mental disorder caused by an imbalance . . ."

I flopped back on the futon. "Save it, Quinn. Let a crazy lady keep a bit of her sense of humor, okay?"

He sat down in a paint-speckled armchair and leaned forward, his elbows resting on his thighs. "Sorry. It's just that you were agitated when you came home last night from your visit to the nursing home and wouldn't talk to me. I was hoping you were feeling better this morning."

"I'm just great, so you can go now."

Quinn stayed where he was, as I knew he would. "I'm not your enemy, Diana." He dropped his head in his hands for a moment before looking over at me. "Besides, I need to talk to you. About Gil."

I sat up quickly. "Is he all right?"

"He's fine. Still not speaking, but he's doing fine. He seems a lot calmer, a lot less anxious. I think Marnie's been a good influence on him."

"I suppose she would be. Sort of like the way bland foods settle your stomach."

He sent me a warning look but didn't say anything, and I wondered if he were giving me a reprieve because of what he had to say next.

Without trying to sound nervous, I asked, "So what's up with Gil?"

I watched Quinn clasp, then unclasp his hands. "I'm taking him back out on the water."

My wounded leg began to throb without mercy, and the pain shot up through my body like a ragged bullet, pounding in my head and flooding my lungs so that I could barely breathe. "You . . . can't," I managed to gasp out.

"I know this is difficult to understand—even more difficult than it is to explain. But I know in my gut that he needs to get back on the water to heal. I'm afraid . . ." He swallowed but his gaze never faltered. "I'm afraid that if we don't make him face this now, we'll never get him back."

I pressed the palm of my hand against my racing heartbeat. "You can't do this. I won't allow it."

He stood, his face darkening. "Yes, I can and I will. Remember—since the accident Gil is legally mine. You have no say whatsoever. I'm only here because I figured I owed it to you because you're his mother."

I stood, too. "You're damned straight I am. And as his mother, I'm begging you not to do this." I felt the tears on my face and I touched them, surprised to feel the wetness. It had been a very long time since I had cried. "You weren't there," I said, feeling the spray of salt water on my face and feeling the pain in my leg. "You don't know what he went through."

"No," he said quietly. "I don't. And nobody's telling me. But our son is suffering and the only thing that I can think of to try that I haven't already is to give him back something that he once loved almost as much as painting."

Quinn stepped toward me, his hand outstretched as if to touch me. I pulled back and he dropped his hand.

"What about his doctors? Have you asked them what they think of this?" My fingers were frantically plucking at my nightgown where the bandage was. I watched my hand as if it belonged to somebody else and heard the panic in her voice. For once I was glad of the medication veil that separated me from reality.

"They think it could help, as long as we take it slowly and gauge his reactions before moving forward. Dr. Hirsch says that if he relives the events in a nonthreatening environment, it could trigger his speech again."

"We?" I asked, that one word sticking in the fog of my mind.

"Yes, Marnie has agreed to come with us. We'll start with exploring the marshes, like we used to, and then Marnie and Gil will help me refurbish the *Highfalutin.*"

I had the absurd urge to start laughing and leave no doubt as to how crazy I really was, but I was too stunned to do anything besides stare at him. I fell back on the futon and rubbed my hand over the throbbing bandage. "And Marnie's going to help you? Willingly?"

A small smile crossed his lips and a fissure of jealousy crept through the fog, mercifully overtaking the pain. "I wouldn't say willingly, exactly, but she's agreed to help." He gave me an odd look. "She says she's doing it for Gil."

His face blurred through my tears. "She should know better than most why none of us should ever go near the ocean again."

"If you're talking about your mother's death, that was an accident. . . ."

"Was it, Quinn? Were you there? How much of an accident can it be when a mother decides to take her two children sailing at night when every weather forecaster is calling for hurricane-force winds?"

He stilled. "You never told me that."

"There's a lot I've never told you. But you should know enough to ensure that your son stays away from the ocean."

He knelt in front of me and took my hands in his, and I had no strength left to pull them away. "Are you talking about the Maitland curse, Diana?"

I kept my head down and didn't answer, glad for the mental haze that softened even heartache.

"We talked about that with your doctor, remember? He told you that there was no such thing. It's just a crutch people use to help them understand why bad things happen."

I looked into his open and trusting face, and pulled my hand away to cup his cheek. "I've faced death twice, Quinn. And the second time our son was with me. Don't do this to him. Don't."

He squeezed my hand and stood. "I'm sorry you don't agree, but I'm going forward with this. We both want what's best for Gil, and I need something more tangible than a family curse to make me change my mind. I promise I'll go slowly, and I'll protect him from danger. And so will Marnie."

I jerked away from him and stood. "Marnie? You think Marnie can protect him?" I again fought the urge to laugh, knowing that once I started I wouldn't be able to stop. "She needs more protection than anybody. You think she's this quiet little mouse of a woman, but I've known her for a very long time, Quinn. I've seen her when she's out on the ocean, and it's like it becomes part of her blood. She feeds off the wildness of the water and wind until she becomes reckless and dangerous. I never entered a sailing race with her because it scared me too much to be on a boat with her."

"Bullshit," he said. "You've never been scared a day in your life."

I walked toward him and my fingers clutched his shirt. "Every single day of my life I'm scared. I'm scared that I will become like my mother. That this disease we share will eat away at me until I no longer recognize reality." I pushed at his chest and he grabbed my hands. "And I'm scared that our son, who is so much like me and her, will one day end up just like us."

He blanched, and I knew he was thinking about all the tests we've had run on Gil, and how the doctors had told us to be vigilant of any cues signaling that our son had inherited more from me than the color of my hair and my ability to put paint on canvas.

He stepped back, putting distance between us.

"And you know I'm right about Marnie, too, don't you?" I asked.

I watched as his eyes flickered to the corner of the room, to the stack of framed pictures covered with layers of sheets and blankets and then secured together with masking tape. I had made very sure that those pictures stayed where they belonged.

Quinn drew a deep breath. "None of that matters right now to Gil. Sailing was his biggest love—more than his painting. And I miss his voice." His own voice broke but he covered it with a clearing of his throat. "This is the only thing I know to do that we haven't tried before. And I'm going to give it a shot." He aimed his blue eyes at me and I felt that little jolt again. "I've got to do it, Diana. I'm sorry if you don't agree, but you know that I won't let anything happen to him." He moved as if to touch me but dropped his hand as if thinking better of it.

He left the room and I fell back on the futon, staring up at the walls, where my strokes of paint had not yet become my voice. Then I closed my eyes and willed the tears to come. But I lay there, dry eyed, and thought about how one could be married to a person for years and never really know them at all.

CHAPTER 9

Marnie

Sedona, Arizona, is known for its spiritual vortices, which offer healing to hurting souls. Being raised by a preacher, I had no dearth of
spiritual knowledge, but when I left the ocean behind me and headed
for the desert, my soul emptied like a breached well.

The first week I was in Arizona, I hired a guide to take me to the
four official vortices in my search to find my soul again. Nestled at the
bottom of a canyon, Sedona is surrounded by towering red sandstone
and limestone cliffs and mesas, sculpted by time into Neolithic shapes
that change from gold and orange to crimson and purple according
to the rising and setting of the sun. They say it's the iron oxide that
gives the red rocks their color, and that also acts as a natural magnet to
conduct earth-based energy. I suppose an empty soul is ready to believe
anything and I dutifully followed my guide.

I don't remember much about my tour except my disappointment
at each supposed vortex in which I was supposed to feel a new energy
and an abiding peace. But they eluded me. At the end, we had a parting ceremony that included a Native American prayer: *I honor Father
Sky; I honor Mother Earth, and all the directions all around. I bring them
into my heart. I give thanks for all the blessings I have received, known and
unknown.* Maybe because the prayer didn't include the water, I didn't
feel as if it had been meant for me.

That night I dreamed of the ocean and allowed its liquid cradle to rock me to sleep. But always, in the deepest recesses of my mind, the powerful tug of the tides threatened to pull me under and thrust me out onto the shores of my old home lost and struggling for breath.

I remembered all this as I stood in the upstairs hallway of my grandfather's house, holding my sister's dinner tray as I contemplated the ocean beyond the glass. *I have come home,* I thought, then shivered. Slowly, I made my way up the attic stairs and knocked on the studio door.

"Diana, it's Marnie. I brought you dinner."

There was absolute silence, and for a moment, I thought she was going to pretend no one was there. Instead, she surprised me by saying, "Just a minute."

I heard the sound of a large piece of fabric being whipped open and then tape being pulled from a dispenser. The tray got heavier in my hand and I knocked again. "This is heavy. Can I just come in and put it on a table? I promise I won't look."

The noises within continued as if I hadn't spoken, and then I heard the sound of the bolt being slid back from the door. Diana opened the door and I tried not to look shocked at her appearance. Her hair was wild and paint-stained, as if she'd spent hours raking her hands through it without any thought to the wet paint on her fingers. She wore a paint-splattered white nightgown with masking tape affixing the shoulder straps to her skin in an apparent attempt to keep the sleeves from falling down and distracting her from her painting.

The room reeked of paint but I could see no visual signs of what she might have been working on. She held the door open wider, and I stepped inside with the tray, my eyes scanning for any partial canvas. Quinn had mentioned that Diana had stopped painting after the accident with Gil and I was eager to see signs that she had moved beyond whatever barrier that had been holding her back.

I faced her. "You didn't come down for dinner again, so I brought this up for you. I thought you might be hungry."

Her gaze flickered over the tray in my hand before she wrinkled her nose. She waved her hand, indicated a small table by a paint-splattered armchair. "Put it over there. And sit down." I did as she said, but hesitated before sitting.

"I won't bite you," she said with the familiar roll of her eyes. "It seems to me that we have some catching up to do."

I sat on the edge of the chair, mindful of wet paint. I watched as she walked over to the sink with a fistful of brushes. She was barefoot, and as I looked at her feet, I felt an involuntary smile creep across my face. Our feet were identical, with the second toe longer than the first and the smallest toe turned slightly inward. We used to laugh, saying that looking at our feet was the only way people could tell we were sisters.

She washed the brushes without speaking, and I allowed my gaze to wander to the canvases stacked against the wall and on every available flat surface in the room. There were also a large number of canvases, wrapped in sheets and masking tape, against the far wall that aroused my curiosity, but I said nothing. Having her invite me in to her studio was rare enough and I didn't want to wear out my welcome already. There had been a hint of desperation in her voice when she'd asked me in, and the old Marnie had responded.

She continued to wash the brushes in silence, so I stood, my attention captured by a stack of canvases standing against the wall behind my chair. I knelt in front of them and began to browse through them. Each one was beautiful and captivating, a riot of color harnessed into a picture that mere mortals could understand. I felt the old pang but continued to look through them, noticing the small portrait of a girl in the background of every painting. I rested them against the wall where I had found them, then moved to another stack that was against the wall, with their backs facing me as if Diana didn't want to see them.

Curious, I knelt in front of these, too, and began thumbing through them. They were beautiful and fine and good, but they weren't genius. For a shocking moment, I thought that maybe they were mine. But as I stared at the paintings, I saw the small portrait of a young woman in the background of each, and I knew they were Diana's. Even mine at my best could never equal Diana's at her worst. It bothered me, this inconsistency in these sets of paintings, both clearly made by the same artist, and I studied them closely again, looking for a clue.

"There's a reason why I have those facing the wall, Marnie." Diana stepped behind me and slammed the stack back against the plaster. "If I wanted people to see them, I'd frame them and show them off."

I stood, embarrassed. "I'm sorry. I was just looking. . . ."

She spoke as if I hadn't said anything. "They're so bad that you could have painted them."

"Ouch," I said, still amazed at how much she could hurt me, and realizing that hearing the truth from her was far worse than thinking it myself.

I headed for the door. "It was a mistake to come in here. I'm leaving."

She grabbed my arm in a firm grip that belied her slender, girllike arms. "I'm sorry. I didn't mean to say that. I'm just upset about . . . about Gil."

I recognized that hint of desperation in her voice again, and I stopped, unable to walk away from her. They say that no matter how old you become, when you are with your siblings, you revert back to childhood. For me, that meant that Diana was the special, delicate, and talented child who needed coddling, and the younger, more serious, and capable Marnie was there to give it to her.

"What about Gil?"

She regarded me through cloudy green eyes. "Quinn says he's going to make Gil get on a sailboat again. And that you're going along with it."

"Yes, that's true. But it's not like we're taking him out tomorrow, Diana. We're just going to navigate the marshes a bit, maybe head down to Cape Romain. And then when we think he's ready, he's going to help Quinn with the restoration of his boat. That's all."

"The *Highfalutin*," she said quietly.

"Yes."

"That was the name of Mama's boat, remember?"

I turned away from her face, unable to look into her eyes and see our mother. "Yes, of course, I remember."

"I named it after hers, you know. So that I'd never forget."

"Funny," I said. "I don't need any reminders to help me remember the night we almost died. The night Mama did die."

"I didn't say that I needed to remember. I said I did it so that I'd never forget. There's a difference, you know."

I began pacing the perimeter of the room to keep my distance from her. "Don't worry about Gil. I'll be with him the entire time. And the boat will be in dry dock, so there's no need to worry." I turned to face her. "Why are you so set on keeping Gil on dry land? Isn't sailing something he loves?"

She stepped close enough so that I could smell the turpentine on her hands and feel her breath on my cheeks. "I've never told anybody what happened the night Mama died, Marnie. Not even Quinn." She leaned closer. "So what Quinn or Gil wants to happen shouldn't matter. They don't know anything. And they certainly don't know why we need to stay away from the water."

I stepped back, unsure of what I saw in her green cat eyes. They were Diana's, and yet they weren't. I had thought they'd looked cloudy before, but it seemed now as if half of her sight was turned inward toward her secrets and her own losses, obscuring a clear vision toward the present and future. It must have been her medication, but I shivered just the same.

She reached for a pack of cigarettes on a nearby table and slid one out. With shaking hands she held it to her mouth and then picked up the lighter.

"Don't!" I shouted, knocking the lighter to the floor. "You've got turpentine on your hands and the room is saturated in paint fumes. Do you want the house to burn down with us in it?"

She looked at me oddly. "It wouldn't be the first time, would it?"

Ignoring her, I said, "Your quarrels with Quinn have nothing to do with me, okay? Leave me out. If Quinn wants to take Gil out in a sailboat, then that's up to you two to decide. I'll be here to help Gil on dry land and to prepare him for the next step. But that's as far as I'll go."

I turned to leave again, but this time I stopped myself as I caught sight of the border at the top of the wall near the ceiling. It looked like a time line with two miniature portraits and birth and death dates beneath. Squinting to read the small print, I read the names Josiah and Rebecca Maitland. Stepping closer, I read the small hand lettering beneath the dates. " 'Death by broken heart and suicide.' " I shrank back. "What is this?"

"It's a history of the Maitlands. And the curse, of course. I figured since I can't paint anymore, this would be my final legacy."

Annoyed, I said, "Don't be so melodramatic. You're still young and you've got lots of years to paint."

She shrugged, the unlit cigarette bobbing in her mouth. "But not if I can only paint shit. I'd rather do wall murals."

I stared at her for a few moments. "You have a son, Diana. Maybe if you spent more time with him instead of painting a morbid mural, you'd feel better. And so would he."

She narrowed her eyes. "You don't know the first thing about me. But I know you. You've always wanted what I had. And that hasn't changed. You see Quinn and Gil, a ready-made family, and you're setting your sights on them."

I was so shocked for a moment that I couldn't find any words. I faced the door, put my hand on the doorknob, and took a deep breath. "I once wanted your talent. And our mother's love. It was always obvious to me that her affections rested solely on you because of your talent and because you were both so much alike. There was never any room for me." I swallowed. "But I have my own life now. I'm a damn fine teacher and I make a difference in troubled kids' lives." I closed my eyes and instead of seeing the vindictive and ravaged woman my sister had become, I saw the image of my sister and me on an old vinyl couch. She had her arm around me while I kept my head buried in her neck as she made everything all right. I softened and heard myself sigh. Without looking at her, I said, "Every once in a while, when I see a beautiful sunset over the desert or an odd-looking cactus that's so ugly it's beautiful, I wish I could create it in paint the way that you can. And I wish, just once, that I could remember our mother looking at me the way I remember her looking at you."

I pulled open the door and she didn't stop me. But before I could close the door behind me, I heard her whisper, "Be careful what you wish for."

I didn't turn around but kept walking, feeling the chill on the back of my neck and remembering what our mother used to tell us about ghosts.

Quinn

I heard the muffled bark of a dog and then the bell on the reception-ist's desk rang impatiently. Putting down my sandwich, I looked at my watch and frowned. My assistant, Vickie, was at lunch and I wasn't expecting my first patient until one. I had hoped to use the extra hour to catch up on the never-ending battle against paperwork.

I left my office and headed toward the reception area, moving a little quicker when I heard the unmistakable whine of a hurt dog. I pushed open the door and spotted Trey Bonner, a longtime resident of McClellanville whose ancestors had lived in the Village pretty much since its beginnings. There were lots of Bonners, and I had trouble keeping their first names straight, but those with pets were easier for me to remember. I could usually recall the dog's name first, and then their owner's weren't too far behind.

Trey was a shrimper and had the muscled arms and strong grip to prove it, as I learned by his handshake, which left the tips of my fingers slightly numb.

"Hello, Dr. Bristow. I don't have an appointment, but I was hoping you might have a few minutes to look at Tahoe here. He's been limping and pretty much miserable all day but he won't let me close enough to see what's wrong."

The German shepherd whimpered as I knelt in front of him, but allowed me to scratch him behind his ears while I did a quick visual assessment. "Is it his back left paw?"

Trey nodded. "He's probably just got a big splinter in there from the dock, but he gets really upset every time I try to get a look."

"Don't take it personally," I said as I stroked the dog's side with one hand while gently squeezing the top of the injured leg, slowly moving down to the paw. "There are some dogs who undergo a complete personality change when they're hurt. And that includes literally biting the hand that feeds them. If you've been with a woman in labor, you'll understand what I mean."

I laughed at my own analogy, but Trey looked at me blankly.

"Guess you had to have been there," I said.

"Yeah, guess so. So what's wrong with my dog?"

I held up the large wooden shard that had been stuck beneath the outer layer of the dog's paw and easy enough to remove with my bare hand. It had been a simple matter of distraction. "You were right. Just a splinter."

"Holy crap. How the hell did you do that?"

"Lots of practice, believe me. And I have the scars to prove it." I gave the wound a swipe with an antiseptic cloth, then scratched the dog behind his large, pointed ears.

Trey laughed. "Well, thanks, Doc. How much do I owe you?"

I waved a hand in dismissal. "Don't worry about it. Glad I could help." I reached over the receptionist's desk, to where Vickie kept the dog treats, and pulled a large rawhide bone out of the basket. "Can he have this?"

"Sure, thanks."

I gave the bone to the dog and waited for Trey to say his goodbyes and leave me to my paperwork. Instead, he folded his arms across his chest and said, "I heard that your sister-in-law is back in town."

I looked at him in surprise. "Marnie? Yeah, she's here for a visit. And that would be my ex-sister-in-law."

Trey nodded. "Yeah, I knew that. But I can't say I ever expected to see Marnie here visiting with her sister."

"What do you mean?"

He shrugged his massive shoulders. "It's just that they didn't really get along. Not after their mama died, anyway."

I watched Tahoe settle down with his bone, working his teeth into the hardened leather, and I quickly forgot about my paperwork. "You knew them back then?"

He gave what I could only describe as a smirk. "Everybody knew the Maitland girls."

My expression must have registered with him because he quickly sobered. "That's not what I meant, Doc. I've known them since we were running around in diapers."

"Really?" I asked, my curiosity piqued. "So you grew up with them."

"Yep. My family lived next door to them until they went to go live with their grandpa." He looked at me as if wondering if he should go on, and when I didn't say anything, he continued. "They had a lot of freedom growing up, because of their parents being what they used to call free spirits. Not a lot of rules, you know? Their mama never married their dad on account of her not wanting her girls to have a last name other than Maitland. Said it would make the Maitland curse easier to find them." He shook his head. "You know how they say there's a thin line between genius and craziness? Well, that was their mama. Real famous painter, you know—they even have a few of her paintings in a museum up north—but crazy as a jaybird."

I had a fleeting thought that I should stop this conversation now. During my years of marriage, I had tried to pry any information about her family from Diana, but she had a way of avoiding the questions entirely or distracting me with sex. I had honored her privacy by never talking about her family with anybody else. But I was no longer married to her, and I found my need to know more hadn't diminished. Maybe it was because of Gil that I became determined now to find the answers. To what I wasn't sure, but the whole Maitland legacy was like a puzzle to me, and I had finally found myself on the verge of discovering where the first pieces fit.

"So you knew them both pretty well."

The dog let out a loud burp and continued to chew. Trey nodded. "It was hard not to. They were pretty much allowed to roam freely as soon as they could walk. The town sort of adopted them, and all the mothers joined in to feed them and make sure they had clean clothes. I remember my own mama packing their lunches and giving them to me to take to school. But I didn't mind. They were beautiful girls, you know?"

I nodded, not yet ready to interrupt him, although I'd begun to think that our conversation had begun to sound more like gossip.

"Yeah, they were gorgeous. As they got older, all the guys sort of drooled over them. They couldn't have been more different in how they looked—one so blond and one so dark. But, boy, were they wild."

That got my attention. I was still trying to reconcile the school-marmish Marnie with the word "wild" when I asked, "You mean Diana was wild. Marnie just doesn't . . . seem the type."

He laughed. "Let me tell you, she's a Maitland through and through. She was a little more subtle about it than Diana, but there were times . . ." He shook his head with a smile but didn't continue as if he'd suddenly remembered that he was speaking out loud. "And you could definitely see it when she was out in a sailboat. Nobody wanted to be on a boat with her because she scared everybody shitless. The saying around here was that she won all those trophies not from being so skilled but from sheer fearlessness."

He lifted his chin at me. "Hey, you were married to Diana. Shouldn't you already know all of this?"

I shook my head. "She never talked to me about it. All I knew was that their dad walked out of their lives when they were still little, and that they were raised by their grandfather after their mother drowned. I only just found out about the night she died. That she took the girls out in the boat during a storm."

Trey bent down to stroke the dog's neck. "I don't think anybody here will ever forget that night. What a tragedy. Miz Maitland had been seeing her doctor for a while and things had become pretty normal—for them, anyway. But for some reason she must have stopped and nobody knew until that night when she flipped out and decided to take a midnight sail in inclement weather."

He straightened and looked at me, his brown eyes darkened with memories. "Their grandpa, well, that was the first time I ever saw a grown man cry. I'd always been scared of him, I guess on account of him being our pastor and me not always following the straight and narrow, if you know what I mean." He lifted his eyebrows. "Anyway, he came down to the Village and was banging on doors hoping to find those girls, but it didn't take long to figure out that the *Highfalutin* was missing and so were all three Maitlands. The coast guard was called and everything. They didn't find Diana and Marnie until the next morning."

"It was called the *Highfalutin*?" I felt sick for a moment, remembering Marnie's face when I'd told her the name of the boat and all the odd looks I received down at the marina when I'd first christened her. I found myself imagining the young girls they had once been, adrift on an angry ocean at night and watching their mother swept away by the storm. A cold, wet hand seemed to grip me and I grabbed the desk behind me to keep my hands from shaking. "And their mother?"

"They figured she went down with the boat. Nice sailboat, too. They only found a few pieces of it—including the parts that the girls had managed to cling on to. That's not so unusual in that kind of a storm, though. Any parts left after the waves got to it would have been pushed way out to sea. Same with Miz Maitland. Nobody really ever expected to find a body, but they searched for weeks before finally giving up. There's a marker for her in the Presbyterian cemetery."

I felt stupid and incompetent all at the same time, realizing how much Diana had kept from me. But I blamed myself for my ignorance. Maybe my own grief had made me impervious to the suffering of others. And maybe that was why Diana had married me.

I felt disoriented, as if I'd stepped on an escalator that had stopped moving. I held out my hand. "Thanks for stopping by, Trey. Give me a call if he continues to favor that paw."

"Thanks, Doc. But one more thing." His expression mirrored the feeling of dread growing in my gut. "Tell Diana she should stay away from the wharf at night. Makes people nervous."

"I'll take care of it," I said, as if I were aware of my ex-wife's nocturnal wanderings. I shook his hand and said goodbye, then thought about how one could be married to a person for years and never really know them at all.

CHAPTER 10

Man's best friends and worst enemies are fire, wind, and rain.
—OLD IRISH PROVERB

Gil

Last spring, before Mama got sick, she bought me a baby orange tree. She took me with her to pick it up, and then I helped her carry it to the highest part of Grandpa's property—the place where you can see the marsh and the ocean at the same time. This was the spot where the first Maitlands lived in a small house while the big house was being built. It burned down at the same time the big house did, and sometimes, when the wind is blowing out to the ocean, I think I can smell smoke.

I held the tree and its burlap root ball while Mama dug a hole with her shovel. She was feeling better, she said, and she wanted to remember it by planting a tree on that spot. When she was done, she wiped her dirty hands on her white pants but didn't seem to notice. Then she put both palms on my cheeks, and I had to remind myself not to back away. I wasn't used to her touching me, and it was like I was testing the temperature of the ocean by diving in headfirst.

Mama put her forehead against mine. "Gil, you might be too young to understand this now. But I just have this feeling . . ." She stopped for a moment and closed her eyes. I wanted to ask her what she was feeling, but I was pretty sure that I already knew. The tree and her bringing me here were a beginning, but they felt like an ending, too. Sort of like being on a sailboat and sailing close to the wind when it suddenly changes. Your sails go slack and you start floundering until you can figure out the new direction of the wind. Or you could just sit there and go nowhere. I looked in Mama's face and felt sorry for her. Even with her medicine, I could see that she couldn't always tell which way the wind was blowing.

She began to tug on my ear like she used to do when I was a baby, but it seemed as if she didn't even know she was doing it. "Maybe later, when you're older and this makes more sense to you, you'll remember what I said. Okay?"

I nodded, not understanding at all.

"I know I haven't been the best mother to you, Gil. And I want you to know that it's always been because of me. It has nothing to do with you." Her mouth turned up in a little smile. "You're a sweet, smart, handsome and talented boy—the kind of son any mother or father would want."

Her hands went to my shoulders, holding tight as if she were afraid I'd run away.

"But sometimes . . ." She closed her eyes again, as if trying to remember what she was trying to say. "You see, we're all born with holes in our lives, and we spend our years on this earth trying to fill them. My art has filled in most of them, and for a while, your father did." She kissed my cheek and smiled into my eyes, which look so much like hers. "And you, too, Gil. I know you might not believe me, but you have filled my life in so many ways." Tears started dripping down her face, and I began to worry that this might be the beginning of one of her episodes. My dad had told me how to watch for them but I wasn't sure. I wanted to think that she had finally decided to become my mother, the way my friends had mothers. And I wondered if that had been the hole I was born with. The hole a mother was meant to fill and why inside of me it was so empty.

She sat back and smiled even though she was still crying. "Every time you look at this tree, I want you to see how strong it is in the wind, how it bends so it won't break. And how it grows stronger each year even though the wind blows and the rain pours down. I want you to think of what I just said every time you come here—especially times when I'm not around. To remind you that you're a Maitland—and that neither fire, rain, or wind has ever succeeded in destroying us. I wanted this tree planted where that first little house burned down to remind you of that." She sniffed and wiped her nose with the back of her hand. "And keep your mind straight and focused when you feel it pulling you in directions you don't want to go."

I didn't really understand, but it wasn't often that Mama would spend time with me, so I went along with it. I kept hoping that she was going to say that it marked a new beginning, and that she and my dad were going to try to work things out. But she didn't say anything about that at all. We stayed there for a long time, looking at the water and letting the wind hit our faces.

It reminded me of sailing but I knew I couldn't say that to her. I wasn't ever allowed to talk about sailing with Mama. I didn't know why, but I was pretty sure it had something to do with all those sailing trophies that nobody dusted or talked about. Once she caught me after I'd pulled them all off the shelf to look at them, and she'd gone a little crazy. When she'd calmed down, she told me something that my grandmother—the one who drowned long before I had been born—had told her. She said that ghosts weren't always people who came back after they were supposed to be dead. Sometimes, ghosts are just shadows of old memories that come back to haunt you just like any dead person. And that was why she didn't want me near the trophies. Because old memories are supposed to be left buried, and making them come alive would be like raising the dead.

We sat there with my little orange tree looking lonely with nothing but scrubby bushes and grass to keep it company, with the sun moving the shadows around us, and I suddenly wanted to paint a picture of my mother. I wanted to paint her with her ghosts, to show her that I saw them, too. The medicine wasn't making them go away, but maybe if she knew she wasn't alone with them, we could both make her better.

I never got a chance to paint that picture. It was only a few days after we'd planted the tree that I was reading on the floor in my great-grandpa's study and Mama was going through the papers in his desk. I'd heard her arguing with my dad about insurance and putting Grandpa in a nursing home, and I figured her going through his stuff had something to do with that.

The room went very quiet and I couldn't hear the shuffling of papers anymore. For a minute I thought Mama had left and forgotten I was in there. I sat up, and when I saw her face, she looked like Richie Kobylt did when my dad and I took him out on our boat and he got seasick.

She fell into the desk chair and the paper she'd been holding in her hand dropped to the floor. She stared at it but didn't pick it up. Her breathing sounded like she had run for a mile, and I started to get worried. I stood and walked toward her at the same time the other part of me wanted to run and get my dad. I stopped in front of her, the toe of my sneaker almost touching the piece of paper she'd dropped on the rug.

Slowly, she lifted her eyes to mine and I froze. I had a flashback to the time I'd stood up on my dad's sailboat at the wrong time and the boom caught me in the forehead. I was lucky I hadn't cracked my skull, but all I could remember was the fear of seeing it swing toward me, and there was nothing I could do to avoid the danger. That was how I felt then, looking into my mother's eyes. And at the same time, I remembered what she'd said about ghosts being the shadows of old memories.

I ran to call my dad, hoping I hadn't waited too long. By the time he showed up, Mama was gone and so was the piece of paper. And that was when I first began believing in ghosts.

Marnie

Quinn stepped into the jon boat and held his hand out to me. I hesitated, thinking again of the desert and its dry comforts the way a man who'd been lost at sea looks at a small room without windows.

I watched as the creek surged at high tide, muddy brown and astonishingly strong. Despite everything, I still saw the beauty of the marsh and found respect for the strength that underlay its loveliness. My grandfather once told me that our Lowcountry marsh was like a mother to the mainland, buffering the continent from frequent storms like a mother would protect her children, and acting as the ocean's incubator by nurturing and nourishing the filter feeders at the bottom of the food chain.

I had liked this analogy, assuring me that nurturing mothers did exist after all, and I found comfort in the knowledge that I had been lucky enough to be born in this place of liquid arms and maternal love.

"Come on," Quinn said, reaching toward me. "We'll just go for a leisurely ride through some of the creeks, okay? All you have to do is relax."

I had asked Quinn to take me out by myself first before bringing Gil so that I would have some idea of my own reactions. I was beginning to doubt my decision, realizing that with Gil there, I could be focusing on him and his insecurities instead of my own.

A shadow of movement above me caught my attention, and I looked up to see a blue heron with outstretched wings gliding over our piece of marsh. I stared up at it, feeling the power of the wind beneath its wings and moved by the solitary grace. I looked back at Quinn, then firmly placed my hand in his and allowed him to pull me into the boat.

It wobbled under my unsteady feet and I had to grab Quinn's shoulders to keep myself from pitching forward into the water. He didn't seem to mind as he smiled approvingly and helped me sit on the middle seat before settling himself on the rear seat, where he could steer the boat.

"That wasn't so bad, was it?"

I clung to the metal seat, mercifully kept cool in the shade of the dock, and nodded, too afraid of any more movement. I felt silly acting like such a novice, as if I'd never been on a boat before. But my feet had become accustomed to desert sand, erasing all memory of sea legs.

Quinn kept the boat stationary for a long while and I was grateful for his courtesy. I trusted him enough that I closed my eyes and tipped my face up toward the sun, its muggy heat like a baptism to me. People in Arizona are always talking about the dry heat, which makes the hundred-degree days supposedly bearable. But here in the marsh, the humid air pulsed and sweated like a living thing, like a mother's heart beating in the womb.

Opening my eyes, I caught Quinn staring at my legs. Self-consciously, I placed my hands over my knees and stared back at him. "What are you looking at?"

His smile didn't give anything away. "I was noticing how white you are. I thought the sun shone all the time in Arizona."

Miffed, I tilted my chin. "It does. I just prefer to stay out of the sun.

It's bad for your skin, you know." I took note of his bronzed face and arms with some satisfaction.

"Pardon me for pointing this out, but all of the pictures of you as a child show a kid with skin dark enough to make her ethnic heritage questionable."

"How could you have seen pictures of me as a child?"

He regarded me with hooded eyes. "Diana has all of your family albums. After we were married, she put all of your mother's photographs into albums."

"And she showed them to you?"

"Not exactly."

I sat back, not understanding.

"I sort of found them and decided since they were pictures of Gil's family, it was all right for me to look."

"Well, that depends. Where did you find them?"

He had the decency to look embarrassed. "In a trunk." He paused for a moment. "In her studio."

I raised my eyebrows.

"For the record, it was Gil who found them, not me."

I remembered the stacks of pictures in our mother's studio and was slightly touched that Diana had thought to put them into albums. I thought of photographs of our parents and felt a longing to see their faces—faces that had long since blurred in my memory so that I could remember colors and expressions, but not a complete picture. It was like remembering the plot of a book without recalling the title.

"Does Diana know that you saw them?"

"Yep. Which is why the trunk is now locked."

I was about to say something else when Quinn interrupted me. "Nice legs by the way," he said as he started the motor, effectively drowning out any response I could have made.

Slowly, he skillfully maneuvered the boat away from the dock, keeping the motor on a low hum as he headed out into the creek. I felt a surge of panic as the boat rocked gently in its own wake.

"Stay on the creeks, okay?" I said. "I don't want to go anywhere near the ICW."

He nodded and again I was grateful that he seemed to understand. The Intracoastal Waterway was a three-thousand-mile highway running down the Eastern seaboard for all watercraft that cut through the creeks and marshes and led from the tidal rivers to the great Atlantic. It had once been my playground but now hovered somewhere near my nightmares as I envisioned the tall boats with their white fiberglass shimmering in the sun. I clung to the seat of our little jon boat a bit tighter than necessary and waited until I could become accustomed to the small ripples knocking into the metal side.

"Would you like something to drink?" He indicated a small red-and-white cooler by his feet.

I was thirsty but wasn't quite ready to relinquish my two-handed hold on my seat. "No, thanks. Maybe later."

He turned his head but not before I saw the smile on his lips.

"What's so funny?" I asked, hating the petulant sound of my voice. All of my hard-earned peace and calm had quickly unraveled as soon as I found myself in this watery territory that my mind had forbidden me to return to.

For a moment I thought he wasn't going to answer. Then, after kicking the motor up a notch, he said, "Do you remember a Trey Bonner?"

I found myself blushing and momentarily forgetting about the water around me and the breeze teasing my face. "Yes, I think so," I said, avoiding Quinn's eyes. "He was in school with Diana and me."

"Really?" he said, and I could tell that he already knew a lot more.

I could feel my flush deepen and I lowered my straw hat over my forehead. "We dated him."

"We?"

"Well, not at the same time, obviously. But both Diana and I dated him."

"Who dated him first?"

I looked down at my lap and at the line where my shorts met the pale skin of my thighs, and remembered my first heartbreak. "I did. I dated him first."

A flash of orange and a loud *cleep* caught my attention from atop an oyster bed off to my right. It was an American oystercatcher, a bird that has piercing yellow eyes and that's about the size of a chicken. I was grateful for the distraction and watched as the bird waited patiently for an oyster to briefly open its two shells to let in water. The animal ignored us as we motored by, and just as we were about to pass him, he quickly inserted his bladelike beak between the shells of an unfortunate oyster, snipping the muscles holding them together and laying open his meal.

"How appropriate," I muttered, remembering Trey.

"Did she steal him from you?"

I jerked my face toward Quinn, having momentarily forgotten that he was there. "That's one way to put it, I guess. But yes, that's pretty much what I called it then." I looked back to where the oystercatcher had now disappeared behind a bend. "She had everything, but wasn't happy if I seemed to having something she didn't."

"But you were close?"

I looked into his eyes, now a piercing blue in the bright sunshine. "Yeah, we were. Odd, isn't it? But it was only the two of us, you know? Our parents weren't really the type you could go running to when you had a problem. Most of the time, they *were* the problem." I smiled to myself. "So, yes, we were close." I watched as a school of menhaden darted beneath the water's surface in silvery clouds and remembered Diana's patience as she taught me how to tie my shoelaces.

"You're not clutching the sides of the boat like a crab anymore. I guess that means you're ready to go a little faster."

Without waiting for me to protest, he increased the speed, creating a spray of water behind us. Two snow-white egrets, startled from their perches by the sudden noise, croaked out their alarm as they took flight away from us. Quinn gunned the motor a little faster and I jerked my head up, knocking my hat into the water. Either he didn't notice or was too intent on teaching me something, but he didn't turn around to get it. I felt my hair blow loose from the ponytail and I lamented its lack of order. I wanted to tell Quinn to stop or at least slow down, but I found myself mute. I had felt the wind on my face again—not the hot dry wind of a desert sand storm, but the warm wind of my home, born of sea salt and the ocean's tides. My breath caught as if I'd rediscovered an old friend whom I long believed gone from my life.

We made our way to wide-open marshland, and I found myself smiling as I recognized where we were, and remembering paddling this way with Diana. And Trey. Cypress trees vaulted skyward along the banks, some wearing veils of five-petaled white blossoms of Cherokee roses like June brides. We passed oyster beds and small terns hugging the sandbars in search of clams. I breathed in the sulfer smell of home, the wind bathing my loosened hair in its aroma, and cloaking me like a skin.

As suddenly as he had quickened our speed, Quinn slowed the boat and then cut the engine. I was out of breath as if I had been swimming instead of riding under the power of a gas motor. My chest rose and fell and I saw Quinn's gaze flicker to my chest before resting on my face again.

We had entered yet another creek, and we were close enough to the bank to hear the sigh of air escaping from the pluff mud as the water sank down with the tide. I watched with delight as small fiddler crabs raced to their holes as if being tugged by an invisible string.

I glanced at Quinn again and found myself holding my breath. He was looking at me oddly, and his face had paled beneath his tan.

"Are you all right?" I asked, leaning forward to feel his forehead with the back of my hand.

He drew back. "I'm fine. It's just . . ."

"Just what?"

"Nothing. It's nothing."

"You look like you've just seen a ghost."

He didn't say anything for a moment. "Maybe I have," he said, then started the engine.

I watched the dark water churning beneath the boat as we headed toward home, and I soon realized that I had removed both hands from my seat bottom and that I was actually close to enjoying the ride.

We didn't speak again until we were back at my grandfather's dock, where we were met by Gil. I was happy to see him, but it meant that I didn't get a chance to ask Quinn what ghost he'd thought he'd seen.

CHAPTER 11

I seem to have been like a child playing on the seashore, finding now and then a prettier shell than ordinary, whilst the great ocean of truth lay undiscovered before me.

—Isaac Newton

Diana

I don't know when it happened that I stopped needing sleep. Somewhere after Marnie's leaving, I think. Marnie's absence was a tangible thing: a constant reminder that I had failed her. I missed the sound of her bare feet coming to my room on stormy nights and the way she always knew when I needed to talk or when I needed silence. I would fight closing my eyes, knowing that when I opened them I'd still be alone. And I missed her almost as much as I was glad she was gone.

In the years since her leaving, I'd learned to cope. I would put on my nightgown and lie in bed with my eyes closed and wish for sleep while listening to the quiet house and the sounds of night outside my window. I missed my sleep, if only because it meant that I no longer dreamed. But maybe that would have happened anyway since I believed that I had no more dreams left.

Since Marnie's return to our grandfather's house, I found it nearly impossible to even lie down and feign sleep. Instead of succumbing to sleep now that Marnie had come home, my body itched to be up and moving, as if tiny bugs crawled beneath the skin urging me up, creating a restlessness in me unfamiliar since the night Gil and I had our accident. I was relieved in a way since the restlessness brought back my need to paint, and I found myself staying up through the night to work on my wall mural.

But sometimes, in the darkest part of the night, even my painting failed me, and I felt compelled to sneak down the stairs and out of the house in search of something—of what, I wasn't sure. I always found myself at the water's edge on the dock or the beach, or sometimes I'd drive into town and wander the wharves where the fishing boats were kept at night, their long net-holding arms stretched out in silent sleep against the darkened sky. I stared into the black waters for a long time, imagining the cold, wet feel of it against my skin and wondered what it would be like to step forward until the water covered me like a cool blanket, rocking me to sleep until no more air filled my lungs. There would be no more pain, no more medicine, no more hate. And no more fear. I longed for refuge, but could only stay on the solid wood of the dock, staring at the water as if it were behind a locked door and I couldn't find the key.

I suppose my wandering to the fishing boats made sense if I stopped to think about it. It was there that I had first learned I could paint, or rather that my mother decided that I could paint. It was also there that I remembered first hating her. She had told Marnie that Marnie's painting had been of the same quality of a monkey dribbling paint from a brush. It had angered me and embarrassed me, and when I'd seen the lost look in Marnie's eyes as she compared her work to mine, I knew that something was gone from me forever and I rightly blamed my mother. When I think back to my youth, it is that day that marks the "before" and "after" of my childhood—the first break in the tethers that bound me to my sister and separated us in our mother's calculating eyes.

I thought my night wanderings had gone undiscovered until a night several weeks after Marnie's return. I couldn't find Quinn's car keys, so I resorted to finding my way in the moonlight to the beach below the house. I sat in the damp sand, glad for the cool breeze against my skin that made me shiver, reminding me that I was alive. I supposed it was for the same reason that I ripped off the bandage on my leg, the dark scab like a gaping hole filled with shadows by the moon and the hot skin cooled by the ocean's breeze. Phosphorescent fish showed off their ethereal scales in the surf, and I felt the old familiar tingle in my fingers as my desire to paint them began to fill the empty well inside of me.

I was deciding if I should go inside to lie awake in my warm bed, or if I should stay there and watch the tempting waves until dawn, when I felt the presence of somebody walking up behind me. I didn't turn around.

"It's three o'clock in the morning, Diana. What the hell are you doing here?"

Quinn's voice was heavy with sleep and I almost felt sorry for being the source of his light sleeping. "I'm trying to get a tan." I grimaced as salt water sprayed over my wound and I was glad of the darkness so I couldn't see Quinn's recrimination.

He surprised me by sitting in the sand next to me. "It's not safe to go wandering at night by yourself near the water, you know."

"Who says?"

"Me, for one. And anybody else who has common sense. And Trey Bonner."

I looked at him for the first time but his face was bathed in shadow. "I wasn't aware that you knew Trey."

"His dog's a patient. I've only seen him a couple of times but he came in today."

"Oh. But why would he be talking about me?" I faced the ocean again, hoping the breeze would cool off my face. I was too old to blush, but talking to my ex-husband about the man I'd soothed my aches with after our divorce made even me wince.

"He asked me to tell you to stay away from the wharf at night. You make people nervous."

"Do I now? Did you tell him that it's none of his business?"

"Actually, I thanked him for telling me."

I didn't say anything, afraid my growing anger would unleash itself on him and I'd never get the courage to ask the question I'd been avoiding since my last visit to the nursing home.

"People are afraid you'll jump, and nobody wants to pull your body up with a shrimp net."

I craved a cigarette and cursed under my breath for forgetting to bring some. Something splashed in the water nearby, and I thought how lucky whatever it was to be able to disappear into the anonymity of the ocean's depths. I stared down at my wounded leg. Quietly, I said, "I wouldn't, you know. Because of Gil. Because of what it would do to him. But that's the only reason."

He didn't say anything for a long time as we stared out at the moonlit waves stealthily creeping up the beach toward us. "I'm sorry, Diana."

"For what?" I asked, craving a cigarette and not wanting to have this conversation. "For the mess I am? You had nothing to do with it. I was born a Maitland, and marrying you couldn't have changed that."

Quinn placed his elbows on drawn-up knees and let his head hang forward. "I'm sorry I couldn't make it better for you."

I felt a surge of tenderness for him and touched his arm. "It's not your fault. Some things just can't be fixed." He looked at me and I pulled away, eager to distance myself from him and from the overwhelming sense of loss whenever I thought about our marriage. I cleared my throat. "Besides, you didn't marry me." A breeze lifted my hair and teased at the wound on my leg. Quietly, I said, "You married a ghost."

Our eyes met in the pale light. "It wasn't like that."

"Yes, it was. Always. Even when we were in bed together, there were always three of us."

He shook his head and turned away from me. "We needed each other, Diana. At least in the beginning."

"No. You needed to fix me. And me, well, I've never needed anybody." I stood quickly, before he could see that I was lying. I stared out to where I knew the horizon lay but saw only smudges of darkness. Rubbing my hands on my arms against the chill, I asked, "Did Marnie say anything to you about sailing again?"

He shook his head. "No. She's actually been pretty strong about insisting that she won't."

"Yeah, well, she probably believes that. But I have a strong feeling that Gil won't get on a boat without her."

He looked up at me, startled. "You've seen that, too?"

"Gil's pretty perceptive. He's probably figured out that getting out under sail would be good for Marnie, too. They're a lot alike, you know, always thinking of others."

He was silent and I wondered whether he was going to ignore the derogatory way I'd said that last part about always thinking of others. "I guess we'll have to wait and see."

"If you want to wait that long. I don't think she's planning on staying very long, and I don't intend to allow Gil anywhere near a sailboat."

Thankfully, he didn't seem to be in the mood to argue about Gil again. He stood, brushing sand off the backs of his legs. "I hadn't really thought about her leaving. She seems so at home here."

"Yes, she does. But sometimes you have to be gone from a place to realize how much you miss it."

Sharp eyes stared back at me. "Like the ocean?"

"Yes," I said, turning away. "Like the ocean. Or the desert." I began to walk toward the path that would lead me home, and I heard Quinn following me. I swallowed thickly, trying to find whatever courage I might still have. "Speaking of Gil, I'd like to take him with me when I visit the nursing home next week. The old lady I've been visiting for over a year now has asked to see him." He didn't answer right away. Nervously, I added, "I guess because I talk so much about him, and I'm always bringing pictures of him to show her. And she's an artist, too." I wanted to bite back my last words, realizing they were the wrong ones to say to Quinn.

Quinn's footsteps stopped, and I stopped, too, turning around to face him. "I think it might be good for him. For us. To be together again alone since . . ."

"No," he said, cutting me off.

"Please," I said, hating the desperation in my voice. "He's my son. . . ."

"No," he said again, and brushed past me to walk up the path.

"Quinn," I shouted, unable to keep the anger from my voice, "you can't keep him from being alone with me forever. I'm his mother."

He abruptly faced me and put his hands on my shoulders, squeezing tightly. "Biologically speaking, yes, you are his mother. But your actions say otherwise. You've shown me one too many times that you can't be counted on to act like a good mother should where our son is concerned."

"Please," I said again, my anger gone and only dark desperation filling the void. "I'm feeling better now. I'm taking my medication. Please."

He released his hold on my shoulders. "Then tell me what happened that night, Diana. Tell me why you went out on the boat in the first place and why neither you nor Gil can or want to talk about it."

I stared at him for a long moment before dropping my eyes to the sand beneath our feet.

"Well, then. There's your answer," he said before turning away from me and walking up the path with long, sure strides.

I stayed where I was for a long time, listening to the rhythm of the waves behind me and remembering that day in my grandfather's library when everything had changed. And how even a mother's love can be a very dangerous thing.

*

Marnie

I sat on the porch across from Gil, watching him furiously scribbling in his sketch pad. His golden head was bent over the pad in his lap, and the intensity of his concentration reminded me so much of his mother. I still had not been able to coax him into painting with watercolors again. I knew he enjoyed it, and was good at it, too. Quinn had shown me some of Gil's framed paintings he'd hung on the walls of his office, and I'd been awed by Gil's use of color and delicate brushwork. Still, though, he could not be persuaded to hold a paintbrush.

While Gil and his affliction remained an enigma to me, I hadn't made much progress in breaking through to him at all. I admit that he did seek my company and enjoyed being with me while I talked about art. But all of my hours in the classroom and all the textbooks I'd read dedicated to teaching the special-needs child didn't seem to apply to my nephew. And sometimes, when I looked in his Maitland eyes, I would see such understanding and intelligence that I wondered if I should be the one to be silent and instead learn from a nine-year-old child.

Always, though, his silence brought my thoughts back to the night he stopped speaking, and made me wonder if knowing the answer to that question was all we needed to bring Gil's voice back.

I glanced around at the whimsically painted chairs and brightly hued flowerpots, trying to picture the morose Diana painting them in her studio with the paint-splattered furniture and the unseen paintings facing the wall. And then I remembered the stack of beautiful pictures that had also been painted by Diana, and once again I wondered at the discrepancy in ability between the two. Without thinking first, I asked, "Did your mother really paint all of these chairs and pots?"

I looked at Gil when he didn't answer, then silently chastised myself when he raised his golden head and stopped drawing. Slowly, he nodded.

Standing, I walked to the blue-and-white polka-dotted pot nearest the front door and picked it up to look at the bottom, not really sure why. Diana's initials and a date were scrawled on the bottom, and I did a quick mental calculation as I slowly placed it down on the porch.

"It's a year older than you are, Gil," I said, smiling. He didn't smile back.

"Are you ready to show me your drawing?" I had been talking about the intricate fretwork that framed the porch and studying the way the sunlight changed the look of it depending on where you were standing and where the sun sat in the sky. I was eager to see his interpretation and maybe, if I even admitted it to myself, to see if his talent surpassed his mother's at his age.

In response, he drew the pad to his chest as he had done before and shook his head.

I forced a smile. "That's fine, Gil. You'll show me when you're ready." I returned to my seat, more hurt than I cared to admit. I glanced back at him again and saw that he hadn't returned to the drawing but was staring down at the pad in his lap. I remembered his silent laughter in the car to McClellanville, and I realized that I hadn't seen him laugh or even smile much since that trip. I leaned back in my chair and studied him through half-closed eyes. "Do you want to hear a story?"

He shrugged, reminding me that he was approaching adolescence and had to show me that a story was too young for him but he'd humor me anyway. I suppressed a smile and closed my eyes, recalling the mobile of the planets on the ceiling in Gil's bedroom, and the fact that he'd grown up without pets, despite the fact that his father was a vet.

"Once upon a time," I began and was rewarded with a roll of his eyes. I pretended to frown at him and began again. "Once upon a time, there was a nine-year-old boy named George. And all he had ever wanted his whole life—more than anything—was a puppy."

I settled in to my story, making it as outrageous as possible and culling on past stories told to a classroom of students and to a younger Diana, who had once believed that she needed me by her side before she could paint.

I was rewarded several times with the twitching of a cheek and once with a full smile. So I upped the stakes and went full-out for the end of the story. "And when George finally held that little puppy in his arms, he realized that through all of those years of pining for a dog, he had never once thought about a name for him.

"Well, being a smart little boy, George was obsessed with science and with outer space and the planets of the solar system in particular. He even had a mobile with each planet made of a different-sized Styrofoam ball. But his favorite of all the planets was the little blue one called Uranus. He wasn't sure why, only that blue was his favorite color and that was the color he'd chosen to paint that planet on his mobile. And that is how he decided on the name for his new puppy.

"However, it wasn't very long before he realized his mistake when George's mother first called out the back door, 'George! Get in here and feed Uranus.' "

I saw Gil's lips quiver.

"And then the next day, his father said, 'George, we need to take Uranus in to get a flea shot.' "

Gil's eyes were clenched tight and his head was shaking with quiet laughter.

I continued. "But the last straw came when the cute little girl from next door came over to see George's new puppy. 'I want to see Uranus,' she said, innocently, only realizing what she'd said after George's face turned beet red. She ran home crying, vowing never to set eyes on George again, lest she be reminded of her embarrassment.

"And that is the story of how a puppy became named just 'U,' since George's mother didn't want to have to buy new monogrammed blankets for the puppy and they couldn't think of another name that started with 'U.' "

Gil's mouth was now open in silent laughter, and I laughed out loud, pleased at my mission accomplished.

Quinn opened the screen door. "Lunch is ready. Come on in and wash up, Gil."

I saw Quinn do a double-take at the flushed skin and wide grin on Gil's face and then turn and look at my matching smile.

I watched as Gil picked up his pad and clutched it to his chest as he walked past his father into the house. I stood to follow, but Quinn stopped me with a hand on my arm.

"Thank you," he said.

I didn't have to ask for what. "You're welcome," I replied, then followed Gil into the house.

My grandfather was already in his spot at the head of the table, but I was surprised to see Diana in the seat next to him, where I usually sat. In the weeks since I had been home, I had stopped expecting her to join us at the table for meals.

"Diana," I said, watching Gil choose the seat farthest from his mother.

"Yes?" She looked at me with bored eyes, as if seeing her at the table wasn't anything out of the ordinary nor was having one's young son avoid you as if you had poison ivy.

"It's good to see you here." I took the seat on the opposite side of the table, next to Gil, who had remained standing until I sat down.

"Is it?" she asked.

I ignored her barb as I helped Gil place his napkin in his lap.

Grandpa held out shaking hands and bowed his head. Diana hesitated for a moment, then took his offered hand while I did the same on his other side. I waited for someone to say the blessing and when none was forthcoming, I said, "Thank you, Lord, for these and all your many other blessings. Amen."

I lifted my head and glanced across the table to find Diana looking at me, and I wondered if she had bowed her head at all. I squeezed my grandfather's hand and let go.

I looked down at the soup in front of me and tried to think of something to say. "Did you make this, Quinn? It smells wonderful."

"Thank you," he said, taking a taste of his, while glancing at Diana over his spoon as an antelope at a watering hole would glance at the nearby pack of lions. "What brings you to the table, Diana?"

Her soup sat untouched in front of her. "I was hungry."

Quinn concentrated on his spoon. "I'm glad you could join us." He took another sip, avoiding her eyes.

After several moments of silence, Quinn sat back in his chair and cleared his throat. "I'm going to go inspect the damage on the *Highfalutin* tomorrow to see what needs to be done to make her seaworthy again. Would anybody like to go with me?"

The silence that followed might have been laughable if I'd not seen Gil's expression. I stared at him for a long moment before I recognized with painful familiarity the look on his face. It was the face of a person who had lost the one thing that mattered most and who had no idea how to get it back.

Diana snorted. "Gee, don't everybody answer at once." She glared at Quinn. "What did you expect? If you'd bother to look around, you'd notice that all of us except for Grandpa here have very good reasons not to ever get aboard a sailboat again. Especially one with the name *Highfalutin*."

To my amazement she picked up a spoon and began feeding our grandfather, her hand shaking almost as much as his. I watched as she fed him and avoided looking at me.

Quinn continued. "She's in dry dock and nowhere near the water. I'm going to need help fixing her up, but I thought maybe Marnie and Gil would like to get a look at her before we start the repairs."

"Hire a carpenter, Quinn. There's no need for you to subject Gil to the torture of seeing it the way it is."

Quinn sent a glowering look toward Diana but addressed his words to Gil. "Remember how we agreed with your aunt Marnie that this was something you wanted to do? And that your doctor thought so, too?"

Gil only paused for a moment before nodding.

Quinn continued. "Dr. Hirsch suggested that it might be reassuring to you to see the boat, to see that she's hurt but can be fixed." He reached a hand out to cover Gil's on the table. "Just like you, right?"

Again Gil nodded, then slowly slid his hand off the table and held it in his lap.

Grandpa waved his hand at his food, indicating that he was done, and Diana let the spoon fall to the bowl with a clatter. Grandpa then began to grunt and point his chin in Quinn's direction. Quinn nodded as if he understood what the old man was trying to say.

"I think your grandfather would like me to quote from the Bible a passage that he recently shared with me." He cleared his throat. " 'If thou faint in the day of adversity, thy strength is small.' "

Diana flopped back in her chair. "What the hell is that supposed to mean? That if at first we don't succeed in dying, then try, try, try again?"

Angrily, I turned on her. "You know that's not what he's trying to say, and you're only succeeding in further alienating your family and frightening your son. Do you think you could try, just once, to think about somebody beside yourself?"

She went deathly still as I watched the color drain from her cheeks. "Oh, believe me, Marnie. I know lots about thinking about others. I've done nothing else for the last sixteen years." Her eyes flickered over to our grandfather. "Haven't I, Grandpa?"

His eyes met hers in an unflinching gaze until she turned away from him. Resigned, she sat back in her chair again, her previous energy gone from her like loose sails on a windless sea. "Fine, then, Quinn. Do what you like. But can I ask that you hire a real carpenter to supervise the restoration? I won't worry as much about Gil working on the boat if I know he's with a professional."

Quinn nodded. "That's a good suggestion, and I was planning on doing that anyway. I thought that while I was in town today I could do some asking around for recommendations."

A mischievous grin teased Diana's lips. "I know a great carpenter. He's actually a shrimper, but in the off season, he runs a woodworking shop, where he makes and sells furniture and stuff like that. He's also worked down at the marina ever since I've known him, helping with boat repairs and renovations."

I felt heat flush my cheeks again and I looked down at my half-eaten soup.

Quinn asked, "Anybody I know?"

"Yes, actually, you do. Trey Bonner. We were just talking about him recently, remember?"

I saw Quinn shoot a quick glance at me, and I mentally flinched, wondering what all Diana had told her ex-husband.

"Great," he said through thinned lips. "I'll see if I can reach him today."

Eager to leave, I glanced over at Gil's plate, happy to see an empty soup bowl and only crumbs remaining of his sandwich.

"Gil and I have plans to go sketch down by the marsh. So, if you'll excuse us . . ."

I didn't wait for anybody to speak but stood before helping Gil retrieve his sketch pad from under his plate and pulling out his chair. I kissed my grandfather on the cheek and ushered Gil from the room.

We had made it to the front porch when I heard Diana call my name. I felt Gil's shoulder stiffen under my hand before he ducked behind me as I turned to face her.

She pretended not to notice her son's aversion to her presence, but I could read the hurt in her eyes. In the years since our mother's death, she had learned to hide her emotions from the outside world. But I knew her like my right hand knew my left, and I reached to touch her arm, knowing before I did so that she would shake it off.

"Yes?" I asked.

"I'd like to paint your portrait."

"Excuse me?"

"Not right now, but while you're here. If I could get you to sit for a few sessions, I'm sure I'd have enough material to paint a full portrait."

I thought about the girl who looked like me and who appeared in all of her paintings but said nothing. This was the first overture she'd made to me since my return, and I didn't want to rebuff her attempt, regardless of how suspicious I might be.

"Are you sure? Aren't there enough people around here for you to paint?"

"Yes. But only one sister."

I felt Gil step out slowly from behind me. "I thought you had quit painting since . . ." I stopped in time, remembering Gil's presence.

"I did. But for some idiotic reason, your face is the only thing I can get excited about painting. Except for my mural, but that doesn't count. But I want to—need to—paint you."

I almost smiled at her dramatic emphasis. But she seemed sincere and the old part of my heart—the only part that still belonged to this place I had called home—tugged at me and willed me to take a chance. I felt Gil's presence beside me and knew that I had to do it for him, too.

"Fine. As long as it doesn't interfere with my lessons with Gil." I smiled at her. "And as long as you eat everything on the food trays I bring up to you."

She looked resigned but pleased. "Fine. I need to get set up in my studio, but I'll let you know when I'm ready to get started."

She turned without saying anything else and I called out to her, "What did you tell Quinn about Trey?"

Pulling open the door, she looked back at me. "Ask him yourself," she said before disappearing inside.

I turned to Gil and wondered if he knew that his expression mirrored my thoughts. Because as eager as I was to find common ground again with my sister, I couldn't help but wonder if her overture had some ulterior motive.

"Come on," I said to Gil as I moved off the porch and headed out toward the marsh, where the ocean met the land and secrets nestled in the cord grass.

CHAPTER 12

The Ponthieva Racemosa *orchid (known also as the shadow witch) does best when planted with other orchids. I have placed mine in the same pot as the fragrant ladies' tresses, yet I've watched the leaves brown and curl and then drop off completely. In a fit of frustration this morning, I ripped the plant out by its roots, determined to start again. But what seldom works in real life will most likely fail in the art of orchid cultivation. Instead of starting all over again, I will repot my orchid and give it special care until it thrives. I won't give up on it.*

—DR. QUINN BRISTOW'S GARDENING JOURNAL

Quinn

I had just finished repotting the *Ponthieva Racemosa*, handling it like I would a newborn kitten, when I heard a timid knock on the door. I knew it was Marnie without turning around through a simple process of elimination: Diana would have barged right in and Gil wouldn't have come at all.

She wore a skirt that fell to midcalf and hid a great pair of legs, a nondescript blouse with a single button left open at the neck, and her ubiquitous bun held tight to the base of her head. I thought back to what Trey Bonner had told me about Marnie's wildness, and I almost smiled but stopped myself when I considered what must have happened to her to make her into the timid mouse of a woman she pretended to be.

I motioned for her to come in and she opened the door. "I hope I'm not bothering you."

"Not at all," I said, standing, then dusting the dirt from my hands and letting brown specks fall on the cream laminate countertop. She watched me, and I had the distinct impression that the untidy countertop was making her uneasy.

She tore her eyes from the counter and stood primly in front of me. "I'd like to come with you to the marina today. To see the boat. If that's all right."

I noticed she didn't say the boat's name. "Sure," I said, glancing down at her clothes. "I thought I'd leave in about half an hour to give me time to clean up a few things here. Will that give you enough time to change?"

"Change? What's wrong with what I have on?"

Besides stating the obvious, I strove to be more tactful. "It would be quicker if we took the jon boat and you might find it more comfortable in shorts."

"Oh," she said, smoothing her hands across her skirt.

"And we'll probably see Trey Bonner. Thought you might want to wear something a little less . . . schoolteacher when you saw him again."

A flash of anger illuminated her eyes and flushed her cheeks, and I knew that I was catching a glimpse into the face of the old Marnie—the Marnie who once fearlessly faced the wind on the open ocean and had been called "wild."

"Why should I care if Trey Bonner sees me? He's a guy I dated a long time ago, end of story."

I knew there was no end to any story involving both Marnie and Diana, but I let it go. "Fine," I said. "Just go put on some shorts."

"I will." She started to leave but turned back to me, then hesitated as if she wasn't sure what she was going to say.

I looked up at her expectantly.

She tugged on her ear as I had seen Diana do countless times. "Diana wants to paint my portrait."

I felt a quick jolt of alarm, but tried not to show it. "Is that a good thing?"

"I don't know. You said that she hasn't been able to paint since her accident with Gil. Except for the wall mural she started in her studio, I haven't seen any evidence that shows that's changed."

I walked toward her and she crossed her arms as if erecting a barrier. "I think you being here has been good for her. Maybe it's made her want to paint again, and you're the most obvious choice. I wouldn't say that she's improved since your return, but she does seem to be taking more of an interest in life. She even asked to take Gil with her to the nursing home next time she visits, which was unexpected. Even before the accident, she didn't spend a lot of time with him."

"Why would she want to bring him to the nursing home?"

I shrugged, not really sure of the answer myself. "I think the old woman's lonely, and it seems to help Diana to help someone else. Diana's been bringing pictures of Gil and telling stories about him, and I guess they both figured it was time to meet him in person. She also mentioned that her friend's an artist, too, which could be why Diana wants to bring Gil. Not that Diana's ever been the biggest advocate for Gil's art, but maybe this is a start."

Marnie pressed her lips together, thinking. "Before the accident— Diana was still painting, right?"

I swiped dirt off the counter and onto the floor before leaning back, her eyes taking in every movement. "If you could call it that. She still sold paintings, and they were certainly better than average. But they weren't her best. Her best work was those paintings she did from the time you left up until the time she gave birth to Gil."

She thought for a moment. "Like the painting I saw in the shop window when I went to the Village with Gil."

"Right." I wondered if I should say more, if I should mention the nature of her sister's work after Marnie's departure, or even the painting that had first introduced me to Diana and which she always accused me of falling in love with before I ever met her. But I said nothing, unsure if there would ever be a right time for Marnie to know.

She continued to stand where she was, making no move to leave. "When was she first diagnosed?"

It was odd talking to Marnie about Diana, about things most sisters knew intimately about the other. But there was very little about the relationship between the Maitland sisters that could be described as normal. I almost felt sorry for the woman standing in front of me begging for information like a seagull scavenging for stray breadcrumbs. "After Gil was born," I answered. "Your grandfather put her under a doctor's care once before, after you left, and he thinks that might have been her first episode. But she wasn't really diagnosed until she became a mother." Marnie blanched and I wondered if I shouldn't have told her what had happened to Diana after Marnie had moved away. But she had wanted to know, and I wouldn't lie to her. "Her doctor said it was probably something that had always been there but that she had learned to suppress, most likely because of what she saw from growing up with your mother. But with the hormonal flood that pregnancy creates, it was too much for her."

"So you had her put on medication, and she was fine?"

"Well, 'fine' is one way of putting it. She didn't have any manic or depressive episodes. But she became . . . flat. And so did her paintings. It killed her a little, I think, selling inferior work for inflated prices. But she stuck to her medication for Gil. She might never have been the perfect mother, but I have never doubted that she loves him."

She gripped the sides of her arms so tightly that the tips of her fingers turned white. "So what happened? What made her go off her medication?"

I shrugged, mentally covering the events of the last year as I had dozens of times already. "It was a normal Saturday. I spent a few hours at my practice in the morning and Gil was with Diana. She wanted to take him to a nursery to get a tree or something—I can't remember what. But I do remember that the last conversation I had with her was about your grandfather. She'd become convinced that he would be better off in a nursing home—although I completely disagreed with her. Regardless, the fact remained that Edward had taken out nursing home insurance several years back, and Diana was going to go through his papers to see what she could find. The next thing I knew, Gil was calling me on the phone to tell me that his mother was flipping out."

I turned away from Marnie, unable to bear her scrutiny, which seemed to take in my story along with all my weaknesses and powerlessness in the face of Diana's illness. I picked up a soft towel and began wiping the green pointed leaves of a white butterfly orchid. "I had to put her in a hospital—that's when I moved in here. She had been taking her meds—I checked—but something sent her over the edge, though to this day she hasn't told me what. Her doctor said that it can happen when a patient's meds need to be adjusted, and has told me what signs to look for to avoid another episode."

Marnie's touch on my back startled me and sent gooseflesh racing down my spine. "But that was last year. Gil's accident was only a few months ago. What's been going on with her in the past year that could culminate with her taking Gil out on a boat during a storm and nearly killing them both?"

I turned on her, anger at myself irrationally directed at her. "I wasn't married to her, remember? I did my best taking care of your grandfather and Gil, and when Diana came home from the hospital, trying to get her to take her meds and making sure she stayed away from her grandfather and son."

She stepped back, her hands clenched at her sides. "Well, you didn't do a good enough job at that, did you?"

"No, I didn't," I said, leaning toward her. "But neither did you, a thousand miles away from here, completely and happily oblivious."

I watched the color drain from her face. "I wouldn't say 'happily,' " she said quietly. "Diana and me, you can't understand . . . you can't understand unless you grew up in our house with a mother whose behavior was so erratic and unpredictable that you never knew if you were going to awake to a slap on the face or a hug. Or if your mother would show up at your school in her pajamas. Or not at all."

"I'm sorry," I said, my anger rapidly deflated in the face of her grief. "I didn't mean to dredge up the past or to hurt you. It's just that since my brother's death, I've become really good at fixing anything that's broken. But I've tried and failed with Diana, and I'm afraid that I can't fix Gil, either."

Her face softened and I took a second look at her. I remember shortly after meeting her how I had thought that she seemed, within the confines of her artistic family, to be a crow in a nest of nightingales. But I suddenly realized that she was neither crow nor nightingale, but the nest that held them all together, the one part that sustained the whole. I wanted to tell her this, but I knew that she wasn't yet ready to hear it.

I held my breath as Marnie stepped closer to me and raised her face to mine. "I think you'll find that people don't always need to be fixed. Sometimes all we need is to be told which way the wind is blowing so we can adjust our sails accordingly. And to be allowed to find our own way." She stood back suddenly as if realizing how close she was. "All of those years with our mother who was never diagnosed. What a waste. I sometimes wonder how different our lives would have been if she had sought treatment."

Her eyes held shadows of terror in them, and I knew she was thinking of the night sixteen years before when she and Diana had lost so much. She was watching me closely, and I felt as if she were challenging me. I remembered her fearlessness, and I wondered what it had taken to suppress it all those years and what it would take to resurrect it.

I stepped closer, my curiosity piqued. "How much do you remember about the night your mother died? When did you know that something was wrong?"

She turned her head away from me and hid her eyes, and I thought for a moment that she wasn't going to answer me. Her voice was quiet when she spoke. "I don't . . . I don't remember everything. I've seen doctors, but nobody has been able to help me recall everything that happened. One doctor said it was a survival mechanism, that my brain is protecting me from things I'm not ready to know, yet." She took a deep breath. "We were so young. But we knew enough that when Mama was in one of her good moods, we needed to keep it that way. We were used to the crazy ideas and the impromptu trips, and her excitement was always contagious. I always hoped that maybe she'd get stuck in the happy part and forget to go back. I don't think that Diana ever had any hope at all."

Marnie walked toward the counter and began methodically swiping the remaining dirt into a cupped hand. "So when Mama got us out of bed and told us that we were going sailing, it sounded like a grand adventure and that maybe this time it would work out and Mama could stay happy."

Marnie stood there with her hand cupped in front of her, a frown wrinkling her forehead. "It was Diana who made sure that I was dressed warmly and had on my boat shoes. Mama never thought of things like that. She wore her nightgown and was barefoot, and I've always wondered why Diana didn't make her change. When we got to the boat, we found that the life jackets were missing, and I was disappointed, thinking that we weren't going to be able to go. But Mama didn't say anything about it, so neither did we."

Her eyes met mine, and for a moment, I could almost feel the sway of a boat beneath my feet and the tremor of fear that coursed between us like a shimmer of lightning.

"The funny thing is, I wasn't scared. I had heard the storm advisory on the radio, so I knew, but I wasn't scared. Diana was. I could feel her body trembling when she held my hand to help me board. I didn't need her help whenever we were on the boat, but I never let her know that the water never frightened me. I became myself whenever I was on the water, just as Diana did when she picked up a brush. But she was my sister." Marnie looked at me as if this last part made sense to me, and oddly enough, it did.

Without even seeming to realize where she was, Marnie began walking around the small greenhouse and tidying up as she spoke, putting trowels at right angles to one another and placing the potted plants in perfect rows, creating order in a world of abstract placement.

"Mama put me on the main sail and she sat at the tiller. She told Diana to just stay out of the way, and I remember how happy that made me." She looked around, searching for more disorder to put to rights. "I was a much better sailor than Diana. It was the only thing I could ever best her at, and I had the trophies to prove it. For a long time I wasn't sure if it was the thrill of moving my boat through wind and water or the joy of capturing my mother's attention that made me want to sail. I suppose it was always a mixture of both."

She looked at me, her hazel eyes staring steadily at me, as if waiting for me to judge her. I said nothing.

"We weren't out to sea more than ten minutes before the wind picked up and the waves became rough enough to splash up over the deck. Diana was so scared that I could hear her teeth chattering over the noise of the storm. I was starting to get scared, too, but I wasn't going to show it." She gave a small laugh but there was no mirth in it. "The things we do for a mother's affections."

She stopped then, her hands gripping the edge of the counter and her fingers bloodless. "And then Mama . . . she wasn't at the tiller anymore. I thought maybe a wave had knocked her away, but I couldn't tell because the rain was coming down hard, making it difficult to see." Her thumbnails scratched at the counter's edge. "I . . . I remember standing up so I could turn around and look down into the water—looking for Mama, I think—when I was hit from behind by something. I knew before I landed in the water that it was the boom and it was my own stupid fault."

She had begun to shiver in the hot and humid greenhouse. "The water was so cold that it knocked the breath out of me. Every time I opened my mouth to get air or to shout for help, I swallowed salt water and I knew, at twelve years old, that I was going to die."

I walked toward her but she turned from me and made her way to my desk, where she began methodically stacking papers and neatly organizing the pens and pencils that lay scattered on the surface. "At the same time, something brushed my leg, and when I whipped around, I saw that it was my mother. She . . . she was only about five feet in front of me. I wasn't sure if she'd been in the water before me or if she'd jumped in after me, but she was there and swimming toward me. I was angry at her for leaving Diana all alone on the boat and was wondering how Diana was going to manage to pull us both out of the water when I spotted Diana about twenty feet away from us in the water. At this point the boat was heeling and filling with water, and one big wave would swamp her. Our only hope would be for the three of us to try to reboard her and begin bailing water while one of us radioed for help."

Marnie stopped, her hands frozen in position in the act of stacking papers, and she stared at a spot in the wall as if it were a screen flashing her past in front of her.

"Did you manage to get back on the boat?" I prompted.

It took her a long time to answer. "I . . . I don't remember," she said, slowly turning to face me. "I've blocked out what else happened that night. I've been to more psychiatrists than I can count, but none of them can get me to remember the rest. All I know is what I've been told, which is that Diana and I were rescued the next morning, clinging to seat cushions from belowdecks. Our mother was never found."

"Does Diana remember?"

She shrugged. "Only that she saw our mother go down. One minute she was there, and the next—gone."

I stepped closer, intrigued by the way Marnie so carefully avoided meeting my eyes. "So your mother drowned and the boat was lost, but you and your sister survived."

She nodded, her eyes focused on my top button.

"Yet, ever since, you and your sister have been at odds with each other. Usually, survivors tend to stick together."

"Usually. But there's nothing about us Maitlands that can be called 'usual,' " she said, placing the stack of papers she held in her hand in the middle of my desk. "I'd better go get changed so we can leave."

I watched her in her sensible flat-soled shoes as she walked to the exit, trying to picture this woman as a twelve-year-old girl fighting a storm in a twenty-four-foot boat and found that I couldn't. Unless I looked into her eyes and saw the woman who hid behind them.

"I don't want to be here," she said, facing the door with her hand on the handle. "I never wanted to come back."

Quietly, she opened the door, then shut it behind her, leaving me to wonder if what Diana had once told me about ghosts was true, and if Marnie had realized it, too.

Diana

My grandfather looked up in surprise as I sat in the rocking chair beside his wheelchair on the great wraparound porch that hugged the front of the house like old, knobbly arms. We watched in silence as Marnie and Quinn made their way down the path that led to the marsh and the dock.

"They're going to the marina. Quinn's taking Marnie to examine the damage to the *Highfalutin*."

Grandpa nodded and tapped his yellow-stained fingers against the closed cover of his Bible. I turned my attention back to Quinn and Marnie, watching as he put a hand in the small of her back as they walked and she pushed a strand of hair behind her ear. I swallowed thickly, my throat suddenly dry, and all I could think of was the old family curse and how apt it was that my prodigal sister should find solace in the arms of my ex-husband.

I must have made some kind of a sound, because I found my grandfather looking at me, his eyes blue and clear and seemingly reading every thought in my head. I'd hated him for it when I was a teenager and living under the same roof with a preacher had been contrary to my wilder inclinations. But after I became a mother, I found it reassuring that someone else could see what was going on inside my head and know enough to hold me back from the edge when I got too close. Except for the last time, when I was already halfway over before he even knew I had leaped.

"I found those papers in your desk."

His expression never changed.

"So you've known all along." I wasn't really surprised. Having raised my mother by himself, he'd had a lot of practice with intuition long before I came to live with him. "You can't be angry with me, though, can you? You've been hiding your own secret all these years."

He kept his gaze focused out toward the ocean as if he weren't listening, but he'd always been a man who heard every word, even those you wished he hadn't.

"I'm not angry now, if that means anything to you. I, of all people, understand why we sometimes have to do something that we don't want to but that we believe is the right thing."

He took a deep breath and moved his hands to his Bible.

"I don't want Marnie to know." He looked at me with those eyes, and I wanted to break down and weep and confess everything. I looked down, ashamed, not able to look him in the face. "Not ever. Because if she knows the truth, then I have nothing left."

Finally, I looked up, and when I saw the tears in his eyes, my shame burned brighter inside me and my whole body ached with it. He had opened his Bible and was holding it up to me, his shaking hand indicating a highlighted passage. With my own shaking fingers, I took the book and read the passage to myself.

The pride of thine heart hath deceived thee, thou that dwellest in the clefts of the rock, whose habitation is high; that saith in his heart, Who shall bring me down to the ground? / Though thou exalt thyself as the eagle, and though thou set thy nest among the stars, thence will I bring thee down, saith the LORD.

My self-righteous anger pushed through, past the shame and sorrow, and I slapped the weathered book closed, dumping it ungraciously in the old man's lap. I turned on him with fury. "You don't know everything. You weren't on that boat with Marnie and Mama. I was. I know things that would break your heart in so many pieces, you and your precious Bible would never be able to put them all back together. You'd be as dead inside as I am. And so would Marnie. So let me keep this piece of poison to myself. And you'd better pray to that God of yours that Marnie never finds out the truth."

I stood suddenly, my rocking chair slamming hard against the face of the house. I ran all the way up to my studio, and then to the window to see if I could catch another glimpse of Quinn and Marnie. But all I saw was the vastness of the marsh where it melted into the ocean, and I settled down to count all the secrets it could hold.

CHAPTER 13

Take any path you please, and ten to one it carries you down to water.

—HENRY MELVILLE

Marnie

I didn't say much on the journey into town, and neither did Quinn. He seemed to know instinctively that I needed this time alone in my thoughts. It might have been in deference to what I had told him about the accident, which only added to my guilt. I had told him more than I'd ever told anyone, including all the shrinks I've seen. But I hadn't told him everything. I have found that there are some things you hold close to your heart and hide from the world. Because if you don't, then you risk the world seeing you as you really are. And that's a very scary thing indeed.

We tied up the jon boat not far from where I'd parked my car when I'd come to the Village with Gil. I still recognized several faces but held back a greeting when I saw that no recognition registered on their faces when they spotted me.

We walked past the post office and the art store, where, thankfully, my sister's painting was no longer sitting out front. As we crossed the street to head in the direction of the Marina, Quinn took my arm. "You're dragging," he said with a smile.

I nodded without reciprocating his smile and increased my pace as eager now to get this over with as I was reluctant to move forward. I stayed back as Quinn went to speak with a man with a name on his shirt and carrying a clipboard; then I followed him as they headed back toward the large wooden shed used for temporary storage behind the marina. With heavy dread I watched as the man unlocked the large wood doors. He slipped off the padlock and walked away with a wave in our direction. I faced Quinn, who stood with his hand on one of the door handles.

"Ready?" he asked.

I nodded, not trusting my voice.

He pulled the doors open one at a time, allowing the sun to slice light into the blackened interior. I felt the blast of warm air on my face, and I felt for a moment as if I knew what it would be like to open a coffin that had been buried for years.

Quinn stepped inside, and a few moments later, I saw the interior dimly outlined by inadequate overhead fixtures before he reappeared at the door. "Are you coming in?"

I nodded, smelling mold and old varnish; then I walked forward, my eyes transfixed on the back corner, where a thirty-foot sailboat sat on jack stands, its keel resting on a thick railway tie. Its mast was gone, taking away its imposing height and making it appear less intimidating. I stepped forward again, noting how scratched and dull the hull was, and the corrosion around the small windows. The metal deck railing had dulled to a matte silver and the visible wood trim was cracked and peeling, the wood splintered and dry like an old woman whose power over the ocean had dispersed beneath the waves.

As I got closer I could read the faded name on the stern and read it out loud. "The *Highfalutin*," I said.

"Yep. That's her. And this is what a boat looks like after it's been cap-sized, dragged to shore, then stored for several months." He shrugged. "I didn't even want to look at her at first, much less refurbish her. It even took me a while to convince myself to turn in the insurance claims."

"I understand," I said, and I knew that he, of all people, would know that I did. But there was something thrumming under my temples, rac-ing through my blood and tingling in my fingertips.

"What are you smiling at?" Quinn asked.

I looked at him, startled to realize that he had moved to stand right next to me. And startled to realize that I really was smiling.

"It's . . . different. I expected it to be the same. The same *Highfalu-*

tin." I swallowed. "My mother's boat, the one I used to race in the club races, was a J/24. Not a big boat—only about a three-thousand-pound displacement, but it was fast. They don't make them anymore, but they made about eleven thousand of them."

He still had that smile on his face, and I felt like an idiot, talking like a sailboat dictionary, until I realized that he again understood my need to talk about boats in a wood-and-fiberglass way, rather than in a head-and-heart way.

"I've seen quite a few J/24's. It's a pretty fast boat."

I nodded, but my eyes were on the tapered hull, which was designed to slice through wind and glide through water. "What kind of a boat is she?" I asked, bolder now. I walked forward and placed my palm on the stern beneath the name, feeling the memory of water.

"She's a Tartan 30. Quite a bit bigger than your J/24. I think she's got about a nine-thousand-pound displacement or so. I liked it because not only is she fast, but there's standing headroom and full-length berths that make cruising on her for a few days pretty comfortable." He smiled at me and I couldn't help but smile back. "And," he said, walking toward the broken rudder, "she's got a fully enclosed head."

"Wow," I said, my eyes diverted to the rudder, which was partially ripped away from the hull. "That's a neat little feature to have in a boat." My voice sounded less than enthusiastic as I stared at the wounded boat, wondering at the fury of the storm that would have snapped the mast and rendered the rudder useless, but left two survivors.

"Hello? Is anybody in here?"

We both turned at the sound of the voice calling us from outside the doors.

Quinn called out, "We're inside—come on in."

I squinted into the bright sunshine, trying to make out the outline of the person moving toward us, the voice vaguely familiar.

Quinn stepped forward with his hand outstretched. "I see you got my message. Glad you could get down here to meet with me."

Recognition hit me at the same moment Trey Bonner turned to face me. He stared at me for a few long moments before his eyes widened.

"Marnie Maitland? Is that really you?" His gaze took in my flat-soled shoes and long walking shorts as well as my tightly held bun and plaid blouse, and in an instant, I wished that I had listened to Quinn and put on something else.

"Hello, Trey. It's been a while." I held out my hand as I'd seen Quinn do, but Trey quickly swept me up in a bear hug, and instead of being annoyed, I felt a little bit of coming home. The warm, solid feel of him and the reassuring faint odor of shrimp had brought me home almost more than anything else since my return.

He released me and held me at arm's length. "You look different," he said. "But good," he added hastily. "I almost didn't recognize you with your hair up. I always remember you wearing it down so it would blow in the wind, and your grandpa was always after you to tie it back or cut it off."

I blushed a little. "I can't believe you remember that."

"There's a lot I remember," he said, making me blush even harder.

He looked pretty much the same—maybe leaner and more muscled, but still the same jet-black hair and dark brown eyes, set off by perpetual sun-bronzed skin. He wore a clean T-shirt and jeans and could easily have been mistaken for someone at least a decade younger. My hand drifted to the neck of my blouse, where I unbuttoned one more button.

"You look good, too, Trey. Do you own your own shrimp boat now?"

He shook his head. "Nope. My life sort of took a different turn. I'm a part investor in my brother's boat, but it's basically his. I help out during the high season sometimes, but most of the time you can find me in my shop."

He stopped, as if he were embarrassed, and I remembered the old Trey as someone who held the important things close to his heart. He'd never been one to brag, instead being more intent on proving himself in actions rather than words.

"What kind of a shop, Trey?"

Shrugging, he said, "Oh, I make things out of wood to sell and my mom works the store. But my real passion"—he lifted his eyebrows and turned toward the *Highfalutin*—"is fixing boats. I've been doing it for a while now and have established a bit of a reputation."

"Really? That's great. Are most of your customers local?"

"Nope. I've got people as far away as California calling me now and business is growing. It's going so well that I'm thinking about hiring an assistant. Maybe getting a bigger place, too."

I smiled up at him. "Sounds like you're really doing well."

"Yep. Hard to believe, huh?" He looked up at the ceiling, and I knew he was recalling the wild nights of two teenagers with restless hearts and a need to escape from the lives they'd been given. "What about you?"

I could almost feel Quinn smirking behind me. "I live in Arizona now and teach art to special-needs children."

"You're an art teacher?"

I could tell he was trying to keep the grin off his face.

"Yes. I enjoy it very much."

"In Arizona. Isn't that pretty much the desert? Guess your plans for sailing in the America's Cup have to wait for now."

I looked down at my sensible shoes. "Come on, Trey. You know I stopped wanting to do that when my mama died."

He touched me gently on the arm. "Yeah, I know. Just thought maybe you'd changed your mind. I still remember . . ." He stopped, looking at me as if he were still seeing the girl I used to be.

"What?" I asked, not sure I wanted to hear his answer.

"Well, you once told me that sailing was like tricking the wind to move your boat. That it was magic that way. Kinda stayed with me, ya know?"

"Yes," I said quietly. "I suppose it would."

Quinn stepped forward and I welcomed his interruption. Indicating the *Highfalutin* he said, "Well, this is the boat. Why don't you come over here and take a look and let me know what you think?"

Quinn let Trey move ahead and then surprised me by putting his arm around my shoulders. We watched as Trey rubbed his hand across the fiberglass of the hull and then used a nearby ladder to hoist himself onto the deck.

"Looks like this boat's been through a lot, Doc." He walked around the deck, chewing on his bottom lip and mumbling to himself. "Lots of sanding and painting, and I think your teak toe rail is either going to have to be completely replaced, or if you want to save some money, you can restore it by hand—but it's a bear of a job." He gave it a gentle kick with the toe of his sneaker. "Let me check out what's belowdecks."

We listened as his feet clattered down the stairs, where he disappeared for about twenty minutes. When he reappeared, he said, "Well, the good news is that the bones of the boat are solid." He wiped his hands on a rag he'd pulled from his back pocket. "Looks like we're going to need some new wiring, a bunch of wood repair and new paint, and the stanchions for the lifelines need rebedding. Plus all the wires that hold up the mast need to be resealed where they attach to the deck. And that's just the stuff I can see right off the bat. I'll give you a more formal estimate and specifics later this week after I've had a chance to do some more investigating and put everything on my computer." He smiled at Quinn. "Plus you might want to think about adding some fun stuff, like an autopilot. And maybe adding an inmast furling mainsail, too. Might as well do it all now while it's up in jack stands, you know?"

He climbed out of the boat and came to stand next to us, sticking the rag back into his pocket. "As soon as you're ready to get started, I'll bring my trailer over and bring her over to my place. After your go-ahead, I can get started this week."

"That's great," Quinn said, looking at me. "Only thing is, I was hoping to get my son involved. He needs . . . he needs to get comfortable being around boats again. His doctor and I both thought that having him assist with restoring the *Highfalutin* would help."

"No problem. I could get the main structural stuff done first, and then when we're ready to start stripping, waxing, and polishing, I'd be more than happy to accept his help—especially with that toe rail. And anybody else who wants to help would be welcome, too," he added, looking pointedly at me. "It gets kinda lonely when it's just you and the wax, you know?"

"I could help," I said, realizing that my participation was inevitable. "I don't think Gil would come unless I was there with him. Assuming I'm still here. I'd like to be back home by Christmas."

"Oh, come on, Marnie. You gotta at least stay until the Blessing of the Fleet in May. And besides, you *are* home."

"This isn't my home anymore, Trey," I said, looking at him and suddenly remembering the taste of warm nights and cocoa butter. "I've taken a leave of absence from my job, and they'll be looking for me to come back, if not by fall, then at least by the second semester." I glanced toward the open doors, feeling suddenly as if I were suffocating. "I'm going to step outside while you two finish up your business. It was great seeing you again, Trey."

He winked. "I hope I'll be seeing a whole lot more of you, Marnie. Oh, and tell Diana that I said hey."

"I'll do that," I said, feeling the old pull of hurt and jealousy—two things I hadn't experienced my entire time spent in Arizona, but that had been pounding me in equal measure ever since I had returned to my grandfather's house.

I waited outside for another twenty minutes or so, my face tilted upward to soak in the sun and warm me. Despite the heat of late summer, being inside with the boat had sent a chill inside my bones, the place where all my fears are kept, and they ached with coldness. I stood in the ninety-five-degree heat and rubbed at my gooseflesh-covered arms until Quinn and Trey appeared.

We said our goodbyes, and after Trey left, Quinn turned to me and surprised me by taking my hands in his. "Your hands are cold." He placed them together in his warm ones. "You did really great in there."

"Better than I expected, anyway."

"No," he said, his blue eyes serious. "Better than anybody who's been through what you have would handle it." He brought my hands up to his mouth and blew on them. "Your hands really are freezing."

I looked into his eyes, seeing for the first time that they were the color of the ocean at sunset, and I felt a fissure of ice melting inside of me. I stepped back, uncomfortable. "Cold hands, warm heart. That's what my mother used to say to me."

He let go of my hands. "Is that true?"

Quinn fell in step beside me as I headed toward the docks. "I don't know. I guess it's better than the alternative, though."

"You mean warm hands, cold heart?"

I stopped to face him. "No. I meant burning hot and cold at the same time. That was my mother's relationship with life, and we can all see where that left her. Diana, too."

"Is that why you try to make yourself so neutral? To make yourself a polar opposite of your mother and your sister? I don't think I've seen that much beige in a woman's wardrobe in my entire life."

I started walking again, quickening my pace.

He managed to stay at my side with long strides. "Because I think that you were once just as passionate as they were. Just because you couldn't paint as well as they could didn't mean that you didn't see things just as vibrantly as they did. You felt things just as deeply. You simply expressed it differently. In your sailing. Your sailing was your way of showing the world your passion. And showing your mother that you were as qualified to be her daughter as Diana was."

Be careful what you wish for. I heard my mother's voice as clearly as if she'd just whispered those words to me. "No," I said, embarrassed to find myself on the verge of tears. "I'm nothing like Diana. My mother always told me so."

He stopped me with a pull on my arm, jerking me around to face him. "But I've seen you. The real Marnie. The way you used to be." He was looking very closely at me, as if searching for my ghost.

"Where?" I asked, not really sure why, but maybe I'd want to go see her. To find if I resembled her at all anymore.

He straightened and dropped his hand, and I tried to decipher the look on his face.

"Just an old picture," he said, shrugging, then turning away to begin walking back to the jon boat.

We were almost home and I was staring at a great blue heron pensively watching the still waters of the marsh when the answer came to me. Quinn's expression had reminded me of the look on Gil's face whenever he saw his mother. Maybe it was simply the father-son resemblance, or maybe they both knew what it was like to want something that had never really existed.

$$\mathbf{\mathcal{O}}$$

Gil

I saw Mama leave in the car not too long after my dad and aunt Marnie left to go into town. Joanna always helps Grandpa into bed at this time, and I think Mama knew this, too, because as soon as the blinds were pulled down in his bedroom, I saw Mama quietly close the back door and walk quickly down to the car. I'm not sure where she got the keys, but if I knew that my dad kept them in the cookie jar in the kitchen, then I figured she knew it, too.

The only thing different about this time was that she had two framed pictures with her. They matched each other, so I thought they were a pair of something, but she had their backs facing me, so I wasn't sure. I watched as she placed them facedown in the trunk of the car and slammed the lid shut before looking around to make sure nobody saw.

I didn't know where she went, and I didn't think anybody else did either or she wouldn't have been sneaking away. All I knew was that I didn't want to be anywhere near her when she got back. It didn't matter if she'd just gone to see her doctor or if she'd been visiting her old friend at the nursing home, 'cause when she got back, she'd be as mad and angry as a mama heron would be if you got too close to her nest.

But she wasn't the only one who could be sneaky. As soon as I saw her leave, I pulled the key from under the hall rug, where she put it, and I got into her studio. I've already seen all those paintings facing the wall and all the ones that aren't, and it was like a mystery that I needed to figure out. I've always loved mysteries. I think it's because I've grown up in this house, where answers hide in all the corners but nobody ever thinks to ask the questions.

Except for me. I've asked my mama and daddy and grandpa all sorts of questions. Like why I never met my aunt Marnie. Or what happened to Grandma. Or why I hear children crying on stormy nights. I stopped asking after a while. As my dad would say about his orchids, why bother to water a flower after it's dead? So I decided to find the answers myself, and that was how I found out about my mama's studio key.

There are things in her locked studio that I've seen before in other parts of the house. She's like one of those scavenger birds I learned about in school, who steals things from other nests to make her own. I found the photo album that I now keep under my bed—the one that has pictures of her and Aunt Marnie when they were little—and two silver candlesticks that have my parents' wedding anniversary date written on them. I know that's the date, because there's a picture of them in their wedding clothes under the couch bed in the studio that's all wrinkled and spotted like it got rained on. But the date that's printed on the back is the same date that's on the candlesticks, so I thought that was what it was.

I also found a little jewelry box that was old and white and had a little ballerina that popped up and spun around when you opened the lid. Inside, wrapped around the ballerina like a hula hoop, was my daddy's wedding ring. I knew it was his, because he used to keep it on his dresser, even though he was divorced, and one day it wasn't there anymore. He asked me if I took it, which is how I knew Mama had it. I didn't tell him. I think I knew even back then that it's not always words that give you answers.

In the jewelry box I also found a tarnished silver chain with half a heart hanging from it. The jagged edge of it was shaped like a lightning bolt and written on it was the word "ever" and underneath it "ters." I couldn't figure out what it meant and I looked in the rest of the jewelry box to see if I could find the other half, but it wasn't in there. The bad thing about being where you're not supposed to be is that you can't ask any questions. So I put the necklace back, deciding that it probably wasn't important enough to know.

On the day that I saw Mama leave with those two pictures, I crept out of my room before Joanna could think to look for me. I slid the key out from under the hallway rug and slipped inside the studio.

I liked the smell in there: the smell of paint and thinner and smoke. I don't think Daddy knew Mama smoked, and she even tried to hide her cigarettes from me, but I knew. Anyway, the smell reminded me of my mother, especially when it's all of her that I got to have. I had learned the hard way what getting close to her could do to me.

I walked around the room, noticing the outlines of a mural circling the wall close to the ceiling that looked like it was going to be people's faces and dates. I was a little surprised when I came to the farthest corner and saw my name but with no picture and no dates yet. I wondered if this would be like the family tree my teacher had assigned for the class last year, but I couldn't tell from what was up there. I'd have to come back soon to check it out. *Another mystery*, I thought, and smiled to myself.

On the back wall, next to some of the paintings that face the wall, was a big locked cabinet that I heard Mama call an "arm-wore." All I knew was that it was always locked and I'd never been able to find the key. Except for that one time. I had already looked at the cabinet and was moving on to the next thing when my brain caught up with what I'd seen: the key sticking out of the lock.

Slowly, I walked over and turned the old-fashioned key, and the wood door just sort of swung open by itself. The hinges squeaked, and I looked over my shoulder, suddenly feeling like somebody was watching me.

It was messy inside, with books, papers, clothes, paint supplies, and bags of cookies, all sort of thrown in together, and I thought then that I knew why my mama never yelled at me to clean up my room. I'd always wanted her to so that I'd know she cared and she noticed and that she was like other moms. But seeing inside the messy cabinet, I sort of understood why maybe she hadn't.

I poked around for a bit, not really seeing anything interesting until I got to the bottom of the first side. Shoved behind an old blanket was one of those plastic bins that I had in my room to keep all my LEGOs sorted. It was big and see-through, and written in her handwriting were the words *Precious Things*.

I slid the box out, careful not to mess up anything that I couldn't put back; then I unsnapped the lid and lifted it off. The first thing I noticed was that it smelled like Grandpa, and that surprised me until I saw at the bottom of the box the small wooden blocks that looked just like the ones that hung in Grandpa's closet. But then I saw what the rest of the stuff in the box was, and I had to sit down because all of a sudden I wanted to cry.

Everything was like a whole sea of pale blue and green, tiny hats and pants and sweaters all folded neatly with tissue paper as if someone had taken a lot of trouble to store them. Really small socks, a silver rattle, and a china box filled with baby teeth were stuck in one corner of the box, the clothing protecting the breakable stuff. A large brown envelope was stuck down the side, and I pulled it out to put flat on my lap. I saw my name written in a big black marker, and I opened the unsealed flap and pulled out all the papers inside.

There were some important-looking papers that I figured were my birth certificate and the record of my baptism. But in the back of the stack were pictures—pictures I had drawn for my mother in art class at school. She hadn't said anything when I'd given them to her, and she'd never put them on the refrigerator. I had long ago figured out that she didn't like my artwork and had probably thrown it away after I gave it to her. By second grade, I'd started throwing it away before I'd left the school building to save her the trouble.

So why was she saving all this stuff if she didn't like it? It was another mystery, and one I'd probably never solve, mostly because I'd discovered that my mother liked to live with unanswered questions. I figured that out as soon as I met my aunt Marnie.

I carefully put everything back in the box, exactly as I had found it, and stuck the box back behind the blanket, backing away a bit to study it to make sure it still looked the same. I was about to close the "arm-wore" when I saw the corner of a piece of paper sticking out from underneath a pile of old smocks on the bottom right shelf. The weird color green of the big writing at the top was what made me notice it, so I reached down and pulled the piece of paper out, and I felt my eyes widen when I recognized it. It was the piece of paper Mama had found in Grandpa's study right before she'd had her last episode, and I almost felt a little sick holding it and wondering how a single piece of paper could be so important.

I read it, not understanding any of it except for my great-grandpa's name and address. I was squinting at the small typing at the bottom of the paper when I heard the front door slam downstairs.

I quickly closed the doors and turned the key in the lock, realizing too late that I still held that piece of paper. My hand was already on the key when I made the decision to keep the letter. Maybe if she never saw it again, she would forget why it was so important, and nobody would have to worry about her seeing it again and having another episode.

Aunt Marnie and my daddy were talking downstairs, and I knew I had to hurry. I looked around the room one last time to make sure I'd put everything back in its place; then I slipped out of the room, remembering to put the key under the carpet before I went down the attic stairs. I ran to my room and stuck the paper under my bed in my own special box, making sure to smooth the bedclothes. Then I went downstairs, my heart beating loud enough that I thought everyone could hear it, and I wondered if that piece of paper was really a mystery, or just the answer to an unasked question.

CHAPTER 14

The more I become decomposed, the more sick and fragile I am, the more I become an artist.

—VINCENT VAN GOGH

Diana

In the years after our accident, Marnie and I were like waves hitting the shore—sometimes in tandem and sometimes in direct opposition, but always two parts of the whole. One cannot have sand without battering waves, and no waves would exist without the sandy bottom of the ocean to sculpt them. We were like this, my sister and I. We both longed to be sky or cloud, something apart from the other, but a twist of fate had made us our mother's daughters, and all the forces of nature couldn't change that.

Marnie was like a puppy in that first year. She would seek me out, waiting to be petted, her eyes full of remorse, grief, and guilt. I indulged her at first, thinking her ignorance was a good thing. But as we got older, her refusal to see the truth and mine to reveal it made her grief laughable and I made her suffer for it. I didn't realize at the time that we would both still be suffering for it all these years later.

I heard the timid knock on the door to my studio and made Marnie wait for a minute while I stretched out my neck muscles, cramped from painting so close to the ceiling, and concentrated on the drugs flowing in my veins to put me in neutral before I called out for her to enter.

I wanted to laugh out loud when I saw her—her hair so tightly held back and her clothes at least a size larger than they should be. What most people don't realize about Marnie is that she's sexy as hell. Whereas I'm built like our mother—skinny with no butt and no boobs—Marnie is small but with long, lean limbs and with a real woman's hips and bust. I think Trey Bonner was the first person to make Marnie realize it, and I had watched in horror as Marnie came into her own during those years, her self-confidence and assurance rising just as quickly as mine deflated without our mother's presence to ensure my rightful place in the pecking order in my sibling relationship. I think that was why I decided that Trey had to be mine, if for no other reason than to reassure myself that I had not become invisible.

Marnie stood patiently in the doorway, her eyes studiously avoiding the paintings stacked against the walls. "Joanna said you'd already eaten breakfast, so I didn't bring anything. Unless you'd like coffee or something?"

"Can't. Not with my medication. Well, I guess I could have the decaffeinated stuff, but what's the point?"

She smiled, her gaze wandering to the mural near the ceiling. Her smile abruptly fell when she realized what she was looking at. "What are you doing here, Diana?"

"I told you. I'm making a history of the Maitland family."

She shook her head. "This isn't a history. It's . . . morbid. Has anybody else seen it?"

"Nope. You're the lucky one."

She continued to stare closely at the painted faces of the Josiah and Rebecca Maitland that lived in my head. They were the faces of my childhood nightmares, and by relegating them to the wall, I had somehow paroled them from my prison. I was rather proud of them, and Marnie's comments annoyed me.

Marnie read out loud the inscription I had painted in calligraphy beneath the portraits. " 'In June 1803, Rebecca Maitland doused her bedclothes with lamp oil, then set herself on fire. Before she succumbed to the flames, she ran down the upstairs hallway of the house to where her children slept, alighting rugs and draperies and efficiently dousing the lives of all but one of her ten children.' "

She was quiet for a few moments as she studied the blond Rebecca, the green eyes so startlingly familiar in their color and intensity, the yellow-white strands of hair blowing behind her as if she stared into the wind.

"She looks like Mama," Marnie said quietly.

I shrugged, not willing to get into it with Marnie. "I used the small oil miniature in Grandpa's room. I could always see a family resemblance between Rebecca and Mama."

"I don't think Gil should see this."

I felt a spark of anger. "He's my son, Marnie. Why do you think I keep my studio locked? Don't you think that I have his best interests at heart?"

She regarded me with her soft hazel eyes. "No. Not really." Her gaze flickered down to my legs, to the large white bandage that covered the wound I would not allow to heal.

I waved my hand impatiently in front of her. "I didn't bring you here to discuss my mothering skills." I pointed at a sheet-draped chair by the window. "Go sit over there and take off your shirt."

"What?"

"Don't be such a prude, Marnie. We both know better than that. And you can keep your bra on if you think you have to. I just want to get your shoulders."

She hesitated. "What are you going to write about me? On the mural."

I shrugged, not sure of the answer myself. "I don't know if I'll put this on the mural. I'm going to paint you on canvas, and then we'll see where it goes from there."

She sat on the edge of the chair and began slowly to unbutton her blouse, each movement unsure, as if she were pulling wires to defuse a bomb.

Impatient with her timidity, I reached behind her and opened the window, then smiled to myself as I watched her shiver. "Take down your hair. I want to see it blowing in the breeze. I have it in my mind to paint you on a sailboat."

I watched as the color drained from her cheeks, and I felt the old tug of remorse. I softened my voice. "It's how I remember you, Marnie." I paused for a moment, taking in her hairstyle and dowdy clothes. "I couldn't paint you any other way because I can only see the real you."

She clutched her blouse closed in front of her chest. "This is the real me now, Diana. I've changed. I've really changed. I'm not the girl you used to know. I started to change the night Mama died, and by the time I left here, the old Marnie was dead."

I knelt in front of her, looking into the eyes that used to ground me when I began to feel the shocks of lightning sparking in my head. I saw the eyes of the sister who looked to me for protection and who I had once loved most in the world. I did not want her to be dead. I could not *allow* her to be dead. And then I thought of Gil and knew that I needed the old Marnie now as much as I ever had.

"No, Marnie. She's still there. I see her. You can't bury her because she's not dead. So let me paint her. And maybe you'll find that you'll recognize her. That you'll want to bring her back."

She stared at her fingers spread out in her lap, the fingers my mother used to say were too short to be an artist's but that I used to think were capable of doing everything else. "I don't think so. But do what you want. I've never been very good at fighting you."

I wanted to tell her that she was wrong, that her resistance had always been the one thing that kept me in check regardless of how much I railed against her. But I stayed silent and rose to my feet to begin mixing my paints while my sister gently began to pull the pins from her hair, one by one.

We didn't speak for an hour, except for my monosyllabic commands to position her in a certain way or to move her head. She kept stealing furtive glances out the open window, where storm clouds had begun to gather. I felt a small thrill, wanting to capture the volatile sky and Marnie's fear, as the wind began to gust through the window and push at her hair, reminding me of the way she had looked that night nearly sixteen years before.

She eventually broke the silence, mostly, I assumed, to distract her from the weather outside the window. "Quinn said that you were planning on putting Grandpa in a nursing home."

I didn't answer, but my brush remained frozen in place over the canvas.

"Is that true?"

"Yes," I said. "Years ago Grandpa insisted that I take out nursing home insurance for him just in case . . . in case I wasn't able to care for him and you wouldn't come home."

She was silent for a moment. "I would have. If he needed me, I would have come home."

"Yeah, well, we had nothing to go on, did we?"

Her lips pursed and she took a deep breath. "So what made you decide that he needed more care?"

I decided to be blunt, if only to stop her from probing further. "For the same reasons why he initially took out the insurance. Because I have no idea how my health will be from one day to the next, and I hadn't heard from you in ten years. I needed to make sure that he would be taken care of. And, after my divorce, I didn't think it fair to dump it all in Quinn's lap."

A strong gust of wind pressed against the house, making it creak and groan like an old man.

"So what made you change your mind?"

I forced myself to remain calm. "I . . . got sick, and all of a sudden, what to do with Grandpa wasn't a priority anymore."

She was scrutinizing me and I could no longer look at her. I made a great show of mixing my paints on the pallet, swirling colors together as if they were memories.

"Quinn said it was sudden, that he had no idea why you had gone off your medication. Only that it coincided with your desire to put Grandpa in a home." She paused. "Was it because of me? Because I wasn't here to help you?"

I didn't answer, preferring her to think it was her fault than to guess at the truth. The back door slammed, and I knew it would be Quinn coming in from the greenhouse. I watched as Marnie glanced out the window, no doubt realizing the same thing.

"He's really great in bed," I said, enjoying her discomfiture.

I was rewarded by a deep blush on Marnie's cheeks.

"I don't think of him that way."

"Sure, you do. He's a good-looking man—and he's single. As long as you don't mind sloppy seconds."

Her eyes widened, but she surprised me by not blushing deeper. Instead, she said, "It didn't seem to bother you when you were dating Trey Bonner."

I tried to hide my smile. "Touché," I said, raising my brush to canvas to try to replicate this enigmatic woman my sister had become, while pretending to myself that blood was no thicker than water and that my heart was too full of hate to allow her back in.

*

Quinn

I was halfway up the stairs to go find Gil when I heard running footsteps coming down the stairs from the attic. I stopped in time to prevent being run over by Marnie. I reached out to grab her arms so she wouldn't run into me and ended up with my body weight thrown forward, pressing her against the wall.

"Are you all right?" She was, after all, running away from her sister's studio, which made my imagination run wild.

She nodded, still trying to catch her breath. "I'm fine. It's just . . . well, one minute I was sitting there quietly and she was painting me, and the next minute she was throwing my shirt at me and telling me that the light was gone and I had to go. She practically threw me out of the room."

"That's not really her, Marnie. You know that, right?"

"Yes," she said quietly. "I know."

It was then that we both realized how close we were standing and that her shirt was wadded in a ball that she was clutching in front of her chest. I watched with interest as color flooded her cheeks as I backed away. I was about to make a comment to lighten the mood when I noticed her hair for the first time.

It was lighter than I had thought, with bold streaks of sun-kissed strands sprinkled liberally through shoulder-length hair. It fell thick and wavy, not the straight hair I had imagined as I'd stared at the tight bun she always wore. Small curls had sprung up around her face to match the unruliness of the rest of her hair, and it appeared almost as if she'd been standing in the wind. Or on a sailboat. This last thought made a memory catch my breath, and I stepped back farther, allowing her to pass.

I was rewarded with a quick flash of cleavage as she darted away from me, forgetting momentarily to cover up her bra with her shirt. I called her back before she'd made it to her room. "I was about to take Gil out crabbing since it looks like that storm is going to just blow right past us. Figured if I got him to spend some time near the water today, the next time we could get him out on the boat. Would you like to come with us?"

She thought for a moment, then nodded. "Sure. Just give me a few minutes to get changed."

"Don't change a thing," I said.

She turned her face away from me but not before I saw her smile right before she closed her door.

Gil and I were waiting on the porch when Marnie joined us. Instead of the bun, she'd compromised with a ponytail and she'd put on her walking shorts. Not ideal, but at least it was better than her school-marm skirts.

"You forgot your shoes," I said, looking at her small pale feet.

She shook her head in mock discouragement and winked at Gil. "Just like a Yankee. You think you need shoes to go crabbing. Well, as any Lowcountry kid can tell you, you don't need them. Unless you want the crabs to point and laugh."

Gil gave one of his soundless laughs as he eagerly kicked off his sneakers and socks. In defeat, I slid out of my Top-Siders and left them on the back porch steps.

Marnie looked behind me. "Where are the nets and lines?"

I looked at her as if she were speaking a foreign language.

"You know, to catch the crabs?"

"Oh, you mean the crab traps?"

"You really are a Yankee, aren't you?"

"Yankee or no, a crab's a crab. You stick the little trap into the water with a little treat and wait for him to go for the bait, and it's crab soup for dinner."

She stared at me for a long time as if she couldn't tell if I were joking or not. Finally, she asked, "You've never caught a crab, have you?"

I shifted uncomfortably. "Well, no. But I figured you'd catch them the same way you catch lobsters."

"Um, no. Maybe Yankee crabs, but not those beautiful blue crabs we have here in the Lowcountry. So why don't you go ahead and try it your way, and Gil and I will do it the right way." She walked past me with her arm around Gil's shoulders, steering him toward the shed in the back of the house. I listened to her chattering to Gil as they walked by, knowing that most of it was intended for me.

"I think it's a sin that a boy born in South Carolina has never been crabbing. Well, we're going to put an end to that sacrilege right here and now, you hear? And if your father ever tries to tell you how to fish anything out of these waters, you call me first, okay? I don't want the other kids laughing at my nephew."

She turned to face me and shouted, "Go find me some chicken necks. I figure you still have the ones from last night you're planning to make soup out of, but we're going to need them for crabbing."

I saluted her like a sailor would salute a captain, and headed inside to the kitchen. When we all met again at the back porch, I saw that Marnie and Gil each held scavenged dip nets and white rope lines weighted with lead sinkers and attached to long poles. Both looked old and dirty, but still usable. I held up the two chicken necks.

She frowned. "They're much better if you've left them outside for a couple of days to rot, but they'll have to do for now." She took them from me one at a time and attached them to the end of the lines with the sinkers. "We're ready," she said, picking up the nets and handing one to Gil. Turning her head back toward me, she said, "You can bring the chicken necks."

"Gee, thanks," I said, picking up the poles and making sure the necks were held out as far as possible in front of me.

I was encouraged when Gil decided to walk with me for most of the trip down to the dock before catching up to walk with Marnie. She'd told me that any structured lessons that she'd planned had fallen by the wayside. She'd found that simply spending time with Gil and talking with him had relaxed him and made him seem like any normal boy. He still wasn't speaking, but he wasn't disappearing into the shadows every time somebody walked near him, so I was calling it progress.

It was also progress that enabled us to walk down to the dock with Gil at all. Marnie had taken him a few times already to sketch, gradually going farther and farther out onto the dock so that he was no longer skittish about it. As long as he didn't have to actually get into the water.

I had made a couple crab traps the day before, and Marnie was kind enough to walk past them without comment on our way to the end of the dock. I watched with admiration as she seemed to walk back in time the minute she'd shown up barefoot. Her walk had become more loose limbed and easy, and her accent became more pronounced the closer we got to the dock, and I had to force myself not to smile and alert her to the fact that I had noticed anything at all.

Marnie grinned as she faced us. "All right, you two. This is a very simple operation. There's really only two things that you have to remember. One."

She held up her first finger, which was a good thing because what she'd said sounded like "Wun," and I hadn't been exactly sure what she'd meant.

"You have to make sure that your shadow doesn't fall anywhere over the water near the bait, or those beautiful little swimmers will swim away so fast it'll make your heads spin off your necks."

She narrowed her eyes at me as I struggled to keep from laughing.

"Two," she said, casting a sidelong glance at me, "you have to be patient. I know that patience isn't a Yankee strong suit, so if you want, you can leave right now and we'll meet you back at the house later with dinner."

"Oh," I said, stretching and yawning loudly. "I think I can manage."

She nodded. "All right, then. Now listen closely so I don't have to repeat myself."

We both watched as Gil sat down cross-legged on the dock and gave her his full attention.

Marnie picked up one of the poles and dangled the chicken neck in front of us. "There's a lot of extra line here, but don't be tempted to use all of it at once. Just peel off enough to get your chicken neck out far enough but make sure that your line is tight. If you feel it jerking a bit, that means they've found their tasty snack and are eating."

Lowering her voice, she stepped a little closer to Gil. "This is where you come in. While they're busy eating, that means they're not paying a lot of attention to anything else. So very, very slowly, start pulling in the line." She made an exaggerated pantomime of her movements, making Gil break out in a broad grin. "If you stop feeling that line jerking, then stop. That means they've gotten suspicious and have stopped eating. Wait a while for them to get comfortable nibbling, then start pulling again.

"As you get them into shallower and shallower water, you have to be extra careful not to cast a shadow on the water over the bait, or your crabs will be history. Remember that they have six legs and can run in any direction, and I would take bets that one of the directions that they won't be running in is toward your soup pot."

I'd stopped looking at Marnie and was now giving Gil my full attention. He was rapt, listening to Marnie's voice, and I realized that somehow the schoolteacher in her had blended with the Lowcountry girl, making her irresistible to both Gil and myself. I listened to her accent and admired her bare toes and zinc-covered nose and saw for the first time what a wonderful teacher she probably was. I had never seen her on a sailboat, but if she approached sailing with the same intensity as teaching, I could only imagine the power of her presence and determination. Diana might have inherited her mother's talent for art, but Marnie had harnessed the ability to seek out her strengths and find her passion there. Maybe it was because she was the second born, an intruder into the bond Diana had with her mother, that had made Marnie seek what lay inside her, rather than relying on what others expected of her. I looked at her with new eyes—eyes that saw the remarkable woman who probably had no idea how incredibly remarkable she was.

Marnie continued. "When you get them to the real shallow water, where they're close enough to the surface that you can see the crabs, that's when you grab your dip net." She picked one up and began stealthily creeping toward Gil, whose eyes were wide-open and whose smile was big enough to catch flies.

"Very, very slowly, and making sure to keep the shadow of the net away from the feasting crabs, you raise your net and then *wham*—you swoop up your crabs, chicken neck and all."

She looked at Gil, whose eyebrows were creased in question. Marnie nodded at him as if she'd heard a verbal question, then said, "Then you hand the net to your daddy and let him take it from there. I'm assuming Yankee crabs are the same as Southern crabs and he'll know what to do next. One can only hope that whatever he knows involves putting the crabs in buckets of salt water to keep them fresh until he's ready to cook them."

"Actually," I said, "I believe that the Southern crabs have better manners than their Northern counterparts. They actually leap from the net into my pot."

Marnie's eyes sparkled, and if I ignored the white nose, I could see the attractive pink coloring of her skin under the hot South Carolina sun.

"You two, go first," she said, handing us each a pole with an attached chicken neck. "I'll supervise."

She showed us where to go, Gil at the end of the dock on one side and me at the other. Then she sat down behind us, with her legs stretched out in front of her, and tilted her head back to catch the sun.

I slowly lowered my chicken neck into the water, watching the bubbles rise up around it. I looked back at Marnie. "You're going to get burned."

She didn't even open her eyes. "Shh. You'll scare away the crabs."

Being careful to keep my shadow off the water, I turned to look at Gil. He stood silently on the dock, looking down into the water and standing absolutely still. I studied him for a long moment, noticing how much he resembled his aunt. It was there in the stubborn chin and the angular shape of their shoulders, as if nothing could ever make them stoop. He caught me looking at him, and he smiled and I swallowed my breath. It was there, too, in his smile. Not like his mother's, which was only ever a half smile turned inward. This was the whole-hearted smile of a person who took joy from life, and searched hard for it when it seemed lost forever.

"Lower," said Marnie quietly, looking at me. "Your pole's too high and the crabs can see it." She pointed her chin at Gil. "They're already tugging on his line, see? He's definitely a Southerner, that boy."

"He's smaller. It's easier for him. . . ."

"Shh," she said again, but a smile teased her lips.

Finally, I felt the reassuring tug at the chicken neck but had to restrain myself from peering over. Marnie pointed to the grease spots that had risen to the top of the water. "That's from the neck—and that's the spot you'll want to aim for when we get them to a little shallower water."

"Guess you've done this before, huh?" I'd meant it as a joke but quickly realized my mistake.

A shadow seemed to fall across the sun, and I realized that it had only been in her eyes. "A few times," she said with a sad smile. "A long time ago."

"Not with Diana, though, huh? She's never even mentioned it or taught Gil."

"Out of all of us kids who would hang around on weekends and go crabbing, I was pretty good at it, but Diana was the best. She was the most patient, and always seemed to know the right moment to scoop with her net." She squinted up at me, her hand on her forehead to block the sun. "She could stand absolutely still for hours, it seemed, and nothing would distract her. It was like she'd allow her mind to wander elsewhere, leaving only her body behind. It was one of those things that set her apart from the rest of us, and a lot of the other kids resented her for it."

"The other kids, but not you?"

She waited a moment before answering. "No, I resented it, too. Sibling rivalry is a rite of passage for most kids. But for us . . ." She shrugged. "I guess we spent a lot of time vying for our mother's attention. I remember thinking how unfair it was that Diana should be the better artist and the better crabber. And Mama, she just . . ."

Marnie stopped suddenly as if she'd already said more than she'd intended.

"She just what?" I prompted.

Looking down at her bare toes, she said, "She just told me to be careful what I wished for."

"Ah," I said, suddenly understanding, but wanting her to say more.

Ignoring me, she went to kneel next to Gil. "Look, see the crabs? They're close enough to the surface now that we can scoop them up with the net."

He looked up at her with a face that was half excitement and half terror.

Reading him correctly, Marnie said, "Not to worry. You keep doing what you're doing and I'll handle the rest, okay? There's no reason for you to get into the water."

Gil nodded, relief bathing his face.

Stealthily, she raised the net, being careful not to cast a shadow over where the crabs were blissfully unaware of impending danger. "Don't move," she whispered to Gil as her net descended into the water, before she raised it up again with a quick snap of her wrist and a white spray of water, neatly catching three large blue and very surprised crabs and one waterlogged chicken neck. "And all of them over five inches, so we're allowed to keep 'em."

Gil jumped up and down in silent joy, then raised his right hand for a high five from Marnie. She gave him a one-armed hug, being careful to hold the net aloft. "You are definitely your aunt's nephew, Gil."

He stopped moving and looked up questioningly at Marnie.

Gently, she clasped his hand and said, "And you're definitely your mother's son."

This made him smile, and I wished, just for a moment, that Diana had been there to see it.

She turned to me. "How are things going over there?"

I turned to my forgotten pole and lifted the line out of the water, the nearly untouched chicken neck still attached. "I guess they could tell I was a Yankee and preferred the other side of the dock."

"Or maybe," Marnie said as she traded my pole for the squirming net, "we're just better crabbers."

She laughed, then turned away with her arm around Gil, looking younger than she had when I'd first seen her step out of her rental car. Still, though, she carried her pain and grief with her as a traveler might carry a suitcase, and it weighted her step and darkened her eyes. I watched them as they walked away, remembering what she'd said about being careful what you wished for, and wondered what the young Marnie Maitland had once wished for and now regretted.

CHAPTER 15

The human heart has hidden treasures,
In secret kept, in silence sealed;
The thoughts, the hopes, the dreams, the pleasures,
Whose charms were broken if revealed.
—CHARLOTTE BRONTË

Marnie

The first time I saw Diana sneak away, I was sketching with Gil. He'd taken me to a site that was familiar to me, the high point of land from which you could see all of the Maitland property. Diana and I went up there often as children, calling it our magical place. We were goddesses there, surveying our world, which included land, sky, and ocean, and for most of our childhoods, we believed that we owned it all.

I never went up there alone, mostly because Diana told me that the bones of the Maitland children burned to death all those years ago were buried there where they died, their father too grief-stricken to bury them in the churchyard. I knew this wasn't true, as I'd seen their graves at the old Presbyterian Church in the Village, but I felt the sadness on the patch of land, as if the Maitland curse was real and strong and could live on in the blades of grass that grew over the scarred earth.

Someone had planted an orange tree and, judging by its size, not that long ago. I asked Gil about it, but he simply stared at me and shrugged. I was in the process of making a mental note to myself to ask Quinn about it when Gil tugged on my arm and pointed toward the house. Diana was exiting through the back door, taking a great deal of time and care to close the door behind her as if she didn't want anybody to hear. I knew she was alone in the house except for Grandpa and Joanna, having just watched Quinn leave in the jon boat for his office. That was when it occurred to me that she would have known this, too, as well as known that Gil and I were gone.

I scrutinized Gil, wondering why he would have called my attention, and when he started moving me down the hill, I figured that he had seen this before and perhaps wanted me to intervene. I began walking quickly but was soon running fast as the possibilities of what Diana could be doing raced through my mind. I shouted to Gil, "Go inside and find Joanna—she'll be with your grandfather—and tell her that I've gone somewhere with Diana." He nodded and I watched as he raced past me toward the house.

I was sprinting now, eager to close the distance to Quinn's car before Diana could. We reached it at the same time, with me gasping for breath and unable to speak for a minute.

She looked annoyed when she spotted me. "What are you doing here? I thought you were with Gil."

"I was," I said, breathing heavily. "But Gil saw you leaving and thought maybe I should know about it."

She raised her eyebrows. "Gil, huh?" She shook her head. "That boy's too smart for his own good." Her voice held a hint of pride.

"Where are you going that you had to sneak away when nobody was looking?"

She looked defiantly at me. "I don't have to tell you anything. It's none of your damned business."

"Maybe not," I said. "But I'm sure Quinn would like to know. He told me you're in a probationary period here, and how well you do will determine how much you're going to be allowed access to Gil. I would guess that he'd want to know where you were heading."

Her chest rose and fell in short deep breaths, but that was the only sign of anger she couldn't keep me from seeing.

"I was just running some errands. I needed a few things—personal items. I didn't think it necessary to get permission to go buy tampons."

I glanced in the backseat and noticed two short stacks of books, a package of charcoal drawing sticks, and a box of Twinkies. I almost grinned at the sight of the box. Twinkies had been a diet staple of our childhood. Where other people's mothers made soup or chicken casserole, our mother would throw a box of Twinkies on the table for supper. She ate them by the boxful, and I suppose we felt lucky that she would share any of them at all. It was the kindness of neighbors that had staved off malnutrition—something I had taken for granted until we'd moved into our grandfather's house and realized what three meals a day were really supposed to be like.

Diana saw me looking at the Twinkie box. "It's still my favorite snack. Reminds me of home, I guess." She smirked and I returned the expression, as only the two of us could ever understand the absolute absurdity of her statement.

I studied her for a moment, still not convinced. "You sure are bringing a lot of supplies with you just to go run errands."

She shrugged. "When I'm through reading a book, I toss it in the car so that I have it when I visit the nursing home. They're always asking for books. And the Twinkies"—she glanced at the box—"well, those are for if I get hungry."

"What's the charcoal for?"

She didn't say anything for a moment. "My friend at the nursing home's an artist. Whenever I find art supplies on sale, I buy them for her and hang on to them until my next visit."

"Well, then," I said. "If you're just running errands, you won't mind if I tag along."

Any other person wouldn't have seen the panic and desperation in the pale green eyes. But she was my sister, as transparent to me as if I were looking at myself in a mirror.

"Suit yourself," she said as she slid into the driver's side and turned the key.

I realized that I didn't have my purse or my cell phone but had no doubt that she would no longer be there if I asked her to wait while I ran and got them. Instead, I opened the passenger's-side door and slid in, barely closing the door before Diana sped off, her wheels spinning on the loose shells of the driveway.

We sped down Highway 17 and I kept glancing nervously at the speedometer. "There're always cops on this road, Diana. You might want to slow down."

Her response was only to lean forward and turn the volume of the stereo up higher so that the heavy rock beat vibrated the speakers.

I flipped the stereo off. "If you get a ticket, don't you think Quinn will find out about it?"

"But I won't get a ticket if I don't get caught. And what's the matter with you? You don't think I can drive?" She began to swerve erratically on the two-lane highway, making me grip the seat and pay close attention to the thankfully sparse traffic. "Am I finally going to make my perfect little sister scream?"

She jerked the steering wheel, careening the car to the right. When it hit the uneven shoulder, the car veered to the left, narrowly missing a car in the oncoming lane.

I was gripped with fear, recalling other times in a car with my sister, but with our mother at the wheel. I couldn't count the number of times she'd piled us in the car, then threatened to drive off a bridge or into a swamp just to make her pain go away. Back then, we thought her pain was from her headaches. It hadn't taken us long to realize that we were the source, and the only way our mother could be well would be if we simply weren't there.

"Stop it, Diana! Stop it!"

She laughed, the sound mimicking our mother's, and she jerked the wheel again. But this time we were on a small bridge over marsh, and my side of the car grazed the cement barrier, the sound of scraping metal somehow bringing Diana back into herself. She pulled off the bridge onto the shoulder of the road and threw the car into PARK. The only sound was our heavy breathing and the occasional buzz of a passing car.

"Are you all right?" she asked, her voice shaking.

I nodded, not at all convinced that was true.

"I'm sorry." Diana leaned forward and rested her forehead on the wheel. "I don't . . . I don't know what comes over me sometimes. It's worse when I'm not on my medication, but even with it, I sometimes feel so . . . angry." She looked surprised, as if she'd finally put a name to the emotion.

She continued. "Angry at everyone—at Mama, at you, at Quinn. And I want to lash out and hurt like I've been hurt." She looked down at the bandage on her leg, which she wore like a badge. "But I always end up hurting myself more."

I turned to her. "What about Gil, Diana? Do you ever get angry with him?" I avoided looking at her bandaged leg or thinking about how afraid Gil was of the water.

She shook her head. "No. Never. Never with Gil."

I leaned toward her. "So tell me what happened that night on the boat with Gil. How did you get hurt?"

"I could never be angry with Gil," she said, my question unanswered. She pulled back out on the highway, even using her turn signal to show her intention of merging into the right lane.

I settled back in my seat until I noticed that she had passed the exit for McClellanville. "You missed the turnoff," I said, turning around in my seat as if to make sure that they hadn't changed the road since I'd last been on it.

"Yep," she said, pushing in the lighter on the dashboard, then rummaging around her purse before pulling out a pack of cigarettes. "Quinn's talked to all the shop owners in the Village, so I have to go to Charleston to get my smokes." She plucked out a cigarette with her teeth, then showed me the empty pack before tossing it in the backseat.

"So you were driving all the way into Charleston just to get a pack of cigarettes."

"Pretty much," she said, holding the lighter to the cigarette before pulling a deep drag.

I wasn't quite sure that I believed her, and I was about to question her further when I had a flash of memory—a memory of our mother throwing a pack of cigarettes into the backseat of her car as we drove with her. But there were bright splashes of orange in the backseat, and I realized that they were the life jackets. The fluorescent color glared at me through my memories and the passage of time, jiggling something loose and making me recall a conversation I'd had with Quinn before we'd gone to look at his boat. About how the life jackets on my mother's boat were missing the night of our accident, and how none of us had thought to question it.

I turned to Diana, seeing the chicken pox scar on the side of her cheek, and remembered the week we both stayed home with Mrs. Crandall because we had chicken pox and nobody knew where our mother was. I had it first, and had given it to Diana, who had a much worse case than me. I remember feeling bad about that, and how I'd tried to apologize, but Diana just thanked me. She thanked me for giving us that week in Mrs. Crandall's house, where people slept in beds when it was dark, and ate real meals at the kitchen table and said prayers before bedtime. She said the only thing I needed to be sorry about was that I wasn't sicker. Then we'd have been able to stay even longer.

"What happened to the life jackets that were on the *Highfalutin*?" I asked. "They were always on the boat except for that night, and I don't remember ever seeing them again."

Diana stared straight ahead, and I thought for a moment that she hadn't heard me, until I saw the tic in her cheek.

"I don't know," she finally answered. "I don't really remember if they were there or not." She kept her gaze directed steadily on the road in front of her. "And I try very, very hard not to remember anything about that night at all. That's why I don't talk about it to anybody. Especially not to you."

It struck me suddenly that this was the first time we had ever said anything about the accident at all to each other. Maybe it had taken all those miles and all those years to stretch between us before I allowed myself the dangerous task of plowing a path through the minefield of memories.

"Diana, we're not young girls anymore. Don't you think it's time we deal with what happened?"

She looked at me for so long that I was tempted to take the wheel to keep us on the road.

"That's where you're wrong, Marnie. I do deal with it. I deal with it every damn day of my life, no matter how hard I try to forget. I can't not deal with it." She crushed her cigarette into the ashtray, then flipped it out the window. "It was easier before you came back. But now you're here and I have to look at you every day, and I have to deal with it again." Her hands trembled on the steering wheel and she shook her head. "Why can't you just leave?"

I swallowed, feeling the prick of tears behind my eyelids. But I blinked them away and straightened my shoulders. "Because Gil needs me. And because I'm just beginning to realize how many unanswered questions I have about our mother's death."

Her trembling fingers reached inside her purse, tossing around the insides before she slammed her fist on the wheel. "Damn it! I need a goddamn cigarette."

I knew I should stop, but I couldn't. So many images and memories were flooding toward the surface now, reminding me of things long since forgotten, and I couldn't let it go. "It was the night that changed our lives, but I don't—or can't—remember all of it. I remember being in the water and then seeing Mama near me, and you were in the water, too. There's more. I just can't . . ." I could feel the cold water and taste the salt in my mouth. But no matter how much I tried, I couldn't see past my hand reaching for my mother.

"Why would she do it, Diana? Why would she take us out in a boat during a storm without life jackets?"

"Because she was crazy, Marnie. Didn't you know?"

I stared at her, surprised at the sudden lightness to her tone, and saw that she was half smiling.

She pressed down on the gas pedal, making the car lurch. "And you never know what a crazy is thinking."

"Stop it, Diana! This isn't funny."

The car slowed. "Actually, it is. But I keep forgetting what a light-weight you've become, so you'll just have to remind me from time to time."

She was silent for a while, and then she said, "Remember when we were little and Daddy took us to the shrimp festival? He bought us those half-heart necklaces that when you put them together it says 'forever sisters.' "

"Yes," I said softly. "I remember."

"I still have mine."

I thought for a moment, wondering if I should tell her how I frequently took it out of my jewelry box and polished it. Instead, I just said, "Me, too."

She glanced into the backseat. "Why don't you grab us a couple of those Twinkies and we'll have one, just like old times?"

The thought should have paralyzed me. Instead it brought back the memory of Diana and me under the covers in her bed, hiding from the dark because the electricity had been shut off, and eating our Twinkies. Looking back, I could sense the terror and hopelessness that drove my sister even back then, but when I was a girl, Diana had been my refuge and I'd had nothing to fear while she was around.

I slipped off my seat belt and grabbed the box, easily slicing it open and pulling out two individually wrapped Twinkies. I gave her one, and then, out of habit, we grasped the little desserts as if they were swords and crossed them.

"Forever sisters," we said in unison, our voices a mixture of sadness and memories.

We sat back in silence, quietly chewing, and watched the road disappear beneath the car.

*

Gil

Ever since I was old enough to behave, my dad liked for me to come to his veterinary practice and watch while he stitched up dogs or set a broken leg. I never thought that blood was gross or that sticking a needle into torn skin was all that bad. I could watch without fainting like a girl or getting sick, and I think this made my dad proud. He'd pull up a short stool for me to stand on so I could get a better look, and then he'd forget all about me as he quickly fixed whatever was broken on the animal he was working on.

When he and Aunt Marnie took me down to the dock to get in the jon boat for the first time since my accident, I felt like he was looking at me like he did those hurt animals. That all he had to do was lay me out on a table and fix what was broken. I don't think he knows that, but he's like that with his orchids, too. Mama once told me that he's on a mission to fix the world, and I want to tell him that most of the world doesn't know it needs fixing and the rest of it probably doesn't care. And sometimes I want to tell him that he should fix himself first and then see if everybody else really seems to be broken.

But I can't tell him any of this, which is why I let him bring me down to the dock. Being in the marsh is a lot different from being in the ocean, so I think I can handle it. Especially since Aunt Marnie and I have been sketching down there, and it's started to feel normal to me again. Even the blue heron whose nest is by our dock looked at me as if she recognized me when I stepped to the end of the dock. Mama once told me that blue herons are good omens, so I took it as a sign.

Daddy got in the boat first, leaving Aunt Marnie and me on the dock. I thought I'd be nervous as I stepped in, but I just did it with one leg first and then the other, and I was done. Daddy hid his surprise pretty well as he turned to help Aunt Marnie into the boat. She'd made sure we all wore life jackets, and mine was a bit too small, as if she'd forgotten how old I was when she'd picked the child-sized one out of the shed.

"Y'all set?" my dad asked.

I nodded and he turned on the motor, starting us at a real low speed. If we were pulling a skier, he would have drowned, we were going so slow. Aunt Marnie took one look at my face and told my dad to go faster, so he did.

We stayed in the shallowest parts, places where you could see the pluff mud on the bottom, and close enough to the edge of the marsh that you could reach out and pull at the tall grass that looked like fingers trying to grab you.

I smiled at my dad and Aunt Marnie because they looked so worried about me and because I really did feel fine on the water. Since my aunt had arrived, I'd felt as if I were learning to draw all over again. Scared at first, and then little by little surprising myself at each little thing I did right. Being on a boat made me less scared of the water, but it didn't really change anything. Just like drawing a shell on the beach didn't change the shell. I still knew what had happened that night on the boat with my mother, and I still couldn't talk about it. My dad had said something about facing my fears, and that was why I had to go out on the boat. But the fear of drowning is nothing compared to other things. And facing that was like staring into the gates of hell. I know about hell because Grandpa told me all about it. It's real. I know because I've seen it.

Aunt Marnie smiled back at me and let go of the sides of her seat, which she'd been holding like somebody who'd never been on a boat before.

"Are you having a good time?"

I nodded and let the wind push at my hair.

"Am I going too fast?" my dad asked.

I shook my head and smiled back at him as he made the motor go a little faster.

Aunt Marnie pulled at the hem of her shorts as if to make them longer. "Your teacher for the upcoming school year called today. I almost told her she had the wrong number when she asked for Gil Maitland."

I looked at her, not understanding.

Daddy said, "Officially it's hyphenated: Maitland-Bristow. But on the school records, to make it easier for Gil, it's just Maitland. Diana wanted it that way."

Her eyebrows wrinkled for a moment before she turned back to me. "Your teacher wanted you to know that she was looking forward to meeting you."

I looked back at the water, trying to picture myself in math class and raising my hand to ask a question. I even opened my mouth to say something, but only air came out. It was as if my mouth didn't know what to do anymore, and I suddenly felt like a bird who'd forgotten how to fly.

Aunt Marnie put a soft hand on my knee while my daddy spoke to me. "Don't worry about it, Gil. You'll be ready when you're ready and not before. I've been thinking, though, about maybe homeschooling you for the first half of the year. Or for however long it takes."

I glanced up at him in time to see Aunt Marnie shoot him a look that said she was as surprised as I was.

Aunt Marnie raised her voice and I could tell she was angry. "Have you thought about who is actually going to be able to stay home with him? Will you be able to fit it in with your practice? Because I don't think Diana would be the best choice."

He looked at her with one of those smiles people wear when they know they've done something wrong. "Well, I was kind of thinking that you'd be the perfect choice. You're a teacher, after all, and you understand Gil. Plus, he likes you."

I smiled broadly at my daddy's prompting and Aunt Marnie rolled her eyes.

"I told you that I'm not planning on staying that long. I've got a life and career back at home, you know."

"You are home," Daddy said, at the same time that I said the words in my head. When Aunt Marnie had been out on the dock crabbing, I thought that she was more at home here than a bird in its nest. I wasn't sure why she'd say any different, except that it had more to do with her and Mama and how they didn't seem to know each other anymore. But when they look at each other, it's like a whole desert of sand sits between them anyway, so I don't think there's any reason for Aunt Marnie to go back to Arizona.

"We'll talk about this later," she said with a look grown-ups use around kids who are old enough to understand what they're saying.

"How about at dinner?" he asked.

She looked confused. "Won't there be young ears at the table, too?"

"Not at a restaurant."

"Why would we be at a restaurant?"

My dad looked at me and I shrugged, as confused as he was about how clueless a smart lady like my aunt Marnie could be.

"Because I would drive us there and we'd go in and sit at a table. Maybe have a glass of wine that a waiter would bring to us. I hear they have food, too. We could actually eat some. After the server brought the food to us."

"Are you asking me out on a date?"

"I could be."

"And what would be the deciding factor?"

"Whether or not you said yes."

I looked from one face to the other and felt embarrassed. They were both glowing like oyster shells in the sun and trying not to smile at each other. It made me want to puke. I looked away from their faces to where Aunt Marnie was still trying to pull the hem of her shorts over her knees. I noticed that my dad kept looking there, too.

"I'll go out to eat with you, but it wouldn't be a date. Just a chance for us to sit down and talk about what's best for Gil."

My dad nudged me with his foot, and I gave Aunt Marnie another big smile. It was then that I noticed that we were heading out of the small creeks and into deeper water, and I felt the breath leave my chest. Aunt Marnie must have noticed, too, because she went still and quiet and her hands gripped the sides of the boat again.

Daddy's lips pressed tight together as he began to quickly steer us into a U-turn. "Damn, I'm sorry. I wasn't paying attention."

I was trying to find the courage to move my leg to step on his foot to remind him that he was not supposed to swear but Aunt Marnie stopped me with a touch on my arm. I looked up at her and saw that she was looking out over the boat toward the deeper water. I turned my head to see what she was seeing and that was when I saw them.

There were three or four dolphins swimming together about twenty feet away from our boat. My dad cut the engine and we bobbed up and down in the boat's wake and watched the dolphins. They were swimming close to the surface, their fins and most of their backs sticking out of the water like angels' wings in a reverse heaven.

Aunt Marnie's voice was quiet when she spoke, as if she were afraid that she'd scare them off. "I haven't seen any dolphins in such a long, long time." She smiled what I call a "secret smile," because it was something in her head that was making her smile and not really the dolphins. "Did Grandpa ever tell you the story about Pelorus Jack?"

I shook my head.

"It's a true story. Pelorus Jack was a dolphin who lived on the other side of the world from us, in New Zealand, about a hundred years ago. They're not sure where he came from or why he was there, but he saved hundreds of lives by guiding ships through a really treacherous pass. They say he probably lost his mother very young, and that's why he didn't follow real dolphin behavior. But for twenty-four years, Pelorus Jack led ships to safety through dangerous rocks and strong currents."

"Whatever happened to him?" Daddy asked.

"No one knows for sure, but they think that he died of old age. Twenty-four years is about the life span of a wild dolphin, so that would make sense." She smiled again, another secret smile. "Diana used to cry thinking that Jack had died alone out in the ocean, so Grandpa told her that God, knowing what a gentle spirit he was, had put him to sleep and then taken him up to heaven, where all animals who have been well loved are allowed to go and where they wait for the people who loved them to join them one day."

My dad looked back at the dolphins. "I never would have thought that Diana could be such a sentimentalist."

Aunt Marnie studied her hands for a moment. "There's probably a lot that you don't know about Diana."

"And you do?"

She looked at my dad for a long time, the only sound that of the dolphins splashing. "I'm her sister" was all she said, as if that explained everything.

My dad nodded, as if he understood, and then we all went back to looking at the dolphins as they swam farther and father away until they were only black dots out on the distant water. I thought about Pelorus Jack as I watched them and how great it would be to have somebody like him to guide you through all the difficult parts that are too tough to go alone.

CHAPTER 16

The lightning flashes through my skull; mine eyeballs ache and ache; my whole beaten brain seems as beheaded, and rolling on some stunning ground.

—Herman Melville

Diana

I sat on the back porch playing chess with my grandfather, our previous argument not forgotten but left simmering on a burner so that we were both aware that its smoke floated in the air around us like a ghost.

As usual I was losing, but I didn't care. I had been worried that he would refuse to see me, and I was so relieved when he agreed to a game that I would have gladly conceded any game. Sitting across black and white squares had been the refuge of my childhood, and I found I could not give it up.

I was staring at one of my bishops, contemplating my next move and wishing I had a cigarette but knowing that I wouldn't dare smoke in front of Grandpa, when the door opened and Marnie stepped out on the porch. She held a page from a sketchbook, the top edge torn and ragged as if it had been hastily ripped from the pad.

We had settled into a wary truce, my sister and I, since our drive into Charleston to buy cigarettes. I'd been furiously angry at having to curtail my plans for the day, but had rediscovered something about my sister when she hadn't said a word to Quinn about me taking the car without his permission.

I faced her as she walked toward me but I didn't smile. There was only so much I could concede to my sister. She kissed our grandfather on the cheek, and then I watched as he took hold of her hand and squeezed it tightly, as if she needed the reassurance to speak with me.

"I'm sorry to interrupt," she said, "but I wanted to show something to Diana."

She held out the paper in her hand and I took it. I stared down at it for a long time before it registered what it was I was looking at.

"It's from Gil," she explained as if I couldn't tell my own son's handiwork. "He made it for you and wanted me to give it to you."

I was almost amused that this same child she spoke about not more than fifteen minutes before had emerged from his father's greenhouse and then made a huge circle around the house to avoid me and the closest entrance to go through the front door.

I met my sister's eyes for a brief moment before returning to the charcoal pencil drawing I held in my hand, the warm breeze gently trying to pry it from my shaking fingers. It was a drawing of the orange tree I had planted with Gil and given to him on a foolishly naive day when I thought that I was on my way to being healed. I should have known even then that any Maitland couldn't have escaped God's ire so completely, and instead of planting the tree, I should have been hunkering down and preparing for the next onslaught. But we are all allowed our foolishness, I thought as I looked down at the exquisite drawing in my hand.

"It's wonderful, isn't it?" Marnie asked, a hint of uncertainty in her voice.

I stared at the delicate strokes of gray and black that created the trunk and branches of the little tree, the shadings that blurred into shadows of light and darkness so that leaves that were flat and one-dimensional on a single sheet of paper, moved and twitched in the wind, and I knew, as if I had ever had any doubt, that I was witnessing genius.

I couldn't speak and remained staring at the piece of paper in my hands long after I had ceased seeing it. There had been a reason why I'd encouraged Gil to sail with his father, to find another passion. We Maitlands have been artists for centuries, our passion and talents surpassed only by the accompanying madness. Some say that there can be no art without a little madness, and we had both in spades. One only had to look at my mother and myself for corroboration.

Since Gil's first preschool crayon drawings, I had known. I never was lucky enough to receive pictures of stick families with a line of blue at the top to indicate sky. Gil brought home fully fleshed renderings of birds and animals, of his great-grandfather and his father, and of the debris left behind by the outgoing tide.

I never framed a single picture, nor stuck any of his artwork on our refrigerator with alphabet magnets. By the time he'd reached first grade, I had taken all of his paints and crayons and thrown them away, and had begun the first of many refusals to his asking if he could go to art camp or take special art classes after school. Even the pleadings of the art teacher at school couldn't sway me. I knew where his art could take him because I'd stared into the darkness long enough, and I wouldn't allow that to happen to my son.

"Don't you like it?" Marnie asked again.

I placed it facedown on the side table next to me. "It's fine," I said, returning my attention to the chessboard.

I could hear the anger in Marnie's voice. "Gil made that just for you, you know. The least you could do is show a little excitement at how talented he is. Don't you think you should frame it or something? It's really special."

"No," I said. Grandpa put a hand on my arm, stopping me from saying anything more. He knew and understood, and that was enough. Later, I would take the picture up to my studio to my locked armoire and place it in the box with all the other precious things that Gil had made for me over the years. But I would never let him know. I couldn't.

Our attention was diverted by the sound of tires on gravel, and we turned to see a bright red pickup truck slowly navigating the dusty driveway. I recognized Trey Bonner after he parked and stepped out of the driver's side.

He took off his baseball cap as he walked toward the steps. "Hello, Reverend," he said, nodding to my grandfather. Then his eyes skipped over me before settling on Marnie. "Ladies."

Marnie pushed a piece of hair behind her ear and smiled. "Hello, Trey. What brings you all the way out here?"

"I just wanted to let Quinn know that I should be done with the major repairs to his boat this week, so if he and Gil wanted to get started with the cosmetic work, we could set up some kind of a schedule."

I couldn't help but smirk. "Couldn't you have taken care of that with a phone call?"

He looked at me with those warm brown eyes, which had been melting hearts, including mine, since high school, but he didn't back away. Which is one of the things that I'd liked about Trey Bonner all along.

"Yeah, I guess I could have, but then I wouldn't have had the pleasure of seeing Marnie again. We haven't seen each other in a while, and I was thinking I might be able to persuade her to go out to dinner with me Wednesday night to catch up."

He turned to Marnie, who was looking as uncomfortable as if she'd sat on a red-ant hill.

"Actually," she said, squirming, "I already have plans."

Both Grandpa and I turned to her and I said, "You do?"

She swallowed. "Yes, actually. Um, Quinn and I wanted to get away somewhere so we could discuss Gil and his plans for the upcoming school year."

I spoke before I could think. "And you didn't think to ask me?"

Trey grinned. "Why should she? You're not married to him anymore, remember?"

Grandpa squeezed my arm but I shook him off. "That's not what I was talking about. I was wondering why I shouldn't be included in talks about my own son." I wanted to tell myself that was really the only reason I was upset. But the thought of Quinn and Marnie together was almost as devastating.

"Because it involved me and how much longer I would be staying. Quinn's been thinking of homeschooling, but that wouldn't be a practical idea unless I were to stay longer than I was planning." Marnie crossed her arms over her chest, making her look like a schoolteacher despite her shorts and bare feet.

"I'm his mother," I said. "Why wouldn't I be the first person considered for even discussing the idea?"

Nobody said anything, and I felt the blood rushing to my face. I stood, knocking the table with the chess pieces, and watched my queen fall forward on her face. "Go to hell," I said as I stumbled away from the table.

"Wait," Trey said, but I ignored him and continued toward the door. "My sister said you left these at the library."

I stopped, feeling suddenly light-headed, and turned around.

He stepped closer. "I forgot to mention that was the other reason I stopped by." He reached into his back pocket and pulled out a thin paperback book and a small tube of denture cream and handed them out to me. "I had to take them out of their bags to fit in my pocket better."

"They're not mine," I said.

He continued to hold them out to me. "Tally was pretty positive they were yours. Said nobody else had been in the psychology section but you. She wasn't sure about the drugstore package but figured it had to be yours because it was with your book."

"They're not mine," I said again as I turned back to the door, threw it open, and walked inside before I had to listen to any more.

I stood still in the quiet house for a moment, waiting for my heart to calm down and my eyes to adjust to the dim interior. I must have stood there for a full minute before I realized that Gil was standing in front of me, standing completely still as if he hoped I wouldn't notice him.

"Hi, sweetheart," I said, reaching a hand out to him but quickly pulling it back when I saw him shrink away from me. Tears pricked the back of my eyes. "Please don't be afraid of me anymore. I'm on my medication again and I'm feeling much better. I never meant . . ." I swallowed. "I would never hurt you. You know that, don't you? It wasn't my fault before. I didn't know what I was doing because I wasn't taking my pills and I was listening to the wrong—" I stopped, knowing that anything I said wouldn't matter to him. All that really mattered were his memories of him and me on the boat in the dark, and nothing could ever change that.

I blinked hard, trying to clear my eyes of the tears. "I love you,

Gil," I said, blinking into the darkness and realizing that I was standing completely alone.

Marnie

I watched Trey's truck pull away and turned to my grandfather. "What do you think that was all about?"

Grandpa was already furiously flipping through his dog-eared Bible until he came to rest on an opened page. He held it up for me to see and pointed out a passage with a yellow-stained finger. I took the book and read the passage out loud. " 'And they will deceive every one his neighbor, and will not speak the truth: they have taught their tongue to speak lies, and weary themselves to commit iniquity.' "

I handed the Bible back to him and then picked up the two items that Trey had placed on Diana's vacated chair. One was a thin book and I flipped it over to read the title. " *'Mental Disorders: Environment or Genetic Predisposition.'* " I showed this to my grandfather and then picked up the second item, a tube of denture cream. "What do you think this is for?" I opened the box and took out the tube to make sure that was what it really was. I knew it wasn't for Grandpa. He still had a mouth full of strong, straight teeth on account of what he called "clean living." I had to agree, seeing as how I'd never seen him touch a drop of alcohol or caffeine.

I picked up the book again and held it out with the cream to my grandfather. "I understand the book and why she might not admit to having purchased it. But I don't understand the cream. I'd say we're both in agreement that she's lying, so I guess I'm just going have to find her and ask her why."

I kissed my grandfather on his cheek again, wondering at the odd look in his eyes. Then I went inside to go find my sister. I saw Gil's picture forgotten on the table on my way out and picked it up, too.

I climbed the stairs to the attic, remembering that she'd always run to her studio when she needed to find a place to lick her wounds. The locked door confirmed my guess. I gave the door a few quick raps. "Diana, it's me. Can I come in?"

I waited for a long time before knocking again with the same result. I was beginning to think that I had guessed wrong when I heard her unlock the door. She didn't open it or say anything, so I knocked again. "Diana? I'm coming in, okay?"

After a long moment without a response, I opened the door. It was stifling in the room. All the windows were closed and the draperies were drawn. The heavy scent of paint and cigarette smoke permeated the air, making it hard to breathe. Huge metal lamps were trained upward toward the ceiling, illuminating Diana's time line. I saw that she'd made a good deal of progress on it, as evidenced by the two new figures that had been painted next to the first two. They, too, had their stories drawn in calligraphy beneath their portraits.

Diana sat on a step stool smoking a cigarette and watching me closely.

"You forgot these," I said, laying down the picture but keeping the tube and the book.

She didn't say anything.

"I get the book, and would like to read it when you're done. Maybe we can discuss it. But what's with the denture cream?" I forced a smile, trying to lighten the atmosphere. "Are you losing your teeth and are embarrassed to tell anybody?"

"Screw you, Marnie," she said as she stabbed her cigarette into an ashtray, then stood. "I use it to mix with my paint for the walls. Gives it more texture so that it's more three-dimensional when seen from across the room."

She snatched the book and the tube out of my hand. "And it's none of your damn business," she said as she opened a desk drawer and threw them both inside.

"Sure it is. Gil's my nephew and you're my sister. I'd definitely be interested in hearing what a professional has to say about my chances of inheriting a mental disorder, not to mention any chances any future children that I might give birth to might have."

"I don't think you need to worry on either account," she said derisively. "Anybody can look at your artwork and tell that you're absolutely normal. Secondly, I wouldn't worry about passing anything on to your children. You'd have to have sex first, and I can't think of any guy who'd willingly bother to get past your ugly school matron clothes and dowdy manner to do the deed with you."

I felt myself flush, but didn't allow myself to take the bait. Arguing with her would accomplish nothing, as I had learned long ago when dealing with my mother. And I remembered what Quinn had said about recognizing the signs of another episode. She was agitated and combative, and I wasn't going to feed her emotional state to the point where she couldn't find the road back anymore.

Ignoring her, I turned to the wall mural. "You've been busy."

She didn't say anything but I heard the click and flare of her cigarette lighter.

I stepped closer, admiring the rich details of the brown-haired man and the blond woman, their clothing style less ancient than Rebecca's and Josiah's before them. My gaze scanned down to their wall and I read aloud. " 'Jonathan Baker and Hannah Maitland.' " I stopped reading and faced my sister. "She didn't change her name either?"

Diana took a long drag from her cigarette. "Nope. Records from the time indicate that since she was the only surviving Maitland child she would keep her name to pass it on to future generations."

"Her husband was very accommodating. Or he must have loved her very much."

Diana shrugged. "Didn't much matter. They had eight children, seven who died before the age of five. The only surviving child was a girl."

"How do you know all this?"

"Mama was interested in genealogy and had started gathering information before . . . before the accident. Last year, I was looking for something and found her notes in the attic. Grandpa had put most of her stuff up there."

Something niggled at the back of my mind, something that wasn't sounding right, but I ignored it, pleased at having found a topic with which to have a civil conversation with my sister. I chose my words carefully, not wanting to set her off again.

"But why paint them on a wall mural? Why not just put it all down in a journal or something?"

She gave me a crooked grin. "I know this sounds strange to you, Marnie, but I'm an artist. It's how I tell my story."

I ignored her insult. Instead, I said, "But what story are you trying to tell?"

Her eyes darkened. "The Maitland curse, of course. What other story could possibly be more interesting?"

I could think of at least a dozen others, but I kept quiet. I turned back to the mural and read what Diana had written beneath Jonathan's and Hannah's portraits. " 'Seven of their eight children died of yellow fever, none of them reaching the age of five. The last child, a girl, was saved by her father when her mother, Hannah, committed suicide by walking into the ocean carrying the baby. He was unable to save his wife.'

"That's so sad," I said quietly, almost feeling the cold water sweeping over my head, my mouth filling with salt water. And then I remembered what had been bothering me before. "There was nothing in the attic, Diana. When we had the leak after Hurricane Hugo, Grandpa got rid of everything up there."

"Then I found them in her room, or here—I don't remember. I just know that they were Mama's papers." She wouldn't meet my eyes. Instead she stood and stubbed out her cigarette and pulled aside the drapes of the large turret window. "I like the light right now. Quickly, take off your shirt and go sit in that chair."

I wasn't going to argue. She needed me. I didn't know how or why, but she did. It was the old and familiar sister's sixth sense, and all the water in the ocean couldn't dilute it. I did as she asked and sat on the edge of the seat, pulling my hair loose until it rested on my shoulders.

"You should wear it like that on your date with Quinn," she said, focusing on mixing her paints.

"It's not a date."

She snorted. "Sure. You know, there's something about how Quinn and I met that—"

She stopped and I looked up at her expectantly. "That what?" I prompted.

"Nothing," she said. "Absolutely nothing."

"He told me that he wanted to buy one of your paintings. That's how you met."

Pausing, she looked at me, her lips pale and thin. "What else did he tell you?"

"That's pretty much it. He says you still have the painting because you'd never sell it to him." I looked around at the crowded walls of her studio. "Is it in here?"

"I have no idea. I might have sold it or thrown it away, even. It wasn't very good." She dropped her brushes on the easel with a clatter and took a deep breath, effectively ending the topic of conversation. "I need you to turn around and sit still, with your profile next to the window."

I did as I was asked, avoiding looking up at the mural, and tried to think of reasons why she would be lying to me.

"Don't close your eyes," she barked.

My eyelids flickered open and I could tell by the new position of the sun that I had been dozing. "Sorry. I'm not sleeping very well. I think it's the humid air." I took a deep breath, smelling salt.

"I don't sleep very well, either. Maybe it's genetic."

Our eyes met briefly, then skittered away.

"Actually," she continued, "it's because I'm worried about Gil. I'm worried that I'm losing him."

She focused on the canvas in front of her, her hand moving the paintbrush in quick dabs.

Diana wouldn't expect me to lie, so I didn't. "I think you're right. I think he's scared to death of you. But I can't help you if you don't tell me what happened that night on the boat with him that started all of this."

Her lips went white as she dabbed a little harder with her paintbrush. "I need to spend more one-on-one time with him, that's all. He just needs to get used to me again."

Forgetting to pose, I turned to face her. "He doesn't want to be in the same room with you when there're other people around. How can you expect him to want to be with you all alone?"

She plopped her paintbrush into a cup of water and faced me. "I'd like to bring him with me to the nursing home. The old lady I visit said she'd like to meet him. She's an artist, too, and I've shown her some of his paintings. She doesn't have any other visitors except for me, and I think it would really be nice for her, as well as giving me an excuse to spend time with Gil."

"Have you talked to Quinn?"

I saw a flash of anger shadow her eyes. "Yes."

"And I'm guessing he said no."

I watched as she made a conscious effort to hold in her temper. She knew as well as I did that lashing out at me would get her nowhere. "I need you to talk to Quinn." Her voice was dry.

"Why do you think he'd listen to me?"

She rolled her eyes. "You're either incredibly stupid, Marnie, or I'm not the only crazy one. He likes you. A lot. The way he looks at you makes me want to puke. But he listens to you, which is the only reason why I'd even tell you what you're too stupid to notice yourself."

I put my shirt on, concentrating on the buttons so that I didn't have to look at the desperation in my poor damaged sister's face. There was so much between us, most of it bad. But there were still all those years where she'd been my brave, strong sister, my protector. And nothing could ever erase that, regardless of the animosity brought about by the events of one night long ago that had fanned out into our lives like the ripples from a single drop of water.

"I'll see what I can do," I said as I buttoned the last button. "I'm not promising anything, but I'll at least talk to him."

Our eyes met for a long time across the room. Finally, Diana spoke. "Why would you do this for me?"

I wasn't sure of the answer myself. My gaze flitted around the room, trying to catch on to something that might give me a concrete answer, until I caught sight of Gil's drawing. I walked to the table where I'd left it and picked it up. I held it out to her. "For Gil. Because you and I both know how much a child needs his mother."

She took the picture without looking at it and I turned to go. I had my hand on the doorknob when she spoke again.

"And no other reason?"

I turned to look at her, and I suddenly knew the answer to her question, just as I knew that she did, too.

"Because you're my sister. And I once loved you best. I guess a person doesn't really ever get over that."

I didn't wait for her answer as I quickly opened the door and let it shut behind me. I was halfway down the hall when I registered her parting words as I left.

"I know," she had said. "I know."

CHAPTER 17

To touch the bow is to rest one's hand on the cosmic nose of things.

—JACK LONDON

Quinn

We took the jon boat into town. It was quicker, and Marnie and Gil both seemed to be okay out in the creeks, as long as I stayed away from deeper water.

I tried not to stare too much at Marnie. It had been my idea to ask Diana for some of her old painting clothes to borrow. Marnie would be getting pretty grimy working on the boat and hadn't brought anything with her that she didn't care about ruining. I'd wanted to argue that point, seeing as how I'd be just as happy to see all of her shapeless dresses and too-long shorts thrown overboard. Besides, she had changed in the short month she'd been back. Her movements were more liquid now, her limbs more at peace within her skin. She moved like a barefoot girl on the sand, all confident strides and sun-bronzed skin. I don't think she realized it yet, but she would. If I had to hold a mirror up to her and point it out to her, she'd see it.

Looking at her now, with a too-tight T-shirt and a pair of cutoff jean shorts, made my breath a little shorter. She sat with her arms folded in front of her and her knees pressed tightly together. Still, she couldn't hide her curves or her slim legs, and I'd even caught Gil giving her a sidelong glance every once in a while. It was good to know that he wasn't blind, too.

"You're fidgeting, you know, and you don't need to. You look fine," I said, trying to get her to relax. "Nobody's going to notice anything different about what you're wearing."

She sent me a withering look. "I look like a sixteen-year-old with nothing in her head except catching a good wind, and not like the twenty-eight-year-old schoolteacher that I am."

"That's not a bad thing, Marnie. Besides, I have a strong feeling that the sixteen-year-old is still in there, waiting for a chance to come out."

She shook her head but didn't say anything, just watched the boat cut through the greenish-brown water of the marsh.

Trey greeted us with a white-toothed grin and a wave as we approached the long aluminum building in the back of his shop on Jeremy Creek. I watched as he gave Marnie an appreciative glance while explaining that half of the building was used for boat storage for out-of-towners and how the other half was relegated to his boat-refurbishing business.

As he pulled open the large door, I was immediately thankful for the air-conditioning. The smells of paint and varnish were strong, the stained cement floor testament to the fact that Trey had a booming business.

Trey followed my gaze. "Just got finished with an Island Packet 38. Now that's a beautiful boat—and fixing one is probably the closest I'll ever get to one, too." He wiped his forehead with the back of his arm. "Had a bashed-in keel from getting a little too up close and personal with some rocks. The guy was snorkeling with his girlfriend and forgot to drop anchor." He shrugged. "Hey, stupidity is what makes up half of my business."

His grin fell from his face as he caught sight of the *Highfalutin* up on jack stands. "I didn't mean . . ."

I waved a hand at him. "I know. Don't worry about it."

I noticed that Marnie and Gil were standing back and Marnie had her arm around Gil's shoulders. I approached and kneeled in front of my son.

"She looks different out of the water, doesn't she?"

Gil nodded and I saw him taking in the missing mast and the stripped hull before moving closer to Marnie. Marnie's eyes met mine and she gave me a nod of encouragement.

"We're not going to think of her as a sailboat at all, okay? This is just a woodworking project for us. We're going to sand and paint, then sand and paint some more. Then we're going to lay carpet and install cabinetry and all the stuff we're going to need in the cabin. The last thing that's going on the boat will be the mast, but that's a long way off and we're not going to have anything to do with that—Mr. Bonner's going to do it." I stood and put my hand on Gil's blond head. "We're carpenters, not sailors, and we're going to make this the best-damn-looking boat there is."

I was reassured when Gil kicked me lightly in the leg.

"Yeah, yeah, I know. I'm not supposed to swear. You win."

He smiled at me, the first big and genuine smile that I'd seen in months, and it was as if the wind had decided to shift behind me instead of head-on. I moved to take his arm but he clung to Marnie, and together they followed me up to the boat.

Trey turned to Marnie and gave a low whistle. "Now that's the Marnie I remember," he said, winking.

Marnie turned to me with a told-you-so look before responding to Trey. "Thanks for noticing, but don't get used to it. These are Diana's clothes."

Trey continued to look at her with a particular gleam in his eyes. "If I were you, I wouldn't give them back."

Gil had been watching this volley with interest, and I steered him to the side of the room to distract him. All of the teak toe rail had been removed from the deck and was covering the floor in one corner of the building. The sides of the railing were beveled, and I knelt in front of one to run my hand along the edge. "I don't know if there's any sander small enough to get all these edges, Gil."

Trey had followed us and spoke from behind me. "That's right. So we're going to have to sand them by hand. Thought it would be a good place to start for you and Gil."

"What about me?" Marnie approached, nervously plucking at her T-shirt, as if to get it to loosen up.

Trey grinned and I thought that it was intended mostly for me. "I thought you and I could start belowdecks. All the wood needs to be stripped, sanded, and revarnished. It's a tight squeeze down there, but I figured since you're pretty small, you and I could handle it."

At first I thought that Marnie would refuse. Instead, she said, "All right. But first I'd like to show Gil the condition it's in now so that he has a good picture of the before and after."

I felt Gil's shoulder stiffen under my hand. I knew what Marnie was trying to accomplish but even I didn't believe she had the skill to get Gil actually on the boat on the first day he'd seen it since the accident.

She held out her hand. "Just you and me, Gil. And I won't let go of your hand if you don't want me to."

Gil stared at her hand for a long moment, then shifted his gaze to the boat. His head moved as his eyes took in the hull and the faded name, then shifted to the stern, where the broken rudder had been removed and was lying on the ground near the back of the boat. I felt a tremor run through him.

He looked again at Marnie before deliberately turning his back to her and moving into my embrace. Marnie smiled and I knew she was as pleased as I was that Gil had turned to me. Getting him on the boat seemed like such a small thing after that. He was my son and I wanted him back, and Marnie understood that.

"That's okay, Gil," she said, smoothing her hand on his hair. "We don't have to do it now. As we work on the boat, you'll get more comfortable being near it. When you think you're ready, just let one of us know, and we'll be happy to take you on board."

Gil kept his head tucked into my waist, but he nodded his head.

"Great," said Trey, rubbing his hands together, "because I really need your help out here with these railings. They're really small spots, and I think your hands are the perfect size to do a good job with the sandpaper."

As much as I hated to do it, I sent Trey a grateful look.

"All right then. Let's go pick out your sandpaper so you can get started." Trey pointed Gil toward shelving on the far side of the building. "And, Marnie, why don't you go with Gil and help him pick out a mask and get yourself one, too? That damn . . . er . . . danged sanding just sends grit up your nose and down your throat."

She nodded and walked away with Gil, sending me a questioning look at the same time I realized that Trey had deliberately left the two of us alone.

"What's up?" I asked, feigning enthusiasm.

A grim expression settled over his rugged face. "Come here. I want you to take a look at something."

He led me over to where the broken rudder lay on its side. He squatted down next to it, and I followed. "Look here," he said, running his finger gently down the rugged break of fiberglass, which looked like some kind of a stress rupture. "What does this look like to you?"

"A broken rudder," I answered, not sure why I was searching for levity. I already had a sick feeling in my gut that this conversation was going to lead me to a place I didn't want to go.

He didn't smile. "What did the accident report say happened to the rudder?"

I tried to think back to a document that at the time I had considered irrelevant in comparison to my ex-wife's physical injuries and my son's inability to speak. "I don't remember exactly—something to do with it hitting something like a rock, or being hit by a strong wave that hit it just right. I believe it was inconclusive."

As I spoke I was looking at the spot where Trey had been running his finger down the jagged line of broken fiberglass that exposed the metal rod underneath. I felt a cold chill steal up my spine.

"I remember what you told me about the accident, and it just seems to me that this kind of damage to the rudder wouldn't happen in open water. See here how the damage is to the trailing edge of the rudder? That means somebody would had to have been backing up pretty fast into something solid to cause this kind of damage. Definitely not something a wave could do. It would have been a hard hit, too, so it's nothing that could have happened accidentally without anybody on the boat knowing about it. I'm talking bone-rattling impact here. And if Diana had been at the helm when it happened, she was an experienced enough sailor to know that her steering ability could be compromised and to keep her docked." He shrugged. "I'm thinking it looks deliberate. And then again I could be completely wrong. Could be there was some kind of really strong wave out there that hit it in the right spot with a big enough force to crack it open." He shrugged again. "Like I said, I just wanted you to take a look at it. Don't think it proves anything, but it certainly raised a question in my own mind."

I nodded, his thoughts echoing my own. "Have you mentioned this to anybody?"

He shook his head. "Nope. Thought you'd want to handle it yourself—assuming there is something to handle."

I nodded, then stood and felt my hands shaking. "For now, though, let's get busy. I suddenly find myself in need of some good, hard labor."

"I know what you mean," he said half to himself, and I noticed that he was looking at Marnie again.

I stepped into his line of vision as I made my way over to join Marnie and Gil, thinking about Diana and wondering how close love and hate could dance together before you could no longer tell them apart.

❧

Diana

I was in my studio when I saw them return. When I saw Quinn's jerky movements as he walked toward the house, I wondered if Marnie had suddenly changed her mind and decided to tell Quinn about my escape the day before. He wasn't one to sit on a feeling and wait for it to rationalize. I started counting the minutes, challenging myself into guessing how long it would take Quinn to find me. Three minutes, twenty seconds later, he burst in the room without knocking, and I smiled to myself, acknowledging how predictable he was. It was one of the things that brought us two opposites together, as if it were some universal truth that a storm would move inland, inadvertently seeking out that which would dissipate its strength until all that was left was a cool breeze.

He left the door open as he entered the room. Then he took an agitated walk around the room, as if unable to focus whatever it was he wanted to say. Finally, he turned to me, his blue eyes darker than I'd ever seen them, and I had a fleeting thought to paint them.

A steely calm seemed to settle over him as he gathered his thoughts. "When we were first married, you told me a story about you and Marnie when you were children, how you would do anything to protect her. Do you remember that?"

Yes, I wanted to say. *Yes, of course I remember. I remember everything that ever happened between us. We were lying naked in bed, and I was telling you about my childhood and how vulnerable Marnie was to our mother's constant criticisms. And how I had slapped Mama once in the face after she'd said something about Marnie's lack of talent and made my sister cry. As a punishment, Mama took all of my paints and brushes away for a month. I told you then that it had been worth it because I loved Marnie most in the world, and I would protect her at all cost. It wasn't until much later, when you no longer pretended to love me, that I realized you had listened to my story not because it had been about me and my childhood but because of something else entirely.*

"No," I said, my heart aching with the memory.

"You told me that you loved Marnie most in the world. You grieved for her when she was gone, and nothing that I said or did could heal that part of you that was gone. And I grieved with you because I remembered what it had been like to lose my brother."

Yes, I remember, I wanted to say, but I remained silent, looking into his beloved face, which was as cold and removed from me now as it had ever been.

"We had lost so much in our lives, and then Gil was born and I was so happy because we both finally had somebody we could love best in this world."

I turned my back to him, watching the greedy sun steal the light from the sky, reminding me of all that I had failed at and how Quinn's words were reminding me of the failure I regretted the most.

He pinched the bridge of his nose between two fingers and clenched his eyes shut. "So how can it be that you would try to hurt our son, the child that we promised to love and protect as long as we lived?"

I had been lost for a while, wondering while he was speaking what any of this had to do with me sneaking away with the car. I think I stopped breathing. All I knew for sure was that there was no more air in the room, as spots formed in front of my eyes. I felt my knees buckle under me, and for a moment I was under the waves, swallowing water, and I felt my mother's arms around me.

Quinn caught me and carried me to the sofa. He left my side for a moment before returning with the warm dregs of a contraband can of Coke. "Sorry. This was all I could find," he said as he lifted the can to my lips.

I turned my head away from him. It was already clearing, but I wanted to see my mother again. But she had gone, taking her warm arms with her. Quinn guided my head back to face him, then lifted me so I could take a sip from the can.

Our eyes met, and he sat back on his heels as I leaned my head back on the cushion. I shivered, still feeling the cold waves of the ocean as Quinn reached behind me to the old moth-eaten blanket that had once been my mother's and placed it over me. I closed my eyes and waited for the spots to go away and then left them closed a little longer, hoping that Quinn would give up and go away. He was still there when I opened my eyes again, as I'd known he would be, and I took some comfort in that.

He looked up as if seeking guidance before he spoke. "What happened, Diana? What happened to you and Gil the night of your accident?"

My bandage itched as if a thousand ants were crawling in and out of the wound, tearing at bits of flesh, but I resisted the urge to scratch. "I've told you and the insurance people everything I remember. We were hit by a giant wave that I thought broke the rudder because suddenly the tiller wouldn't work. I tried to reach Gil in time, but another wave swamped the boat, taking down the mast and throwing me against the deck, where I must have blacked out. The next thing I remember, we were being rescued by the coast guard. I had Gil's shirt wrapped around my leg so it wouldn't bleed." I closed my eyes, seeing the face of my sweet, brave son. "He'd learned that in Cub Scouts. . . ." My voice broke and I couldn't speak. Everything I'd told Quinn had been true, but the weight of the words that I couldn't say weighed down my tongue, making it stick to the bottom of my mouth.

His face seemed to turn in on itself like a crumpled piece of paper. "But why, Diana? Why would you take him out in the first place?"

I reached for him like a drowning man would reach for shore, and he lifted me, as I'd known he would, and placed me on his lap, his arms wrapped around me and my mother's blanket. He'd always been that way for me: the solid earth I always strived to find beneath my own quicksand. I buried my face in his neck and smelled the old familiar smell and missed him all over again.

"You can't understand unless you've been there. Without my medication . . . it's like it's all darkness. Nothing looks or tastes or feels the way you know it's supposed to. And you find yourself doing things that you know don't make sense but you're doing them anyway. I heard . . . I heard my mother's voice, Quinn." I raised my face, unsure of what else I should say. But the answering calmness in his eyes gave me the courage I needed. Almost in a whisper, I said, "She reminded me about the Maitland curse, and . . ." I swallowed, wishing now for the oblivion of my illness, instead of the stark reality I was forced to face.

"And what, Diana? What else did she say?"

I took a deep, shuddering breath, forcing out the words before I could think to hold them back. "She said that Gil was the last Maitland, and the curse could all end with him."

His arms stiffened around me and his face paled. "Why didn't you tell me this before?"

"Because after the accident I got better, so it didn't matter anymore. And I didn't want to scare you and make you worry more than you already were." I swallowed thickly, desperation grabbing hold of my thoughts and my voice, making me spin words as a spider might spin a web. "But I know that's not real, Quinn. I know it was my sickness talking to me. I won't ever let that happen again. See, look." I pressed my hands to my chest as if he could see past the flesh to my heart. "I'm taking care of myself now. I'm taking my medicine and trying to eat more. And I love Gil. More than anything else in this world. I could never hurt him. You know that, Quinn. I could never hurt our son."

He pulled away, holding my face in his hands and looking at me with those beloved eyes, and I felt a fresh wave of grief over the desire that was no longer there in those blue depths. I had never seen shades of that elusive emotion love, despite his efforts, but I'd been satisfied with his physical need for me, and for a long time, that had been enough. Eventually, though, like a house built on shifting sand, the foundation of our marriage had crumbled, tossing us into the open sea. Quinn had found solid ground again, but all I could do was founder. I often wondered if my discovery in my grandfather's study that day would have been so devastating to me if I'd still had Quinn to fall back on. It made it easier in a way to place some of the blame on Quinn, and I wasn't yet ready to release him from his guilt.

"So it was an accident, then."

It wasn't really a question, but I nodded anyway, wanting nothing more than to lay my head on his shoulder again and block out the sound of my mother's voice.

"I believe you," he said, gathering me in his arms again.

But I heard the uncertainty in his voice, and I had a fleeting thought that he was merely trying to patch up a broken spot in his life, with the same result as putting duct tape on a gaping hole in a ship's hull. I pressed myself against him, hoping to make him forget his doubts, but I had once again overestimated his feelings for me.

He pulled away. "No, Diana. You know it's not that way between us anymore."

I tugged my T-shirt off over my head. "Come on, Quinn. For old time's sake. Just this once."

I tried to ignore the pity in his eyes as he leaned forward and gave me a soft kiss on my lips. "No, Diana, that's not what you need, and you and I both know it."

We both turned at a sound from the doorway. Marnie stood there at the open door with a tray of iced tea in two glasses and a plate of sandwiches.

"I'm sorry," she said, her eyes everywhere but on us. "I thought we were going to be working on my portrait now, but I'll come back later."

She turned away abruptly, the tea sloshing out over the edge of the glasses, but not before I'd seen the look in her eyes.

Quinn stood, then threw the blanket back over me. "I'd better go talk to her."

"Yes, you do that," I said, remembering the look in Marnie's eyes and feeling not all that sorry. I watched him leave me to go to her, and the grief and sadness returned to me, engulfing me like a frigid wave from the deepest part of the ocean.

Gil

When I was in fourth grade, our science class studied sharks. Since we all live near the ocean, I kinda wondered why the teachers would make us really think about fish with sharp teeth that swam in the same water that most of us liked to boogie board in, but I didn't say anything. Even back then, I wasn't much of a talker.

Anyway, we were all assigned a research paper where we had to pick a type of shark and then write about a typical behavior. I picked the sand tiger shark, but only because Richie Kobylt had pushed to the front of the line and got the great white and Laura Gray had wanted to do the bull shark, and I couldn't take that from her even if she was behind me in line.

So I picked the sand tiger shark and headed right for the library so I could write the best research paper the teacher had ever seen and maybe even impress Laura Gray.

I learned a lot about the sand tiger shark (*Carcharias taurus*). I learned that their babies are called pups and that the mama doesn't stick around to take care of the pups after they're born. And I also learned that sand tiger shark pups do something called "adelphophagy." That's a Latin word that means "eating one's brother." It's when one of the larger and stronger pups inside the mama eats its smaller and weaker siblings.

I got an A on my project, but I stopped wishing for a brother or sister after that. And now, ever since Aunt Marnie's come back, it's made me wonder if a kind of adelphophagy happens with people, too. Because from what I've seen, sometimes when sisters grow up, there doesn't seem to be a way for both of them to be happy as long as the other one is around. It's as if they decided back in their mommy's tummy that there was only room for one of them.

Maybe that's why Aunt Marnie moved to the desert. Or maybe it's why she came back. All I know is it's like when they're walking around by themselves, they're only half a person. But when they're together, they're whole again. I want to go get a huge mirror and put it in front of them so that they can both see it, too. Or at least see that neither one of them is the bigger or stronger one; they're both when they're standing together.

CHAPTER 18

Last night I saw St. Elmo's stars
With their glittering lanterns all at play.
On the tops of masts and the tips of spars,
And knew we should have foul weather today.
—Henry Wadsworth Longfellow

Marnie

I'd felt like a child avoiding Quinn for the rest of the next two days, the parts of his conversation with Diana that I had overheard playing over and over in my head. Diana stayed in her room, apparently working on her morbid mural, which made avoiding her easy. It was almost five o'clock in the afternoon on the second day before I realized that I was acting as I had when I was sixteen and seen Trey Bonner kissing Diana behind the shrimp nets out on the wharf. Besides, I'd heard enough of their conversation to know what was really going on in addition to the fact that it wasn't like I was dating Quinn, anyway. I suppose it was simply old habit that would raise the familiar specter of jealousy between Diana and me, and I was old enough now to lay it to rest.

I showered and dressed, then put on a sundress that I had brought with me for reasons that even I didn't know. It was lower cut than I was used to, and had a snug, gathered waistline that emphasized all my good points and hid everything else. It was made of a bright yellow cotton piqué material, and when I'd seen the dress in the store, it had reminded me of one of a similar fabric that my mother had owned, and I'd felt compelled to try it on. The color and the texture had reminded me so much of home that I probably would have bought it even if it hadn't fit as well as it did. I paid for it without looking at the price tag and had never even put it on my body again since I'd brought it home from the store.

I slipped the dress over my head, enjoying the way the cool cotton felt against my bare skin, and I wanted to see what I looked like in a full-length mirror. I remembered the cheval mirror in my mother's old room, so I went down the hall in the hopes of it still being there. The door was closed as it had been since her death, and I opened it slowly, with the old ghost stories that Diana used to tell me whispering around my head.

The room had remained pretty much untouched since the days of my mother's girlhood, despite the fact that it had been Diana's room, too. It was full of pink and ruffles and the stale smell of old perfume. Mama's doll collection still sat on a low hutch by the window, and her books waited on the antique bookcase opposite the virginal twin bed.

It was an innocent-looking child's room, but I still shivered, remembering the woman this child had grown into. I couldn't help but spin around the room and imagine that all of Mama's demons had somehow been given birth in here.

The cheval mirror sat in the same corner it had been in for more than fifty years, and I walked over to it to see my reflection more clearly. I'd brought two different shoes with me to see which worked best, and I slipped one on each foot before taking turns lifting up one foot and then the other. I was still trying to choose between the espadrille and the high-heeled slide when my gaze caught on a blank spot over my mother's bed.

I turned to face it, trying to recall why it looked so different. The other three walls were bare, as they had been since I was ten and my mother had gone on a rampage and burned all of her artwork. *Oh, yes,* I remembered. *My blue herons.* The two paintings I'd entered into the art competition that had been hung in my mother's house and then moved into this room after her death were gone.

Just like the walls downstairs in the front parlor, there were rectangles of darker paint on the wall, which gave testament to how long they had hung in their spot over the bed. I looked around at the pink chenille bedspread and chiffon drapes—two items that had remained in this room since long before my birth—and tried to think of a reason why those two pictures would be missing.

The door swayed open, making me start, until I saw that it was Quinn.

"Looking for ghosts?" he asked with a tentative smile.

He wore a light blue oxford cloth button-down shirt that showed off his tan and his eyes, and my mouth went a little dry. "I might be," I answered with a similar smile.

"Need any help?"

"No, thank you," I said, my smile fading. "I don't seem to have any trouble finding them on my own."

His face grew serious as he took a step into the room. "Marnie?"

I stopped where I was, suddenly cautious and fervently hoping he wasn't going to bring up the scene in Diana's studio. "Yes?"

"Are you still planning on going on the nondate with me?"

"Yes, of course. I'm ready to go. Why—have you changed your mind?"

"That would depend."

I swallowed, my throat even drier than before. "On what?"

"On whether or not you wore the same pair of shoes instead of one of each." He looked pointedly down at my feet and I felt an annoying sense of relief.

"Oh, right. I'd forgotten." I stepped forward to move past him. "Let me go get my other shoe and I'll meet you downstairs."

He put a hand on my arm. "I like your hair down like that. You should wear it that way more often."

I felt myself blush at his close perusal. "I'll see you downstairs," I said as I brushed past him and walked quickly down the hallway to my bedroom.

The late-summer air was balmy and carried with it the heady scent of the marsh. Quinn paused at the bottom of the front steps. "We could take the car or the boat—you pick."

I felt the air pushing at me, nudging me toward the dock, the rich odor of the water and the grasses filling the air around me. "If you promise not to get lost in the dark, let's take the boat."

He indicated for me to begin walking. "I'm not worried. You know the creeks blindfolded like the back of your hand."

I glanced back at him. "I never told you that."

"Nope. But your sister did."

I didn't say anything, hoping that by not mentioning Diana's name, Quinn wouldn't mention the conversation I'd overheard between them.

"About yesterday afternoon," he began.

I shrunk inside. "Please. Don't," I said. "What you and Diana do is none of my business."

I felt his eyes on me but I didn't look up. "Yes, it is."

I remained silent, afraid to ask why.

He didn't say anything more until we were both in the boat heading away from the dock. He kept the motor on low so we could still hear the singing tree frogs and the squawking of a night heron on the hunt. I was lulled by the warm air and the gentle sway of the boat until his voice shook me out of my reverie.

"Diana told me that she heard your mother's voice before she took Gil out on the boat that night."

I sat up straight, my hands clenching the sides of the boat. "Have you told her doctor?"

"Not yet, but I've scheduled an appointment for both of us next week." He looked away for a moment. "I thought you should know."

"Thank you," I said softly. "Thank you for telling me." My thoughts went back to the missing pictures on the wall of my mother's room, as if the darkened spots should tell me something more. "But that was before she went back on her medication, right?"

"Yes, and Diana pointed that out to me, too. But still . . ." He looked at me. "Your mother wasn't the sort to deliberately hurt her children, was she?"

I shivered, suddenly cold. Quinn noticed and gave me his jacket to drape around my bare shoulders. "Not deliberately, no. She did cruel things," I said, remembering the ill-fated trip to Disney World, "but never intentionally malicious. We knew she was . . . ill. And we knew to take everything with that in mind." I looked up at the fullness of the moon, its maternal roundness embracing the marsh around us. "But she also loved us," I added quietly, remembering the two pictures she'd framed and hung on her wall after I had thrown them away, knowing that they weren't as good as Diana's.

"Did she love you equally?"

I stared up at the moon again, watching as it cast its light unevenly over the water and blades of grass, and created striped shadows of darkness and light beneath the old cypress trees. "No. She didn't."

Something splashed in the water nearby and I froze, the sound reminding me of something I thought I'd forgotten, something I didn't want to remember.

As if from far away, I heard Quinn's voice calling my name, and felt his hands on my shoulders, shaking me.

"Marnie, are you all right?"

I managed to nod. "I'm . . . fine. Just remembering something, that's all."

He idled the engine and took both of my hands in his. "Your hands are like ice," he said.

I shivered again, my teeth clenched tight to keep them from chattering, my head turning as if to hear another voice. I thought that if I reached out my hand, I could touch her, my mother. But all I could feel were her hands slowly letting me go. And then pushing me away in the frigid water.

"Marnie!"

I don't know how many times he'd said my name before I heard him.

"Yes, I'm here," I said, my teeth chattering. "I'm fine."

He blew on my hands, then rubbed them with his own. "I can take you home if you need me to."

I shook my head. "No, really, that's not necessary. I just had a sort of déjà vu or something." I forced a smile as I looked up at him. "I'm hungry—let's go eat."

He moved back to the engine, and we were under way again as I turned my face into the warm wind, trying to thaw my skin and my memories.

We docked the boat at Leland Marina and took a leisurely stroll to the Crab Pot Restaurant, its claim to fame being that it was once reviewed favorably in the venerable *New York Times*. What it lacked in linen and candlelight, it more than made up for in the best Southern seafood anywhere. Before I'd even stepped through the front door, my appetite had returned, and I was ready for their famed she-crab soup.

Without asking me, Quinn ordered a bottle of wine. "You look like you need it," he explained as he helped me into my seat.

"Thanks," I said, not really realizing how much I meant it until I tasted the first calming sip.

Quinn leaned forward, looking at me oddly.

"What?"

"Your hair. Did I mention how much I like it down like that?"

"Yes, actually. You did." Self-conscious now, I brushed my hand over the side of my hair, and flipped it behind my shoulders.

He continued to look at me. Finally, he said, "There's something I haven't told you. . . ."

"Marnie Maitland? Is that you?"

We both turned at the sound of my name, and I smiled when I recognized Kathy Arasi, my childhood friend. Diana and I hadn't had many close friends growing up on account of us trying to keep our mother's behavior to ourselves and other mothers wanting to keep their children away from us. And we had each other, neither one of us ever really feeling the need to seek outside friendship.

But Kathy had been different. An only child, the daughter of a local judge and a schoolteacher, she was wise beyond her years and usually sought out whatever others avoided. Thus, I became a pet project for her. She'd move her lunch tray next to mine in the cafeteria, and squeeze in next to me in the reading circle during library class. She'd be the only person to volunteer to be my gym partner and bullied others into letting me on their team during kickball out on the playground.

I stood and allowed myself to be enveloped in her hug. She'd always been slender, but she could put a lot of punch in her hugs. In a home where there wasn't a lot of touching, it had been one of the things I'd liked most about Kathy.

"I didn't know you were back," she said, holding me at arm's length. "And look at you—you're even more beautiful than when you left. Isn't she, Quinn?"

Quinn, having no idea what I must have looked like before, raised his glass. "I'll drink to that."

"So are you back for good? How long have you been here? I can't believe you haven't called me." In typical Kathy fashion, she never paused long enough between questions to wait for an answer. She hugged me again, then held me out for inspection. "So how long you here for?"

I glanced at Quinn. "It's all kind of up in the air right now. I had planned to be gone by September, but I just extended my leave of absence from work through the first semester. I'm enjoying spending time with my nephew, Gil."

She shook her head and clucked her tongue like a mother hen. "Bless his heart. I haven't seen him since the accident, but I heard he's still working on getting better. He's lucky he's got you. You were always such a nurturer, you know. I don't think Diana would have made it to adulthood if you hadn't been there for her. She really depended on you keeping her grounded, you know." She smiled her toothy grin, making me wonder if maybe she should go into politics. "Of course, we know you both depended on neighbors for your dinner, but Diana always had you."

I looked at her, feeling confused. I had never seen it that way at all. I had survived our childhood and our mother because of Diana and not the other way around. I was spared from having to respond by Kathy opening her mouth again.

"But you have to stay for the Shrimp Festival and the Blessing of the Fleet. It's on May seventh next year. And don't forget Charleston Race Week is the first week in April, and I know you must be dying to see it—or even enter! Now that you've reconciled with Diana and come home, I can't imagine that you'd want to miss it. Or ever leave again. Remember at high school graduation how you were voted 'Most Lowcountry' and 'Least likely to ever live anywhere else'?" She slapped her hand on her leg. "And don't forget 'Most likely to win the America's Cup.' I've got a bunch of laughs over that through the years, seeing as you live in the desert now. But I always knew you'd be back, Marnie Maitland. You and the ocean—just can't ever imagine that you could stand to be parted."

I stared at Kathy for a long moment, rolling her words back in my mind to determine if there had been a question and if I were required to answer it. "The Race Week—that's in April," I interjected. "I really don't plan to stay past—"

"And not only that, but I'm starting a new women's group and calling it Women Who Launch—isn't that a hoot?—and we'll meet every week during good weather to go sailing. You simply have to join us."

Quinn spoke quickly, as if he were afraid this might be his only chance to get a word in. "It will all depend on Gil. I know that Marnie wouldn't leave him until he's better."

Kathy turned her attention to Quinn, a sympathetic look on her face. "Bless his heart," she said again. "How difficult this must be for you."

"I imagine it's a lot more difficult for Gil than it is for us," I said quietly, "but he seems to really be getting better."

"That's wonderful. And poor Diana, to be involved in two boating accidents but lucky enough to survive them both. Her guardian angel sure is looking after her," Kathy said, beaming.

Quinn sent me an uneasy glance. "I wouldn't exactly call her lucky."

Kathy flushed. "No, I guess not. I was just saying that she's a survivor, that's all." She squeezed my hand. "You both are."

"Thanks," I said.

"Well, I'll let you two eat. It was so great seeing you again, Marnie. I'm going to give you a call this week so that we can get together for lunch and catch up."

"That'll be great," I said as I resumed my seat and my eyes caught Quinn's amused ones.

Kathy turned to leave, then stopped. "Oh, wait—I almost forgot. Would you please let Diana know that I'm sorry I missed her when she stopped into the library but Tally Deushane—remember Trey Bonner's little half sister? I'm training her right now at the library. Anyway, Tally said that she looked through every single book Diana had checked out in the last month at the library but didn't find the piece of paper Diana thinks she misplaced. I know she only asked Tally to look through the one book—what was it?" She tapped a long fingernail against her chin. "I think it was *Modern Psychiatry* or something like that, but anyway I looked through that one really well again and then just decided to be really thorough and looked through all of the books we had a record of her checking out in the last four weeks or so. Tally could tell she was really upset and this was important to Diana, so please let her know that we did everything we could."

Quinn's hand gripped the stem of the wineglass so tightly that I was afraid it would snap. "When was she at the library?"

"This was yesterday evening—right before closing, which was why I missed her, because I had to leave early for a tennis match. I'd expected her earlier—she stops by just about every Wednesday at about the same time—but she said that she got sidetracked yesterday and couldn't get the car."

I put a hand over Quinn's. "Did she say what the paper was?"

"No, she didn't. But she was really upset. Tally asked her if she wanted her to call Quinn to come get her, but that got her even more agitated, so she didn't." Kathy's forehead wrinkled. "I hope I didn't do anything wrong."

"Not at all. Thanks for letting us know, and I'll be sure to tell Diana that you and Tally did everything you could to find it."

"Great." She gave us a smile of relief. "You two eat now, and I'll talk to you later this week." She waved a few fingers, then left to go find her party.

Quinn's eyes were hard. "Do you have any idea what she's talking about?"

I shook my head. "Not about the paper, anyway."

Our waiter decided that was the opportune moment to bring us bread and tell us about the day's specials, and I looked at him with gratitude, hoping Quinn would have forgotten what he was about to say by the time our waiter left our table with our order. I was wrong.

"What do you know about her taking the car to go to the library every Wednesday? It just occurred to me that I have office hours every Wednesday afternoon and I always take the boat unless it's raining."

"I didn't know about her trips to the library."

"But you did know about her taking the car when I wasn't aware of it." It wasn't a question.

I took a long sip of my wine. "Gil told me."

He raised an eyebrow.

"I have a feeling Gil sees and hears a lot more than we would guess. He and I were sketching outside earlier this week, and he pointed her out to me as she was sneaking out the back door before heading for the car. I got in with her and we took a ride. To Charleston. To buy cigarettes."

"Cigarettes?"

"Yes. She said that you've spoken to all the folks in town who sell them and told them not to sell them to her. So she's been forced to sneak away into Charleston."

"Bullshit," he said. His eyes flickered over my face. "Pardon me. I forgot your delicate Southern ears. But either way you say it, she's lying."

"But why . . . ?" I thought about the Twinkies, the art supplies, and the books in the backseat, but nothing made sense.

He shrugged. "Who knows with Diana? However, knowing what I do know, I think it's simply a matter of passive aggression. She can't stand to be told what to do, so she takes the car when she thinks I won't notice. She feels better because she's gained a little bit of freedom, and I feel better because I'm kept in the dark and happily believing that I'm still in control of her movements and protecting Gil."

"Is that why you do it, Quinn? To protect Gil?" I sat back to allow our waiter to place my soup in front of me. "Or to punish Diana for something she has no control over?"

I thought he'd be angry, but instead a smile slowly spread over his face, and the impact was enough to convince me of what it was that had first attracted Diana to Dr. Quinn Bristow.

"I guess I shouldn't be surprised at you sticking up for her, and I'm glad. Diana doesn't have too many friends, and it's nice to know she has an ally."

He poured another glass of wine for both of us, and I looked away from the intensity of his gaze. I focused on the deep red of the liquid as I brought it to my lips and then set the glass back down on the table. "We used to say that to each other, that we were more than sisters. We were always sisters first, but we were also allies—the two of us against the world."

"Well, she's got me, too, whether or not she realizes it. She's Gil's mother and I owe that to her. But my first responsibility will always be to Gil, and at the moment it's protecting him from her until she's stable again."

"But she is," I said, pushing away my almost-empty soup bowl and leaning toward him. "She's taking her medication without complaint and trying so hard to please you." I paused for a moment, measuring my next words. "She wants to start taking Gil with her to visit at the nursing home. She thinks it would be a good opportunity for the two of them to bond again, and it would also help the old woman she visits."

"Absolutely not. It's only been three months since the accident, and I still can't seem to get a clear answer from her as to what happened. I do think it was an accident—but it was still her fault because of her bad judgment. How will I know when she's past making bad judgment calls at the expense of our son?"

"Then let me go with them," I said, not sure if I'd had the thought before. "I don't think Gil will get better until he's mended his relationship with his mother. Maybe this is the way to do it—for them both to have something together. And I can be there for both of them."

"No," he said, shaking his head as if to convince himself, but I'd seen the wavering in his eyes. "If you'd only known the terror I felt when I found out where they'd gone . . ."

I reached out my hand and touched his. "But I do, Quinn. Except you were lucky—they never did find my mother."

Our main courses arrived and we both sat back in our chairs, our eyes locked until the waiter had moved away.

"I . . . I could stay. Until Gil is better. If you let me do this for Diana, I'll stay as long as I'm needed."

He raised an eyebrow as a half smile creased his face. "I could make sure that's a very long time."

I felt my cheeks flushing. "She's my sister," I said, trying to convince myself of my reasons as much as convince him. I kept seeing the image in my mind of the three of us in the water, and I could feel my mother's arms pushing me away and then swimming toward Diana. It haunted me as old ghosts do, and I knew that Diana would be the only person who could explain why I was remembering things now that were perhaps better left on the ocean floor.

"All right," he said, his eyes never leaving my face. "But you have to promise me that you will not let her go off with Gil on her own."

"I promise," I said, taking another sip of my wine, and I wondered how it was still possible to taste the ocean in your mouth after so many years.

Quinn

The marsh at night has an ethereal feel, where the lush smells and throaty sounds creep under your skin and into your blood, so that you become a part of the saltwater creeks and estuaries, an arm reaching out to the ocean where all things eventually flowed. I wondered if Marnie knew this—knew that if you were born by the ocean, you were destined to return to the place that nourished you. Before there was a Diana and a Gil for her to come back to, there had been the ocean, biding its time, waiting for its prodigal daughter.

We didn't talk on the ride back, each of us content to listen to the marsh music. She didn't object when I took her hand to help her out of the boat and didn't let it go. When we reached the fork in the path that determined whether we would go up to the house or down to the beach, I pulled her toward the beach and she resisted.

"Come on," I said gently. "The moon's out and I won't let go of your hand."

She stood still, not answering.

"It's not only Diana and Gil who need to face their fears, Marnie."

She hesitated just for a moment before allowing me to lead her down toward the beach.

"Are you afraid of anything, Dr. Bristow?"

"Lots of things," I answered carefully. "Of making a mistake with one of my patients. Being late with my taxes. Walking into a room with my fly down."

She bumped into me. "No, really. I'm serious. I'm talking fear as in the fear of speaking, or the fear of the ocean, or the fear of not knowing what your brain might tell you to do."

"Why do you want to know?"

"Because if I know that you're a real human being with real fears, then I won't be ashamed to let you see mine."

We had reached the bottom of the steps, the short expanse of beach splayed before us like an open fan as the ocean waited beyond the sand like a chained dog. "I'm afraid of heights," I admitted.

Her hand trembled within mine, and I gripped it tighter as we continued to move toward the water. She kept talking as if the words would keep her fear at bay. "Because of your brother's accident?"

"Yes, I think so. Before he fell, I'd never had a problem with heights. There was something about sitting high in a tree and looking at the rooftops around you. At least there is until you watch your brother slip on the branch below yours just as he's reaching for your hand."

We'd stopped walking, still safely on the soft sand that the encroaching tide hadn't yet claimed.

"I grabbed the cuff of his T-shirt, then heard it rip. It happened so fast that all I could do was stare at the cuff in my hand and wonder where Sean had gone." I looked up at the unforgiving moon, all light with no warmth. "My parents weren't home and the neighbors lived too far away to hear me shout. I waited up in the tree, holding that damned cuff and seeing my brother's body on the ground. There wasn't a thing I could do. I was absolutely powerless. And even now I wonder if it's the fear of being powerless and not of heights that keeps me on the ground. Because I can still feel how wonderful and freeing it is up on a mountain, or skydiving, or even up on a ship's mast. But I think I can run away from the fear by putting myself in control of every aspect of my life."

"By solving other people's problems. By fixing them."

"Pretty much," I said, aware of how her skin glowed in the moonlight. "But I think I'm beginning to understand that running away from fear doesn't make it go away. It's still there, waiting around the corner, and I figure one day I'm going to catch up to it and finally face it." I touched her cheek with the tip of my finger, feeling liquid moon. "Like you running to the desert, Marnie. Sooner or later, you were bound to find the water again."

Her hair blew softly in the night breeze and reminded me of what I had been about to tell her at dinner. But the moment had passed and I had lost my courage. And then she'd mentioned Diana, and I realized that I would probably never tell Marnie the truth about me and Diana. As she had told me herself, they were sisters, and that one word carried an ocean of meaning, which I couldn't cross.

She looked at me, her eyes luminous, but she wasn't seeing me. "The night of the accident, we saw Saint Elmo's fire. It was sudden, just these ghostly blue flames that appeared like magic and lit the mast like a candle. And I wasn't scared—because Grandpa had told me that Saint Elmo was the patron saint of sailors and that when he appeared I'd be safe."

The tide moved up and an incoming wave teased our legs with warm droplets. I still held her hand and felt the trembling there, but she didn't step back.

"But the rational part of my mind also told me that if I was seeing Saint Elmo's fire, then there was a bad storm approaching." She turned away toward the water, as if trying to see her boat, to call it home. "I told Mama, but she ignored me. She acted as if she hadn't even heard me."

Marnie bit her lip. "The funny thing is, I've never remembered that part about Saint Elmo's fire until now. And I wonder . . ." She stopped, looking down at the wet sand at our feet, the water reflecting the moon's intense gaze. She looked up at me again. "And I wonder if it's because of what you said, about running from my fear. Maybe it's not the water I'm afraid of. Maybe it's remembering what really happened that night that I've been running from all this time."

I stepped closer to her, and I thought I could smell the sun on her skin. "Whatever it is, Marnie, you don't have to face it alone."

She tilted her face up to mine, and it was the most natural thing in the world for me to pull her closer and press my lips to hers. She tasted of wine and salt air, and in my arms she felt just like the girl I'd seen all those years ago with the wind in her hair and defiance in her eyes.

Her arms came around my neck as she pressed her body close to mine before pulling her head away. "In the restaurant, you were about to tell me something. Something you were saying you should have told me before."

"I don't remember what it was," I said, pulling her closer to me again as the waves crept even closer, encircling our feet like the fire of Saint Elmo, dancing and leaping until finally retreating from where it had come.

CHAPTER 19

Wide sea, that one continuous murmur breeds
Along the pebbled shore of memory!
—JOHN KEATS

Marnie

Autumn in the Lowcountry comes slowly, its inhabitants usually notified of the changing season by the appearance of migratory birds from the north and the disappearance of the blue crabs as they seek the warmer waters off the ocean floor. I watched as the strong winds plucked the tussocks of straw-colored seeds off the tips of the cordgrass, painting the marsh yellow until that faded, too, as winter robbed the marsh of all its color, leaving only dried browns and pale greens to remind you of the vibrant life that once teemed there. It was as if the marsh were in mourning, waiting for its rebirth. I think that was why I made my daily pilgrimage down to the dock to witness this hibernation, feeling as if something inside me was also waiting—waiting for the spring rains to unfurl the parts of me that had remained shriveled for so long.

The repairs on the *Highfalutin* were going well, with most of the outer work completed. We still hadn't been able to convince Gil to go on board, but Trey had managed to move Gil's work space closer and closer to the boat so that now he was near enough to touch it. He didn't cling to me anymore or shrink back from the boat when we entered the work area, although I noticed that he never put the boat behind him. It was as if he needed to keep an eye on it, unsure of when it might pounce.

Gil still hadn't spoken a word since my return, although I noticed the absence of words less and less. It was as if he had honed onto methods of communication that made clear his intentions without drawing attention to the fact that he hadn't uttered a word. He continued to sketch in his pad but as yet hadn't shown anything to me, and I still hadn't convinced him to return to his watercolors. Occasionally I would find the torn pieces of paper that had fallen from the spiral wires at the top of his pad, and I assumed these pictures went under the door to his mother's room. I never saw them, but once in a while I'd find the telltale scraps of white paper clinging to the carpet on the floor outside her studio.

As for Diana, we kept to our wary truce. She continued to paint my portrait, but not let me see it, and she'd added more ill-fated couples and their children to the Maitland mural: a soldier of the Civil War who'd made it home only to succumb to scarlet fever within a month, taking three of his four children with him, and a steamboat explosion that had taken a father and pregnant mother away from the only surviving child who'd been left at home. I had to admit that the sheer number of tragedies that had befallen our family did leave me with second thoughts about scoffing at the Maitland curse, but, as I futilely tried to explain to Diana, the last three centuries were centuries without antibiotics, fire alarms, or air bags, and higher mortality rates weren't exactly unexpected. Still, when she wasn't looking, I'd read the carefully calligraphied words and feel the goose bumps on my neck, as if a cold breath had blown against my skin.

We talked more now, but there were still things that were off limits: the night of our accident and the circumstances surrounding her last breakdown. And when I'd asked her about the piece of paper Tally Deushane had searched for in Diana's library books, I'd received a blank look of such innocence and confusion it made me wonder if Diana had missed her true artistic calling. But I'd seen her ransacked armoire, and I knew without a doubt that she was lying. I couldn't help but wonder if I really wanted to know the truth after all.

I wondered, too, if our truce had somehow been fortified by the fact that I'd secured Quinn's permission to have Gil accompany Diana on her nursing home visits. What neither she nor I had factored in, though, was Gil's resistance to the idea. Even though I promised I would be with him, he still refused to go. As with the boat, I knew it would take time, but hopefully before summer, when I'd been given my last ultimatum to return to my job or lose it forever. I suppose that was why I continued to keep the rental car, although I rarely used it. It was nice to know I still had the option of leaving.

I looked up at the gray October sky and shivered, pulling my sweater closer as I walked away from the dock to the greenhouse. We didn't have a designated meeting time, but Quinn always seemed to be waiting for me after my morning walks.

I tapped on the glass before entering, noticing the new grow lights that were placed about six inches from the plants, then tipped down toward the pots. A fan blew a gentle breeze through the small space to discourage insects and bacteria, and I stepped out of its direct path to avoid any kind of wind. Despite the cloudy day, it was brighter in the greenhouse since Quinn had removed the shade cloth that covered the greenhouse in summer to prevent his orchids from frying in the hot sun.

My years in the desert had made me forget the changes in seasons. As much as I hated the chill and damp of the Lowcountry winters and the cold blow of the nor'easters, I'd missed the cooling of the summer's end and the changes of color. The desert had made me forget that everything changes after a while.

Quinn stood at the large sink, filling his watering can. He looked at me and smiled as I entered, causing an uneasy jump somewhere between my throat and stomach.

"Good morning," he said, putting the can down on the counter, then moving toward me.

"Grow lights?" I asked, keeping my sweater-clad arms wrapped tightly around me.

"Yep. There's not enough sunlight hours for the orchids on cloudy days like this, so I try to help them out."

I nodded, glancing down the rows of pots with their parental lights beaming at them from above. "Why orchids, Quinn?" I stepped around him to walk down the first row of plants, pretending to study them.

He thought for a moment. "I guess one reason would be because they're temperamental and can be difficult to grow."

I raised my head to look at him. "Like being married to Diana wasn't enough conflict in your life?"

"Maybe," he said, leaning back against the door with a half smile, as if he knew why I had put an entire row of orchids between us.

"That's one reason. What's another?"

"Because my mother loves orchids."

"Loves?" I repeated, noting the present tense. "So your mother's still alive?"

"Yes—both of my parents are, actually. They live in Massachusetts, not too far from the house my brother and I grew up in."

"Oh," I said wiping off a stray water droplet from a green pointed leaf. "I just assumed they had both passed because you never talk about them."

He straightened, then moved back toward the sink. "There's not a lot to talk about there."

"Have they ever seen Gil?"

He shook his head. "No. My dad's too ill to travel."

I didn't point out the obvious that traveling goes both ways.

"Why do you ask?"

I looked up, startled to find that he had moved next to me again, blocking my way.

I shrugged, feeling that jumping sensation again. "I don't know. I was just thinking that I would like to see my parents again . . . if I could. I guess as I get older, I find myself wondering how I'd see my parents through a woman's eyes instead of a child's."

He reached up and tugged on my ponytail, pulling it loose. "In my experience, people stay pretty much the same." He eyed me closely, making me squirm. "Except for you, Marnie Maitland. You're not the same girl you used to be, are you? The brave Marnie whose fearlessness won so many races. The Marnie who used to let her hair run wild in the wind."

I swallowed and my eyes met his. We hadn't kissed since the night of our dinner at the Crab Pot. It was as if by mutual agreement that we

blamed the wine and retreated to a platonic relationship that was as full
of discussions about Gil, the boat, and the weather as it was of tension
between us—a tension as taut as fishing wire. And always, always the
specter of my sister haunted us; a ghost we could both see but had no
idea how to exorcise.

A fleeting thought grabbed hold of me, as I smoothed my loosened
hair behind my shoulders. "How would you know what I looked like?
We didn't meet until a few months ago."

He gazed silently at me for a long moment. Finally, he said, "Really?
It seems as if we've known each other for a lot longer than that."

"But you knew what I looked like. Did Diana talk about me?"

Quinn hesitated just for a moment and then nodded. "That was
why I almost didn't recognize you when you showed up. I guess I was
expecting warrior Marnie."

"And you got me instead," I said, thinking of the beautiful Diana
with her blond hair and waiflike figure and how she was everything I
wasn't.

"And that's not such a bad thing." The corner of his lips quirked up
in a familiar half smile. "Who else could tell the story of the legendary
Uranus the dog to my son in such an eloquent way?"

I blushed. "Nobody was supposed to hear that but Gil."

Quinn was smiling fully now. "No, but I enjoyed it just the same."

I tilted my face up to his as he leaned toward me, but I pulled back
as the greenhouse door blew open and Diana walked in, bringing the
chill winter wind with her.

"I hope you know that the walls are see-through and everybody can
see what you're up to in here." She wore jeans and a spaghetti-strap
top, accentuating the thinness of her arms, her bare skin marked with
splotches of paint.

"Good morning to you, too, Diana," said Quinn, not stepping back
from me. "Aren't you cold?"

"Not at all. I'm quite warm, actually. I've been painting since midnight, and it's really worked me up into a sweat."

Her face glowed as she fidgeted around the potted orchids, flitting
like an unsettled butterfly, while Quinn and I exchanged glances.

Quinn moved toward her. "Did you take your medicine this morning?"

Diana turned on him, her previously ecstatic face now turned to fury. "Of course I did. How could I not? Joanna practically forces them down my throat every morning. So, yes, Warden, I took my damn pills."

I stepped forward. "He's just trying to help you, Diana. Even I thought something was up with the way you're acting. If he hadn't said anything, I certainly would have."

She turned to me, her eyes hard. "Why is it, Marnie, that you have to take everything from me? Haven't you taken enough? Is there anything left for me?"

I met her gaze, afraid to look at Quinn. She was beautiful in her fury, her green eyes large and clear, her bones as thin and delicate as a bird's. I had hated her for that a long time ago, and it hit me as odd that I would be having this conversation with a woman who was everything I always wished I could be. "I've never taken anything from you, Diana."

She didn't look away. "Have you ever once wondered how we both ended up in the water that night?"

I jerked back as if hit; memories of that night were always a physical thing for me. I shivered in my sweater. "I was hit by the boom—that's all I remember. And then . . ." I blinked hard, feeling the salty water sting my eyes. "And then I saw Mama and you in the water."

"Had you ever in your life as a sailor been stupid enough to get hit by the boom?"

"No." I shook my head, trying to clear it of her words and old memories that didn't seem to fit. "But what has this got to do with anything?"

"Nothing. Nothing at all," she said softly. Her attention had shifted to the door behind my shoulder, and I watched her anger seep out of her like a deflating balloon. Her entire face softened, and I knew before I heard the tapping on the door that Gil was there.

Quinn opened the door and ruffled Gil's hair as he stepped into the greenhouse. I watched as he took in his mother's presence, and was relieved when he didn't shrink back from her.

"Hi, Gil," Diana said, squatting to get down to eye level with him.
He regarded her with matching solemn green eyes.

"I haven't seen a lot of you lately."

Gil remained where he was but he didn't hide behind me or his
father, so I counted that as progress.

"My friend at the nursing home was asking about you yesterday.
I've been showing her the drawings you've made for me, and she really
wants to meet you."

This was pretty much the same tack I'd been using for weeks, and I
wondered if Diana would have better luck.

Gil studied his mother before reaching into his back pocket and
drawing out a piece of white paper that had been folded into a small
square. He hesitated only for a moment before handing it to her.

Still squatting, Diana slowly opened the paper and her smile slowly
faded. "That's nice, Gil. That's real nice. Thank you." Without showing
it to anybody else, she folded it back up and put it in her own pocket.
"Well, then," she said, standing. "I guess I'd better get back to work."

"Wait," I said. "I've been meaning to ask you something. Remember
those two framed prints of the blue herons that I painted for the art
competition when we were in high school?"

I thought I saw something flicker behind her eyes, and I continued.
"They were always hanging in Mama's room but they're not there now.
I was wondering if you had any idea what had happened to them."

She wrinkled her forehead in concentration. "I vaguely remember
them—just vaguely. But I have no idea where they are now. Probably
sold when Grandpa took everything out of the attic."

"After Hurricane Hugo."

"Right. Something like that."

I nodded as she put her hand on the door handle before pausing.
Slowly, she turned to face Quinn and me. "Have you told Marnie how
we met, yet? Have you told her about the painting?"

Diana didn't wait for an answer. The three of us stood watching as
Diana walked through the door, snapping it shut behind her.

Diana

When Marnie and I were about six and eight, my mother took us to Pawleys Island for a day at the beach. It was during one of our mother's fleeting bouts of wellness, and neither Marnie nor I had the heart to explain to our mother that living near the water as we did, Marnie and I already spent more time near the beach than we did in our own beds.

We'd felt so normal: the three of us with our brightly colored beach bags with matching towels that we'd stopped by to purchase from one of the tourist shops in Litchfield Beach. My mother had also purchased zinc oxide for my nose and a hideous sun hat for my head, and I held my tongue from telling her that I preferred her when she was being crazy.

She kept me under the rented umbrella the whole time, making sure I was coated with the zinc oxide and the sun lotion with the highest degree of protection. I watched as Marnie sat on the beach and built sand castles and chased the waves, her olive skin turning a light brown under the sun's rays.

I envied her her dark hair and brown skin, her freedom to run into the surf without worrying if her sun hat was going to stay on, and the strong capable hands that couldn't paint a boat on the water but could build a sand castle that withstood the incoming tide. But mostly I envied the way our mother watched her. I had always felt as if my mother and I were apart from others, but never from Marnie. But for the first time I saw what my mother saw: I was the flawed child and the dark-haired girl with the skin that browned in the sun was the child to be envied.

As I shut the greenhouse door behind me, with the picture of the three of them standing so closely together, I wondered not for the first time exactly what I was fighting against. Maybe there comes a time in every woman's life when pride and old hurts lose their sting. But all I had to do was think of Mama and how she had looked at Marnie, and I was drowning again in a sea of my own making.

I found Grandpa on the back porch in one of the rockers, his hands folded neatly on top of his opened Bible. In the last months I'd found myself both avoiding him because of his inability to condemn me and seeking him out for his peaceful acceptance of.everything I was, including my sins.

I tucked the heavy blankets around his shoulders and legs, making sure he couldn't feel the wind. I was impervious to it, it seemed, but by the way he hunkered down into the folds of the blanket, I could tell the wind whipped into his old bones.

Straightening, I asked, "Do you believe in life after death, Grandpa?"

His clear eyes regarded me silently. And then, almost imperceptibly, he nodded.

I leaned against the porch railing and crossed my arms as I looked out toward the ocean. "I don't believe in a lot of the stuff you used to preach from the pulpit, but I do believe that there's life after death." I turned my head to face him. "After all, I have proof, don't I?"

He continued to stare silently, his blue eyes watery, and I thought that it might not have been from the wind. His hands remained still, resting on his Bible.

"I think Gil knows. You remember that paper I found in your library? Somehow, he found it. He just gave me a drawing of it while I was standing there with Marnie and Quinn." I couldn't help but smile. "It was sheer innocence or just plain brilliance on Gil's part—I haven't figured out which. Either way, he didn't inherit either trait from his mother, did he?"

I slid off the railing and moved to the chair next to my grandfather. I rocked back and forth, the movement jarring instead of comforting. Maybe because it felt too much like being on a boat. I craved a cigarette and started patting my pockets before I remembered that I was with my grandfather. I've always found it amusing that no matter how old you get, you'll always be a little girl to your teachers and the people who raised you.

"I hated to sail. Did I ever tell you that?"

He shook his head.

"Remember how Daddy bought us our first little Sunfish? I hated that damn thing and didn't want to have anything to do with it. And then Marnie got up on it and was able to coax the wind into the sails and go whipping off into the waves. It was like she was a magician and all she had to do was conjure the wind. It was all so damned effortless for her. When I got up on it, I'd slide off or capsize like an uncoordinated fool. But all I had to do was watch Marnie taming the wind with her hair blowing behind her like some masthead and I'd climb back on, pretending to love it and not to notice all the bruises on my legs."

I felt my grandfather tugging at my arm, and I resisted looking at him at first, knowing he would press the Bible into my hands again and make me read from Scripture something about Cain and Abel. He didn't give up, and eventually I turned to him, surprised to see not the Bible, but his proffered hand.

I put my hand in his and squeezed and felt his gentle squeeze back. I tilted my face so he couldn't see my tears, but we sat there for a long time, our hands clasped while we turned away from the ocean and watched the sleeping marsh, instead, all of us, it seemed, waiting for something to happen.

*

Gil

Before Grandpa had his last stroke, when all of a sudden he couldn't talk or move his hands very well, he used to teach me sailing knots. I was really good at it, and he said it was because I had long fingers like my mama's, which made it easier to hold a part of the rope while twisting another part at the same time.

I learned them all: loop knots, hitches, stopper knots, and even some that are just done because they're fun to look at. Grandpa made me learn them by closing my eyes and using just my fingers while I listened to him give instructions. He said it was a trick he picked up when he was in the Navy: how it's better when you're trying to focus on just one thing like hearing or seeing, that you block out everything else. I think that's why I'm a much better listener now that my mouth has stopped working. I'm learning how to read lips, too, because people always talk slowly to you if they think there's something wrong with you. So I stare at their lips, waiting for them to finish talking and that's how I learned.

I think that not talking has made me think more, too. Mama was tearing apart the house looking for something, and it didn't take me very long to figure out what it was. Only it didn't make any sense why that piece of paper was so important to her. And then I remembered hearing Aunt Marnie and Mama talking about the leak in the attic after Hurricane Hugo and getting rid of all the stuff up there, and everything just sort of made sense. It was like in the cartoons when a giant light-bulb goes off over somebody's head. So I drew a picture that had some of the words from the piece of paper on it and gave it to her. I didn't give her the piece of paper because it will hurt Aunt Marnie. I knew this because I heard Mama saying that to Grandpa. But I wanted to let her know that I had it and it was safe. I also figured that I'd be having to go with Mama soon to the nursing home to visit her friend.

I lay in bed that night and closed my eyes, my fingers feeling the scratchiness of the imaginary rope in my hands as I tied a bowline. It has a fixed loop at the end and then a stopper knot when you're done so that it doesn't ever slip or come loose. *Under, around, through, then up and around and through, tuck in end and pull tight.*

The great thing about bowlines is that besides being strong and stable and easy to tie, they're also quick and easy to untie. I think about Mama when I'm tying bowlines; she's strong and capable when she's feeling well, but she's just as easy to come undone. And I'm beginning to think that her ends are frayed, and starting to unravel. I guess that's why I'd better go with her and Aunt Marnie to see the old lady, because it seems to mean so much to her. And maybe I'll see her as strong and capable again, and then I can become the son she used to think she didn't want.

CHAPTER 20

In my research I've discovered that there are over 28,000 species of orchids. That means that they're the most genetically changing group of plants on earth and one of the most adaptable. Some Australian orchids grow completely underground, and several jungle orchids grow in trees. But I'm left to wonder if a genetic component in those wandering orchids ever craves the soil of their ancestors and if they might flourish better if they're ever returned to where they started out.

—From the gardening journal of Dr. Quinn Bristow

Marnie

I tapped on Gil's door. When there was no answer, I thought he might have fallen asleep, so I opened the door just in time to see him sliding a clear plastic box under his bed. He turned around abruptly, his face registering guilt, so I smiled reassuringly at him.

"It's okay to have private things, Gil. As long as you're not doing anything that would hurt somebody, it's all right to have personal things that you keep private." I thought back on my training with children who had special needs and amended my statement with "But it's also okay to share with somebody you trust."

He simply sat on the floor with his back to the bed and stared at me blankly.

I held out my hand to him. "Come on, it's time to go. We're going to the nursing home this afternoon, remember?"

He nodded and allowed me to pull him off the floor. I wasn't completely sure what had changed his mind, but for Diana's sake, I was pleased and relieved. I'd still go with them, but this marked a change in their relationship. It was a bittersweet realization for me, as I considered what Gil's continual progress would mean to my departure date.

When we came down the steps, Diana wasn't there, but Quinn was. He sat on the sofa in the front parlor with a stack of paintings leaning against the coffee table in front of him. After Diana's cryptic words in the greenhouse the day before about a painting, Quinn had only responded that he would show me later and explain everything then. I assumed this was later.

He stood as we entered the room. He smiled at me briefly before turning his attention to his son. Regardless of all the butterflies in my stomach that his smile had somehow managed to let loose, it was nothing compared to the warm feelings engendered by his constant regard and devotion to his son.

Quinn knelt in front of Gil. "Are you all set to go with your mama and aunt Marnie?"

Gil nodded.

"If you have any questions or worries, Aunt Marnie will be there." Quinn glanced at Gil's ever-present sketchbook. "And I'm glad you're taking that. You can always write something down if you need to tell Aunt Marnie something."

Gil nodded again, chewing on his lower lip. It was full and rounded like his father's, the only thing in his face that didn't come directly from his mother. I fleetingly wondered about the vagaries of genetics and the possibility of what other components from Quinn had been wired into his son.

"Good," Quinn said as he stood and ruffled Gil's hair again.

I walked toward the stack of paintings, disappointed that they had been placed against the sofa face-first so that I couldn't see them. "What are these?"

His face was taut, carefully devoid of all expression, as if he were afraid to give anything away. "I said that I would show you, remember?"

He picked up the first painting and walked over to one of the dark rectangles on the wall before flipping it over and hanging it on the nail that already protruded from the plaster.

Slowly, I moved toward the painting, my breath hovering somewhere between my chest and my mouth. "Oh" was all I could say as I stared at the Diana and Marnie I had once known long ago: two little girls in pigtails on the beach gathering shells. The small Diana was as fair as her sister was dark, but their profiles, turned toward each other, were like two halves of the same face.

Without saying anything, Quinn picked up each picture and began hanging them in the spots where they belonged, each frame fitting into its designated slot like a piece of a jigsaw puzzle. Slowly, I walked around the perimeter of the room studying each painting, and it almost felt as if I were dying and being shown parts of my past life. But instead of a movie, my life had been relegated to oils and watercolors and forced to fit inside rectangular frames.

The next painting was of an older Diana and Marnie, barefoot and wearing cutoff jeans and T-shirts knotted about the waist. They were on the dock crabbing, their backs to each other and holding their poles on opposite ends of the dock. Both wore their hair loose, like dark and blond halos dancing around their heads. Again their faces were in profile: two sides of the same coin.

There was a painting of us sitting in the rocking chairs on the front porch and another of us down on the beach digging for clams; there was even one of Diana with an easel while I sat on the grass, looking toward the ocean. In all of them only half of each face was visible, and even I began to believe that neither girl was whole without the other.

As I continued around the room, I saw the first individual portraits. It was as if the artist had seen that as we got older, she and the subject began growing apart. The first one I noticed was me on my Sunfish. You could see the tip of Diana's yellow one on the edge of the picture, but it was easily overlooked in the painting that overwhelmed the viewer with the bright colors of the boat, my bathing suit, the unrelenting blue sky, and the rolling aqua of the ocean's waves.

There was even a self-portrait of Diana in her studio as she stood painting on an unseen canvas propped on her easel, the chaos of her studio depicted honestly in the background of the painting. I looked from one to the other, astonished; even in these paintings, only the sides of our faces were visible.

I had to swallow several times before I found my voice. "Where did these come from?"

Quinn selected the last portrait from the pile. "From Diana's studio. She'd taken them off these walls when she heard you were returning. I convinced her to let me rehang them."

"You convinced her?"

He gave a quick glance toward Gil, who was sitting on the sofa with his elbows on his knees, pretending not to listen. "Let's just say that I made her believe that hanging these pictures here would directly influence my decision to allow Gil to go with her on her next visit to see her friend."

"But we had a deal! You'd already decided to let him go."

He smiled that disturbing half smile again. "She didn't know that."

I was about to say something when he lifted the painting in his hand and affixed it to its spot on the wall. I lost my breath again as I stared at a portrait similar to the one I'd seen in the store window in Mc-Clellanville. This was a scene from the marina, with the shrimp boats packed tightly together at the dock during the off season. But the sky was an ominous gray with red streaks bleeding through the fat clumps of cloud. *Red sky at morning, sailors take warning.* Almost as an afterthought, a figure had been painted into the corner opposite the shrimp boats. Her back was to the viewer, but it was unmistakably me and I was looking off into the distance at where a boat in full sail appeared to be sailing off into the darkening sky.

I shivered and turned away from its awful beauty and found Quinn looking intently at me. "What do you think?" he asked quietly.

"Diana's an incredible artist," I said. "I've always known that, of course. It's just . . ."

I spun around the room, taking in the myriad sizes and scenes like a person looking into a kaleidoscope waiting for the jumbled colored shapes to form a picture. It was then that I realized that each one of these framed portraits was not so much about me and the years of my girlhood; they were about Diana's perspective of me. The first paintings had been of us together as children, and then several more as we grew older. But the constant was that we were always together. The first portrait of me in which I appeared alone, I was sitting on the dock and staring out toward the water. Once again, I was only seen in profile, but I was completely alone. And when you looked at my expression, there was something in my face that spoke of loss and infinite grief. I would have been about twelve in the portrait—about the same age I had been when our mother drowned.

I continued studying all the portraits while Quinn sat down next to Gil, his arm around his small shoulders. In the following portraits on the wall, I continued to be alone but my figure became smaller and smaller as if in the artist's eye I had been moving farther and farther away from her, until I could be relegated to a small space of her canvas—gone, yet hovering always in the corner of her consciousness.

I faced the couch, noticing the huge blank rectangle on the wall. "Where's this one?"

Quinn's face remained closed. "She can't find it, so she thinks she might have sold it."

"Oh," I said, disappointed. "What was it of?"

"You," he said simply.

I glanced around the room one more time. "Yes, I suppose it would have to have been." It was odd staring at myself in every incarnation of my childhood and girlhood. And as I looked at the ones of Diana and of me, my heart tightened as it does when I think about something important I lost and don't ever expect to find again. I felt the unmistakable urge to cry.

Quinn stood and I turned to face the picture of Diana and me collecting seashells so he couldn't see my face.

"These are her most valuable works. You wouldn't believe the calls we get from dealers, but she's made it clear that she'll never sell them." He put his hand on my shoulder, and the sudden warmth there drew me to him until my head was pressed against his chest. "She started painting these right after you left, before I'd even met her. She'd sold quite a few before she decided that they weren't for sale anymore."

I looked up at him, warmth and understanding meeting my gaze. "She once told me that your leaving felt like a defection to her—almost as if you'd been playing a game of chess and you'd picked up all your pieces and gone home."

I pressed my forehead against his collarbone, reassured by the firm, warm presence of him. "But she didn't even like me anymore. She changed after Mama's death, and things got worse and worse after that. It was like she was another person, always accusing me of being blind, of not seeing things the way they really were. And when I tried to apologize"—I stopped to swallow the lump that had lodged itself in my throat—"it made her even more angry. I never expected this," I said, straightening and sweeping my arms out to indicate the vast array of my sister's talent and memories splayed across four walls. Except for the one glaring omission over the sofa.

"You certainly didn't waste any time."

The three of us turned to see Diana as she came down the stairs, her hair combed discreetly back in a low ponytail, and wearing a modest skirt and buttoned-up cream cashmere sweater with low-heeled pumps. If I hadn't intimately known every article of clothing that I had brought with me from Arizona, I would have sworn that she'd stolen everything she wore from my closet.

Quinn slowly moved away from me. "I told you that I was going to rehang them all, so this shouldn't come as too much of a surprise."

Diana's lips were pale as if she were pressing them too tightly together as she moved into the room and stood by Gil on the sofa.

"They're beautiful, Diana. Truly beautiful." I wasn't lying; they really were her best work. But everything else that needed to be said hovered between us like a persistent ghost.

"I know," she said, not meeting my eyes. "I doubt I'll ever paint like that again."

Neither Quinn nor I said anything as she turned to Gil. "Are you ready to go?"

He nodded. For a moment I thought that Diana might offer him her hand, and felt relief when she didn't.

"Let's go then," she said, and led the way out the door. "We'll be back by five," she called over her shoulder to Quinn.

I hesitated for a moment, unwilling to leave my rediscovered childhood and sister, whom I had once loved the most. I turned around to look at the portrait of the two girls on the rocking chairs for one quick glance before heading out the door behind Gil, letting the screen door shut softly behind me.

∅

Diana

I didn't know that my hands were shaking until I tried to open the car door. I had to give it three tries before I was able to pull the handle out far enough to release it. I went immediately to the passenger's side, not wanting to get into an argument in front of Gil with Marnie about driving.

It took me a few moments to realize that we weren't moving. I looked over at Marnie, who was busy looking at me.

"Where am I going?" she asked.

"North Charleston. Just take Highway Seventeen and go over the Cooper River Bridge. I'll give you directions once we get there."

She nodded and pulled the car onto the gravel drive. As happy as I was that Gil was with me, and that he had come willingly, I settled down uncomfortably for the forty-five-minute trip. I had never wanted Marnie to see those paintings. The first one I had done, the painting of Marnie and me as little girls collecting shells on the beach, had been started in a blind panic the day Marnie had left for college in Arizona. I started painting, and soon found that I couldn't stop. I painted day and night, giving up food and sleep just so I could paint. It soothed my grief like an ointment to a wound, and I felt neither fatigue nor hunger as long as I was painting.

It was my grandfather who realized I was having my first manic episode. He'd had plenty of experience with recognizing the signs, after all. He committed me to a hospital where I could be treated, and left me there for a month. He visited daily, bringing me books and magazines and even smuggling in Twinkies. But he would not bring me my paints and brushes, and I wouldn't let him talk about Marnie. I felt that by putting her in oil on canvas, I had exorcised her from my head and heart. And for a long time after I was released, I came to believe that to be true.

Of course, being a Maitland, I should have realized that sooner or later my sister would come back to haunt me. And she did, just not in the way anyone would have expected.

"What's your friend's name? I'd like to know what to call her when I meet her." Marnie's voice broke into my thoughts.

"You're not going to meet her, so don't worry about it."

"What do you mean? Aren't we going to the nursing home to see her now?"

"Yes, but she doesn't want to meet you. Only Gil." Even I cringed at the harshness of my own words. "It's nothing personal. It's just that she's a bit of a recluse and doesn't really like to meet strangers. She only wants to meet Gil because she's heard so much about him and likes the pictures I've been bringing in to show her." I glanced back at Gil and gave him a smile. He didn't smile back, but he didn't look terrified, either, so that was a definite improvement.

"Is that why you're dressed that way?" There was the trace of a smile in her voice.

"You mean like you?"

I watched her chew on her inside cheek. She'd been doing that since she was about four years old and had been told by our grandfather to bite her tongue before she said anything she would regret later. Her cheek was as good as she could manage at the time, and it stuck.

Without looking at me, she said, "No. Just like you but with more fashion sense. I'm glad you've finally realized that cutoff jeans really aren't for every occasion."

"Touché," I said under my breath, grudgingly admiring the way she'd learned to stand up for herself. "She just thinks that everybody's a little too wild these days and appreciates a conservative demeanor. That's why Gil's in khakis and a button-down shirt, too."

She nodded. "That'll show her."

"Yes, it will."

"But she doesn't know Gil, so technically he's a stranger, too."

I closed my eyes, wishing that she would just stop talking. "Not re-

ally. I've been telling her about Gil for almost a year. She knows everything about him. She knows about the Maitland curse, too."

She looked at me, startled. "Why would you even tell her such a
thing?"

"Because it's true."

"You mean because Mama thought it was true."

I turned away from her and concentrated on the bleached gray asphalt of the highway. "Because maybe it really is."

She shook her head and was silent for a moment. "I brought her a
book. . . ."

"Great. I'll make sure I give it to her and say it's from you." I continued to stare out my window.

"It's Pat Conroy's latest. It just came out last week, so I wouldn't
think she's already read it. I assumed she's from the Lowcountry and
would enjoy it."

"Yes," I said. "Yes, she is." I closed my eyes, trying to signal to her
that I was tired of talking.

"Those paintings . . ."

I kept my eyes closed, hoping she'd stop.

"Quinn said you started doing them right after I left. Before your
first episode."

She was quiet for a long time and I thought she was finished. Finally
she said, "I'm sorry, Diana. I'm so very sorry. As inadequate as that word
is, it's all I have to give to you for playing any part in . . ."

I wanted to fill in "my craziness," but I kept quiet, my eyelids closed
against the light and Marnie's discerning gaze.

"I'm sorry," she said again, her voice heavy with tears and containing
more hurt and pain than could be held within the boundaries of the
ocean's floor.

It's too late, I wanted to say, but she wouldn't know what I was talking about. She'd think it had to do with the paintings and how I went
a little crazy when she abandoned me. But the one thing she should be
sorry for she'd never know, and I had every intention of carrying that
knowledge to my grave.

I continued to pretend to be asleep as Marnie drove. I heard her swallow before she spoke to Gil, and I felt a flash of warmth where my heart had once been. Marnie was the one who'd always been concerned about others' feelings, and even now, despite her own mood, she didn't want Gil to be left out.

"Do you want to hear a story?" she asked.

I pictured Gil rolling his eyes. He was getting to be that age where stories weren't cool anymore, but he still loved to hear them. My father, when he was around and before he disappeared from our lives for good, had been a great storyteller. There had been nothing Marnie and I had loved better as little girls than curling up in his lap and listening to his silly stories. It was the only way he knew how to communicate with us, and for a while, it was enough.

But as we grew older, and our mother grew less predictable, the stories grew fewer and fewer. And then one day, he was just gone, and I never really knew to miss him except when I was in need of a lap to curl up into and listen to a story.

"This is a story about soldiers in the last great war," Marnie continued, and I moved my face toward the window so she couldn't see my smile. This one had been my favorite.

"Well, the hero of our story is a young man by the name of Peter Parts who wanted to join the Army. But even though he was brave, strong, and smart, there was no recruiting station that would have anything to do with him. And it took him a whole year of trying before some nice sergeant pulled him aside and let him know the truth. You know what that was, Gil?"

I pictured Gil shrugging and Marnie glancing in the rearview mirror. "Well, it was on account of nobody wanting to have Private Parts in their regiment."

I heard the distinct sound of a snort coming from the backseat, and it took all the strength I had not to turn around and to continue feigning sleep. That one sound had been the first I'd heard out of my son's mouth in almost six months, and I felt as I had when he was a baby and had taken his first step.

I knew that Marnie had heard it, too. Through half-closed eyes, I watched her as she gripped the steering wheel a little bit tighter. I kept smiling as I listened to the old story about how Peter Parts changed his name to Peter Payne until he became Major Payne and then eventually had to report to General Lee Asinine. I must have snorted, too, at one point, because Marnie elbowed me in the side of my arm, chiding me, I thought, for pretending to be asleep.

Marnie found a parking spot near the front entrance of the nursing home, and we all piled out of the car, each of us with a small stack of books in our hands. I led the way as Marnie followed with Gil, who, I was surprised to see, didn't seem to be showing any trepidation about being alone with me for an hour.

Susan Goldsmith, the residential manager, met us at the reception desk and stood as I made introductions. She was a tall, slender lady about my age with a regal smile.

"Good to see you again, Diana. She's been waiting all day. We had to give her something to sleep last night, because she was so excited about today that she couldn't sleep. But she's awake and alert now and expecting you."

"Great," I said, motioning Gil to come with me but being careful not to touch him. I indicated the plush sitting room near the reception desk outfitted with several comfortable leather couches and a few side tables scattered with magazines. A drink dispenser hummed in the far corner, disguised by a large ficus. "Marnie can wait here."

Susan raised an elegant eyebrow. "Your sister won't be joining you?"

I shook my head. "No. You know how she gets when she's around strangers."

I didn't wait for a reply, as I added the books Marnie carried to my pile and then ushered Gil away from Marnie and into the familiar corridor I had been walking down for over a year. After carefully adjusting Gil's collar so that I had limited contact with him, I knelt in front of him.

"Thank you for coming with me today. I like it that we're together again."

He stared solemnly at me with familiar green eyes.

"Don't be scared, all right? We're just going to talk for a while, and if she asks you any questions, I can help you answer them, so don't feel like you're being put on the spot." I reached my hand up to brush the hair off his forehead and he flinched. I let my hand fall, angry at myself.

I straightened and brushed at the knees of my skirt. "She might want to talk about your pictures, okay? She really likes them, and I've put a few in frames for her. I thought you might like that."

My palms felt sweaty and I rubbed them against my skirt. "Are you ready?"

He took a quick look behind him down the hall, and I knew he was hoping to catch sight of Marnie. Then he looked back up at me and nodded.

"Great," I said. "If you get scared or nervous, just pretend you're as brave and strong and smart as Private Parts."

That got me a snort as I turned to knock on the door, and I suddenly felt better than I had in a very long time.

*

Gil

After I got back from the nursing home, I went straight up to my room and pulled out the box that I kept under my bed. It was like my mama's box that had that label on it that read "precious things" because I kept all my important stuff in there—my favorite marbles, a shark's tooth I'd found on the beach, a picture of my parents when they got married, and a few other things that I thought were pretty cool or important for some reason. I unbuttoned my shirt and pulled out a wrapped Twinkie that was only a little bit squished, and stuck it in the box.

I took out that piece of paper that I had taken from Mama's armwore and looked at it closely. I stared at the writing at the top, and all of a sudden everything sort of made sense. It was like looking into the view finder on a camera and playing with the focus button until everything becomes sharp and clear.

I stuck the paper on top before closing the box and putting it back under the bed, knowing that I would probably be looking at it again just to make sure that I was right. Then I grabbed my sketch pad and pencils and went up to the orange tree on the hill and started drawing while trying to figure out why Mama had lied to the old lady about not bringing her Twinkies when I knew there was an entire box sitting out in the car.

And I was almost done with my drawing before I realized that I hadn't remembered to be afraid of Mama once the whole time we were at the old people's home. I figured that was a good reason to celebrate, so I took out the other Twinkie I'd hidden in my shirt and began to eat it, and wondered again why my mama would have lied.

CHAPTER 21

❧

I must go down to the seas again, to the lonely sea and the sky,
And all I ask is a tall ship and a star to steer her by,
And the wheel's kick and the wind's song and the white sail's shaking,
And a gray mist on the sea's face, and a gray dawn breaking.

—JOHN MASEFIELD

Quinn

My brother, Sean, used to tell me that the tides were caused by the breathing in and out of a huge sea monster. I accepted this for a long time, figuring that was a lot more credible than believing that tides were caused by the gravitational pulls of the moon and sun dragging a bulge of water around the planet.

But I had also believed that Sean and I would be brothers forever, raising our families near each other and teaching our children how to sail on the same boat. Looking back, I wish that I had known then how quickly the unbelievable can become believable, and I would have learned that much sooner that the tides do move at the whim of the sun and moon.

It was damp and chilly in the jon boat as Marnie, Gil, and I maneuvered our way through the sleeping marsh toward town. An early-morning fog had begun to dissipate, already hanging filmy necklaces around the tops of the tall cypress trees. The sounds of our motor and the slapping water against the old oyster beds were the only noises as we made our way to the marina.

The large doors to Trey's boatyard were propped open to allow in the colder air, but he'd taken off his shirt to work on sanding the hull of a twenty-two-foot Tanzer. I watched as Marnie paused beside me long enough to admire Trey's exposed chest before turning her attention to Gil.

"Look, Gil," she said, leading him over to the side of the building where the *Highfalutin* sat on her jack stands, her fresh coat of paint gleaming under the fluorescent lights. "It looks like the outside is just about all ready to go."

"Just about," said Trey as he approached. Thankfully, he'd thrown on a T-shirt, and he wore a healthy layer of sawdust in his hair and face, the outline of his goggles giving him a surprised-chipmunk look. From the appreciative look Marnie gave him, it didn't seem that she'd noticed.

"Hey, big guy." Trey tussled Gil's hair, and Gil smiled up at him, creating an irrational pang of what I could only describe as jealousy. Trey was an okay kind of guy for his type, I guess. I was grateful to him because of how he'd gone out of his way to work with Gil and include him on lots of the little projects involved with repairing the boat. It was only that I knew he was the one Diana had turned to after our divorce, and I couldn't get that out of my head. And the way that Marnie looked at him sometimes didn't help, either.

"Well, we were able to get a lot of painting done on account of that bit of warm weather we had last week. Otherwise, it would have had to wait until next spring. But before we can do the interior painting, I've got to remove all the teak trimming from the cockpit and around the cabin, get it sanded and revarnished. I'll definitely need a hand with that, and I was thinking of Gil because he did just a great job with the toe rail."

Trey walked over to a cardboard box sitting on the floor next to the wall. "Look what came in this week." He stuck his hand in, pulled out a layer of bubble wrap and foam peanuts, then lifted something out of the box using two hands. "We got our new tiller. I was able to find this and a few other parts from a guy I found on the Internet. All came from another Tartan 30 he'd gutted." He winked at Gil. "Gotta have a shiny new tiller to match the shiny new varnish, don't you think?"

Gil's eyes widened as Trey held up the object for Gil to inspect.

"If you help me attach it, I'll let you show me some of your sailing knots. Your dad said you're a real pro."

Gil glanced at me, then back to the tiller, and I knew from the expression on his face the exact moment that he realized that to attach the tiller he'd need to get up onto the boat, since its location sat on the stern portion of the deck.

Marnie stepped closer to him. "We can go check it out first, if you like. See how you feel on board, right here in this building without any water anywhere. And I'll be with you."

Gil glanced at me, and I recognized the look in his eyes he'd had when I'd allowed him to man the jib sail all by himself for the first time: a look of fear mixed with hope and excitement. It was his nature to be cautious; he'd learned that from me. Why else would I have climbed a thirty-foot tree that I had no idea how to get down from if I hadn't taught him that? Because it was also in my nature to challenge whatever limitations I had.

I touched his shoulder. "I have two minor surgeries scheduled this afternoon, and if you agree to help Mr. Bonner with the tiller, I'll let you scrub in and watch."

He rolled his eyes at me as I'd known he would and then focused on the boat again. Bribery had never worked on Gil, even as a baby. I could almost hear his mind working him past whatever barrier had imposed itself there. I knew that there were several for him, and that he could only hurdle one at a time. But here was a place to start, and I knew that he recognized it, too.

Marnie's eyes met mine for a moment, and it occurred to me that her thoughts had probably very closely mirrored my own.

"I'll go first," she said and I looked up, startled to realize that she hadn't been on the boat yet, either. I suppose I was so focused on Gil that I hadn't noticed, although of late I'd been very aware of her whenever she was near.

As if to move before her body changed its mind, she walked toward the stationary boat. Even without its mast, it looked huge out of the water, overwhelming Marnie as she stood next to it. Without looking back, she used the ladder Trey had temporarily mounted onto the back of the boat to allow for easy access, and hoisted herself up.

Peering down at us, she wrinkled her nose. "Smells like new carpet up here." Despite the lightness of her tone, her voice came out in a slightly higher pitch.

Trey put his hands on his hips and smiled up at her, and I thought he looked like the Jolly Green Giant on a can of asparagus. "Nope—not new carpet. New upholstery in the cabin. I know it's a bit premature, but the fabric came in early, and I figured I'd get it done to surprise you. Guess it won't be much of a surprise now."

"No, I guess not," she said absently as she looked around, her hands gripping the newly polished handrail. Her knuckles appeared white in the fluorescent glow.

She stood still, her hands not moving from their spot on the rail, and closed her eyes. It seemed like she swayed for a moment, as if waves gently prodded the bow in the age-old rocking movement mimicked by mothers everywhere.

Gil was watching her, too, and I had a sudden flashback to when he was four or five and we'd been out on the *Highfalutin* all day. His nose and cheeks were pink despite the sun block I'd continued to apply, but he kept resisting my suggestion that we turn back and go home. Diana had been restless and morose, staying in her studio much of the time, and Gil hadn't really seen her in a week. I remembered him telling me, in his sweet young voice, that he missed his mother the same way the tides miss the moon.

The only thing that would make him think of anything else was sailing, so we took the boat out every day. My shoulders ached and my skin was blistered and peeled, but none of it mattered if it meant seeing my son smile again.

It was only after the third day that I realized what it was that had so pacified Gil. Whether we were zipping through the waves or biding our time with slack sails, the water held us and the boat in its maternal arms, rocking us in its watery rhythm and perhaps even reminding Gil of his mother as she had rocked him as a baby, or even before that in her womb. The sailboat had become like a mother surrogate to him— something I could never tell Diana. There was nothing she despised more than sailing, and to have her son cling to it in her absence would have done more harm than good.

But as I watched Marnie's face and then Gil's, it occurred to me that maybe that was what sailing was all about: the going back to the place you came from. Maybe that was what made great sailors. I enjoyed sailing, but mine had been a methodical learning of it. Gil's skills came all from instinct, from knowing the wind before it blew and understanding the temperament of the waves beneath the hull. I imagined it was this way with Marnie, too.

That was why when he took a step forward, I didn't move. Purposefully, he strode to the stern and climbed the ladder as he'd seen Marnie do. He paused at the top and looked at his aunt.

She held out her hand to him as he stepped onto the deck of the boat and moved to stand beside her, clutching her hand. They both gave such triumphant smiles that it almost made me want to let out a loud whoop. But I stood still, watching in awe as they both seemed to adjust to their new position.

"Looking good, you two," said Trey. "I'd say you're ready to hit the waves."

A matching look of utter panic swept over their faces and stole their smiles.

Marnie forced her lips to curl upward. "I think you're being a little premature."

Gil had backed away, heading for the ladder that would take him off the boat. Nobody tried to stop him.

Trey approached the boat and looked up at her. "Bull, Marnie. Anybody who could ever sail a boat like you should never be away from one." He faced me. "You ever seen her sail?"

I cleared my throat. "Not exactly," I said, watching as her eyes moved to my face. "But I've seen the trophies."

"There you have it, Marnie. Two people who think you should be under sails again."

I wasn't sure where he'd reached his conclusion, but I did agree that she needed to be back on a boat.

Marnie moved to follow Gil off the boat.

Trey said, "How about I take you out on my boat? She's not as grand as the *Highfalutin*, but she's a great little twenty-two-footer. Get your feet wet again, so to speak."

She turned to face Trey, and I could read the word "no" on her lips, but he interrupted her.

"Think what a great example you'd be for Gil, here. Maybe if you went first, it would be easier for him to follow in your footsteps."

I admired Trey's brilliant mind for a moment. Marnie and Gil looked at each other, and I was caught again by their similarity, which had nothing to do with coloring or the shapes of their noses but everything to do with great loss and the will of a soul strong enough to fight back. "I could go, too, if that would make it any easier for you."

Trey gave me a sidelong glance. "Actually, three people crewing her would be a crowd. But the two of you are more than welcome to take her out."

I found myself liking him a little bit more. "If you can trust us with your boat, that might be a really great idea."

"I've never seen you sail, Doctor, but I'd trust Marnie in my boat with a blindfold on. She's a little crazy when there's a wind chasing her, but she knows what she's doing."

Marnie blushed and looked down at her feet. "You wouldn't say that now. I don't think I could tell the difference between a jib sail and a mainsail anymore."

Trey snorted. "I don't believe you. Besides, sailing's a lot like riding a bicycle—you just don't forget how. Especially you, Marnie Maitland. I bet you still pee salt water."

She looked at him with a shocked expression before laughing. "I can't believe you still remember that."

"Remember what?" I asked.

Sheepishly, she explained, "Before a junior regatta, I was being teased by the crew of a competing boat. I'm not really sure why, except that my boat wasn't as nice as theirs and because I was small for my age. They asked me if I'd need floaties on my arms and if I'd ever actually been in the water before."

Trey was laughing out loud now and Marnie grinned reluctantly.

Smiling back, I asked, "So what did you say to them?"

Her cheeks and the tip of her nose reddened slightly. "I told them that I'd been sailing so long that when I peed, it was salt water."

Trey wiped his eyes. "You should have seen the looks on their little snooty faces—it was priceless."

I laughed. "So did you win?"

"Damn straight I did," she said, smiling up at me and making me remember what her lips tasted like.

Impulsively, I asked, "So do you want to go sailing with me?"

I held my breath while I waited for her answer. The light faded from her eyes. "No," she said after a moment. "It's one thing to stand on the boat in here. But it's a whole different world out there on the Atlantic."

"That's the whole point of sailing," I said softly.

"Stop it," she said, keeping her voice down to avoid alarming Gil, who was studying an assortment of winches and rigging that Trey had accumulated on shelves in the corner. "You don't understand what it's like."

"Maybe I do," I said before turning away from her, as eager to leave her to her thoughts as she was. I knew my anger was irrational; what had happened to her on a sailboat was beyond comprehension. Yet when I'd seen her face as she stood on the deck of my boat, all arguments were moot. I had seen that face before, of course. It had been a long time ago, but even time can't erase the memory of two elements captured together that seemed to belong together like the sun and the sky. The Marnie she was trying to be was an awkward fit, like a young girl trying on her mother's shoes. Yet Marnie seemed blind to it, and I was at a loss as to how to make her see.

I stripped off my jacket. "Okay, Trey. Show me what tools I should use, and I'll start removing the teak in the cabin. If Gil wants, he can help me after he helps you with that tiller, and then you and Marnie can start the sanding."

"Sounds like a plan," Trey said as he moved toward the stacked metal shelves.

I was halfway up the ladder when Trey called out to me, "Hey, Dr. Bristow, my brother wanted me to ask you if you wanted to go parasailing again. He said you bought a series of three lessons but have only been up once. It's too cold now, but he said he's already booking up for spring, so he wanted to let you know."

I avoided looking in Marnie's direction. "I'll let him know, thanks."

"You want to come with me, Gil?" I stood at the top of the ladder and stretched my hand out. "Trust me—this is the easier part. Of course, if you really enjoy sanding, you can stay and help. Or you can come with me."

He hesitated only a moment before following me. He put his hand in mine and I pulled him aboard. As we waited for Trey to bring us our tools, I had plenty of time to think about fear and how most people wore its mask one way or another.

◗

Marnie

Every muscle in my back and arms ached from bending over strips of wood and methodically and painstakingly sanding the tops and edges of every single piece. Tomorrow I had the restaining and varnishing to do, and my muscles ached in anticipation.

Quinn and Gil had left earlier for his office appointments, and I looked at my watch after cleaning up and realized I still had about an hour before they would be ready to leave for home. I watched as Trey approached me, wiping his hands with an old rag and reminding me what it had been about him that had attracted me all those years ago.

"All done?"

"Yes, although even if I weren't, I'd probably have to lie to you so that you wouldn't make me do any more sanding."

He glanced over at the strips of wood lying on the large worktables behind me. "Yep, that's a tough job. Good for the soul, though."

I raised an eyebrow.

"It's the kind of job that keeps your hands busy so your mind can sort of work things out. Like knitting, but harder."

I laughed. "Yeah, something like that."

His smile faded softly as he regarded me. "Guess I couldn't interest you in a drink or something to eat while you wait, huh?"

"No, probably not."

"I didn't think so, but thought I'd try anyway."

I smiled up at him. "You're a great guy, Trey, and when I was seventeen, you were everything I needed. But I'm not that girl anymore."

"No, you're not. And there's that Diana thing, too."

"Yeah, that, too. Hard to forget a heartbreak caused by your sister sleeping with your boyfriend."

His dark face colored even darker. "I'm sorry about that. I don't think you ever gave me the chance to apologize, but I am sorry. I'm not even sure how that happened, embarrassing as that sounds." He grinned sheepishly at me. "It's just that Diana, well, you know how she can be."

"Yeah," I said softly, "I know." I stood on my tiptoes and leaned forward to kiss him on the cheek. "Apology accepted."

He kicked his toe into the ground. "Too little too late, I guess, but thank you."

"I'll see you tomorrow."

"Sure thing."

I was almost out of the door when he said, "Dr. Bristow's a great guy. You can't go wrong by him."

"He is a great guy," I admitted. "But he's my sister's ex-husband."

He smiled that old smile again, and I was once again reminded of how nice it had once been to be sixteen and Trey Bonner's girlfriend. "Hey, it wouldn't be like it hadn't been done before."

"Bye, Trey. See you tomorrow," I said as I left, shaking my head.

I decided to visit the little library on Baker Street to see if they had the next Nelson DeMille novel. Quinn, Gil, my grandfather, and I spent most evenings sitting in the family room reading in front of the fireplace, where the smell of pine logs brought me home almost more than anything else had since I'd returned. But I'd long since finished the novel I'd brought to read on the plane from Arizona, and there were only so many issues of the *Journal of the American Veterinary Medical Association* that I could read more than once.

I loved the smell of libraries—the comforting mixture of old books and floor polish made all the stronger by the pervading hush. I strolled over to the popular fiction area and began perusing the shelves, picking up a couple of novels as backups in case I didn't find the one I was looking for.

"Miss Maitland?"

I turned around quickly, startled enough to drop a book. The young girl with the dark hair pulled back in a French twist and an iPod hanging around her neck bent down easily to retrieve it and handed it to me. "I'm sorry. Didn't mean to scare you." She smiled at me with bright brown eyes accented by black cat's-eye glasses, something about her looking oddly familiar.

"Do I know you?" I asked.

"Sort of. I'm Tally Deushane, Trey's half sister. I didn't expect you to recognize me. I think the last time you saw me I was about eight years old."

"Oh, my gosh—Tally! And you're right. I wouldn't recognize you. I think you were in jumpers and pigtails when I saw you last." She was very petite, even shorter than my own five feet four inches, and curvy. I recognized her brother in her eyes, and smiled.

She smiled back, her pale skin telling me that she probably spent a lot more time in the library than at the beach. "You're probably right. Didn't have a lot of fashion sense back then. I sort of make my own fashion statement now."

I eyed her eclectic look of striped leggings under a short skirt, Converse sneakers, and T-shirt that read "I Love Nerds," and had to agree.

Continuing, she said, "I knew it was you because Trey's mentioned that you've been working on a boat with him, so I knew you were in town. Plus your sister's in here a lot and you look alike."

"We look alike? I don't think anybody's ever said that before."

She shrugged her narrow shoulders. "Yeah, well, I notice things about people that most don't. Looking like somebody doesn't always have to be about hair color and eye color."

"No," I said, admiring her astute observations. "It really doesn't, does it?" I looked at her carefully. "So what about you? I figure you have to be about seventeen now, right? Any plans for after graduation?"

"Well, I've got another year of high school, but my mom's taking me college shopping over spring break to check out a few schools. I'm looking to major in English/creative writing and journalism."

"College, huh?"

"Yeah. I'll be the first in my family."

"That's great, Tally. To know what you want to do is really great."

Her dark eyes bored steadily into mine, reminding me again of her brother. "Trey said that you used to want to win the America's Cup. But you're a teacher now. How long did it take you to figure that out?"

I thought for a moment. "Sometimes things figure themselves out for you. I guess you can say that's what happened to me."

"It's not too late, you know. To win the America's Cup."

I looked into her young, innocent face, trying to remember when I used to be the same way but found that I couldn't. Too much had happened to me since then, too much experience and living had obscured my vision of the old dreams. But, I was beginning to realize, what was left wasn't all that bad or even regretful. I loved teaching; it made me humble and great all at the same time, as changing a child's life can do to a person. And I had even begun to believe that had I lived my life at the helm of a sailboat, getting better and better at cheating the wind, I might never have truly discovered that.

"I know," I said, "but I can't say that's what I really want anymore."

She nodded, then held up her hand. "Before I forget, I want to give you your sister's purse. She left it last time she was here. She hasn't called for it yet, but I figure it's only a matter of time before she realizes where she left it."

"Oh, thanks," I said, curious as to when Diana had been to town last without either Quinn or me knowing. I wondered why she hadn't just asked me to stop by the library on our way back from the nursing home.

"Here it is," said Tally, handing over Diana's large canvas tote, which doubled as her handbag. "She checked out a book, too, so I just stuck it inside. I hope that's all right."

"Of course. And thank you—I know Diana will appreciate it."

"No problem. Glad I could help."

"And good luck with school. Try to take it easy—it can be a little overwhelming."

"Too late," she said, placing an iPod earbud in her left ear. "I'm president of the Latin club and have a few speech competitions coming up with the National Forensics League, as well as trying to complete my Girl Scout Gold Award before graduation." She smiled brightly. "I'm too busy to be overwhelmed."

I laughed and we said our goodbyes. After checking out a thick DeMille hardcover, I left. I still had another twenty minutes to spare, so I took my time walking down the tree-lined streets of McClellanville, admiring the beautiful old wood-framed houses and the long arms of the live oaks with their shawls of Spanish moss, which almost made me forget the arid desert of my adopted home. I must have been looking up to admire one of the trees, because I didn't see the large exposed root that protruded from the cracks in the sidewalk. I stumbled and went sprawling, my book and Diana's purse flying in opposite directions. I hoped against all odds that nobody had seen me.

My knee stung where I had scraped it against the ground, and my hands were covered in dirt and scratches where I'd tried to break my fall. But other than a bit of bruised pride, I seemed to be okay. After brushing the dirt off my hands as best as I could, I gathered my library book, then grabbed hold of one of Diana's purse handles and lifted it up. Unfortunately, during its flight the contents had shifted and the book that Tally had so thoughtfully placed inside fell out, accompanied by several sheets of heavy white paper, which had been folded in half.

I picked up the book, and caught a glance at the title: *Post-Traumatic Stress and Repressed Memories: Rediscovering Your Hidden Past.* My hand froze on the book, and I had to resist the impulse to open it up to see if Diana had highlighted anything or folded down the corners of pages. Her purse had always been like her teenage diary, completely off limits, where not even a sister would dare venture. Although technically Diana hadn't placed the book inside, I knew that if she'd wanted me to see it, she would have had me stop off at the library on our way home the previous day.

Before I could change my mind, I hastily shoved the book into her purse, then bent to retrieve the folded papers. In the fall from the purse and the slight November breeze, the pages had opened at the crease, so when I picked them up, the top page was staring up at me.

I could tell by the torn edge at the top of the pages that they had been taken from Gil's sketch pad, but I would have known it was his work even without that clue. The penciled drawing was of a sailboat so completely lifelike and detailed that I wondered if he had sketched it from memory or had made a trip back to town to sit and sketch the *Highfalutin*. Even without the name written in dark lead on the page, I would have known it to be the boat we'd been working on for months, complete with full mast and functioning rudder.

Curious, I flipped to the next page. Again, this was a sketch of Quinn's sailboat, but this was a closer view of the deck and of two people on board. It was definitely Gil and Diana; their likenesses were almost uncanny in the gray-and-white drawing. They were both smiling and leaning back against the starboard side of the boat as the depiction of the full sails and frothing water gave the impression of movement.

Without any compunction now, I flipped to the third drawing, my hand held suspended in midair. This drawing was almost identical to the one before it, except in this one the sky had darkened and the waves were higher, lashing up over the deck. The two people were in the same position, but Gil was looking skyward and Diana was looking at Gil. Neither was smiling.

Almost with dread, I flipped the last one to the top of the small pile, barely aware of my library book and Diana's purse sliding to the ground at my feet. This drawing was of the same view as the one before except now the sky was completely dark and the wind had gone out of the sails. Tall waves surrounded the boat in a dangerous game of monkey-in-the-middle. But the most arresting thing about this final drawing was that there were now three figures on the deck: the first two identifiable again as Diana and Gil. The third person, however, was harder to discern: neither male nor female, the hair covered by a fisherman's knit hat and the face turned toward Diana and away from the viewer. Diana's expression was blank, but from the raised hand of the third figure, it was obvious that Diana was receiving some sort of instruction.

I stared at it for a long time, trying to make sense of it. Then I slowly returned it to the bottom of the stack. When I did so, a smaller piece of paper fluttered to the ground. I retrieved it and saw from the jagged top that it had been from another page of Gil's sketch pad, but it had been ripped in half with only the top of the mainsail and its rigging visible. I flipped through the pages again to see if I had misplaced the fifth and final drawing, but there was nothing more.

Unsettled, I folded the pages again and stuck them in Diana's purse. After retrieving my book, I continued walking toward Quinn's veterinary practice, not even aware of the scenery anymore. My mind kept going back and forth from Diana's library book to the drawings. Why would she want a book on repressed memories? It was obvious to me from the drawings that Gil had no such affliction. I was on the front walk in front of Quinn's building before it occurred to me that maybe it wasn't Gil's memories that were concerning Diana; maybe it was somebody else's entirely.

I walked thoughtfully up the steps to the front door, letting myself in and allowing the door to swing shut behind me.

CHAPTER 22

Once more
Upon the waters!
Yet once more!
And the waves
Bound beneath me
As a steed that
Knows his rider.
—Lord Byron

Diana

It was barely past dawn when Marnie tapped on my studio door. I'd been awake all night again painting, but I'd made sure to pull on fresh clothes to hide this fact from my sister. I'm sure that Quinn had already schooled her in the signs and symptoms to look for in another "episode," as he liked to call them, and I didn't want to set off any alarm bells. That's not to say that I didn't sense something brewing inside of me; I'd become something of a barometer, sensing things in the atmosphere that others couldn't. But this time it was different. I wasn't sensing changes inside me; I was sensing changes in those around me, and I wasn't sure if I should be so content to be left behind.

"Come in," I called, and Marnie entered the studio. She had changed in her months here. Her movements were more fluid and less planned; her clothing choices came from my bag of discarded clothes that were now too big for me, instead of from her own closet. More skin and less teacher is how I described it to myself. I would never say that out loud to her, as it would send her right back into her baggy denim dresses. Secretly, I admired her adaptation to the landscape; she was a Lowcountry girl again, the girl from the paintings whose absence had deprived me of half my soul.

She held up a breakfast tray, and from one wrist dangled my straw purse. I looked at it with alarm.

She placed the tray on a table and then held the purse out to me. "Tally Deushane gave it to me to give to you. She said you left it at the library."

I looked back at my easel, trying not to show either the relief or the anxiety that was currently flooding my bloodstream. "Thanks," I said, keeping my voice calm. "Just dump it on the chair over there. Then come here and sit down. I wanted you here early to catch this light, so hurry up before we lose it. I'm not hungry, so you wasted your time bringing a tray."

Without saying anything, she did as I asked, then sat on the stool I had placed by the window, the buttery light of early morning bathing her hair and skin in its glow. I wished she could see herself now, see her the way I saw her. But she had never had the artist's eye, and I'd never felt the need to share it with her. Our mother had seen Marnie this way, too, and I closed my eyes for a moment, not wanting to remember.

Marnie unbuttoned her blouse and took it off before sliding the band out of her ponytail so her hair could fall across her shoulders. I started to relax, thinking she wasn't going to say anything, so when she did speak, it startled me.

"When did you go to the library, Diana? You had your purse with you when we went to visit your friend."

I decided not to lie, although I didn't think she needed to know the whole truth, either. "Last night. I realized after we got home that I forgot to stop at the library to pick up a book that had come in for me. I didn't want to bother you, so I just went by myself."

"You know you're not supposed to do that." She shook her head, then looked back at the chair where she'd dumped my straw bag. "I got the book for you. Tally said you'd checked it out already, so she stuck it in your purse."

I didn't say anything as I carefully studied her face, trying to read her. For the first time in my life, I couldn't read every thought on her face. "Thank you," I said hesitantly.

She looked out the window to where the moon could still be seen in the flaming morning sky. "I'm just curious as to why you would read such a book. Do you think Gil has any repressed memories of his accident?"

I paused with my paintbrush held expectantly over the canvas. "I'm willing to look at anything, really. Anything that might give me a clue as to why he won't speak."

She was silent for several minutes and I was hoping that she'd finished talking.

"Maybe I can read it when you're done with it. Since I've come back here, I've found that I'm recalling things that I never remembered before." She faced me, her eyes alight. "Like when we saw Saint Elmo's fire the night of our accident. I'd completely forgotten about it until . . ." She looked down at her hands, and I saw the telltale blush on her cheeks.

"Until what?" I asked, remembering how I'd seen her and Quinn walk down to the beach together.

She shook her head. "Until recently. And other little things, too."

My hand remained frozen, suspended over the canvas. "Like what?"

"Like how all three of us were in the water, not just me. I remembered being hit in the back by the boom and landing in the water, but I couldn't understand how you and Mama got there, too, when the boat hadn't yet capsized."

I shrugged. "There was so much happening. I think I must have seen you go over and jumped in to help you. But I was never as good of a swimmer as you. Mama must have jumped in to save us both."

Marnie continued to stare out the window as the light drifted over the marsh and up to the house, painting the winter with a brush of spring. But none of the sun's warmth was able to reach the chill that had somehow taken hold of me.

She faced me. "But the one thing that I can't make myself remember is what happened when Mama reached me. I think I remember, but I just . . . I just can't accept it as the truth."

I gave up any pretense of painting and placed my brush in the cup. "What *do* you remember?"

Her eyes had the same haunted look they'd had after the accident and until the day she'd moved away. I had hoped it was gone forever.

"I remember"—her eyes met mine and I couldn't look away—"I remember Mama pushing me away and then swimming toward you."

For a long moment I couldn't speak, the long years of unspoken words somehow jumbled together in my throat. "I'm sure you're mistaken. Maybe she went to grab for you and missed, and the waves just pushed her to me. Remember," I said, looking down at my paints, "she was the one who drowned. Not us."

"So why have you been blaming me all these years for her death?"

The ice crackled around my heart. "What? Why would you say that?"

"Ever since we got out of the hospital and moved in here with Grandpa, you've hated me, as if I had been the one who killed Mama."

I wanted to throw my head back and shout with laughter, but I was too stunned to do either. "She drowned, Marnie. Neither one of us killed her."

"Then why did you change? Why couldn't you stand to be in the same room with me after the accident? What had I done to make you so angry with me?"

I slowly mixed my paints again on my pallet to keep my hands busy and stop them from shaking. "I think that almost dying can change a person. Maybe I was angry because it didn't seem to change you at all."

"But it did," she said softly. "I lost a lot that night. I can't even say that losing our mother was the worst of it—we both know she wasn't the best mother, although I think in her way that she loved us." She closed her eyes and sighed. "But I'd also lost the two things that I had loved the most: my passion for sailing"—her eyelids flew open—"and you. I lost you that night, too. I found that to lose the thing that matters the most is like a kind of death. I think that's why I moved to the desert, where everything appears dead or dying. It suited my soul for a long time."

"But not anymore?" I asked through frozen lips.

She didn't answer my question. Instead, her eyes flickered down to my leg, where the bandage was still visible beneath the hem of my shorts. "Why do you still wear that? If your wound hasn't healed by now, you should be seeing a doctor about it."

"Please don't concern yourself with things that have nothing to do with you, okay, Marnie? I never asked for your help before, and I don't need it now, either. Just stay out of my life, okay?"

I flinched at my own words, but Marnie just sat there, regarding me solemnly. I knew she wouldn't ask me any more questions, at least for now. She'd always been the patient one, biding her time until she knew she could get what she was after.

A small smile tweaked her lips, surprising us both. "Too late, Diana. I'm your sister."

The dark pall in the room seemed to have dissipated with the morning fog, and I found myself answering with a smile of my own as I turned back to the canvas. "That you are," I said as I lifted my paintbrush and began to paint.

I painted in silence for almost half an hour before Marnie spoke again.

"You're almost done with your mural."

I glanced up at the painted time line at the top of the walls, to where I had reached our grandparents' generation. I had just started the painting of our grandmother, the one whose automobile accident was still considered a suicide by some, and had begun my outlines of our mother, Marnie, and me. On the fourth wall, all by himself, I'd left Gil's space with only his face sketched in and his birth date.

"Why are we up there?" she asked, annoying me by getting off her stool.

I dropped my brush in the cup, the dirty water splattering my shirt. "We're Maitlands, aren't we?"

"Yes, but we're not cursed. We're survivors, remember? And so is Gil."

She seemed genuinely upset, so I searched for something to say to calm her down. "Why should it matter to you? You don't believe in the curse anyway."

"No, I don't. But this is just too morbid, seeing my name up on the wall with the dead."

"I'll paint you smiling then, okay?"

"I'm serious, Diana."

"Me, too. Look, this is my studio and my art project. Please keep your comments about my paintings to yourself."

She sat down again, her shoulders rounded in defeat. She was usually such an easy person to read, my Marnie, that I almost felt as if I were cheating whenever we argued. Almost.

I began drying my brush on an old towel, squeezing out the water and feeling it soak through to my shaking fingers. "I need you to take me in to Charleston again. Gil needs new clothes. And I was hoping afterward we could stop at the nursing home."

"So soon? But we were just there."

"I know, and I wouldn't bother you if I didn't have to. It's just that my friend has become obsessed with this curse thing, and I'm eager for her to get to know Gil so that she can see that he's more Bristow than Maitland, that he's nothing like me at all."

"But why should it matter, Diana?"

I couldn't meet her eyes. Staring down at the murky water in the cup, I said, "I don't know, but it just does. And it's not harming him, you know. Spending time with me is a good thing, and he enjoyed himself when we went before. He enjoyed being with me. And I think he got a kick out of listening to somebody he's not related to praising his artwork."

I knew she wouldn't argue with that; I'd seen it in her face and secretly congratulated myself on hitting the bull's-eye.

"Fine," she said, pulling on her blouse and beginning to button it. She yawned. "And maybe you can tell me why on earth you had me come here so danged early."

"Because you're going sailing today."

She looked at me with alarm.

"And in case you didn't return, I wanted to make sure I had the chance to paint you one last time."

She skipped the last of her buttons and strode quickly to the door. "Go to hell," she said before she slammed the door behind her.

"I'm already there," I said quietly to the closed door.

I waited for a long moment before walking over to my purse. I pulled the book out and looked inside, seeing what I was searching for. I slid out the folded sketchbook pages and flattened them out. I knew she'd seen them; I could tell by the way her eyes kept darting back to the purse when we were talking about the book. But she hadn't said anything.

I went to the armoire and unlocked the door, then slid out my "precious things" box. I lifted the lid and placed Gil's drawings on top, then closed and locked the door again, hiding the key this time and hoping nobody else would ever see them.

✺

Marnie

Quinn was already waiting for me on the back porch by the time I came downstairs. I wore sweat pants and a sweatshirt, a Windbreaker, and boat shoes—all new. I was grateful that Quinn didn't even suggest that I dig around in the closets of the old house, as aware as I was of the old ghosts that I might find.

My Windbreaker rustled as I slowly made my way down the stairs, a sound I had once loved, as I'd contemplated how lucky I was to live in South Carolina, where such a thing as all-year sailing existed. As unpredictable as our winter weather was, it was currently a balmy sixty degrees outside, although I was chilled to the bone, as if it were cold enough to turn the ocean to ice.

I stopped short when I spied my grandfather in his wheelchair by the door. I heard Joanna bustling around in the kitchen, explaining how he'd come down the stairs. I kissed him on the cheek, his bristled jaw and warm breath doing nothing to thaw me. "Good morning. What are you doing up so early?"

As I'd expected, he thrust his Bible up to me, his gnarled finger pointing at a highlighted passage. I read it aloud. " 'Therefore snares are round about thee, and sudden fear troubleth thee; Or darkness, that thou canst not see; and abundance of waters cover thee.' "

I read it again to myself, trying to understand what he was attempting to tell me. I had a sudden recollection of him sliding the newspaper classifieds toward me one morning at breakfast a few months before I turned sixteen. I'd been horrified to see that they were of boats for sale. He'd explained that it was within his means to either get me a used car or a used boat for my birthday and that he'd leave the choice up to me. I'd picked the car without hesitation, and it was that same car that had driven me out of McClellanville for the last time two years later. But I'd never forgotten the look of disappointment in his eyes when he'd handed me the car keys.

"What are you trying to tell me, Grandpa?"

He looked at me with his pale blue eyes reflecting the light from the front window. He grunted and motioned me with his hands to come closer. I did as he asked and felt him grip my hands tightly as he grunted again. I closed my eyes, feeling the sting of the tears behind the lids. "I am afraid. I am so afraid."

He nodded, then let go of my hands while he quickly turned the tissuelike pages of the old Bible, finally coming to rest on a passage and thrusting it up into my hands again. I smiled softly as I read the old words that I had learned by heart as a young girl. " 'But whoso hearkeneth unto me shall dwell safely, and shall be quiet from fear of evil.' "

I wiped my eyes with the back of my hand. Quietly I said, "It's not evil I fear, Grandpa. It's the water. It's the things I'm afraid it'll make me remember."

He did the oddest thing then; he pulled me down by the hands again until his mouth was by my ear, and he grunted a word that sounded very much like "good." Then he let go of my hands and turned away, like he used to do when Diana and I fought and he refused to take sides. Except this time I wasn't sure who I was supposed to be fighting.

I said goodbye and left, relieved to find Quinn on the other side of the door. "Are you ready?" he asked, his blue eyes sparkling in the morning sun.

"I'm here," I replied. "I'm not sure if I'm ready, but I'm here."

He surprised me by taking hold of my chin and kissing me. He tasted of minty toothpaste and crisp morning air, and I didn't want him to stop.

"What was that for?" I asked, more pleased than stunned.

"For you. For being so brave. For facing your fears."

"I'm not doing this for me. I'm doing this for Gil." I blinked into the sun before turning back to him. "And for you."

"For me?"

"You once told me that you were afraid of heights, but I overheard Trey asking you about the parasailing you've been doing with his brother. I think flying over the water with a thin scrap of nylon is a whole lot scarier than sitting on something with sails that floats."

He grinned that grin that had a way of warming me up from the inside out. " 'Something with sails that floats.' That's one way to describe sailing, I guess."

"But why would you go parasailing?"

"Because I had to. I still don't like heights, but at least I know I can do it again if I ever had to."

He led me off the steps and we walked slowly down to the dock. "Gil's waiting for us. He wanted to watch us sail and brought his sketch pad. I told him that if he got bored, Trey would bring him back home."

"Great," I said, catching sight of the small figure at the end of the dock. He turned and looked at me with his mother's eyes, and I stumbled.

Quinn caught my arm. "You all right?"

"Fine," I said, remembering the sketches Gil had given to Diana. I stopped abruptly. "Quinn, was there anybody else on the boat the night that Gil and Diana had their accident?"

He shook his head. "No. And I can say that without any doubt, because there were eyewitnesses of them getting into the boat, and it was definitely just the two of them."

We resumed walking as I kept my eye on Gil, who looked up at us and smiled when we approached. He was so different from the skittish boy I'd first met, but I was frustrated at how I'd come no closer to prying loose his secrets and his words.

Quinn got in first, then helped us both into the small boat. We were quiet in the morning chill as Quinn started the engine and pushed us away from the dock. I was silent as we skirted the deeper water, and it wasn't until I felt a tug on my sleeve that I realized what it was I'd been searching for.

Gil pointed off the starboard side at the two telltale fins that sluiced through the murky water. I felt relief, somehow. "Don't dolphins migrate?"

Quinn shrugged. "Not like whales, no. But they usually leave in the fall to follow their food source. Maybe these two stayed just for you." He flashed me a grin.

The dolphins danced around each other in the water, as if their ties to this lush place were too strong, the pull of home somehow keeping them grounded here like a compass that had found true north.

They skittered away with a splash of water and then were gone, seeking deeper waters. I felt strangely comforted by their presence, and I found myself softly thawing.

Trey met us at the marina, smiling broadly and not looking the least bit worried that he was about to send his boat out with a woman who hadn't sailed in almost sixteen years and a man whose boat he was currently repairing. *You once told me that sailing was like tricking the wind to move your boat.* Remembering his words made me smile, and he looked at me curiously.

"You must be excited," he said as we drew up to the dock.

With Gil present, I had to watch my words and hold back what I really wanted to say. "Those wouldn't be my exact words, no."

He helped Gil out of the boat and onto the dock, then got in the boat with us. "I'll take you over to the *Pelorus* and pick you up when you're done."

I followed his gaze to a twenty-two-foot Catalina moored about fifty yards away. "You named your boat the *Pelorus?*"

"Sure did. Remember that story you used to tell about that dolphin? I thought he was a smart and strong enough dolphin to name my boat after."

I nodded, feeling strangely assured. Then I focused my attention on Gil. "You can come with us if you want, you know. There's room in the cabin if you'd rather not be up on deck with your dad and me." I wasn't sure why I had made the offer, knowing there would be Diana to deal with if Gil said yes. But I thought facing her anger would be a small price to pay if it meant Gil would speak again.

Gil regarded me with large, knowing eyes, and it was almost as if I'd heard him say, *You first.*

"All right," I said, rubbing his head. "Today it's my turn, but the next time is yours." The jon boat pulled away from the dock, and I felt my heart sink low in my chest. "Bye," I shouted with a lot more enthusiasm than I felt.

Gil seemed so small all by himself on the dock, but before I could ask Quinn to turn back, I saw Gil flip his thumb upward, and I smiled, relaxing into the wind.

Trey drew alongside the *Pelorus.* "You ready?"

"Are *you* ready?" I asked, trying to sound flippant but not quite hiding the panic in my voice. "We're taking your boat, remember?"

"No worries in the world," he said as he offered me his hand as I stood up and reached for the shrouds at the beam. Without thinking, I pulled myself aboard and stepped down into the cockpit, then looked for Quinn.

Trey pulled away. "All the gear's already been stowed on board—your life vests, the emergency kit, and some drinks in the cooler—so you're all set. No outboard motor on this boat, so you'll have to use your sailing skills right off the bat to get her from her mooring and out onto the ICW. I'll keep an eye on Gil. Y'all have fun, and I'll be ready to come out and get you when you return."

Quinn gave Trey a mock salute, then climbed aboard to stand next to me. "How are you doing?" he asked, and I knew in that moment that if I asked to go back he would take me. But I thought of Gil's hopeful face and Quinn deciding to go parasailing, and I couldn't ask him. My ghosts were close now. The only way I could face them would be out on the open water, where they waited for me. I thought of Diana, too, how she didn't want me to do this although she hadn't told me. We were sisters, after all, and she didn't need to tell me in words. But her reluctance made me all the more determined to end my struggle with pain and grief and memories.

You once told me that sailing was like tricking the wind to move your boat. I smiled again, remembering Trey's words. "I'm fine," I said, meaning it more than I expected.

I looked around to inspect the boat for the first time. Trey had removed the sail cover, hanked on the jib, and attached the sheets and halyards so that the sails impatiently waited in the breeze, begging to be hoisted. I began to feel the familiar thrumming in my veins as I turned my face into the wind, the best indicator of wind direction despite the yarn telltales on the shrouds. My body took over from my brain, my limbs seeming to move from memory as I settled myself next to the tiller, preparing to move us away from the docks into Jeremy Creek, then to the Intracoastal before finally heading out into open water.

My fear seemed lost in the cool breeze as I began to hoist the mainsail, pulling on the halyard as hard as I could until the sail was as high as possible, then made the halyard fast to its cleat, relishing the familiar slip and groove of the lines through my fingers. Then I moved to the jib sail and hoisted away until it was absolutely straight, with no scallops between the hanks as my mother had shown me to do a million years ago. Satisfied, I made the halyard fast to its cleat and stowed it neatly. Checking to make sure the centerboard was down and the sails luffing freely, I gave Quinn the signal that it was time to slip the mooring pendant.

I pulled the jib sheet tight to force the bow away from the mooring as Quinn moved forward and released the line. When the boat fell about forty-five degrees off the wind, I trimmed the mainsail to stop the boat from turning and to begin our movement forward. I felt the pull of the wind as the sails filled like pregnant bellies while the liquid movement beneath my feet reminded me again of the memory of water. I turned my face into the wind once more and heard a yelp of glee, surprised to find that it had come from my own mouth.

Gripping the side rail, I watched as Quinn walked down the windward side of the deck to join me in the cockpit. I felt the saltwater spray on my face and opened my mouth to shout again. My eyes met Quinn's, and he gave me a quick nod, making my chest tighten in unfamiliar ways. *He understands,* I thought, thinking that I knew, too, why he had gone parasailing after he had once been trapped high up in a tree while his brother's body lay beneath it. I did shout then, cutting loose the power the grief had held over me and letting it go into the oceanborne wind. I wasn't cured; my fears still waited in my pockets until I rediscovered them after a season of forgetting. But at last I knew as the wind caught my hair and teased my face, I had finally found my way home.

CHAPTER 23

The sail, the play of its pulse so like our own lives: so thin and yet so full of life, so noiseless when it labors hardest, so noisy and impatient when least effective.

—Henry David Thoreau

Quinn

I took a weeklong class trip to Italy once when I was a senior in high school. In Florence, we'd gone to the Uffizzi Museum, where they had a special Leonardo da Vinci exhibit showing the inventor's greatest achievements in science, aviation, and art. Splattered among the exhibits were quotes from da Vinci, the one I remember most being something about finding the one thing in life that made your soul sing. And when I saw Marnie Maitland on the open water in a sailboat, I knew that she, at least, had found it.

We stayed on the water for almost two hours, skirting the coast and never straying too far from the shore. Except for commands to adjust our sails as our course changed, we didn't exchange words during the entire time. There was no need. Her hands and feet were her language as she moved about the boat, trimming the mainsail and commanding the wind. We spent the first twenty minutes or so becoming accustomed to the *Pelorus*, testing the fine line between the boat's heel and her sail performance. As Marnie became more comfortable, we began sailing closer and closer to the wind, while I went along for the ride, trimming the jib and hanging on tightly as the boat heeled dangerously close to capsizing. Watching her, I finally began to understand why Trey Bonner had called her wild, and I began to recognize the woman I had once seen all those years ago and with whom I had fallen inexplicably in love.

Marnie put the boat through its paces as she sailed in various directions, finally setting the course with the wind behind us to minimize the wind chill on our faces. She seemed to be lost in a different world in a different time as we sailed along in silence for almost an hour.

My nose had become numb from the November wind, and I was about to suggest that we return to the dock when I caught a look on Marnie's face. At first I thought she'd seen something in the water—something she didn't want to. I knew her attention had strayed when the leech began to oscillate and the boom lifted, both signs of sailing too close to an accidental jibe and a sure way to damage the rigging or be knocked overboard by a wayward boom. I was alarmed because I spotted it before her. Her eyes were focused behind her, but not seeing, and when I called her name, she didn't respond. It was only when the jib flopped over that she sprang into action, steering the boat out of danger as smooth as the incoming tide. But I'd seen the expression on her face and wondered if finally, after all of her running from the water, her memories had finally caught up to her.

"Are you ready to go back?"

She nodded, concentrating on the sails again, but her movements had become rote and she'd begun to sneak glances toward land.

With teamwork, we efficiently maneuvered the boat back to its mooring and lowered the sails as we waited for Trey to come out and pick us up. I'd expected Gil to come with him, but my son remained on the dock as if he, too, had sensed something from Marnie. I looked at her again and felt suddenly as if I'd been in an elevator that had dropped several stories before abruptly stopping.

I helped her into the jon boat and felt her fingers trembling in my hand before she let go and reached for Trey's outstretched hand. I climbed in after her and sat on the front bench seat.

"How'd it go?" asked Trey, unaware of the undercurrents that seemed heavy enough to swamp the small boat.

"It was wonderful," I said, sensing Marnie nodding in agreement.

"Did you get to practice a few tight maneuvers?"

She shot a quick glance at me. "The wind was perfect for a little running. Thank you for letting us borrow your *Pelorus*. She's a great little boat."

Her words were so flat and so inadequate to describe what I had just witnessed that I wondered if she'd seen something in the water, after all.

"You're welcome—anytime," he said, a puzzled frown creasing his forehead.

We reached the dock, and a waiting Gil and his wide smile faded as he caught sight of Marnie. Quickly flipping his sketch pad closed, he traded places with Trey in the jon boat.

Trey gave him a high-five as they passed. "It was fun hanging out with you, Gil. Hope your dad and your aunt don't have to deal with the sugar rush after what you had for lunch."

Even that remark didn't elicit much of a smile from Marnie. We said our thanks and goodbyes, then pulled off from the dock toward home.

Unwilling to ask Marnie about her sudden change of mood in front of Gil, I instead focused on my son.

"You should have seen your aunt Marnie, Gil. She may be small, but she's a great sailor."

Gil smiled brightly.

"Did it make you want to go out on the water again?" I asked.

He glanced over at Marnie and she smiled at him. "I won't lie to you, Gil. I was about as nervous as a turtle in a horse race when I got on that boat. But sailing keeps you so busy that it's easy to forget about everything else in your head. By the time we were out there and zipping along, you know what I felt like?"

Both Gil and I focused our undivided attention on her. She looked up at the sky as if seeking help in finding words that eluded her. "It was like finding an old friend I'd been looking for, for a long, long time."

Gil continued to regard her solemnly, as if he, too, couldn't believe the inadequacy of her words, because he'd been there and knew what it was like to feel the wind in your hair and on your face. He knew. Sailing was what made Marnie's soul sing.

"She's almost as good as you, huh?"

Gil looked at me with laughter in his eyes and shook his head.

"I don't know about that. I think you could certainly give her a run for her money." I turned to focus on the marsh, pretending to study the fauna as I navigated the small boat. "The Rockville Regatta is coming up in the spring, you know. It's not a qualifying race or anything, but they have family races where crews of all ages can race. I thought it might be something fun for the three of us to enter."

I felt the stony silence behind me and didn't turn around.

Finally Marnie, her voice sounding as if it had been brushed over sand said, "That's a great idea, Quinn. But I've never seen Gil sail. I just don't know if he'd be good enough to crew with me."

"That's a real good point, Marnie. I guess you couldn't just take my word that he's an excellent sailor and would be a superb addition to our crew."

"No," she said, her voice still dry and strained. "I'd really need to see all crew members in action before hiring them on. I've seen you now, so I'd say you can join. But I don't know about a third member. . . ."

Gil slapped my leg, and I turned to him, pretending to be startled. "What, Gil? You want to give it a try on Mr. Bonner's boat?"

He hesitated for a long moment. He glanced at Marnie, but her face remained neutral, as if she knew that Gil's decision had to come from him without coercion from anybody else. Her eyes met mine above his head and my chest tightened.

Slowly, Gil nodded.

"So that's a yes?"

Gil nodded again, this time without hesitation.

"Great. That's good news. I'll call Mr. Bonner tomorrow and see if he'll let us borrow his boat again. It'll be fun." And, I added to myself, I'd have to talk to Diana again. I didn't relish that conversation at all.

I looked at Marnie and Gil and almost wanted to laugh at how their dark expressions didn't really translate into fun. I turned toward the marsh once more, recalling Marnie's face the way it had been when we'd first set sail, determined now to see it again. "It'll be fun," I said again, more to convince myself than anybody else.

When we reached our dock, I helped Gil and Marnie out of the boat, and then Marnie and I fell into step behind Gil. When we got close enough to the house to see the porch, Gil spotted his great-grandfather bundled up in a rocker and ran ahead of us. I slowed my pace to match Marnie's.

"Thank you for today, Quinn. I never thought I'd do that again. I never thought that I'd *want* to do it again."

I regarded her closely. "But what happened out there? You were so happy, and then all of a sudden, you couldn't wait to get to dry land again."

She looked at me sharply. "There's not a lot you miss, is there?"

"No, not really." I tried to lighten the tone but she didn't smile. "Did you remember something? For a moment out there, I thought you'd seen a ghost."

Her face blanched. "Maybe I did." She shook her head and smiled tightly. "Actually, I just didn't want to keep Gil waiting much longer." She stopped walking and faced me. "But thank you, Quinn. It *was* marvelous. It's just going to take more than one afternoon, that's all."

"I never thought it wouldn't. Even I signed up for three parasailing lessons, after all. Doing just the one sounded a little conceited on my part." I reached for her hands and they felt cold. "I want you to go again as soon as possible. When I take Gil out, I want you to go with us."

"That will be too soon. . . ."

I pulled her a little closer. "I don't think it will be soon enough. I finally saw the real Marnie out there. She was strong and brave and a damn fine sailor. Maybe if you told me what it is that's bothering you . . ."

She pulled away and began walking ahead of me. "I told you it was nothing—just nerves, maybe. I'll let you know if I'll be ready to go again with Gil, assuming Diana ever says yes."

I caught up to her and matched my stride to hers, but remained silent as I listened to the pine needles crunching under our feet, and smelled their soft aroma that always reminded me of Christmas.

"Diana wanted to go to the nursing home again today with Gil and me. I said I'd ask you."

"But she was just there a few days ago."

"I know, but apparently her friend is obsessed with the Maitland curse—I guess Diana's been filling her head with stories for months now. But now Diana is almost as obsessed with demonstrating how different Gil is from her and the rest of the Maitlands. It's like she wants to prove that the curse ended with Gil, that he's mostly Bristow, I guess, and unable to pass it on to his offspring."

"I've never understood this whole curse thing. When Diana's healthy, she has always been pretty rational in her thinking except where this silly curse is involved."

"It's not her fault, really. Our mother pretty much drummed it into us from the moment we could talk, although it was mostly aimed at Diana."

"Really? Why was that?"

Marnie shrugged. "I figured because Mama always called her more Maitland than me. She had the blond hair and the artistic talent to go with it, so I guess it made sense." She was silent for a moment. "I was so jealous of her. Knowing what I know now, it was petty and stupid, but for a young girl, it was devastating to be so different from your mother in every way that you wanted to be like her. And then having a sister who was everything you weren't." She smiled to herself but didn't say anything.

"What?" I prompted.

She paused for a moment. "Mama once told me to be careful what I wished for. I was never really sure what she meant."

We had reached the back porch, which had recently been vacated by Gil and his great-grandfather, the chairs swaying gently as a reminder of their recent occupation.

I stood on the bottom step. "Did it ever occur to you when you were a girl that it was the other way around for Diana?"

Her eyebrows pulled together. "What do you mean?"

"That it was she who envied you."

"But that's silly. I didn't have anything to be envied."

I stepped onto the porch so that I stood in front of her. "No. Just everything that Diana didn't have. Like your mother's unconditional love."

Marnie shook her head. "Diana had that more than anything."

"Actually, from what I've learned from Diana and from you, it would seem that your mother's love was very conditional with Diana. She had to be a better artist. She had to ignore her illness and pretend it didn't exist. But you were free to be you, to strike out in any direction you wanted to, and you did. That is the one thing Diana never did have. And I think that was what she always wanted the most."

Marnie looked up into the winter sky, the sun's glare making her eyes seem transparent. "I've never seen it that way before." Her voice sounded far away. "Today, when we were on the boat . . ." She faced me, her eyes haunted.

"What, Marnie? What did you see?"

She shook her head. "I'm . . . I'm not sure. I just think that I'm finally beginning to understand what my mother meant when she told me to be careful what I wished for."

I watched as her eyes clouded over before she pressed the pads of her fingers against her eyelids. I wanted to hold her, but stayed where I was. She was strong enough to face her own demons, and we both knew it. I just hoped that she knew that I would be here waiting for her when she was ready. "What is it?" I asked again.

She didn't answer right away, but turned to the door and opened it. With her back to me, she said, "Call Trey right away and see how soon we can get the boat again. I'll be there with Gil."

She let the door shut behind her as she walked back to me, put her hands on my shoulders, and kissed me. "Thank you," she said, her eyes serious and her lips roughened by the wind.

"You're welcome," I said to her retreating back, unsure what I'd done to deserve her thanks, but hoping I could figure it out so I could do it again soon.

Marnie

I sat in the driver's seat, my gaze switching from Diana's tight-lipped form beside me to Gil's white face in the back. We'd been at the nursing home for two hours, long enough for me to have fallen asleep on the couch in the reception room. I came awake seeing Gil's wide-eyed face hovering over me and hearing Diana's agitated voice in the hallway. When I looked through the doorway, I saw Diana approaching with a nurse.

"We need to go now." Both Diana and the nurse were unsmiling.

I sat up suddenly, my head spinning. "Is everything all right?"

"Just fine. Let's go." She faced the nurse. "Tell her . . . tell her I'm not sure when we'll be able to come back."

The nurse's face creased with concern. "You know how much she looks forward to your visits." The nurse glanced at Gil. "And she's especially enjoyed getting to know your son."

"Yes, well . . ." Diana pulled on her gloves. "It's almost Christmas, and it's always crazy busy for me. Let's just wait and see." Diana began walking toward the exit, not even checking behind her to see if Gil and I were following. If I hadn't been so concerned about what had just happened, I would have found it amusing, since I was the one with the car key.

I said goodbye to the nurse, then rushed to follow Diana out to the parking lot.

As we slid into our seats, I asked, "What was that all about?"

She was staring out her window, and I thought for a moment that she wasn't going to answer. Finally she said, "Sailing." She didn't look at me, but I saw her cheek muscles move in either a smile or a frown. "Damn. I wish I had a cigarette." She glanced in the rearview mirror to see if Gil had heard her.

"Sailing?"

"Yeah. Seems everybody's got sailing on the brain these days. I happened to mention to her that Quinn wants to take Gil out on the boat again. She went kind of ballistic."

My hand paused on the key in the ignition. "Did she misinterpret something you said?"

"No." Her fingers plucked at the spot on her jeans where I could see the slight bump of her bandage. "She knew exactly what I said."

"But why would that make your friend upset?"

Diana finally looked at me, in her eyes an odd mixture of anger and fear. And for a moment, I almost thought that her anger was directed at me.

"It's because of the Maitland curse. She takes it very seriously."

I started the engine, ready to dismiss the entire conversation now that it had taken a turn into ridiculousness. "But we don't, so it doesn't really matter, right?"

She didn't answer, so I turned to her, aware of how pale her skin had become.

"Right?" I repeated.

"Maybe it *is* real, Marnie. Did you ever think of that? You've seen the wall mural—how can all that happening to one family ever be called coincidence? And Grandpa's been preaching for years that the sins of the father will haunt his children and his children's children for generations."

"Diana, you're starting to scare me." I pulled the car over to a parking spot near the exit. "Firstly, our family is nobody else's damn business, okay? Secondly, Grandpa has also always preached that God gave us free will. What you and I decide to do with our lives is completely up to us. We're not governed by anything as arbitrary as a curse, assuming such a thing existed. All right?"

Her fingers continued to pluck at her jeans. "I don't want Gil to get on a sailboat. Not ever."

I looked in the rearview mirror, recalling that Gil was in the car with us and listening to every word.

"He loves it, Diana. Quinn said that Gil loved sailing more than his art. And that's saying a lot. Don't take that from him because of what some old lady seems to think about a nonexistent curse. It has nothing to do with Gil—or with you or me. But it has everything to do with your son and helping him find his voice again."

She swiped the back of her hands across her eyes. "I'm his mother, and I don't want him on a sailboat, and that's it. It's for his own good."

I looked in the rearview mirror and saw Gil staring out the side window, his profile mirroring the stubborn set of his mother's, and I almost smiled. I started the engine again. "I'll let you discuss it with Quinn. Let's go home now."

"No. Let's drive into downtown. I've got some Christmas shopping I might as well do while we're here."

I stared at her for a moment, wondering how such a rational comment could follow so closely any talk about family curses. "Fine," I said, putting the car into gear. I recalled the memory I'd had while out on the *Pelorus* with Quinn and the questions I had for Diana that I hadn't been able to bring myself to ask. I glanced back at Gil again and knew that whatever I needed to know about the night my mother died would have to wait.

❧

Gil

When I was very young, when my parents were still married and my great-grandfather wasn't in a wheelchair all the time, everybody was careful about keeping me away from the water. But it seemed to me, even back then, that I was meant to be in the water. There was something about it that made me think of being rocked by my mother, the sound of the waves like a lullaby I remembered from when I was too small to remember anything else except the sound of my mother's voice.

Then my father began taking me sailing with him, and it was like that book about these kids who find a whole different world in a wardrobe. That was what sailing was to me. And all that time I spent on the water I never once remembered that I was supposed to be afraid.

Mama never said it out loud, but I knew that she hated sailing. I knew she could sail since I'd seen all those pictures of her and my aunt Marnie in the photo album under my bed. But she never went sailing with me and my dad, and my dad never asked her, either, like he knew what the answer would be anyway.

That was why when Mama asked me to go sailing with her that night, I didn't think to say no. I'd figured she'd finally decided that I was good enough to go with her, and I decided that I was going to show her how good I really was.

It didn't take me very long to figure out why we were really on that boat at night during a storm, and I knew that it had something to do with that piece of paper she'd found in Grandpa's study. Because it was right after that time in the study when she started looking at me in a different way, like how a mother bird with one worm would look at her nest filled with empty beaks.

That night I learned about making choices, both bad and good. And I learned how hard it is to lose the thing you love the most. But I also learned that sometimes you can find strength where you never thought you had any. That was why when I was listening to Aunt Marnie and Mama arguing in the car that I decided it didn't really matter if they wanted me to go sailing or not. It wasn't about them. It never was. It was about finding my way back to the water, where I had once thought I'd lost everything, but where maybe I needed to go to get it all back.

CHAPTER 24

Marnie

As Christmas approached, the weather grew colder, and there were no more chances to go sailing. But there was a waiting in the air—a suspension of action that seemed to freeze us as much as the cold winds that blew off the Atlantic. Gil, in his wordless and enigmatic way, waited with impatience and trepidation for his turn on the deck of the *Pelorus*. Quinn waited for the restoration of the *Highfalutin* to be completed while also waiting for Diana to allow Gil out on a boat again. His appeals to Diana were subtle but unsuccessful. I wondered why he waited for her approval, but knew in the end that it was because he was Quinn; he would never risk damaging his relationship with Diana or with his son. I suppose this was because of his relationship with his parents, honed from loss and profound grief over his brother's death, and I couldn't imagine Quinn any other way.

I wasn't sure what Diana was waiting for. She continued to work on the wall mural, but now she kept it covered with billowing sheets that blocked my view without touching the paint. She also refused all of my requests to see my portrait, telling me that she would show me when she'd finished. I wondered sometimes if this waiting time for her was spent in deciding when the right moment would be to unveil both of her masterpieces. As I sat by the window while she painted me, I couldn't help but imagine that there must be some big secret she was waiting to reveal. I suppose my own waiting time was spent anticipating the same thing.

Christmas morning dawned chilly and rainy; the scene outside our windows was one of solid gray. I didn't cringe anymore from the sight of rain, but all the nerves in my skin tingled under the surface, sensing its presence like an apparition.

I walked down the stairs, following the scent of roasting turkey and apple pie, feeling as giddy as a child. But there were no cookies for Santa or any other holiday traditions besides the opening of presents and the wonderful turkey dinner prepared by Quinn. He'd informed me that a year before Gil had approached him and calmly explained that there was no reason for his parents to stay up late on Christmas Eve to put together toys and lay out presents from Santa. Apparently Gil had ceased to believe in Santa following a forage into Quinn's desk drawer to find a stapler when he had emerged instead with Gil's letters to Santa, neatly tied with a ribbon. As sad as I'd been to hear that Gil's childhood had grown a bit shorter, the story had also had the effect of fluttering my heart with the detail of Quinn keeping the letters and tying them with a ribbon.

Gil sat between Diana and Quinn on the sofa in the front parlor while I tried to focus on how happy I was to see Gil not cringing from his mother. He seemed comfortable in her presence as long as other people were around, but he avoided being alone with her, as if by being with alone with her, they would both have to face the ghosts that haunted the space between them.

As I had as a child and without having been asked to resume my role, I reached under the tree and handed out the wrapped presents, then waited as we each opened one present in turn, starting with my grandfather and then working around the circle. Gil's eyes danced with anticipation as he waited his turn while Diana opened the new set of paintbrushes from me, and I opened a box filled with new clothes from Diana. I raised my eyebrow at the skimpy tops and even skimpier shorts and thanked her, wondering at my own anticipation of warm weather so I might try them out.

Grandpa received a hand-knitted scarf, new gloves, and a large package of colored highlighters. Quinn got a thick sweater, an Atlanta Braves hat, and a new gardening journal. I opened Quinn's gift to me with a little trepidation. I had given him a set of new clay pots for his greenhouse, an idea that had seemed like a good one at the time. But I guess my practicality as a teacher had taken over as evidenced by Diana's brushes, my grandfather's scarf, and Quinn's pots. I cringed inside as I opened the small square box on my lap.

I held my breath as I pulled out the delicate silver chain with the silver crab charm dangling from it. I smiled, knowing exactly why he had given it to me.

"It's to remind you of the day you taught a Yankee how to catch blue crabs. And also to remind you that you'll always be a Lowcountry girl at heart, no matter where you are."

I looked down to blink away the sting in my eyes.

Diana stood. "Here, let me put it on you."

Brushing aside my hair, she clasped the chain behind my neck before letting my hair fall back into place. I felt the cool silver of the charm like a finger on my pulse.

To change the subject, I looked back at the tree. "Is that all, then?"

It was Quinn's turn to stand. "No. There's one more, but I didn't put it under the tree." He reached underneath the sofa and brought out a large shirt box wrapped brightly in red snowman paper. "This is for Gil."

He crossed the room and placed it in Gil's lap. "Before you open this, I want you to know that it's for later. But I wanted you to have it now so you'll have something to look forward to."

Gil tore into the paper as children do, then flung the lid aside and stopped. I almost expected to hear him shriek. He held up a bright yellow Windbreaker and matching sailor's cap, both embroidered in navy blue with the word *Highfalutin* on them. I'd seen Quinn in a matching jacket and cap, and I smiled at the mental image of them on the deck of their boat, sailing into the wind with their bright yellow sleeves flapping.

Gil beamed his thanks to his dad, then quickly stood and began putting the jacket over his pajamas. He set the hat on his head and looked at his dad, who nodded with approval before slowly looking over at Diana.

"Well, don't you look handsome?" she said. "And just in time with all this cold, wet weather we've been having."

Quinn cleared his throat. "Or when it's warmer. It's always chillier out on the water."

Diana faced Quinn. "I think you misunderstood. He's not sailing again, ever. Period. As long as I'm his mother, he does not have permission to go out on a sailboat. It's too dangerous, and I can't have you risking the life of our son because of some stupid desire to chase the wind in a boat pulled by sheets."

Quinn's face darkened. "Diana, you said you would think about it in the spring. He's ready to go now, but agreed to wait. And don't think for one minute that I would let anything happen to him while he was with me out on the water."

His words hit their mark and I saw Diana swallow. She looked down at her hands and tried to flake off yellow paint that was stuck on her thumbnail. Quietly she said, "I'm his mother. And I said no." She looked back up at him with a defiant glare.

I watched as Quinn bit back his words. "This isn't the time to discuss it, but we will discuss it later." He walked over to Gil and tugged the brim of the cap down. "In the meantime, you can wear the jacket and hat whenever you want. They're not just for sailing."

Gil nodded, all the excitement in his eyes dimmed like an extinguished candle.

Diana stood and smoothed down her shirt. "I have something for you, Quinn. It was too big to wrap, so I didn't put it under the tree. Hang on and I'll go get it."

As she left the room, I caught sight of her face. Not for the first time since my return, I was unable to read her expression. All I knew was that she deliberately avoided looking at me as she walked past me toward the dining room.

She came back carrying a large framed portrait, about the size of the empty rectangle on the wall behind the sofa, the back of it facing us in the room. She put it down with a heavy thud. My grandfather grunted and I saw him shake his head at Diana.

"It's all right, Grandpa. I'm fine with it. And it's time."

She looked down at the unseen portrait for a moment before focusing her attention on me. "I don't know how much Quinn has told you about how we met."

Quinn was on his feet again. "No, Diana. Please don't. . . ."

"It's mine to give, Quinn. I never let you have it, remember?"

He sent me a quick glance before looking back at Diana. "This isn't just about you and me, Diana. We need to talk about this first."

She threw her head back and laughed. "No, it's not. It never was, was it? It's always been the three of us."

Quinn took a step forward. "Diana, please. Can't we just talk about it first?"

"No. I want Marnie to know. And I think you want her to know, too."

I stood. "Would somebody please tell me what's going on here?"

Diana nodded. "If the two of you would please sit down, I'll explain."

Reluctantly Quinn sat and I did the same. Gil and my grandfather remained where they were, watching us intently.

"After you left, Marnie, I became a bit obsessive with my painting." She indicated the paintings around her. "It's really what made my career take off, so I think I probably owe you a huge thanks.

"But the first portrait of you that I painted, I couldn't stand to have around me. It reminded me too much of what I had lost, of how much I once loved you."

How much I once loved you. Her use of the past tense was no surprise to me; the only surprise was how much it still hurt me.

"I didn't want to sell it, either, but I didn't want to look at it every day. So I lent it to Pam Taekens to hang in her antiques store on South Pinckney. She hung it behind the counter where she kept her cash register, and after a while began to keep a tally of how many offers she received to buy it."

She sent me a brittle smile. "I just couldn't part with it. Giving you up had almost killed me. I couldn't give this last part of you away." Turning to Quinn, she said, "Do you want to finish this story or should I?"

He was looking at me and didn't turn away when he answered her.

"You've done such a great job so far, why don't you just go ahead and finish?"

Diana leaned against the rolled arm of the sofa, its fabric frayed from years of use and of existing in a house with no woman to take care of the details. "Quinn was one of those people. Pam said he came in nearly every day, upping his offer each time. Eventually, he convinced her to give his name and number to me so I could contact him." She pursed her lips and slid a sidelong glance in Quinn's direction. "Pam had described him in such detail that I decided that I would pay him a house call. So I picked up the painting, stuck it into the backseat of my car, and showed up on his doorstep."

I looked at the back of the painting, at the metal hooks and wire hanger that dipped across the back, and felt my palms sweat. I glanced around the room, wondering if anybody else could hear the pounding of my heart. My gaze slid up to Quinn, and I found him watching me steadily.

Diana continued. "So he opened his door and saw me standing there on his doorstep with the painting, and that was it." She stole a look at Gil. "We were married three months later."

I licked my dry, cracked lips, suddenly thirsty, my eyes back on the painting.

Diana leaned back on the sofa's arm, swinging her legs casually, but her pale fingertips gave her away by the way they gripped the fading fabric. "Why don't you go ahead and hang it where it belongs, Quinn, so Marnie can see it?"

He dragged his deep blue gaze from me to Diana. Without saying anything, he hoisted the painting up, flipped it over, then hung it on the picture hooks protruding from the wall above the sofa before stepping back to allow me to see it.

My first thought was *Who is that girl?* She was young and beautiful, and her face was the unlined and open face of a girl who had not yet discovered how the edge of loss spreads out into your life like spilled paint. It wasn't until I recognized the shirt and the earrings that I realized *That's me.*

It was on the deck of my mother's boat, the first *Highfalutin.*

There were blurred images of other crew members, but the eyes of the viewer were drawn to the figure manning the tiller at the stern of the boat. Placing the figure there was redundant; it was clear by the way she leaned forward and pressed her face into the wind that she was in charge of where the boat was heading. She wore a white blouse that had been knotted at her midsection and that billowed in the wind, the paint strokes making the fabric vibrantly alive. I could almost smell the varnish of the wood and feel the crispness of the flapping sails that framed the top of the portrait. But the girl in the painting—I couldn't call her me, after all; this girl was young and strong and hopeful. Three things that I had ceased to be almost sixteen years before.

Her long thick hair bled streaks of brown into the wind, highlighted by the backdrop of aqua waves. The sails were trimmed tight, as if the boat were running with the wind, and from the light in the girl's eyes, it was apparent to the observer that she had succeeded in tricking the wind into moving her boat. Her body was one with the wind and sea, a sensual portrait as captivating and revealing as if the subject had been completely naked.

Diana came to stand beside me. "It was the first and only time I painted your entire face. I think that's why I didn't like it, because I couldn't stand to think that you could possibly be whole when I thought of myself as missing half of myself."

I wanted to cry and scream and wrap her in my arms and tell her how much I had missed her, too, and how much I loved her still. She was my sister, and that one word spoke all my truths. But I did none of those things. The miles of desert still stood between us, an ocean of sand that could easily drown anyone unprepared to cross it.

Instead, I turned to her. "But what has this to do with Quinn?" My blood seemed to run sluggishly through my veins as I considered the possibilities and remembered how he'd once answered my question about how he and Diana met. *I fell in love with one of her paintings.*

She looked at Quinn as she answered me. "It didn't take me long to realize that it wasn't the painting he'd fallen in love with. But by then it was too late. I was in love with him, enough to make myself try to convince him that I was a good enough second choice. I'm pretty good at convincing, aren't I, Quinn?"

Diana approached the painting and appraised its position on the wall before tilting it slightly to the right. "There was only so much lying to myself I was prepared to do. So, after Gil was born, and I had my little 'episode,' as Quinn likes to call it, I decided to let him go." She turned to face the room. "But I kept the painting. I was willing to lose my heart and my self-respect to my ex-husband, but I wasn't going to let him have my soul, too."

The room was silent except for the crackling of the fire in the fireplace, and I imagined I could hear the press of the moisture-laden gray clouds pushing against the sides of the old house—the same house that had witnessed the lives and deaths of generations of Maitlands. And I thought of the years without my sister, wondering if the pain in my chest had been the absence of the other half of my soul.

"So I'm giving it to you now, Quinn. It's time."

She looked at me and I wondered if she'd felt the same as I had, that we were all waiting for something. And that maybe she'd finally realized what that something was.

Diana walked over to Quinn and kissed him on the cheek. "Merry Christmas, Quinn. I'm going up to my studio now, and I won't be down for dinner, so please don't call me. I'll come down again when I'm ready." She pressed a kiss against the top of Gil's head, then began to leave the room. But Grandpa shot out his arm, grabbing her wrist as she passed by his wheelchair. They looked at each other for a long moment until Diana quickly shook her head. Without another word, she bent to kiss his cheek and he released her.

Quinn stood, studiously avoiding looking at me. To nobody in particular, he said, "I need to get back to the kitchen. I'll let you know when dinner is ready."

Gil had sat back down on the floor and was taking off his new Windbreaker, his fingers tracing the embroidered stitches on the front. I looked up at my grandfather, who was gazing steadily back at me. I felt suddenly as if I had been handed a challenge; Diana had gone first and now it was my turn. Except that I had no idea what it was I was supposed to do.

I glanced out the window to see if the clouds had dissipated, but they were as thick and heavy as before, pressing still against the old house, waiting.

✍

Quinn

I closed the blinds in my living room, not really sure if I was blocking something from getting in, or avoiding looking out. I didn't expect any visitors to the old caretaker's cottage behind the house that I'd renovated. Still, the act of closing my blinds separated the day from the night and blocked the sun from peering too early into the four rooms of the tiny house.

As I prepared for bed, I contemplated the last twenty-four hours and felt my ears burn as I remembered not only the unveiling of the painting, but everything that had happened afterward.

It had been an odd Christmas dinner. Diana remained in her room, leaving just Grandpa, Gil, Marnie, and me to sit around the large dining room table. Joanna had gone back to Atlanta to be with her family for the holidays, leaving only Marnie and myself to create a conversation composed entirely of asking to pass the bread or commenting on the different tastes of the different dishes. Not that I tasted anything. I could have eaten cardboard and I wouldn't have known. I had never wanted Gil to speak as much as I did the entire hour we sat at the dining room table, made much worse by the fact that I couldn't even look Marnie in the eye.

I had just taken off my shirt and begun fumbling with the button on my pants when I heard a soft rapping on the door. I walked to the front of the house and pulled aside the curtain on the door's side window. Marnie stood on the other side, shivering in her bathrobe, her legs bare and her feet covered in bedroom slippers.

I pulled the door open. "What is it? Is it Gil? Or Grandpa?" I took her arm and pulled her inside.

"No, no. They're fine. Everyone's fine. I just . . . couldn't sleep." She bit her lip. "I needed to talk to you."

I thought again of the painting, and how I'd felt when I'd first seen it. "About what?" I ventured, not wanting to take the lead in this conversation.

Her gaze slid down to my chest and I remembered that I wasn't wearing a shirt. I crossed my arms in front of me.

She raised an eyebrow and almost smiled. "About how you and Diana met."

"Oh. Well." My eyes took in her bare legs and thin bathrobe. "Can I get you some coffee to warm you up first?"

"Um, sure. Yes. Thank you."

I indicated the sofa for her to sit and then moved to the tiny kitchen area separated by a bar. She sat and slid off her slippers, pulling her bare feet up underneath her. "May I?" she asked, indicating the afghan on the back of the couch. I nodded and she pulled it around her shoulders and I noticed that her teeth were chattering. I wondered if it was really because of the cold. While waiting for the coffee to brew, I went back to my bedroom and threw my shirt on, not bothering with the buttons.

When the coffee was ready, I brought two steaming mugs over to the table in front of the sofa before sitting down next to her. "It's decaf," I said, smiling nervously and not really knowing why.

"The painting," she started and I watched her pale cheeks flush. She moved her hand to the back of her head as if to pat a bun before realizing that her hair streamed down her back and shoulders. Instead, she used the movement to tuck her hair behind her ear.

She forced her eyes to my face. "You told me that you fell in love with the painting. Is that really what happened?"

I shook my head, unable to take my gaze from hers. "No."

"No?"

I shook my head again and reached for her hands. They were cold yet they sent waves of heat through the veins of my arms, warming my blood. "No." I smiled at her uncertainly. "The painting was beautiful and mesmerizing, but it was the subject that held my attention." I closed my eyes, remembering the first time I'd seen it. I had been brand-new to the Lowcountry, filled with grief and disappointment, but still hopeful enough that I would find whatever it was I needed to fix my life that had seemed so irreparably broken ever since Sean had fallen from the tree. It was a Sunday afternoon, and I entered the antiques shop more out of boredom than any desire to purchase anything, and I'd seen the painting immediately, placed in a prominent position on the wall behind the cash register.

The woman in the portrait was beautiful, but not because of her physical attributes. She was beautiful because of the way she faced the wind without fear, how she didn't look behind her but stayed her course despite the tall waves whipping around her. She was in control and strong and everything I had once been but couldn't seem to find my way back to. Like a siren from the sea, she'd reached out from the canvas, and I thought I'd felt my broken soul slowly begin to gather its pieces together.

I looked at Marnie now, seeing her as the woman I'd come to know: not as a siren with all the answers, but as a woman of strength and determination and flaws, a woman who faced her fears because she thought it would help a wounded little boy. I touched her face. "In the portrait I saw a woman who was everything I wasn't. I wanted to know her so she could tell me her secret. I felt like I could see the soul of the woman, which led me to believe that it must have been a self-portrait of the artist because nobody could paint the soul of another person with such clarity."

I felt her cheek crease under my palm as she smiled.

"When the owner told me that it had been painted by the subject's sister, I understood. I'd felt the same way about my brother. But that only made me more determined to own it."

"And then Diana showed up at your door with the painting."

"Yes. She told me that you lived out west and were never coming back. That you lived in the desert and never sailed anymore. My first thought was *What a waste*." I ran my finger along her jawbone, feeling the fineness of it that hid the determination under the pale skin.

"What was your second thought?" Her eyes were wide and luminous in the dim light of the single lamp by the sofa.

"That Diana was real and she was standing on my doorstep. And when she turned her face a certain way, it reminded me of you—of the girl in the painting—the way she held her head like a golden goddess on the prow of a ship. The resemblance is there, you know. Even now I'd say that the two of you have more in common than not. You're both pretty remarkable, and I've thought more than once in the past few years how much I would have liked to meet your mother and congratulate her on producing two such women as you and Diana."

Marnie went still, her eyes like darkened hollows as she sat back away from the light. "She had nothing to do with it. Diana and I were pretty much left alone to raise ourselves."

"But if that were true, I doubt you and Diana would have become the people you are today."

A small laugh came from the darkened corner of the sofa. "There you go again, Dr. Bristow, trying to fix things." She leaned forward, touching my arm and moving into the light again. "She was a terrible mother. That's not to say that she didn't love us—she did. She just had no idea how. She made a lot of mistakes."

I paused, feeling the hurt seething from her warm skin heating the air around her. "We all do. It's only when we don't learn from them that they become permanent."

Marnie tilted her head to the side, the same way Gil does when he has a question. "So what happened next? Diana showed up at your doorstep and you wanted the painting, so you invited her inside."

I shrugged, not wanting to share any details and aware that details weren't what Marnie wanted anyway. "She was charming and sexy and proceeded to make me believe that I was falling in love with her."

"Did you? Fall in love with her?"

"I suppose I did, for a time. Like when she was pregnant with Gil and we were both so happy. I thought that I'd finally found whatever it was that I'd been searching for since Sean died. I think, though, that I forced the pieces to fit. I think that Diana knew it, too. She became frantic trying to make it work, which only made things worse, really. And then Gil was born and she realized she couldn't hide her illness from me anymore."

It was Marnie's turn to touch my face, her fingertips brushing the stubble on my cheeks and chin. "But you stayed with her. You tried to help her."

"Don't say that like I'm a hero or something. She was my wife and the mother of my son. And she's worthy of being loved. But there's something inside of her, beyond her illness, that eats away at her, that makes her turn away from the very love she searches for as if she's unworthy of it. Something so dark and consuming that she'd never talk to me about it."

Her brow creased. "I remember that. When she was a young girl, she kept it hidden better. But after Mama died, she was unreachable." Her eyes met mine. "Something was broken inside of her that you couldn't fix no matter how hard you tried."

I realized that we'd let our untouched coffee grow cold. "Something like that." I reached for her hands again. "I'm glad you came back. It's made a world of difference to Gil—not to mention Diana and your grandfather, too. You're meant to be here, I think." Her robe gaped open at the neck, and I saw she wore the necklace I had given her. The silver crab winked in the light, recalling cold, dark waters and the unseen life that teemed there.

Marnie leaned toward me, and the set of her jaw and the look in her eyes reminded me again of the girl in the portrait. I leaned forward, too, eager to meet her halfway.

"I wouldn't be here if I thought it would hurt Diana. I think by giving you the painting that she was making it clear that it was okay with her." Her cheeks pinkened.

"That what was okay?"

Her blush deepened as she opened her mouth to say something more, but I silenced her with my lips against hers. I thought of the first time I'd kissed her, on the beach with the water teasing our legs and her arms trembling around my neck. But there was no fear in her now as she let me gently press her back against the sofa. As she kissed me, I remembered, too, how her lips had tasted like salt and how she'd talked about Saint Elmo's fire. I touched her neck where the silver charm lay, and thought again of the girl in the portrait and how the woman in my arms had far exceeded the expectations of a young man foolish enough to imagine himself in love with paint and canvas.

Yet still, as she moved beneath me, I felt the presence of the heavy clouds outside, and the sleeping marsh and the ocean's tides—all of them suspended in motion, hovering on the periphery of our lives. Marnie stilled for a moment and looked into my eyes as if she'd felt it, too. Then she pressed her forehead against my chest, and I held her there for a long moment, straining to hear the tides move again. But everything remained suspended while Marnie and I lost ourselves in each other and the outside world held its breath, waiting.

$$\wp$$

Gil

I lay in my bed with my eyes closed, but I was still awake. I felt the lump under my pillow where I'd folded up my jacket and my hat, afraid that my mama would sneak in after I was asleep and take them if I left them where she could see them. It was late; my dad had long since finished banging around the dishes in the kitchen as he cleaned up by himself. Aunt Marnie had asked to help, but Daddy said no. He said he'd appreciate it if she'd help Grandpa get ready for bed, instead. I could tell that they were both relieved that they didn't have to spend any time together in the small kitchen.

They were acting really weird. It started when Mama brought out that painting from her studio. I'd seen it before, of course, but I guess I'd never really studied it. From the way that Daddy and Aunt Marnie were staring at it, and if I hadn't seen it myself, I would have sworn that Aunt Marnie was naked in it or something. And when I looked at the face in the painting, *really* looked, I could see that in a way, she sort of was.

The house was still and quiet and I closed my eyes, hoping that sleep would come. But the house made its nighttime sounds, making me think of a sleeping cat that's waiting at a mouse hole. It seemed that everybody was waiting for something to happen. Even the weather outside was asleep, the sun waiting to shine but not yet ready.

I got out of bed and pulled out the jacket and hat from under my pillow. I put them on and looked at myself in the long mirror on the back of the closet door. In the dim glow from my night-light, I couldn't really see the yellow and the navy blue. But what I did see was a sailboat on the water, with me on deck. I could almost feel the waves roll under my feet, the oak of my bedroom floor looking like teak in the yellow light.

Mr. Bonner had stopped by on Christmas Eve to deliver a fruitcake that his little sister, Tally, had made for us. I'm one of those weird people who actually likes fruitcake, and I'm pretty sure she'd made it just for me. Before Mama got sick, we'd go to the library a lot, and Tally would take me over to the kids' section, where she helped me find books. Mama spent a lot of time at the library because she doesn't like to bring the books home. She said it's because she's afraid she'll lose them, but I think it's because she doesn't want anybody else to know what she's reading. So Tally and I have become friends, and that was why she sent the fruitcake.

I guess Mr. Bonner and my dad forgot I was there because they started talking about the *Highfalutin*, something Daddy never does when I'm around. Mr. Bonner said that she was ready to go, and that the week after Christmas was going to be warm enough to be spring but without the wind gusts. Perfect sailing weather, he'd called it. I was lying on the sofa pretending to be asleep when Daddy mentioned it to Mama. He made the same arguments that he had before—that I was ready and that I wanted to, which is true. What he didn't say is that I needed to. Probably because he doesn't know it yet. But I do. Like when the fiddler crabs know when it's time to return to the marsh in the spring, I felt the pull toward the water.

Mama didn't even argue. She just said no, as if her opinion mattered more than Daddy's or Aunt Marnie's. Or even mine. I think it's because of her sickness that Daddy feels we need to be gentle with her, and lots of times I agree with him. But not about this. Only Mama knows how I became afraid and why I can't speak the truth. I figure if I can find the courage to go back to the water, she can find the courage to tell the truth. And then we will both be better.

I took off the jacket and hat and folded them up under my pillow again. Then I went back to bed and pulled the covers over my head, listening once more to the still house as we all lay in our beds beneath the quiet roof and waited.

CHAPTER 25

The fishermen know that the sea is dangerous and the storm terrible, but they have never found these dangers sufficient reasons for remaining ashore.

—VINCENT VAN GOGH

Diana

I couldn't sleep again. I'd forgotten how long it had been since I'd been able to sleep through a single night, and if I thought about it, I could probably trace it back to when I first started having the dreams shortly after Marnie's return. In them, my feet would be submerged in water as I searched in the darkness for something precious I had lost. I would wake up with a damp pillow and dried tears on my cheeks, remembering only that I had cried simply because I couldn't remember what it was that I was looking for. All I retained from the dream was a lingering sense of loss, like being aware of a present set high on a shelf I couldn't reach. Sleep became a perilous journey, and I'd grown to expect spending the night in quiet wakefulness, listening to the sounds of a sleeping house.

But last night had been different. I'd first heard Gil jump out of his bed, and then a short while later, his squeaking bedsprings told me that he'd returned to it. But then I'd heard Marnie's door quietly open and close. I wasn't surprised, of course; she and Quinn together was as inevitable as summer following spring. What did surprise me, though, was that I didn't feel the expected hurt. As I'd watched Marnie walk up the path to Quinn's cottage in her nubby pink bathrobe, I'd felt only relief. Relief and an abiding peace that covered me as unexpectedly as the incoming tide. It was as if a part of my past could finally be put away and locked with a key, and two of my biggest failures forever relegated to my distant past.

I stayed where I was at the window, waiting for dawn, unsure what I should do next. My mural was complete and so was Marnie's portrait. It wouldn't be what she'd expect at all, but it was what I'd needed. As I stared at the still-wet paint, my head and hands felt heavy, as if I were pushing them through water. Looking at the canvas was like waking from my dream, except now I could see what it was that I had lost and how close I'd come to never finding it again.

I stood and moved to the bookshelf I kept in the corner of my studio. It was filled with all the books I had ever owned. I'd never been a huge reader like Marnie, but after she'd learned to read, it was to her voice that I fell asleep every night. Even now, when I pick up *Anne of Green Gables* or *National Velvet*, I hear Marnie's voice reading to me. I have those books still, an innocent part of my childhood I shared with my sister that I could never give up.

My fingers skimmed over the bindings until they came to rest on the book I was looking for. It was a thick and heavy volume, its spine cracked from being held open by small hands again and again, the pages bent and yellowed. I pulled out *The Hunchback of Notre Dame* and flipped to chapter thirteen, skimming the lines until I'd found the passage I was looking for. I read it once out loud, then closed my eyes and recited it from memory.

I carried the book back to my easel and set it opened at the right page on the small table next to the easel, and wondered if I would have the courage to ask Marnie to read from it again. And I thought of my grandfather and all his Bible verses and not one of them had touched the heart of the matter quite like this one. But maybe that was because I couldn't hear them being read by Marnie's voice.

I studied the painting again, seeing everything with more clarity than I had experienced since before Gil's birth. It was as if by painting it, I had become aware that keeping the truth to myself was more damaging to me than it could ever have been to Marnie. And I knew that lying beneath the truth beat the heart of the matter: Marnie had never abandoned me; I had simply let her go.

Stretching, I stood and glanced out the tall turret window and caught a flash of yellow heading toward the path leading to the dock. I'd heard Marnie return, which meant Quinn would be up, too. Maybe he'd decided to get an early start at his office and was taking the jon boat. I yawned, amazed at how tired I felt; the completion of the painting and its revelations to me were like permission to finally rest. I lay down on the daybed and pulled a blanket up to my shoulders, then closed my eyes. And when the dream came, I was searching again. Except this time, I finally knew what I was searching for.

❧

Marnie

I showered and dressed slowly, my skin feeling pleasantly sore as I slathered myself with soap, then pulled on my clothes. The clouds had completely disappeared, giving us a day that was more straight out of April than the day after Christmas. I wore jeans, and put on one of the new shirts that Diana had given me, giving into the impulse to throw a light sweater over it.

Trey had called to say that he was putting the *Highfalutin* in the water if we were up for some sailing, as the weather forecast called for highs in the seventies and no precipitation for the rest of the week.

We were still waiting for Diana to come around and grant her permission to allow Gil to sail, but I didn't know how much longer we could hold out. It was obvious to both Quinn and myself that the key to unlocking Gil's speech lay somewhere on the deck of the boat under full sails.

I'd promised Gil a trip down to the dock to see the boat in the water and to sketch her, so I slid on my sneakers and approached his door. I knocked twice, waiting for a few moments before knocking again. When there was no response, I turned the handle, then slowly opened the door, calling his name.

"Gil?" I stepped into the room. The bed was unmade but slept in, his pajamas lying on the floor. I picked them up and folded them before placing them at the bottom of the bed. As I turned to leave, I spotted his sketch pad on his desk and went over to pick it up. I didn't open it since Gil seemed to consider it his private domain and hadn't chosen to share any of his pictures with me as of yet. But I figured if I ran into him elsewhere in the house we could just leave without having to wait for him to go get his pad.

I went from empty room to empty room, wondering where everybody was. I knew Quinn said he needed to stop in the greenhouse before he came to get my grandfather up and give him breakfast. I told him that I would take over the responsibility but he'd said no, saying that time spent with my grandfather was some of the most peaceful and thought-provoking moments of his entire day.

The door to Diana's studio was shut, and I imagined she'd be working and not happy about being disturbed. I figured Gil must have gone to the greenhouse to help Quinn, so I poured myself a bowl of cereal and waited for somebody to appear.

I was putting my dishes into the dishwasher when the kitchen door opened at the same time Diana padded barefoot into the room, wearing an oversized T-shirt and rubbing sleep from her eyes. I was saved from any embarrassing conversation with Quinn in front of Diana when I realized that Gil wasn't with either one of them.

"Where's Gil?" I asked.

Diana looked at her paint-splattered watch. "It's only eight thirty. He's probably still asleep."

I looked at her in alarm. "No, he's not. I already checked his room, and he's not in there."

Quinn's expression remained neutral. "Let me get your grandfather up and fed. Then I'll go look around outside, see if I can find Gil. He likes to wander around a lot, but he knows to be careful. Chances are he'll show up any minute now wanting something to eat."

"Make sure you look up on the hill where we planted his orange tree. He likes to go up there to think." Diana's fingers scratched at her bandage. "I'm going upstairs to throw on some clothes, and then I'll help you look."

Diana left and Quinn followed after a discreet kiss, and I was left standing in the middle of the kitchen, alone again and unable to sit down and do nothing. Still carrying Gil's sketch pad, I went up the stairs and into Gil's room again in the hopes of finding some sort of clue as to where he could be, like a missing easel or even a book from beside his bed.

Everything seemed normal and accounted for. I was disappointed to see his oil paints and brushes untouched on his easel, where they'd been since I arrived. Noticing his unmade bed again, I decided to make it to keep me busy. I placed the sketch pad on the nightstand and stepped closer to the bed to pull the covers up when my toe struck something hard. Stepping back, I looked down at the dust ruffle, noticing something square and solid poking out from under the bed.

Curious, I bent down and slid out a clear plastic box, the unlatched lid catching on the fabric of the dust ruffle and sliding off onto the floor. I picked up the lid to reattach it before replacing the box under the bed, but the piece of paper on top caught my attention.

It was yellow and thin, as if it were part of a form that had once been in triplicate. Printed in red type at the bottom right corner were the words *Patient Copy*. I read the name of the company on the letterhead, running the name around in my head like a ball in a pinball machine, waiting for it to land in the right spot. My gaze drifted down the page, my eyes catching sight of a familiar name at the same time I recognized the letterhead. It was the name of the nursing home that I had been visiting with Diana and Gil. But that second name—the name on the line that started with *Patient's Name*, I knew that one, too. A cold chill blew on the back of my neck, and I jerked upright, knocking the sketch pad onto the floor. A loose paper flew from between the pages, and I recognized it immediately as the missing half of the page that had been in Diana's purse and I froze.

In the other four sketches, the face of the third person on the boat with Diana and Gil had been obscured. But in this sketch, the face was peering out at me, leaving no doubt as to the identity of the third person. Brittle air filled my lungs as I tried to concentrate on breathing in and out, all the while thinking to myself *So this is what it's like to see a ghost.*

I ran out of the room, calling for Diana. I threw open the door of her bedroom to find it still and untouched, the room of a child long gone from a house. I backed out of the room and ran to the attic stairs. Her studio door was still shut, but I knew before going inside that I wouldn't find her.

The sheets had been pulled from the mural and from my portrait, exposing all to the morning light filtering in through the large windows. I stared up at the mural, at all the familiar faces of the dead, the same face in each portrait that Diana had borrowed from our mother's photo. *Of course,* I thought. *Gil would have known how to get in here and would have seen the mural. And his grandmother's face . . .*

I walked to the end of the mural, to where Gil's picture sat by itself, his birthdate neatly stenciled beneath it. A bit farther down the line, my picture was painted next to Diana's and our mother's. There was no calligraphied story beneath these last three portraits; only the years of our births were documented with a single dash to show no death dates.

I backed away, my breath coming in heavy gasps, as if I'd run a long, long way. The room appeared to be getting smaller, and I forced myself to take deeper breaths, concentrating on breathing the air back into my lungs. *Breathe in. Breathe out. Breathe in.* I backed into her easel and a heavy book that had been propped open next to it slid to the floor. I managed to catch it before it fell all the way and held it up to the opened page, sure I already knew what it was before I looked. My eyes skimmed the words that I knew by heart. *Do you know what friendship is . . . it is to be brother and sister; two souls which touch without mingling, two fingers on one hand.*

"Diana." I said her name softly, seeing her as I had once seen her long ago as I looked at our reflections in a mirror as she braided my hair. Her hair had been as fair as mine was dark, her limbs as long and gangly as mine were small and more compact. *Twins,* she'd said, and for a moment, I'd thought she was joking. But when I looked at her reflection, she'd been serious. *Two souls which touch without mingling, two fingers on one hand. Yes,* I'd said then. "Yes," I said aloud now in the quiet room, wanting my sister back and trying not to think of all the years and the gossamer reasons that had separated us.

I looked down at the papers in my hand, knowing that I held part of the

answers I sought, but not able to put any of the pieces together. "Diana!"
I called her name loudly in frustration, not expecting an answer.

I was about to leave to search for her elsewhere when I remembered
the portrait. Turning slowly, I faced the uncovered canvas. My vision
narrowed for a moment as the sensation of falling created a weightless-
ness in my limbs, and I wondered for a moment if this was what dying
felt like. I lifted my hand, surprised to find that my fingers weren't
translucent after all.

On the canvas, painted in rich grays and blacks, wasn't a portrait of
me; it was a portrait from a moment in my life that had forever altered
me and my relationship with Diana. In the bold splashes of color, the
artist had depicted a storm at sea. And in the middle of the storm, its
mast snapped in two, was my mother's boat.

I listened carefully in the quiet room, not hearing the muffled quiet
in the sunlit room, but instead remembering the sound of the howling
wind through the sails and rigging. And I remembered how I'd known
that the mast had broken because all of a sudden the howling of the
wind had just . . . stopped. I closed my eyes, recalling something else,
something brushing the edge of my memory the way a soft breeze teases
the tall marsh grass.

I looked at the painting again, my eyes drawn to the wheel. *Where's
Mama?* I remembered now, looking for her to tell her that the mast was
gone, as if she couldn't tell herself. But I'd been too shocked at what was
happening to make any sense. *But where was Mama?*

And then I remembered. I saw her just as clearly as if she'd been
standing in front of me. She'd brought Diana out of the cockpit, and
they were both at the deck rails at the side of the boat near the shrouds.
Mama had her hands on Diana's shoulders, and Diana was grabbing
Mama by the forearms as if she were fighting her. The wind pushed
seawater into my eyes, and I blinked them shut. And when I opened
them again, Diana was gone.

The wind and ocean knocked the boat into a semicircle, and I
turned around to see if I could find Diana in the angry arms of the
ocean. The next thing I remember was my breath being knocked out

of me as the boom hit me square in the back and pushed me into the white-tipped waves.

I struggled to stay atop the waves as a chilling thought crept into my brain: *Where were our life jackets?* And then Mama was in the water and swimming toward me, and with relief I fought not to sink. When she reached me, she drew me into her arms as if in a hug, and she said something in my ear that I couldn't hear. And then she pushed me away from her.

I studied the painting again, noticing the abstract swaths of color that only hinted at what the objects depicted were, the boat being the most recognizable. But then I saw the figures in the water. My face was white against the dark sea and my hair, and I was floating on top of the seat cushion from the cockpit. *Yes. I remember. Somebody must have thrown it to me from the boat.*

I stepped back, trying to get a better grasp of the painting. And when I did, I think I stopped breathing. There, almost hidden by the black waves and swirling rain, were two figures struggling to reach a single life preserver. Both were long-limbed and blond, and I couldn't tell them apart. All that remained unclear was who eventually reached the life preserver.

Tears fell down my cheeks in the empty room as I finally recognized the heavy weight I'd carried around all these years. The feeling of my mother's hands slowly letting me go had haunted me as much as any ghost, its whispered words and ethereal footsteps following me until I'd gone to the desert and was able to bury it in the sand. Until now.

I raced out of the room and down the steps, stopping in the kitchen, where Quinn was helping Grandpa with his breakfast.

I knelt in front of the wheelchair. Grandpa's hand reached out to me, wiping the tears I wasn't aware I was still crying. "You knew," I said, surprised that I felt no anger toward him. "All this time, you knew."

His eyes met mine, but he made no movement, not even to reach for the Bible that lay closed and silent in his lap.

I stood as Quinn removed the plate from in front of Grandpa. "What's going on, Marnie?"

"I don't know yet. I just need to find Diana." I felt myself close to panic, as if time were running out.

"I heard the back door slam about thirty minutes ago. I thought it was you going out to look for Gil." I made to leave, but he held my arm. "What's wrong? What can I do to help?"

I touched his face, warmed by his look of concern. "I've got to fix this myself, okay? I need to find Diana. If you see her or Gil, call me right away. I'll have my cell phone."

He held my arm for a moment longer, then reluctantly let it go. "Call me if you need me. I'll be here." He pulled me to him and kissed me quickly.

I looked from him to my grandfather, surprised to find them wearing matching expressions of love and concern. "I'll be all right," I said, more to reassure myself than anybody else. Then I grabbed my purse and keys and ran from the house, letting the door slam shut behind me.

CHAPTER 26

And the sea shall grant all men new hope, as sleep brings dreams of home.

—CHRISTOPHER COLUMBUS

Marnie

When I reached the carport, I realized that Quinn's car was gone. I began dialing my cell phone to call Quinn to let him know, then slowly hung up. I was haunted still by what I'd seen in Diana's studio and needed to talk to her before Quinn intervened. And now that she was finished with the painting and the mural, I knew that there was only one place she would go.

I jumped in my rental car and headed out toward Highway 17 toward Charleston, remembering the route I had followed before with Diana and Gil. I pulled into a front spot in the parking lot of the nursing home, only one of ten cars or so; another of them was Quinn's.

When the nurse at the front desk greeted me, I lost my courage for a moment, unsure of myself. When the nurse asked again if she could help me, I forced a smile.

"I'm here to see Meredith Maitland."

"Oh, yes. I thought I recognized you. Your sister is already here. She's in room seventy-nine, but I suppose you already know that."

"Yes," I said, my lips numb. *I've been so close. This whole time, I've been so close and never knew it.*

My joints felt stiff and heavy as I went down the hallway, reading the numbers on the other doors like a condemned man counts down the minutes to his execution. My eyes barely registered the burnt orange carpeting and green doors, wondering what kind of punishment it must be for an artist to be confined in a place devoid of any grace or beauty.

My fist paused in midair in front of the door to room seventy-nine, poised to strike. Gathering my courage, I allowed it to come down in three hard rasps.

There was a short pause, and then Diana's voice said, "Come in."

Slowly I turned the knob and pushed open the door before stepping into a narrow foyer. At first glance, it looked like a regular apartment: the small galley kitchen to my left, the plain white paint on the walls, the heavy-duty neutral carpet on the floors. There were hotel-quality couches and lamps placed in a sitting area that faced me as I entered, but when I turned toward what must have been the bedroom door, all semblance of a hotel ended.

I followed Diana's voice, like a fireman scenting smoke, passing a Formica dining table with an opened box of Twinkies sitting on top, and entered a small bedroom. In here, attempts had been made to make it feel more apartmentlike, but the hospital bed and the emergency button on the wall next to the metal walker signaled that the person who lived here was elderly and most likely infirm.

The bed was empty, and I pivoted toward the sound of Diana's voice in the corner of the room, where two fake leather club chairs had been placed in an effort to appear homey, but succeeded only in reminding its occupant that she was far from home.

Diana stood, but the old lady sitting in the other chair with a cane resting on the stuffed arm remained seated. I felt her eyes on me—eyes that I knew were just like Diana's—but I couldn't look at her yet. Instead, my attention was drawn to the only artwork on the stark white walls: two watercolors, each showing a blue heron in a different pose, in matching frames with my signature in the corner of each one.

"Did Quinn find Gil yet?"

I squinted in concentration, wondering how Diana could ask such a normal question, given the circumstances.

I touched my purse, realizing that I didn't have my phone. "No," I answered. "Quinn said he'd call me when Gil showed up, but I left my phone in the car."

She nodded, then took a deep breath, squaring her shoulders in the old familiar way she had when she needed to appear smug and confident but she really felt neither. "Sorry to have left without saying anything, but I knew that Quinn wouldn't let me go, and it was urgent that I get here. I finished my mural and your portrait, although you probably already know that since you're here."

I reached into my purse and pulled out the admittance form and Gil's picture, and showed them to her. "I found these in Gil's room."

Her pale eyebrows arched in surprise. "Oh. Oh," she said again as if something new had occurred to her. She stared down at the form. "I've been looking for this."

"Yes, I imagine you have." Finally, I turned to the old woman sitting in the other chair. Her hair was held back in a long braid, as thick as when I'd last seen it, yet now completely white. Her hands, resting in her lap, were fisted into tight balls with large, round, arthritic knuckles, the once beautiful fingers now useless. She regarded me silently, her green eyes cloudy but alert, watching me intently. *I love you,* she had said. I remembered now. When she had let me go on that night in the water, she had said that to me.

"Mama?" I said, wanting to touch her, but stopped by the look in her eyes. I suppose there's something in all of us that makes us want our mothers during the difficult times in our lives, regardless of how well one was mothered in the first place.

"Sit down, Marnie." Diana indicated her vacated chair.

Gratefully I sat, not taking my eyes off my mother's face. Her skin was pale, her eyebrows almost nonexistent in the thick lines and wrinkles that spoke of her years in the sun and on the water. "What happened? You . . . drowned."

My mother blinked twice, her eyes bright, then glanced away.

I forced myself to look at my sister. "How long have you known?"

Diana sat back against the bed. "Since about a year and a half ago. I was going through Grandpa's desk, looking for an insurance policy he had that would cover him if we decided to put him in an assisted living facility, and I found a copy of Mama's admission form."

I tried to sort through the questions racing through my head. A year and a half ago would have been when Quinn said she'd gone off her medication and had her most recent bipolar episode. "But how did Mama get here?" I put my hands on my head, as if that would still my thoughts. "Oh, my God, Diana. Why didn't you tell me?"

Diana faced our mother as she answered me. "Because then I'd have to tell you what happened the night we thought our mother drowned. And why I've hated you ever since." The old woman flinched under Diana's scrutiny. "I was supposed to die that night, you see. Mama had it all planned so that I would die. And then you had to get yourself knocked into the water."

"What? What are you talking about?" And then I remembered the life jackets and the painting in Diana's study, and I suddenly felt sick.

"Diana, no. Please don't." My mother's voice was the same, still. But it lacked the power she had once used to command our obedience.

Diana turned on her. "Don't what? Tell her that you made a choice that night—a choice about which daughter should live and which one should die?"

"Stop it!" I stood. "Stop it, Diana. Why are you doing this? She's an old woman. Why would you be doing this?"

Diana went very still. "Because I thought you wanted to know the truth. The truth I've been hiding from you all these years. The truth that she chose you that night because you were the untainted one. She knew, even back then, that I was blemished with the Maitland curse, and that we would all be better off if it ended with me." She was shaking, her eyes wild.

"That can't be. You were her golden child—the gifted, beautiful one who looked just like her. She never had any time for me."

Diana jerked herself off the bed and barked out a hysterical laugh. I took a step backward, my legs pressed against the chair. "Do you know why you aren't a good artist, Marnie? Because you aren't very observant. You miss all the details, including the most important ones. Like how Mama could barely tolerate my presence because I was so much like her—in the bad ways as well as the good. And you," she said as she pressed the heels of her hands against her forehead, "you were every-thing I wasn't."

My mother sat in her chair, shaking her head from side to side. "No, no, no, no."

I moved to kneel in front of her and placed my hands over her ruined fingers. "It's all right, Mama. Diana's confused. . . ."

Diana moved to stand behind me. "Tell her, Mama. Tell her the truth. And then maybe she'll understand why I couldn't stand the sight of her after the accident. Because I had been forced to learn what it was like to lose the thing that mattered the most to me—my mother's love—and to know that it had never been mine to begin with." She stepped to my side so I could see her face, pinched and wounded with the years of secrets. "It had always belonged to you, Marnie. To the sister who I always thought was the other half of my soul, the sister who betrayed me without even knowing it."

The sun from the window behind her caught the side of her face, and she seemed old all of a sudden, the unforgiving light highlighting the fine lines and wrinkles around her eyes and mouth, marking her resemblance to the old woman in the chair. "Tell her, Mama," she said again, her voice hard. "Maybe if she hears it from you, she'll believe it."

At first, I didn't think Mama had heard her. She sat so still, with her head bowed. But when she raised her head, she looked at me with dry eyes, and for a moment, I thought I recognized the woman who had been my mother for such a short time, and who, despite everything, was still the woman who had given birth to me and who had framed my amateurish paintings and hung them on her wall. *I love you*, she had said.

"Tell me," I said, squeezing her hands. "Tell me what really happened."

She looked down at our clasped hands and nodded. Then she began to speak in a near monotone as if she had long since rehearsed the words she would say to me and had bled the emotion from them to make them easier to hear.

"I wasn't well. I never really had been. Your grandfather would have me committed, but they would drug me up so badly that I couldn't paint, so I'd find a way to get out. But I couldn't get well, and I learned to seek the uneasy times, because that's when I would do my best work.

It didn't matter to me during those times that I was a mother with two daughters who needed me. This disease does that to a person—makes them unable to see any logical reason in anything."

Diana left for a moment and returned with a glass of water. Mama took it without looking at her.

"The night of the storm, I'd gone off my medication, because I decided it was time to feel real life again. I knew there was a storm coming, but I didn't care. And I can't even say that any of it wasn't planned. A few weeks before, I'd taken the life jackets out of the boat and thrown them into the car. You two drove around with those life jackets and never said a thing. Probably because you were scared of me, but there you have it. I went to the marina that morning and put them in a Dumpster. I was looking for a grand adventure. And maybe"—she took a sip of her water—"and maybe to show you girls a little bit of my life—how I lived it every day without the safety net of a life jacket. But Diana already knew that, of course. I'd already started to see the first signs in her that she had inherited this sickness from me. If she didn't already know what it was like living without safety nets, she soon would."

My knees ached and I sat back on the floor, hearing the steady rhythm of my heart as I focused on my breathing.

"I don't know when I decided what was going to happen that night. In my mind, looking back, everything took on a logical progression. I think it began when the mast broke, and we no longer had control of the boat. It was like a sign to me, the broken mast symbolized my entire life—I'd been set adrift in life without the tools to steer my boat."

She took another sip of water and paused for a long moment. "And then I looked over at Marnie, so competent and levelheaded. I think I knew then that if I left Marnie alone on the boat, she'd be safe. All I needed to do was to get Diana in the water and then follow her. Diana was always so thin—she didn't weigh more than a hundred pounds—and I didn't have too hard of a time knocking her overboard. But before I could jump in after her, I saw the boom swing across the boat and slam into you, knocking you overboard."

She closed her eyes, but they remained as dry and emotionless as her voice. "I knew then that you'd seen me and Diana, and that you weren't paying attention because you were looking for Diana in the water. I was so angry with you, that you couldn't see that I was trying, for once, to make everything better for you."

I fell back, scrambling across the carpet to get as far away from her as I could. "No, Mama. Please stop. I don't want to hear any more." My tears tasted salty on my tongue, reminding me again of the water and of that night.

Diana kept her gaze on our mother. "Keep going. You haven't gotten to the best part yet."

I put my hands over my ears, but it wasn't enough to block out the strange monotone of my mother's voice.

"I picked up a seat cushion from the boat and threw it to you, but you didn't see it. I jumped in and swam to you so that I could lead you to it. I held you in my arms for what I knew would be the last time, and then I pushed you away from me and toward the seat cushion. There were straps on the bottom of it so that you could stick your hands in and use it to float."

I remembered again my mother's hands slowly pushing me away. But this time I remembered, too, the bright orange seat cushion bobbing toward me in the storm-tossed ocean. *I picked up a seat cushion from the boat and threw it to you, but you didn't see it.* "Oh, God," I sobbed and covered my face with my hands.

"And then I spotted another cushion that must have fallen in the water because the boat was heeling sharply now. Diana was swimming toward it and I had to stop her. I was a strong swimmer—much better than Diana—and I reached her before she could get to the cushion. She struggled with me, but I held her back. Except this time she must have known that she was fighting for her life, because she didn't give up. The waves were so high and the wind so strong that it was hard to hold on to her and to keep her head underwater."

I stole a glance at Diana. She was trembling, her face ashen, and I wondered if that was how she'd been when she'd first heard our mother's story. I thought of all the years that marked the distance between us, the events of that long-ago night filling them in ways that I had never understood.

My mother paused and her eyes were far away, as if she were not just seeing the night sixteen years before, but was actually *there*. I thought that if I turned my head, I'd see the wrecked boat and feel the lash of the water against my face. I shut my eyes and listened again as my mother resumed her tale.

"I remember thinking that what I was doing was wrong, that this was my child, and that I should love her, even though she was flawed." Her eyes flickered and then settled on Diana. "But this disease—the *real* curse of this family—it robs you of everything. Even the ability to think clearly when your own children are in danger. Or to remember that you were responsible for getting them there in the first place."

She drained the glass of water before continuing. "Somehow, Diana released her arms and swung back and hit me in the head with her elbow, making me let go of her. I was exhausted from struggling with her in the water, and I didn't have the strength to go after her. So I lay back in the water and began to think of dying.

"But then something hit me in the shoulder—I think it was a door hatch or something that had broken off of the boat—and I knew it was a sign to me. A sign that I was supposed to live. You see, no matter how much faith I put in the Maitland curse, I was the daughter of a preacher. And all those years of his fire-and-brimstone sermons had been drummed into me so that they were as much a part of me as breathing. I figured I was meant to survive, regardless of what happened to my children, so that I could suffer for my sins."

She looked down at her gnarled hands, at the fingers that had once belonged to an artist who could hold a brush and create brushstrokes of beauty. And I wondered if she considered them now as part of her atonement. A drop of moisture fell from her face and onto a swollen knuckle, bathing it in salt water, as if it were a reminder of her sin.

I cleared my throat. "What happened to you next? How did you end up here?"

She shrugged, but continued to look down at her hands. "I don't know how long I drifted out to sea, pushed at the whim of the storm so that I had no idea which way was land. Around dawn, I was spotted by a Florida fishing boat. They took me to a hospital, where I faked amnesia and then escaped, taking my roommate's clothes with me so I'd have something to wear. When my body wasn't found, your grandfather hired a private detective, and I guess it wasn't too hard to find me. I'd been living in an artists' colony in the panhandle and using my real name. I suppose I wanted to be found."

Slowly she looked up, her gaze meeting mine. "He had me institutionalized, knowing that if he called the authorities they might take you and your sister away. And then about ten years ago, he moved me here so that I could have a little more freedom while still receiving medical care. But in return I had to promise never to contact either one of you."

Diana sank back down on the bed, her teeth chattering. "Until I found a copy of the admission form in Grandpa's desk."

I pressed the heels of my hands against my eyes, hoping to stop myself from crying. This woman didn't deserve my tears. "That night, when you hugged me and then pushed me away, I didn't know that you were pushing me toward something. I've always thought that it was pure luck that I found something to float on. But I thought you'd pushed me away so that you could go save Diana."

A thought washed over the back of my brain, a stray thought that tapped at my memory, pressing me to bring it forward. And then I remembered what it was. I looked back at my mother. "You said something to me. Before you pushed me away, you said something to me. I've never been able to recall what it was until today. Do you remember what it was?"

"Yes," she said, her voice thick with tears. "I said 'I love you,' because I did and because I still do. I know it's hard to believe after all you've been through because of me, but it's true. I was never a good mother, but I did love you. Both of you."

I forced myself to stand and began walking in circles around the small room, seeing the starkness of it and wondering again if this was part of my mother's penance.

I turned on Diana. "Why didn't you tell me? All of these years I thought you hated me for something I'd done. That our mother had tried to hurt us both by taking us out in the boat that night and that you blamed me. If you'd just told me . . ." I shook my head as if to clear it and make this room and everything I'd just heard go away.

"Oh, Marnie, don't you see? She chose you. *You.* How could I not hate you for that? Our own mother chose you to live and me to die. I couldn't live with that. In my stupid, jealous way, I thought it would be easier to have you believe that it was your fault than live with the truth."

I stared at her, seeing her with my old eyes, and understanding her more than I wanted to. "So why now? Why have you decided that it's time to let me know the truth?"

Diana drew in a deep shuddering breath. "Because I'm not angry anymore. Because of the portrait. When I finished it, I realized why I had felt compelled to paint it in the first place. It has something to do with working out the events of that night, I think, but mostly it showed me that you had nothing to do with what happened. That it wasn't your fault our mother was ill. That you're still my sister and that I should have never let you go."

I thought of Victor Hugo's words again, and despite myself, I felt the corner of my lips turn up. Softly, I said, " '. . . two souls which touch without mingling, two fingers on one hand.' "

My smile fell as I considered one more thing. "What about Gil? What happened on the boat with Gil?"

Diana and my mother flashed each other a look, and I knew.

"When you found Mama again, she started talking about the Maitland curse, didn't she?"

Diana shook her head. "It wasn't like that. It was just that seeing her again—it was such a shock. And I'd forgotten to take my medication and I wasn't feeling right, and then I came to see Mama for the first time. When she told me what she'd done, it all seemed to make sense to me in some very bizarre way. I showed Mama a picture of Gil, and she made some comment about how much he looks like me, and that was all it took. I became obsessed with the idea of this family curse.

"Even Mama was alarmed. That was why she gave me all of her papers—the ones Grandpa brought her from the attic. She thought if I had the facts I would understand that it wasn't something as arbitrary as a curse, but an inherited trait that is now not only recognizable but treatable as well. I think in my heart I knew she was right, but my head was telling me different things entirely. That was when I got the idea to do the time line mural. To show everybody that I wasn't crazy, that I had proof that the curse existed." She shook her head. "It's almost funny, really, that I knew from experience that my illness was treatable, but that didn't stop me from obsessing over the curse. I almost felt justified because I could paint again, *really* paint without the fog from the medication to ruin it.

"And then I decided one night to try to finish what Mama started. Gil was so much like me, it seemed obvious that he was destined to be cursed with this sickness as I was and as our mother was. And that without us, it would just be you. You who didn't look like a Maitland, at all."

My head throbbed. I looked at my mother, who had turned to stare out the window, a view I could see was the side portion of another cement building. Her chest fluttered with her quick indrawn breaths as she listened to Diana's words, but she seemed unable to look at either one of us, reminding me of what a cold ghost guilt can be.

"So what did you do to Gil, Diana? What did you do to that precious little boy?"

Her fingers plucked at the bandage under her skirt, the bandage I now realized she wore as a reminder. "I took him out on his father's boat. I remember how excited he was to be doing anything with me, that the guilt almost made me take him back. But in my manic state, I was convinced I was doing the right thing." A haunting half smile touched her lips. "But Gil is a lot brighter and a lot stronger than I gave him credit for. I had deliberately damaged the rudder the day before by backing it into rocks, knowing it wouldn't take much to disable the tiller if it were stressed from a storm. I guess I'd underestimated his sailing skills, because he knew immediately what to do with the sails to get us under power again. The storm was slow in coming, and I couldn't rely on it to swamp the boat, and we were making too much headway with the sails." She swallowed, and I noticed that her hand shook as she tucked her hair behind her ears. "I stood there facing him, paralyzed, wondering how to get him in the water at the same time I was horrified that I could even think it. And I remember"—she shuddered as if she couldn't continue—"I remember him looking at me with those eyes, and I knew then that he was aware of what I was thinking. I can't remember what happened next. Either I moved toward him and caught my footing on a fairlead, or I let go at the wrong time and lost my balance, but I ended up slipping and falling down while Gil held on to me to keep me from falling overboard. But the turnbuckles on the shrouds—Quinn had just replaced them and hadn't wrapped them in tape yet—I fell on them and cut open my thigh, making it bleed really badly. I must have lost a lot of blood and passed out, because the next thing I remember, I had Gil's shirt tied around my thigh like a tourniquet and a coast guard boat was pulling us aboard."

She put her head in her hands. "Quinn had me hospitalized. And ever since he's made sure I've stayed on my medication. And Gil"—her eyes gazed up toward the ceiling—"Gil has been told all of his life to speak the truth, that liars go to hell. He'd rather not speak than to be forced to tell a lie." Her voice broke. "Because he could never tell the truth that I had tried to kill him. For some stupid reason, my son still loves me."

My head throbbed as I tried to absorb everything I'd heard. "But why have you been bringing him here to see Mama?"

"Because I'm trying to convince us both that Gil isn't that much like me at all. That this . . . affliction . . . has passed him by completely." She shrugged her thin shoulders again. "I cannot stand to see this happening to him."

I stood and stumbled backward toward the door. "I can't be here with both of you right now. I need to go, to be alone." My back hit the door as my hand fumbled for the knob. I twisted the handle and ran out into the corridor, not even bothering to see if I had closed the door.

I made it to the parking lot and out of sight of prying eyes before I knelt in front of an overgrown hedge and threw up, expelling from me every piece of poison I had just ingested. My skin felt clammy and cool, but the only thing I could think of was getting home to Gil and letting him know that I knew the truth so that he didn't have to hold it in any longer.

When I reached my car, my cell phone had just stopped ringing. I flipped it open and noticed that I had missed eight calls from Quinn. I was just about to hit the REDIAL button when I saw Diana rush through the doors, taking her cell phone away from her ear and snapping it shut.

"That was Quinn," she said, slightly breathless and her skin even paler than before. "He can't find Gil anywhere. The jon boat's missing, and Quinn thinks Gil may have gone to the marina. Quinn wasn't left with a car to use, so he's called Trey to come get him and take him there. He's been trying to reach you to see if you can get there any quicker."

I began fumbling for my car keys in my purse. "Trey put the *Highfalutin* in the water yesterday, and Gil must have overheard Quinn talking with Trey about it. Surely he wouldn't . . ." I stopped, too afraid to finish my thought. "Damn it!" I shouted, tossing things out of my purse in a desperate attempt to find my keys.

Diana held up Quinn's key chain. "Here. Take these."

I grabbed them from her. "Thanks," I said, heading for her car. When she slid into the passenger seat, I looked at her in surprise. "I don't remember asking you to come along."

"He's my son, Marnie. Even if I have to tie myself to the bumper, I'm going. Now. So you pick."

I took a deep breath and then stabbed the key into the ignition. "Fine." I backed out of the parking spot and sped out of the lot with squealing tires. I ignored the speedometer as I pressed the gas pedal down as far as I could manage without flying off the road. By the time we reached Highway 17, I let it down all the way. Diana and I hadn't said a word for almost fifteen minutes, and when I glanced at her, I saw the muscles in her jaw working.

"Why wouldn't you let him go sailing? That's why he's doing this, you know—because you forbade him to sail. If you knew that he loved it this much, why wouldn't you let him?"

She turned away from me and didn't answer.

All the anger and emotions dredged up in the last few hours consumed me as I skidded to a stop on the side of the road. "Get out. Answer me or get out of the car. What you did to Gil nullifies your right to keep anything about him from me. Do you understand? I'm his advocate here, and you'd better tell me everything I want to know. Right now."

Her eyes were the only remaining color in her face as she went absolutely still. A car passed on the highway, its motor droning as it sped by. Her voice was barely audible when she spoke. "Because I've cheated death twice. If there is a curse, then I think I've tested it enough—don't you think? If something happened to Gil now, I couldn't live with myself. It would all be my fault." She dropped her face in her hands and began gasping out huge sobs, her thin shoulders shaking. "I love him, Marnie. I know you don't believe me, but I do. He is my whole life. I've just tried to limit my exposure to him so I wouldn't corrupt him, like our mother did to me."

I sat still, understanding the truth of her words. I looked away from her for a moment, trying to think clearly, but all I could think about was how she had been the one to hold my hand when I'd broken my leg falling off a pier when I was seven.

I opened my arms to her and held her while she cried. "It's going to be all right, Diana. Nothing's going to happen to Gil. I won't let it."

She looked up at me as if she believed every word, and I wished that I could be as sure as I sounded.

"Let's go," I said, flooring the gas pedal again, listening to the grind of the wheels on the loose asphalt as I shot onto the highway.

Diana's hand fisted into a ball on the seat between us, and I lifted mine to put on top of hers. I turned toward the windshield again, wondering if the same words were going through her head, too: *two souls which touch without mingling, two fingers on one hand.*

CHAPTER 27

So we beat on, boats against the current, borne back ceaselessly into the past.

—F. Scott Fitzgerald

Gil

I looked at my watch again for what must have been the hundredth time, waiting for Mr. Crumbley to leave the marina office. Most days he was on the water, teaching people how to sail, but today he was in his office, probably doing all that stuff my dad calls "paperwork." Unluckily for me, he had a corner office with a view of most of the marina—including me. Everybody called him Captain Dave, but Daddy said I was to call him Mr. Crumbley since I was just a kid. I once heard Mama call him Captain McHottie, but she made me promise never to repeat it, and I haven't. Which was okay with me, since I didn't know what it meant, anyway.

I watched as he walked down the dock toward me, his sunglasses making him look really cool. He'd already come out to the dock twice to ask me what I was doing and to see if I needed anything. The last time he'd given me a bag of sunflower seeds, and I ate a few and fed the rest to the gulls and other birds that flew over the marina as I passed the time. I looked up at Mr. Crumbley and smiled, ready for his questions.

"Still waiting?"

I nodded.

"Your dad?"

I nodded again.

"He's going to take you for a sail as soon as he's done at his office, huh?"

I nodded.

Mr. Crumbley looked at his watch and then out toward the water. "The wind's really picking up, so if you're going to sail, you should go soon. And I just checked the NOAA on my computer for the updated weather forecast. Barometric pressure's dropping, so things could get dicey later on. I'm sure your daddy knows that, but make sure you let him know just in case, all right?"

I nodded, trying to look as responsible as I could.

"All right, then." He cleared his throat, wrinkling his forehead while he looked out over the water. "Something's definitely coming in." He zipped up his Windbreaker and smiled at me. "I'm heading out for lunch and locking up the office because there's nobody else here today. Are you sure you don't need anything before I go?"

I shook my head.

He looked at me for a long moment. "All right, then. But stay away from the water until your daddy gets here, okay?"

I nodded one more time, giving him a salute and making him smile.

After he left, I waited a few more minutes to make sure that he wasn't coming back. Feeling the breeze now, I zipped up my new yellow jacket, and then moved down the dock until I was next to the *Highfalutin*. With a deep breath, I stepped onto the boat at the widest part of the deck, holding on to the shrouds like my daddy taught me as I stepped over the lifelines, making sure I didn't step on the teak toe rail that I remembered sanding. My muscles hurt at the memory, and I promised myself that I would do whatever was possible to make sure that the toe rail remained in as perfect shape as possible for a long, long time.

I stood where I was for a minute, remembering the last time I'd been on the boat when it was about to set sail. I'd been with Mama then, when she'd been sick, and I'd been too selfish to notice because all I wanted to do was to sail and to be with her. I sometimes wondered if that was why I wouldn't talk about it, because I thought it was all my fault. And I wondered, too, if a mother could still love you even after she did something really terrible. I thought that the answer could be yes. I still loved her, after all, although I couldn't tell her. I guess it's the same part of the heart that makes you love someone no matter what they've done as the part that makes you forgive them for it.

As fast as I could, I went down the list in my head of what to do to prepare to sail, almost hearing my daddy's voice telling them to me, one by one. I unzipped the mainsail cover and attached the main halyard, adding two wraps around the hoisting winch. I released the boom vang so when I hoisted the mainsail, the boom would be free to rise. Daddy forgot to do that once, and I learned a lot of cuss words as he tried to get the sail up all the way and couldn't.

I checked to make sure the winch handle was secure in its holder so it wouldn't be lost overboard. I'd learned that one the hard way as I'd had to listen to at least a million lectures from my dad about what happened when the winch handle wasn't secured and how much they cost to replace.

I checked the wind indicator at the top of the mast and turned my face into the wind to determine which spring line to undo last. If I screwed that part up and put a scratch or dent on my dad's newly painted boat from letting it get banged against the dock, he'd probably be pissed off enough to not allow me on the boat for the rest of the year. I slipped the spring lines off the boat and tossed them onto the dock, feeling pretty good about how I'd remembered everything so far.

Moving to the helm, I turned on the engine, running through the NIL drill in my head, which my daddy had drummed into me: engine in neutral, throttle in idle, no lines in the water near the prop. I waited for the engine to pee—not that I would say that out loud in front of any other adults, but that's what Daddy called it when the engine started spitting out water like it's supposed to. After casting the bow and stern lines, I began to back the thirty-foot boat out of the slip.

I glanced down the dock to make sure Mr. Crumbley hadn't come back or that my mama or daddy and aunt Marnie hadn't figured out where I was, yet. It was okay for them to be there when I got back, as proof that I was such a good sailor that I could handle the *Highfalutin* all by myself. But if they showed up now, while I had to motor slowly out of the marina, they'd be able to stop me. I took in the fenders and threw them in the cockpit, knowing that leaving them on would be like a flashing sign that said *inexperienced sailor on board.* I had done that the first time I'd gone sailing with my daddy, and I'd never done it again.

As I motored out into Jeremy Creek and headed toward the ICW, I looked toward the coast line as Daddy had taught me to do, to check for bending trees or windsocks and flags to determine the direction of the wind near the shore. Grandpa had once told me that like oil paint and watercolors are Mama's mediums as an artist, the wind plays that part for the sailor. Most important, he'd said, a good sailor would never forget it. I also noticed that all the gulls and other birds that I had been feeding earlier were suddenly gone. The sky was quiet, and I tried to remember what my dad had told me that meant, but I couldn't. I was too excited about sailing again to try to remember something unimportant like missing birds.

Despite the warmer weather, there weren't a lot of boats out on account of it still being December. That was fine with me. Not that I thought I might hit another boat, but in McClellanville where everybody knows everybody else, word would get back too quickly. As I got onto the ICW, I caught a stiff breeze, and I realized how much cooler it had become. I looked up at the sky, surprised to see there was little blue left and a thick gray cover of clouds had arrived to block out the sun.

I wasn't worried. Whatever Mama might think, I was a good sailor. I'd never piloted a boat by myself in bad weather, but I knew that I could. There was something about being at the helm of a boat that changed you inside; like when Popeye eats spinach, I could feel my brain and muscles getting smarter and stronger. When the wind filled my sails, I became like Superman: afraid of nothing and able to do anything.

As I approached open water, I checked my compass. I was going to stick to the course my dad and I had sailed before, and the one he'd used when he'd taken Aunt Marnie out on Mr. Bonner's Catalina. Not too far out, but far enough into deep water to make the sailing exciting. I told my dad once that there wasn't anything better or more exciting in life than being under sail in fast winds. He'd said that there was one thing, but that I was too young to know what that was. That was a

few years ago, and I still haven't figured out anything better, so I guess
Daddy must have been wrong.

I set my course about forty-five degrees off the wind and then
pushed the autopilot button like my dad had showed me. Of all the
neat stuff he'd had Mr. Bonner add to the boat while it was in the shop,
this was the coolest. Daddy had decided not to replace the old sails
this season so he could buy the autopilot instead. I definitely thought
it was worth it since it let me pay attention to the sails without worrying about steering. The autopilot could even correct itself if the boat's
direction changed, which was a lot easier than me having to mess with
it, too.

I released the main sheet about twelve inches for slack on the boom,
then moved to the middeck to hoist the mainsail. As I walked toward
the boom, the boat bumped over some waves, and I lost my balance for
just a second, because I'd forgotten to keep one hand on the boat like
my dad had told me to do about a thousand times. I was glad he wasn't
there to see it and yell at me, and I didn't need him to. I figured almost
falling off the boat would be a good enough reason to try to do better.

After a deep breath, I hoisted the main, checking to make sure it was
flat without any creases. Satisfied that the shape looked good enough, I
walked to the bow, holding on to the boat with one hand this time, to
make sure the jib was ready to roll out. I felt like that guy in the movie
Titanic, except I wouldn't be so stupid as to let go with both hands at
the bow of the boat just to tell the water that I was king of the world. I
went back to the cockpit and unfurled the jib and watched as it caught
the wind, pushing my boat across the waves.

I was sailing close to the wind and heeling slightly when I noticed
that the water had taken on a darker texture. I felt a bubble of something like fear explode in my chest as the boat began to take on a little
speed, heeling steeply enough that I could hear the fenders in the cockpit tumbling over each other and hitting the opposite side with a thud.
I looked up at the sky and my mouth went totally dry. Half of the sky
almost looked like night, and the black clouds were rolling toward me.

I wasn't scared yet, but I knew that I needed to turn around quickly
to head back to the marina. I prepared to tack, trying really hard to

ignore the blackening water and darkening sky around me. I picked out my new point of reference on the land to steer toward and got ready to tack by making sure the jibsheets were uncleated and ready to run off the winch. I directed the autopilot to tack without any problems and released the jibsheet, trying not to think too much about how far away from land I was.

I was getting ready to tack again when a sudden gust hit the boat hard enough that it sounded like the slap of a hand. I swear I thought the bones in my face were rattling from the force, and it occurred to me for the first time to think that my daddy being angry with me might not be the worst thing about being on the boat today without his permission. The boat rolled violently to a sharp angle, straining the small electric motor of the autopilot as it fought to control the course.

The force of the wind had knocked me down in the cockpit, my knees hitting the hard seats and hurting worse than when I had jumped off Richie Kobylt's diving board and hit the board on the way down. The boat was heeling almost straight out of the water, making it hard to climb around in the cockpit. I could almost hear my heart beating in my chest when I saw that my point of land reference was gone, and that I was facing toward open water now. I blinked, feeling like I just stepped off a roller coaster and couldn't remember where I was supposed to be.

A beeping sound came from the stern and I looked back to see a red light blinking on the autopilot. I wasn't sure what it meant, but I knew it wasn't good. *Shit*. It didn't count as a bad word because I hadn't said it out loud, but I felt a little better after thinking it. If I could just douse the sails first, then I could turn off the autopilot and steer my way back to land. Getting down on my hands and knees so I'd have more balance, I crawled over to release the sheets, my knees hurting me so bad that I felt tears prick my eyes. I wiped them away with my sleeve just as I figured out it wasn't just the pain that was making me cry.

I spied the jibsheets and blinked for a moment just to make sure I wasn't imagining anything. Daddy had once told me about something called "panic," and I wished that he was there so I could tell him in person that I was pretty sure I knew what it was now. The jib had been backwinded when the boat had rounded up through the wind, and my only hope now was to release it. I struggled to hang on to the sloping cockpit as I struggled to reach the cleat. I could only use one hand since I had to hang on to the boat with the other, but my hands were wet and cold and kept slipping on the metal grip. I stretched out my fingers as far as they could go, barely grazing the line with my fingernail, and tried unsuccessfully to pry it up off its cleat but instead bent my fingernail backward, breaking it off. For a moment I thought I saw stars in my eyes from the pain. I pounded the deck with the palm of my hand only because I couldn't think of anything else to do.

The wind increased to a howl—something I'd never heard before on a boat and something I definitely didn't want to ever hear again. The autopilot continued to beep, and I looked at it the way I think a fish looks at you as you pull it out of the water on your hook. I started to shake then, knowing that I had no control over the boat. The boat heeled even more under the shouting wind, and I might have shouted, too, but I couldn't hear anything over the sound as the wind raced through the old sails, shredding them as easily as I could poke holes through a tissue. I watched as water came over the side rail and sloshed into the companionway and into the cabin below.

With the boat taking in water, I knew that it was only a matter of time before it capsized. What I didn't know was how long it would take. I was soaked through now from the rain and shivering from the cold, and I felt like a baby because I wanted my mama. I guess there's always a part of a person that will want his mama no matter how old he gets. I was real scared now, figuring I was about to die and how I wished I had told everyone that I loved them. And I wish I could have told Mama that I had forgiven her. I hadn't realized that I had until I'd stepped on the boat, remembering how she once held me close when I was almost too small to remember, and rocked me to sleep. I closed my eyes and my thoughts began hopping about in my head, starting with planting the orange tree with my mama and ending with how I'd never had a puppy even though my daddy's a vet.

My eyes popped open as the boat tilted more, and my hand slipped, making me scramble with my hurt knees to grab hold of something.

My hands slipped once, then twice, until my frozen fingers finally caught hold of the companionway. I saw the cabin was halfway filled with water, and that was when I remembered the life jackets in the locker down below. I didn't have much time now, as the water had begun pouring in pretty fast, so I reached my hand inside the locker and grabbed the first jacket my fingers touched. I quickly stuck my arms in it, taking turns holding on to the stairway. I struggled to get my arms in the holes, which seemed much too small, and then with the fasteners in the front, squeezing them across my chest and unable to get them to meet. As my feet became submerged in the icy water, I realized that I had grabbed a small life jacket, probably the one I had worn two summers ago and since outgrown.

I opened my mouth to scream, but no sound came. Or maybe it did. The ripped sails and rigging jostled in the roaring wind as the growing waves slapped at the boat with more and more anger, blinding me with pain and fear. I closed my eyes, hoping to see my family once more, but pretty sure I wouldn't. I figured this would be the time to start praying and thought about my great-grandfather's highlighted Bible, and the twenty-third psalm. I really suck at memorizing things but I figured God would give me some slack, considering. *The Lord is my shepherd,* I began, then stopped because I was crying too hard. I was crying because I figured I was going to die, and crying, too, because I was a coward for not speaking the truth before it was too late. I should have loved my mother enough to trust her with telling the truth herself. I closed my eyes again and prayed this time to be given a second chance; and I swore that I would never take a stupid boat out by myself ever again.

"Gil!"

I opened my eyes, blinking back the sting of the salt water, wondering if I'd imagined the voice.

"Gil!"

The waves were high enough now to be hitting me in the face, and I knew it would only be minutes before the spreader tips and the mast were below the surface. I pulled myself up to the side rail and waved my hand, hoping they'd see the bright orange of the life vest.

"Gil—we see you. Hang on. I'm coming to get you!"

Mama! I could barely make out the medium-sized motorboat that I recognized as Mr. Bonner's rocking in the high waves near my sinking boat, and I almost fell off then as my knees inside my soaking-wet jeans turned into jelly. I opened my mouth again to shout, and ended up choking on a mouthful of salt water. I waved my hand again so they'd know I'd heard. I could make out two people on the boat, and I knew that one was my mother and my knees almost gave way again.

They drew alongside as close as they could get without bumping into me. "Can you get to the back of the boat?" Mama stood on a swimming platform at the rear of the motorboat, her blond hair almost black in the rain, but I recognized her just the same. Aunt Marnie had been at the wheel but came back now to stand next to Mama.

I looked toward the stern, trying not to notice the steep angle of the deck, and nodded. Even I could tell that it was probably the safest place to get off the boat. Slowly, ignoring how cold I was and how slippery the metal railing felt under my numb fingers, I made my way to the stern. I tried very hard not to think of the last time Mama and I had been on a boat and what had happened. Things had changed. I think it had something to do with the mural she'd painted on the wall of her studio, as if she were trying to figure something out. And I think she had. If I hadn't known it before, I knew it now, because Mama was here to save me.

Mama yelled, "Don't move! I'm coming for you, so wait until I tell you to jump, okay?"

I nodded, hoping she wouldn't see that my life jacket was way too small. But I was a good swimmer and had the Cub Scout badge to prove it.

Aunt Marnie moved the boat a little closer, fighting the waves that kept tugging it away. Mama jumped into the water and I could see her below me, moving up and down with the waves. She shouted up at me, "I want you to jump right to me—it's not very far. Get ready to go when I count to three!"

I took deep breaths and listened as Mama called out the numbers. "One! Two! Three!"

Taking a deep breath, I jumped into the frigid waves, the boat shuddering under my feet as the mast disappeared beneath the darkened water, exposing the hull. A large wave must have hit the boat as I jumped so that I landed farther away from Mama than I was supposed to. The large waves were pushing me farther and farther out toward open water.

"Gil!" I heard my mother scream as I rose up on a wave in time to see her dive under a large swell. She emerged a few feet from me, and I saw that her teeth were chattering at the same time I noticed she was smiling. "It's okay, Gil. I'm going to get you to the boat and you'll be fine."

Aunt Marnie stood at the back of the motorboat, holding a tethered life preserver. "Diana—take this."

The ring sailed over the waves and landed just a few feet from me. I reached out my hand to grab it, but a large swell swept it back in the direction it had come from. I watched as Aunt Marnie began hauling in the line to try again, and knew as I watched her that it couldn't help us and that we couldn't wait for her to try again.

Mama grabbed hold of my life jacket, and her smile slipped as she must have realized how small it was. It was then that I noticed she wasn't wearing her own life jacket and that mine could barely hold me up and definitely not the two of us. We would have to swim together, not relying on anything to keep us on top of the water. She began tugging on me, and I kicked hard to help propel us both toward the motorboat. We were swimming against the waves, and no matter how hard I kicked, the motorboat seemed farther and farther away. Aunt Marnie was on the swimming platform now, calling for us, and I tried to kick harder but I was too cold and tired and wanted to just give up.

"Come on, Gil," my mother yelled to me, tugging on my jacket. "We can do it. It's just a little bit farther."

I was so numb and tired, I couldn't even nod to let her know I'd heard her.

"Gil, we're there. I just need you to grab on to Aunt Marnie's hand for me."

I nodded, seeing Aunt Marnie's face above me with her hand outstretched. I knew if I could grab on to something, Mama wouldn't have to hold me up anymore, and I stuck my hand out and grasped the plastic step of the ladder. Surprise registered in my frozen brain that I was holding on. Aunt Marnie grabbed the back of my jacket and began hauling me up, almost dropping me as the unfastened jacket started to slide off my arms. With one strong shove, she moved me to the floor of the boat, then turned back around to the platform.

"Diana—give me your hand."

I struggled to a stand behind Aunt Marnie and watched as my mother reached her hand out of the water, her skin as white as a sail.

A huge wave lifted Mama, and for a moment, she was even with the deck. I remember her eyes widening with surprise as it seemed she could just take a step and end up on the platform. But then the wave slammed down, and I watched as her head went down with it, hitting the edge of the swimming platform with a loud crack.

"Mama!" I screamed.

I ran to stand next to Aunt Marnie, avoiding the pink stain on the edge of the white platform, which vanished as a wave washed over it. There was no sign of my mother as we looked out into the water.

"You stay here, Gil. Do you hear me? I'm going in but I'm not letting go of the life preserver, okay?"

Off the port side of the boat, my mother's face floated to the surface. The water rinsed the bloody gash that ran across her forehead, but her eyes were open, and they seemed to be looking for something.

"Aunt Marnie—over there!"

Aunt Marnie swam to the spot where I was pointing. I didn't let my eyes off my mother, and she kept looking at me, too. "Mama!" I shouted again, trying to get used to my mouth forming words. "Aunt Marnie's coming. Hang on!"

Her eyes were drifting shut as Aunt Marnie struggled in the waves, getting closer but still so far away. "Hurry, Aunt Marnie—hurry!"

My mother was trying to swim, but her arms were too slow, and I could see she was hurt and tired. I remembered praying for second chances and wondered if there were any limits on how long a second chance could last. I leaned over the railing as far as I could go. "I love you, Mama. I never stopped. So please, please hang on!"

Suddenly, her eyes opened wide, and she looked right at me as if she had finally found what she was looking for. She moved her lips, but I couldn't hear what she said, and then, just like a person closing a door, she shut her eyes like she was going to sleep and drifted beneath the waves.

"Mama! No, Mama!" I ran to the edge of the swimming platform.

"Don't come in the water, Gil—I need you to stay on the boat!" Aunt Marnie's voice was broken by the wind, but I knew what she said made sense. If we were both in the water, there was a good chance that nobody would be able to get back on board.

I stared out at the empty spot of water where I'd last seen my mother, and I thought then of the time when I'd been very small and had been lost in the grocery store. I'd run down all the aisles shouting for my mother, believing that she'd left me and that I couldn't stand thinking that I might have to live without her. I felt that way now as I pressed myself against the railing, looking for a pale face or a flash of her brown jacket, but all I could see was cold black water, the edges white and bubbly like curtains folding themselves around something precious.

Aunt Marnie reached the spot where I continued to point to show where I'd last seen my mother. She frantically looked around her, then began to undo the fasteners on her life jacket, and I felt myself grow even colder as I watched her let go of the life preserver and dive under the waves to search for my mother.

I stood there for a long time watching Aunt Marnie dive again and again. I couldn't hear her, but I knew she was crying. The life preserver had drifted away, and I'd already pulled it in to get ready to throw to her when I saw that she was too tired to dive anymore.

"Aunt Marnie—here!" I tossed it to her, using everything I'd ever learned in the backyard of my house throwing a baseball to my dad, and it landed within arm's reach. She grabbed it and I began hauling her toward the boat.

When she'd climbed on the platform, she reached for me, and we hugged each other in the rain while we both watched the troubled waters around the boat, waiting to be sure that Mama wouldn't be coming up to the surface again.

Finally, Aunt Marnie kissed me on my forehead and brought me down to the cockpit, where she threw an itchy blue blanket over me to try to keep me warm. Then she went back to the wheel and headed toward home. I held on to the side of the bunk to keep from being knocked off as my teeth continued to chatter, long after I had warmed up.

It wasn't until we were almost at the dock that I figured out what Mama had said to me the last time I'd seen her. *I love you,* she had said. I said her name out loud again, liking the way it sounded, and then I cried like the baby she had once rocked in her arms until we reached the marina and the safety of home.

EPILOGUE

For all at last return to the sea—to Oceanus, the ocean river, like the ever-flowing river of time, the beginning and the end.

—RACHEL CARSON

Marnie

Spring blossoms early in the Lowcountry. The first rains of March drenched the dormant seedlings and fertilized the coastal estuaries, feeding the tidewater plankton and algae and bringing hosts of hungry marine creatures back to the wetlands. The fiddler crabs and periwinkle snails returned to populate the mudbanks and to feed and mate, while the snapping shrimp began their nightly rhythm, a staccato bass underscoring the sounds of the tree frogs and crickets as they made their marsh music.

It was the ceaseless cycle of life, death, and rebirth, and I relished it all this spring more than before, the greening of the marshlands like a benediction to me. For all of us, really: for Quinn and Gil, and my grandfather, too. We had moved out from under the shadow of Diana's illness and the darkness it created in all of our lives, and we were now ready to banish the shadows from the corners.

Quinn's boat was lost, and I can't help but think that maybe it was for the best. Quinn and I discussed it with Gil and decided that maybe later in the summer, when we'd all given ourselves more time to heal, we would pick out a new boat together. We haven't decided yet, but I think we will christen her *Diana*.

I haven't been back yet to see my mother. There's still so much forgiveness I'm not prepared to give. But it will come. I suppose that's part of the healing. I know it will come because I have Quinn and Gil with me now, and with them I can do anything. Quinn pushes me in the right direction, just as I push him toward a reconciliation with his own parents, and one day it will happen. But not today.

They've never recovered Diana's body. I try not to think of that when I picture my beautiful sister as I knew her, with her golden hair and bright green eyes, who could coax little miracles out of oil paint and canvas. She is the mother of the boy I love like my own son, and I see her whenever I look in his face. We're planning a memorial service for her up on the hill by the orange tree she once planted with Gil so that he might always remember her. I wonder if, even then, she knew. I try not to think of why she wasn't wearing her life jacket when she jumped in the water to try to save Gil. I'd handed her one when we'd boarded Trey's boat, and it never occurred to me to notice whether she'd put it on.

I feel her with me still, my sister. My ghost. She is there next to me, and sometimes I think if I just turn my head quickly enough, I can see her, with her beautiful blond hair dancing behind her in the wind, her elegant fingers gripping a paintbrush while a secret smile haunts her lips. I miss her. I suppose I always will.

We went to the McClellanville Shrimp Festival and Blessing of the Fleet yesterday. It's always warm in May, but there was just enough of a breeze to make it comfortable. Quinn pushed Grandpa's wheelchair, while I walked beside my grandfather, holding his hand and supervising Gil with his new black-and-white puppy, U-dog. Only a select few know the origins of the name, but it always brings a smile to Gil's face whenever somebody asks. I didn't really care what he called the dog; I loved hearing Gil's voice too much for it to matter.

Trawlers festooned with colorful flags and pennants slowly paraded down Jeremy Creek to receive the prayers of the local clergy. A man wearing a kilt and playing the bagpipes led the procession of three local clergymen, and silence settled as they gave their blessings to the fishermen for a safe and bountiful season. And then the mournful wail of the bagpipe lilted over the crowds of people and the flag-bedecked shrimp boats as the floral wreaths were dropped into the water as a memorial to those souls lost at sea.

I tried to hide my tears from Gil, but he slid his hand into mine and pressed it hard while he blinked back his own. He's older now. How odd to see the maturity of a young man's face on the body of a child, but he is still our Gil. He's returned to painting, and he wants to sail again. I love him for that. His courage is his Maitland legacy, along with his ability to re-create the world with paints and pencils, and his inherent knowledge of how to trick the wind into moving his boat. And that is all.

A young blond-haired girl named Laura Gray came up to Gil and asked him about his puppy. Quinn and I let the two of them run off to one of the tents selling ice cream, more happy than either one of us could express that the young man inside him could still be the boy he was meant to be.

My grandfather seems older now, too. Quinn plays chess with him, and I sit and talk with him, but there are no recriminations from me. I don't know if I would have done things any differently, and for his constant love for both myself and Diana, I will always be grateful. Gil is his joy, and the two of them sit for hours on the porch, witnessing the encroaching summer together and the changes it brings to the marsh, both of them understanding more than most the eternal circle of life.

As we were getting ready to leave the festival, Tally Deushane ran up to me to let me know she'd picked her top three colleges to apply to. And then she told me that she was writing a story for the Archibald Rutledge Academy's *Pirate Press* on past graduates, and she'd come across my senior yearbook, where I'd been voted least likely to leave the Lowcountry. She was looking for a quote she could put in the paper.

"What made you come back?" she asked.

I looked out at the boats docked along Jeremy Creek, where the water was fed by the vast Atlantic Ocean, the same waters that nourished my beloved marsh, and I thought for a long moment. I almost told her what Diana had once said to me, that surrounding myself with a lot of desert was like sitting in quicksand, that sooner or later the water would find me and suck me under. Instead, I turned to Tally's young, eager face and said simply, "I missed the water."

She'd smiled and thanked me before leaving, and I had looked at Quinn, sensing his question.

"Yes," I said, "I'm home to stay."

He kissed me then, and I felt the blood run in and out of my veins, nourishing my heart and my soul, like the ocean's tides flooding the marsh with life-giving sustenance, then bringing it home again.

Photo by Picture Perfect Photography

Karen White is the author of seven previous books. She lives with her family near Atlanta, Georgia. Visit her Web site at www.karen-white.com.

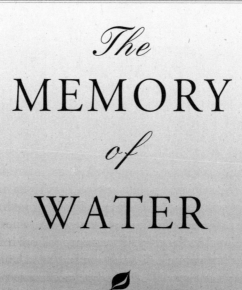

The
MEMORY
of
WATER

KAREN WHITE

This Conversation Guide is intended to enrich the
individual reading experience, as well as encourage us
to explore these topics together—because books,
and life, are meant for sharing.

A CONVERSATION
WITH KAREN WHITE

Q. Sailing and boats play a prominent role in this novel. Do you sail?

A. Until I wrote this book, I had never been on a sailboat before, but I'd always admired sailboats and sailors from afar whenever I'd see them out on the water. To research this book I had to do a lot of reading and ended up taking a few sailing lessons on a local lake. While doing my research, I discovered that the more I learned, the more I realized that I didn't know! Sailing is certainly an art form and something that would take years in which to develop a proficiency. Maybe when I retire!

Q. The relationship between Marnie and Diana is very complex. How would you explain the complexities of the relationship between sisters? Do you have sisters of your own?

A. I grew up with three brothers and my endless wish was always for a sister, I suppose that's why I've always been fascinated by the subject of the relationship between sisters and why I always seem to write about them.

Now that I have children of my own (a daughter and a son), I am similarly fascinated with the relationship between siblings and the power of sibling rivalry. Although I could never imagine having a "favorite child," I wanted to explore this concept in a book, and take it to its farthest degree (a mother who seemingly pits the sisters against each other) and watch the fallout by how my characters—in this case two sisters who considered each other an ally in an otherwise dysfunctional family—reacted.

Q. Gil is a fascinating boy. Who or what was your inspiration for his character?

A. I love young children, finding their forthrightness and honesty both disarming and charming, which makes them ideal characters to place in a book. I have found in my own experience that children usually say it like it is and see the adults around them with a clarity unmuddled by social mores or prejudices. This makes them sort of the microscope characters in my books; through their eyes the readers see the other characters as they really are.

Q. In this novel, your character Diana is suffering from a mental illness. What interested you about this illness in particular? What kind of research did you do?

A. Before I wrote this book, I read an article in a magazine about two sisters who grew up with a mother who had bipolar disorder. It was a story that was both heartbreaking and inspiring as I read about how the sisters clung together as a defensive device against their mother's abuse and neglect. When I decided to write *The Memory of Water*, I couldn't find the article, but the crux of the story stuck with me enough that I was able to borrow the emotions I had when reading the article and use them in my book.

Luckily, there are lots of articles and books out there on the subject of bipolar disorder—including my textbook with case studies from my college course in abnormal psychology. As I found while researching how to sail, that it would take years to get a firm hold on my subject, it was apparent that the complexities of this disease could never be fully fleshed out in a single novel. However, I hope to at least convey part of the emotional cost of living with a loved family member afflicted with the disease.

Q. This book is written differently from your previous novels in that the perspective is continuously rotating between the characters. What made you decide to write this way? Did you find it difficult to keep track of their individual voices?

A. I don't think I consciously set out to write the book in any particular way. When I started I had four very distinct character voices in my head, and each one came to me in first person as if they were all vying to be heard. I realized that each one had an important role to play in the book, and then I had to sit down and figure out the best way to do them all justice.

By using the different viewpoints, all told in first person, I was better able to get inside the characters' heads—especially Gil's, who is mute throughout the book. Using a rotating first-person viewpoint allowed me to literally "change hats" for each character—much like an actor does, I suppose—and become a different person as I wrote each scene. Not that writing is ever easy, but I found this to be a very useful tool in keeping each character separate in my mind.

Q. Diana's paintings also play a central role in this novel. Do you have a personal interest in painting?

A. As with sailing, the ability to paint has been something I've always admired from afar but am hopelessly inadequate at when it comes to creating anything recognizable on canvas.

However, as an artist in a different medium, I identify with other artists—singers, musicians, painters, even sailors—understanding what it means to find that part inside of yourself that needs to be expressed and then being blessed enough to be able to express it in a public way. In the book, Quinn refers to this when he says that when watching Marnie sail, she has found the thing that makes her soul sing. That is the thing that I believe all artists search for and what binds us all together.

Q. *What message would you like readers to take away from this story?*

A. My books are always about families muddling through difficult lives and finding their way—much, I would think, like us real people do.

I hope at the end of *The Memory of Water*, my readers will close the book feeling uplifted and hopeful that even the toughest obstacles can be overcome by forgiveness and by a family's unconditional love.

Q. *Water is a recurring theme in many of your novels. What does water mean to you? How is it important in your life?*

A. To my great disappointment, I have never lived (yet!) near a large body of water. Not even a creek has ever graced my backyard. But from my first glimpse of the Gulf of Mexico while visiting my grandmother's house in the Florida panhandle when I was a small child, I have felt an affinity for the water. There is something restful, beautiful, and eternal about the ocean and other large bodies of water—even something a little bit frightening about the unseen depths. But whatever it is, it pulls at me. The coast of the South Carolina Lowcountry especially draws me; it might be the smell of the pluff mud or the ethereal beauty of the old cedars and live oaks. I sometimes think it's because the landscape of the ocean hasn't really changed all that much through the centuries. Perhaps I, being a history lover, find staring at the ocean a bit like traveling through time, seeing the exact same thing as someone standing in the same place saw hundreds of years ago when the world was a much different place, and so many stories were yet to be told.

QUESTIONS
FOR DISCUSSION

1. Water is a central theme in this novel and has a different significance for each of the characters. To whom is water important and why?

2. Painting is Diana's passion. After that night on the boat with her son, she is unable to paint again until her sister returns. What is the significance of this?

3. Quinn feels that helping to restore the boat will help Gil to heal. Why is this?

4. Marnie and Diana feel equal amounts of love and resentment toward each other. Why is this and how are they able to mend their relationship?

5. What is the significance of the time line that Diana has painted in her studio? How is this a reflection of her mental health?

6. It is mentioned several times throughout the story that Marnie and Gil are very much alike. How so? How are they different?

7. How is Diana's painting related to her mental illness? How does it reflect her relationship with her sister?

8. Gil has refused to speak since the incident on the boat with his mother. What is his reasoning for this, and why does he finally decide to speak?

9. Their mother plays an important role throughout the book that we learn about through Marnie's and Diana's memories. How is she significant to whom Marnie has become? How so for Diana?

10. Quinn and Marnie gradually develop a relationship as the book develops. How is Diana's painting related to this?

11. What is the significance of Diana naming the boat the *Highfalutin*?

12. What role does the orange tree play in the relationship between Diana and Gil?